Get-To-Read Publications

About the author:

Michael Wuertz was born in Copenhagen in August 1970. He is educated as an aerospace engineer, having worked for The Boeing Company and Airbus, as well being a private licensed pilot. Heroes Banging Fat is Michael's second book.

m.wuertz@engineworks.de

Michael Wuertz

HEROES BANGING FAT

ﮩ

Thriller

Get-To-Read Publications

First published in Germany 2018 by epubli.com

2nd edition

A Get-To-Read Publications

All characters in this publication are fictitious and any resemblance to real persons, living or dead, is purely coincidental.

ISBN 978-3-746723-01-3

Typeset by Get-To-Read Publications

Hamburg, Germany

Printed and bound in Germany by epubli.com

Verlagsgruppe Holtzbrinck

Other books by Michael Wuertz

Death by Breed

I dedicate this work
to all you handsome
readers out there

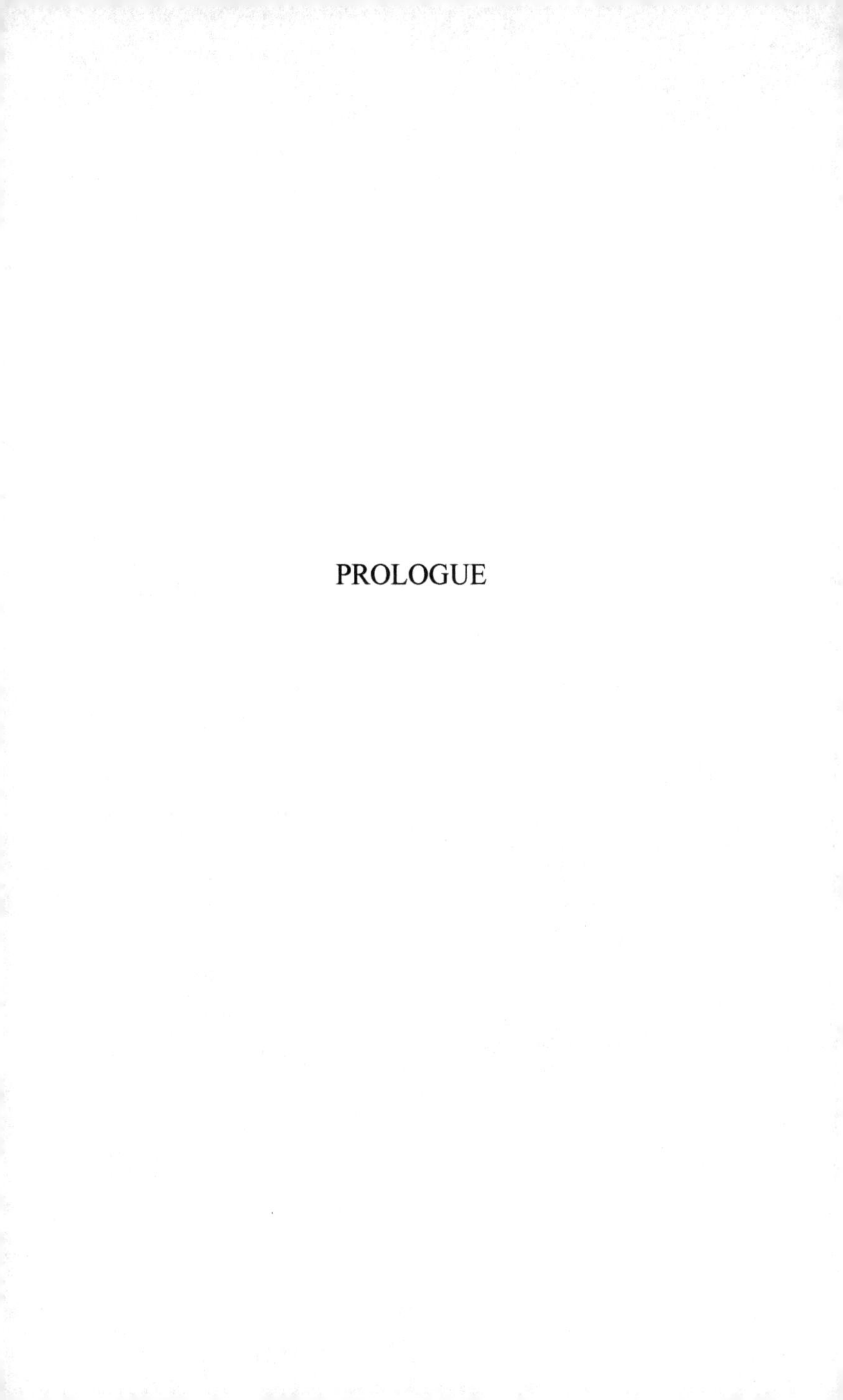

PROLOGUE

'THANK YOU FOR JOINING this morning, Ms. Seymour. It has been a while since you were last in our morning show. And a lot of things seem to have changed since then. The United Kingdom is a kind of on its' way out of the European Union. And now, polls, and our viewers, seem to react allergically to you. Your ratings have never been as low as they are today. How do you respond to people when they compare you to other politicians?'

'Oh well. I guess it's all part of politics. You can't satisfy all. Everyone seems to have an opinion about everything these days – being experts.'

'Our viewers have selected you to be the most obnoxious politician ever to be elected in the modern political history of the United Kingdom. What would you say to an impressive title like that?'

'As a politician you need to take some beatings once in a while. Some people obviously don't understand that what we're doing is in their best interests – as well as society's. People watching this show, as we all know, are not very educated. And most of them who are watching right now, obviously don't have anything else to do, such as going to work, or contributing to the well-being of the United Kingdom. Except of course, all the hard-working housewives out there, fulfilling their roles. The rest, the fat ones, the ones The Party is dealing with, dislike our politics anyway. You know … the ones who are too lazy to lose weight in order to be fit for the labour market.'

'Wouldn't that depend on what side of the argument you stand, Ms. Seymour? And doesn't politics work in the opposite way? I mean, if you want to remain in Parliament, you should speak the language of the people, not attack them.'

'But we do speak the language of the people. They're fed up with fat people. Firstly, most fat people aren't that very well educated. And due to their size, it's difficult for many to find jobs and be able to handle the pressure in the labour market. How often do you find highly paid fat managers? Or fat people in positions where important decision have to be made? Most fat people are on social welfare, which is very expensive for all of us, so I think we can agree that fat people are a wasted resource in the global battle for maintaining our welfare system and its benefits. Many fat people don't contribute to society at all other than taking up resources from hard-working and decent people. They're inefficient and even worse; they lack the self-discipline to do anything about it.'

'I'm sure many of our viewers would strongly disagree with those accusations, Ms. Seymour.'

'That's not right! According to the latest statistics ...'

'Which I have right here. To quickly update our newcomers. Statistics show in spite of Ms. Seymours and her political party's unpopularity that, she has picked up a lot of speed lately and gained five percent last month. And if new-elections were to be held today, she would win a majority of votes. This makes The Party even more popular than the Independence Party.'

'Mr. Dunham! I can tell you that our own statistics show that a lot of voters come from the Tories and from the Independence Party. The reason is simple: Contrary to other parties, our politics provide people with hopes for a better future. We're the ones who will lead this great old nation back to its strong roots and make our Kingdom great again. Not the others.'

'Moving on ... wouldn't you call it racism to discriminate against people just because they're obese?'

'Our followers, the decent hard-working people, understand we're wasting a major resource here. So I would say of course not. We're not trying to discriminate against anyone. Educated people understand this. And remember; there are a lot of fat people among our followers who have joined The Party and agree with our policies. Today they use our WeighForLife program which prepares them to return to society and assist in building a new great and strong United Kingdom.'

'There have been rumours that these obese people are practically forced to work for free inside The Party.'

'Of course they aren't. They've agreed to pay back what they've taken from society by being so fat and lazy and what they've taken away from all the decent hard-working people out there. So I don't see that it's unfair for them to contribute to The Party with half their earnings. They do it gladly. You must consider that the money they spend on supporting The Party goes to programs like WeightForLife, which assists other fat people to be able to return to society and get out of their social poverty.'

'Some would compare that with organisations such as Scientology.'

'Saying that is absolutely ridiculous! You should rather consider what would happen if all fat people had a goal in life rather than watching your stupid show every morning while stuffing bacon and butter into their mouths. Hopefully this interview inspires many to enter our WeightForLife program. Because, there they have plenty of other people who are in the same miserable situation as they are, with whom to share their problems. Our WeightForLife progam is a win-win situation for everyone. For them, for society, and for the individuals who want to do something for the United Kingdom instead of sitting on their fat behinds, unhappy with what they are listening to right now. The Party is their chance to start over.'

'We have a viewer on the line who wants to ask you a question, Ms. Seymour.'

'Go ahead.'

'Ms. Seymour! My name is Patty Griffith. I would like to know; why are you doing this to us? Don't you think there are more important matters than people being obese? I read yesterday about how many people view being obese as the most awful thing that a human can be. This has really gotten to me. I have struggled with my weight for many years. So I'm certainly not one to glamorize being overweight and am sometimes ashamed of not being able to cope with my problem. But what I want to say is; what about a murderer? Or paedophile? Or people who are disrespectful, like you? All you value in people, Ms. Seymour, is their appearance. Nothing else.'

'I've clearly stated my reasons. I've said …'

'Why do you attack body shape? You probably don't even know a single obese person. Have you ever taken the time to talk to obese people? Have you ever tried to understand their situation?'

'I was one myself. I know how it is to be fat. And I managed to do something about it. What's your excuse?'

'I find it upsetting how the public actually accepts you harassing people about being overweight. Today, you're not allowed to bad mouth coloured people, immigrants, or whatever. Or to make fun of someone in a wheelchair. You'd be lynched in public! Society would view these actions as despicable, distasteful, unlawful. But obese people …'

'It's not my fault you fat people can't get your act together and lose weight. Disabled people cannot be blamed for their handicaps and coloured people for being black. And then there are immigrants and refugees who come to our country because they have fled from some regime or war or want a better life. But you fat people, you do nothing but put food into your mouths. Don't come here and tell me it's the world's fault that you can't eat wisely and take care of your body.'

'So you say it's okay to hurt our feelings? That we're not humans because we're obese? You're the one who isn't human Ms. Seymour! What do you say about that?'

'By God! Don't take it so personal. I'm not the one who lacks self-discipline. I'm not the one who puts a burden on society with high social costs, expensive hospital bills and so on.'

'You're so pathetic Ms. Seymour! I'm a good Christian! I'm a great friend! A great daughter! A good sister! I'm a great and kind-hearted person who gives when I can and lives my life without hurting others. And no, I refuse to take part in this stupid thing you call 'WeightForLife', giving half my earnings to your insane party. Why are you doing this to us?'

'Because it's for your own good. It's for society's good. How many times do I have to repeat myself? The more fat people like you we can convert to normal decent people, the sooner we can get our Kingdom back on track. We need every single citizen to do this. If you don't understand this, you're the one who is a pathetic loser. A fat pathetic loser who ...'

'Right now, I'd like to show you how hard an overweight person can slam you on the side of your face ...'

'Ms. Fat person. I recommend you to take up our WeightForLife program.'

'Phew! Ladies. Time has luckily run out. Thank you for calling-in, Ms. Griffith. And I would like to thank you for coming on our show this morning Ms. Seymour. Let's see what the future holds for all of us. Only time can tell.'

'I thank you for the invitation.'

'After the break we'll return with a young man whose life changed overnight when he was diagnosed with cancer. He will tell us about his fight to stay alive, although, he knew he would eventually lose this battle. It is a heartbreaking story. And now a word from our sponsors.'

EPISODE 1

THREE EXTREMELY FAT MEN

CHAPTER 1

ANDY GREEN GETS INTO HIS old yellow metallic completely rusted Toyota Corolla. The chassis gives in bending to its driver's side caused by the overweight body that suffers from many years of malnutrition. He takes a mistrustful stare at his watch stuck to the dashboard with some old chewing gum confirming that, once again, he is running late. He is always running late. So what is the use of pretending he will be on time this time?

Andy Green sighs while turning the ignition key. Right at this moment, he ought to be at The Special Council's headquarters somewhere downtown. But an urgent private matter has come up. And when private matters like these appear, which they often do in his life, it will not be the day he checks-in with his employer.

Though. Getting fired. That will never happen.

The old yellow Toyota complains while cranking up to idle. The surplus of unburned fuel spills out the tailpipe with loud thuds. It takes a few attempts before the engine finally ignites. At least now the little car starts every time after the battery pack was expanded from one to three last year. Even on days where the Seattle winter bites off people's behinds it now starts.

Andy Green takes a look in his rear view mirror. The blueish white fog making the Seattle panorama with its skyscrapers disappear for a few seconds has vaporized indicating that all systems are go. He steps hard on the accelerator, making the engine choke a couple of times, before it picks-up speed to cope with the steep hill up to the highway. The little Japanese car is an absolute workhorse. And apart from a blue toxic gas cloud appearing after every startup it is a car in perfect condition.

Then to his surprise the engine dies.

Andy Green turns the ignition key one more time. The engine immediately fires up and the car blasts the 50 meters up the hill.

From his home in Kirkland, he proceeds to Interstate 520 leading to the Evergreen Point Floating Bridge continuing to downtown Seattle via the I-5. The highway is as usual congested at this time of the day. Or so he suddenly remembers. The congesting, starting from the border of Canada and carving its route all the way down to the Mexican border where only God knows how often drivers complain about the traffic jams, had he been a little wiser which no one can blame him of being, he certainly would have taken the Metro to the airport. It is a forty-five minute ride and actually quite comfortable. Because with the congested I-5, it will probably take two hours making him arrive late for sure and with alcohol fumes still hanging around his head from yesterday evening like a thick fog, it certainly would had been a better choice to let someone else do the driving.

At least this evening Seattle shows itself from it's good side. An old colleague and very appreciated friend could not have selected a better time to drop by for a visit. It is a perfect Seattle summer day. People living in Seattle says it rains a lot. But only to keep visitors from moving here so they have their city for themselves, because statistically, Seattle gets less rain than Miami and New York though no one really believes it. The Emerald City as it is called, located between Puget Sound and Lake Washington in King County, is popular because it provides near-to everything. Food comes fresh from the ocean. Meat is raised on the plateau's before the mountain ranges and so are vegetables, providing fresh produce for the region making Seattle a popular place for gourmets. Then there is the Space Needle. The tower with the hopelessly expensive entrance fee that only tourists pay. The Space Needle provides a spectacular view of the Cascade Mountains to the East and the Olympic mountains to the West where in summer, or at least for a transitional period, people can be seen skiing down the mountain slopes in the morning and kite-surfing at Alki Beach later in the afternoon. Then there is Washington's approval of Obama Care, the healthcare that Donald Trump tried to thwart, and there is legalized marijuana which gives the night-life a boost for students and people from all over the world. Seattle is always a place where people like to settle. They get jobs with Microsoft, Boeing, Amazon, Starbucks, FedEx and Nintendo, companies that help keep the city rich and livable. He is proud of being born and raised in this city where he has spent most of his youth also smoking his share of weed. And that before crackpots at Town Hall ever came up with the idea of legalizing it. With his parents he has had the privilege of exploring much of the world. So seen from this perspective, he can surely say that Seattle is not a bad place to live, to find a beautiful woman, to marry and raise six children.

He turns off the highway onto the ramp going to Tacoma Airport. The congestion was not as bad as anticipated. He forgot that the traffic moves north to Everett at noon on Fridays. Chris Campbell is arriving today from England and will stay until Sunday night while he is traveling through. His call was a little surprising and on rather short notice. But it is always nice to hear his friend's voice. Since the man left The Special Council for a job in the corporate world a few years ago they don't see each other as often any longer. In a sad way it makes their friendship more or less based on random visits now and then.

At Tacoma airport it is impossible to find a place to park. It is the crackpots down at Town Hall attempting to copy all these European cities and their public transportation systems. They should do the right thing instead of doing the wrong thing by not expanding the road system. It's kind of insane but they truly want people to give up their cars for the public transportation system. He finally finds a spot to park, gets out of the car and goes into Arrivals and looks up at the information board. He sees that Chris' plane has already landed – although, with a delay of ninety minutes, meaning that he impressed himself today by actually being on-time.

He sends a text message to find out where his friend is. The return message says in the coffee shop at the end of the terminal.

'Chris! How are you?' asks an excited Andy Green when they meet. They hug and give each other a couple of friendly claps on their backs.

'I'm just fine. And you?'

'Can't complain. I was surprised about your sudden call since you normally call far in advance. I had to skip work to prepare for your stay.'

'Ha ha. You sounded a bit drunk when I called you yesterday evening!'

'I admit I was. It was finally a beautiful day here and you can't miss out on enjoying it to its fullest with a few drinks to celebrate.'

'I know that feeling. London can be pretty depressing once in a while too.'

Then Andy Green looks at Chris Campbell with curiosity. 'You're really here on short notice. It makes me wonder what's going on. What brings you to the West Coast and Seattle? It couldn't possibly be me.'

'Well ... Yes and no. Something urgent has come up,' explains Chris.

Andy notices that his friend seems unusually nervous.

'You seem to be not quite yourself, buddy. I got the same feeling when you called.'

'You're right, I'm not myself these days. Something has come up in The

Special Council and that's why I'm here.'

'The Special Council? Didn't you transfer to the corporate world?'

'Yes. But in the last two weeks my work situation has changed. You and I are going to work together again.'

'Wow! That sounds good! Then we can have fun like in the old days.'

'I thought you'd say that. But it's a little more serious than that. There was a big problem in the corporate world. So the Old Man has hauled me back in.'

'Damn! I thought we'd be able to have some fun now that you're finally here again.'

'We will. But first we need to talk. Then we can have fun afterwards.'

'Okay. How can I help?'

'It's the Old Man. He needs your division to do us a favour in London.'

'Aha, I see. You're the messenger this time?'

'That's the reason I'm here.'

'Okay. But this is not the place to talk. Let's go to the car.'

ON THE way to the parking lot, the two rather obese men chit-chat about this and that although for Andy Green the mood is not quite what it used to be. He senses that his English buddy seems unusually heavy-hearted.

'You said you got plans for us?'

'Ha ha. That's the Chris Cambell I know. You'd better believe it. I've got big plans for us this weekend.'

'It'd be great to go to that bar again … What was it called … Rob Roy?'

'No, this time we're going somewhere else. There's a new place called Wilma's Junkyard. It's supposed be awesome.'

'Sounds like a lot of alcohol.'

'Believe it! Shall we bring your luggage to your hotel? Or we can keep it in my car and head straight to Wilma's.'

'It's getting kind of late. Let's keep it in your car. I see you still have your little Japanese servant,' says Chris while pointing it out in the parking lot.

'They don't build them like this anymore.'

'How come a hardcore Republican like you sticks to a Japanese-built car instead of an American?'

'You ask me that every time you're here! The answer is the same: After three American cars, I've had enough.'

'Why don't you buy a German one? Or at least a Tesla?'

'Because my salary says 'Too expensive' and my bank statement says 'Stick to what you've got'.'

'Yes, life is expensive, isn't it?'

They put Chris' luggage at the rear. When they enter the car their summoned weight levels the car to its knees. Andy pushes the accelerator to the floor making the engine start with the usual loud thud and bluish cloud. The car barely picks up speed going up the ramp to the Interstate.

'Wow! What've you got in those bags?' jokes Andy. 'And ... uh ... be careful with the window. If you put it down we won't get it up again. We'll have to put up with the heat.'

'You should definitely buy a new car.'

'Are you hungry? We want to eat first, right? I'm thinking about Naked City on Greenwood Avenue. Best burgers in town. They brew their own beer, too.'

'Really! Let's do it.'

'But Chris! What's going on? Tell me now!'

'We might as well get it over with. We're having one.'

Andy doesn't answer.

'This one is different though,' continues Chris. 'It's from the Western world.'

'Not some Banana Republic?'

'No.'

'So. It could be serious?'

'We've intercepted a conversation regarding people like us.'

'Are you saying that The Special Council has been exposed?'

'I formulated that wrongly. What I meant was; the conversation regarded to overweight people like us, not The Special Council.'

'Whew, for a moment there, you made me nervous.'

'Have you ever heard about Victoria Seymour? The one who was elected Prime Minister after Brexit? You've probably heard the United Kingdom is in the process of leaving the European Union?'

'Are you referring to this beautiful slim middle-aged woman? She looks a little like Sarah Palin, right?'

'That's her.'

'The newspapers don't write much about her over here. People were more or less baffled about the United Kingdom's decision to leave the European Union. Her election campaign was more or less a copy of what has been going on over here. None of our political analyzers expected her to reach power. And in all honesty. I think it caught us all by surprise that a woman like her could win an election in the United Kingdom.'

'But it has happened. And the Old Man has just put her on his observation list.'

'Oh, that's bad. Bad for her. What's the reason her getting on it?'

'According to the Old Man, the elites here and there have failed to see the writing on the wall. They've been too busy with themselves after the 2008 financial crisis. So the pendulum is swinging to the far right. And it's fair to say; I don't mind, because something need to change in our societies. Just like me, the Old Man says that change is good but that the pendulum may be going a little too far-right and that this could come to influence democracy in the United Kingdom.'

'That's not good of course.'

'Now, this is the background for the Old Man's decision: People elected Victoria Seymour and her party because they're fed up with the establishment and the political elite. Her coming to power was nothing but a protest vote. You might not have noticed but after she came to power, other European right-wing politicians running for office, haven't had much of a chance – apart from Five Star Movement in Italy, which seems to disappoint their voters. In a way many Europeans have come to realize that with the election of Victoria Seymour, neither Marine Le Pen from France, Geert Wilders from Holland, Donald Trump and Five Star Movement is the solution to solve their problems. In spite of this people do still select them in the hopes for change.'

'I do understand.'

'But Victoria Seymour is different. The woman is super clever, she's intelligent and she and her political party actually know how to run a country. I've read her political manifesto for the United Kingdom and it's actually quite good! But the Old Man and his team expected the Tories to win the election which is only bad news if you're an immigrant or a refugee or come from the working-class. Victoria Seymour honestly thinks she won the election on campaigning against fat. But she didn't. She only won because people from all over society wanted to punish the established parties.'

'Yes, it's a dangerous trend. I'm not really sure if people are aware how much they endanger their democracy by doing this,' remarks Andy.

'Exactly! And as it turns out. It seems Victoria Seymour thinks she's found the recipe for her success with this fat thing because she doesn't need to play to the xenophobia of immigrants, Muslims or whatever. Everyone can hate obesity without being called a racist.'

'I'm insulted.'

'We both should be.'

'So, why exactly did the Old Man put her on the observation list?'

'She and her team are starting to mess around with the constitution …'

'In the United Kingdom you don't have a constitution.'

'That's correct. What I meant was the doctrine of Parliamentary Sovereignty. She's asking about whether it's even valid anymore especially now that we're no longer in the European Union. More than 16.000 laws from the European Union have to be taken out of the United Kingdom legal system and be rewritten. Inarguable, she's using the instability caused by Brexit to insert her own laws, which could make her and The Party untouchable. They're sneaking in new Acts of Parliament while keeping the press and others busy with this obesity thing.'

'That's a rather clever move. She sounds like a good politician.'

'The Old Man and the Continent Teams are starting to worry about the political future of the United Kingdom. Now that the European Union has been thrown out, there's no one to hold the politicians accountable for their actions – except for the Courts, which she'll probably figure out how to fix. In general politicians in the United Kingdom are somewhat overworked due to Brexit. And the political system is on the brink of collapse. The Special Council has projected that there's a chance of one of the most democratic countries in the world might come to suffer markedly with Victoria Seymour at power. The Old Man thinks it's her objectives of following her life's dream of being at power and one of those to decide everything for everyone else that may trigger an unfortunate scenario.'

'Wow. I had no idea about the seriousness of the situation. It sounds like trouble could be brewing for European stability.'

'Exactly! Had Marine Le Pen won the election in France after Victoria Seymour we would need to consider taking her out as well. Some of our experts have calculated that, had she won, then the chances of some kind of armed conflict in Europe within the next couple of years could had become reality.'

'Take out Le Pen, you say? Hm. Today's political campaigns are driven by feelings rather than facts and statistics. People don't realize that this way of campaigning actually weakens the democracy they take for granted. I guess Victoria Seymour has been repeating things so often that people now believe in her nonsense.'

'I think reality for her and the United Kingdom are starting to blur a little. Some obese people like us actually now believe they're a burden to society.'

'That's ridiculous! Who can possibly believe obesity can be held responsible for the world's problems?'

'Sometimes this world surprises in unexpected ways.'

Andy needs some time to digest what he has heard. After taking a deep breath he sums up. 'Admittedly, I haven't followed the political situation especially much in the United Kingdom. I mean, over here, we have our own issues. But you need to tell me how Victoria Seymour has succeeded in turning the problem of mass immigration into blaming obesity for the problems in the United Kingdom?'

'Because after Brexit nobody wants to be called a racist. Obese people are of all colors, tribes, income classes and nationalities. Blaming the Jews and black people, that train departed long ago. Victoria Seymour is a formidable speaker and when you listen to her, you melt. She's quite good at manipulating people.'

'I believe there have been similar cases throughout history.'

'Indeed. But the problem is she *does* actually have a point. Obesity *is* a problem for society. She's got good ideas about how to change and improve on society. But who's interested? That was her problem. If people don't know they're worse off now than before you first have to convince them that they are, and in that process, find a scapegoat. Without anyone to blame the masses can't unite. The Old Man cares less about what she says. It's what she *does* that may lead to a condition which could damage democracy in the United Kingdom. It's really unfortunately but with the short-comings of the government there are people out there who think Victoria Seymour's obesity accusations are absolutely correct.'

'It diverts people's attention away from the real problems. That's the real problem. And I guess the middle-class likes to blame the upper class and elites when things aren't as lovely as they would like them to be. Poor people would blame everyone who's got money. Everybody must appreciate a woman like Victoria Seymour.'

'Exactly. It's a mess! The woman is a political paradox. And this is where the Old Man sees things in the future escalating. The rhetoric will eventually backfire and the consequences may be severe for the United Kingdom. There's also always the chance that this unrest will ripple on to other European Union member nations.'

'How severe is the current damage?'

'Currently within limits. But enough for the Old Man to want to get rid of her. The Continent teams have unanimously agreed to execute an FDAR.'

'Shit! I knew you'd come to this.'

'This is why I've come to you. We want your people to carry it out.'

'Does the Old Man want her taken out here in the United States?'

'She's going to meet your President in six months.'

'Then we'll take him out as well. Ha ha. Has my boss been informed?'

'That's what we need to do tomorrow. The Old Man wanted to relay the message via carrier instead of our conventional communication procedures.'

'Yeah, that's probably better so.'

Chris Campbell sighs. The man is deeply relieved to get this off his chest.

Andy notices it. A stone has fallen from his friend’s heart. Assignments like FDARs are not only complicated but also rather complex to prepare and execute. In spite of the vast research, analysis and preparation that goes into any FDAR, nothing can guarantee the outcome. Being the 'self-nominated' protectors of Democracy, which in itself is a difficult job, then the maintenance of democracies is even worse. It is a painstaking process to prevent powerful people with the wrong intentions from abusing the naivety any democracy possesses. Generations of people in the Western world have grown up with democracy and have come to take it for granted, not realizing that it is something that should never be taken for granted.

But okay, that's why the Old Man established The Special Council. Now when business is settled they can have some fun. At least before the hard work for preparation of the FDAR starts.

'So, where are we going again?' asks Chris.

'Wilma's Junkyard. We need to try it out. No place has a worse reputation in Seattle. For us it's a perfect match! I've been waiting for a chance to check it out.'

'And I'm your chance!'

'You certainly are.'

'Where is it?'

'Belltown. Someone told me they have awesome cocktails there.'

'I'm all excited! Let's go.'

WILMA'S JUNKYARD turns out to be the biggest pigsty east of the Seattle Space Needle – and much worse than its reputation. All kinds of folks gather there. It doesn't matter if you're rich or poor, fat or thin, married or single, old or young, black, white, yellow or red, Republican, Democrat or Independent. You can come dressed in suit and tie or naked like the skimpily dressed waitresses moving in and out of the crowd taking orders and serving drinks and food. Flashing lights go on and off from disco balls hung from the ceiling sending colorful rays to the dance floor and lasers throw beams of blue, green and red lines all over, temporarily blinding the patrons as they speed by. The atmosphere is far from relaxed on the dance floor where young woman and men hang from polished stainless steel poles, wearing very little enticing the audience's three sexual orientations. The DJ's selection of music on this night turns out to be what the crowd wants. Amateur strippers mingle with the audience using the floor to stage their own show showing what they have learned the last couple of months. They are here not only to perform but also to give the place an even worse reputation than it already has. The mood, the alcohol, the legal weed and the drugs which will probably never get legalized, are certainly the reason for the magic taking place here tonight. Bill Gates would love this place.

'And you still think this is something for us?' asks Chris.

'I must say, I'm a bit surprised myself.'

'We should've gone to Naked City.'

'And miss this? Not for the world! Seattle is truly turning into a place where to people can escape.'

'So, I guess I'm in the right place, then.'

A girl heads in their direction. 'Hey you! What do you losers want to drink?' shouts a loud voice now in front of them. It's a waitress wearing a pretty big E-size bra. As she stops in front of them, the inertia of both boobs continues, almost slamming Chris and Andy against the wall.

'For starters, how about a couple of Mojitos,' suggests Andy. 'What do you say, Chris?'

'Works good for me.'

A young woman nearby jumps off a table, crashing into the dancing crowd. People are quick to catch her and put her back on the table. People are obviously used to fallen angels around here.

'Do not, I repeat, do not tell Betty that I was here, okay?' demands Andy.

'I believe this place would get me in trouble, too.'

'At least your wife is more than 5 thousand miles from here!'

'Your drinks are ready.'

'That was fast!' responds Chris.

'They look great. Do we want to order two more, Chris?'

'Sure, why not?'

CHAPTER 2

THE SCENT OF SEAWATER anesthetizes Mason Sanders' nostrils. It makes him glimpse. The panorama view to the Town Hall and its square at the Marina is what makes this terrace the best in Piran. Mason Sanders bought his exclusive penthouse seven years ago. It took ages to renovate the building and it was a damn expensive venture. But as the result shows, it has been worth the investment, and worth the wait for the job to be fully completed. In this part of Slovenia, outdoor life can be enjoyed almost year round because of the mild, steady weather. He really loves this place.

Mason Sanders moves his attention from the Town Hall and its square to the exclusive yachts and local fishing boats at the Marina. They explain well the prosperity the region has always had. Piran is located at the beginning of the Balkans in the North-Eastern part of the Adriatic Sea. Its' residents call their town the 'Pearl by the Ocean'. It is an old town consisting mainly of compact houses with narrow, medieval Italian style streets once influenced by trade between the Austrian-Hungarian empire and the neighboring towns of Venice and Trieste. Once local fishermen and servants and their families lived in Piran. But today the city is no longer for average people but for those who have enough money to let their homes stand empty in the winter and sometimes even in the summer. The city of Piran is a popular place and after the annexation of Slovenia to the European Union, the city of Piran has become even more popular among rich people.

Mason Sanders takes a towel from a nearby sun-lounger and wipes the sweat from his forehead. The weather is warmer than usual. There are no clouds on the sky and the sun is shining as never before which is somehow the opposite of his current financial situation – which in recent time seems to be going in the completely wrong direction. Summer thunderstorms used to brew all morning over the ocean and then dump their contents within ten or fifteen minutes in the late afternoon. But for the last three months, the weather has been warm and quite dry and unbearable like a drought. Not a single drop of water has come out of the sky this year. Plants have dried out and animal life has suffered. Buses and trucks sink into the asphalt leaving huge wheel holes and even bike tyres soften. The water situation has become more or less critical.

Nothing is as it once was.

Mason Sanders throws the towel back onto the sun-lounger. Today, he will return to London, where he has his business. What is happening in the United Kingdom at the moment, is not good, and might even cost him his future and luxurious life. The new Prime Minister and First Lord of the Treasure and Minister for the Civil Service, Victoria Seymour, is really giving obese people like him an unnecessarily hard time.

He looks down once again at the town square in front of the Town Hall to people sitting at tables dining under sun shades. He adores this place. If they knew what trouble he is in they would certainly sympathize with him.

'Lost in thought again?' he hears a voice behind his back say. Then two arms try to grasp his rather big waist.

It is Mason Sanders girlfriend.

'I was deep in my own thoughts.'

'I noticed,' says Mason's girlfriend.

'What a shame I'll have to go back to London. I'll miss you.'

'Don't worry. I'll take care of everything around here.'

'Why now? Why now when everything is going as it should?'

'I'm sure you'll solve the problems at ImplantSkills. It's just temporary.'

'Oh no! Look at that.' Mason points down at the town square.

A woman in a fur coat walks through the square her high heels clicking rapidly on the stones. Click, click, click.

'Can you believe it?' he asks.

'How can anyone dress up in fur on the hottest day of the century?' she laughs.

'That's something!'

'It's getting a little strange around here, isn't it?' she states.

'It certainly is.'

Mason observes the woman in the square. His girlfriend's choice of words make sense. Strangeness does seem to follow money. The more uncreative rich people are, the more weird tastes they tend to have. Most of the young woman in town seem to have nothing better to do than to shop, meet other girlfriends, eat, drink coffee and go to the beach dressed in their expensive bikinis. The expensive designer clothes, the jewelry, the boats and exclusive penthouses, the private jets. If it's a young girl, it certainly isn't hers but belongs to her Sugar Daddy or father. Most of the girls who live here would never think of themselves as being well-paid luxury items who can be replaced at the wink of an eye. They think they are too valuable for this ever to happen or at least for this season. Even his own girlfriend, standing at his side, looking out over the balcony; young, wrinkle-free, fit and curvy and way too young at only half his age, can be replaced. She is here because of the money, his status, influence and social rank – or at least this is what he thinks. Why else would a 54-year old man, weighing approximately 157 kilograms and born naturally ugly, be able to attract a girl like this? He is very well aware of the fact that he is not exactly the beauty his mother dreamt of.

Mason Sanders looks at his girfriend with a quick, distrustful glance. She is twenty-seven. They somehow always are twenty-seven. She reminds him a great deal of himself from back then. Ambitious, persuasive, persevering, stubborn and ultimately seeking success. Contrary to other girls (and there have been plenty), she does not spend money on worthless shopping or wear fur on the hottest day of the year. No, she has used his influence to start up an own company with an innovative idea she has. The move surprised him and he accepted it. But if she remains at his side when she is successful and he not, that only time will tell.

'Isn't that Mehdi Hanachi down there?' asks Mason's girlfriend, pointing to a small brown-colored man crossing the town square with steps almost as quick as the woman in fur.

"It certainly is,' agrees Mason, waving in an attempt to get the man's attention. But the good looking Arabic gentleman fails to notice them.

'Say? Why don't we go down to his cafe and drink a coffee? You can pack later.'

The idea appeals to Mason Sanders. Usually before he leaves on a business trip there is the compulsory round of sex on the kitchen table, then the dip in the ocean to remove the smell of sex before heading to the Cafe Casa Piran like two wet dogs to drink the best coffee in Piran. They would finally return to the apartment to dress and drink a Pornstar Martini while waiting for the taxi to the airport. He has done this all so often through out the years (with whatever babe he was keeping) that he has stopped counting.

But today is different. Yes, today is certainly different. Today he is beginning to feel the strain that routine has put on his life. A strain that he would gladly do without. A strain that he does not want to continue too much longer. It would be nice to discover that his girlfriend is actually there for him. And not his money.

'That's an excellent suggestion, Yulia,' agrees Mason. 'Let's go down to Cafe Casa Piran and have a cup of coffee.'

ANDY GREEN wakes up with a monumental hangover. If a Friday night can cause so much havoc on a Saturday morning, how will the world look tomorrow morning when they drink tonight? The bed is warm and cozy and so is the body beside him. But instead of the soft body of his wife, which is almost as big as the one beside him right now, this bloke has neither his wife's beautiful eyes, the long blond hair nor the voluptuous breasts he still adores after twenty-five years of marriage and half a dozen children. How that hairy beast ended up here in his bed, he doesn't remember. Any other day, he would have waked up with his wife, but when Chris is in town, his wife knows it is smarter to spend the weekend with her parents in Redmond.

And not without reason. Chris shouldn't be here. He has a room reserved at a hotel downtown.

Andy gets out of bed. When he passes to the other side of the bed, he notices through the window that his little Japanese car is parked exactly where it should be.

'Hm.'

It should be parked downtown where they left it last night, but it's parked in front of the house. What happened? Who was driving? How did it get there? These questions could plague him all day. He slams Chris hard on his big, naked, obese butt.

'Hey, wake up! It's a new dawn. We need a de-tox drink.'

'… what …?'

'Wake up!'

'My head! What happened …?'

'Wilma's Junkyard lived up to its reputation.'

'Did we go there?'

'We certainly did.'

'That was really something ... wasn't it? How did we get home?'

'That's bothering me, too.'

'Uhm. I might have been the one driving. You were too drunk.'

'And you were not? Get up! We need a solid breakfast to sober up.'

'Wow, where do you get your energy from, Andy? And by the way, you ought to put more water into your bed. My bones hurt. Especially my head.'

'Your head isn't a bone. Say, didn't I reserve a hotel room? Now get up!'

'You did. But I forgot the name of the hotel. And so did you.'

'While you get dressed, I'll fetch us a couple of beers and order us a huge breakfast.'

'Aye to that.'

'MASON! So nice to see you again,' shouts Mehdi Hanachi moving in their direction through Cafe Casa Piran. 'Has it been a year already?' asks the middle-aged Libyan man who was doomed to die in one of Gaddafi's dead-prisons, tortured multiple times by the dictators brutal henchmen and today still not shedding tears over the death of his former leader. Piran would never be the same without this gossip channel – and its coffee. Mehdi Hanachi recognizes the new Sweetheart at Mason Sander's side. 'Oh, where are my manners,' he excuses himself and gives her a kiss on both cheeks. He doesn't realize that it's actually the same girl as from last year.

'But Mehdi. You two already know each other.'

'Oh yes. I'm so sorry. He says, offering his excuses. My mistake. You know how it is around here ...'

'No offence taken,' she replies.

'How have you been, Mehdi?' asks Mason Sanders. 'How's business?'

'Can't complain. I finally bought the supermarket at the Marina. So, now I can afford to also live in Piran. I made a small profit last year and am thinking about buying a pizza restaurant.'

Mason Sanders laughs. 'Pizza is certainly something missing around here.'

'I hear your sarcasm,' says Mehdi Hanachi, winking an eye. 'It's going to be excellent pizza. Deep-pan pizza, not this flat Italian crap.'

'And the opening date?'

'Only the Almighty God knows. The efficiency of the Slovenian authorities isn't the fastest.'

'I remember that from the time I modernized my apartment.'

'Oh, where are my manners? Cappuccino as usual?'

'Yes, please.'

'And you?'

'Me too, please. Mason, I forgot my purse. I'll run back quickly and get it,' informs Mason girlfriend.

'Sure. See you in a moment, Yulia.'

'So …' Mehdi Hanachi says, leaning a little closer after Yulia has left.

'I understand she's the same as last year.'

'She is. She's different from the others. She's got brains, you know?'

'Still, you know very well how the rabbits breed around here.'

'Sure …' Mason Sanders hesitates for a few second. 'But, she'll be gone soon, anyway.'

'Really? Why?'

Mason Sanders hesitates. 'I'm ... Well … things are not going so well at the moment.'

'With you two? Are you having trouble?'

'No. Not her and me. We've had an incidence at ImplantSkills.'

'An incidence?'

'ImplantSkills' bank accounts have all been hacked and our cash stolen.'

'So what? Doesn't the bank provide you with back-up capital? At least until the theft has been resolved?'

'No, they don't. They've started a 40 day investigation. Meanwhile, our accounts have been frozen.'

'But, how're you going to survive, then? You need cash. It's not your fault that the bank has been exposed to a cyberattack.'

Mason's face turns truly worried. The facial expression catches Mehdi Hanachi totally off-guard. It is an expression he is not used to seeing in the gentleman he appreciates so much. All the fun times they have had together, the invitations to the great parties, the deep talks about life and this and that, especially the financial contribution he got when he was establishing his cafe. Damn! This man deserves all the help he can get.

'I …' stutters Mason Sanders before continuing, 'I can't shake the feeling that someone is intentionally putting stones in my way. Now I need to find investors, or we need to make an Initial Product Offering, but that simply takes too long.'

'Wow. That does seem to be a serious situation.'

'It is.'

'But I don't understand. There must be addresses on the bank transactions to show where the money has gone so it can be traced.'

'And that's the problem. Right after the transfers were made, the information was deleted from the bank's servers.'

'That shouldn't be possible.'

'The bank says it must have been an inside job. You cannot do anything like this from the outside unless you know how the transaction protocols are designed. You need direct access to be able to manipulate the databases.'

'Oh boy. The hackers could have deleted anything.'

'That's why I believe it must be a targeted attack, specifically done to hit ImplantSkills – or me.'

'So, while the bank figures out what happened can't they give you a credit line to keep the company afloat? I mean …'

'That's the beauty of the scheme. As long as the bank can't figure out where the money went, they're not obligated to loan us money. We do use more than one bank. But, in theory, it now looks like we're insolvent. The capital we require is too high-risk under the current circumstances. Banks don't loan to companies that are on the brink of insolvency. So, you see, no one sees themselves in a position to loan us anything, unless private investors.'

'Gee. So much for banks. And investors?'

'I don't really want to have investors. They're all so damn greedy. But a woman called me yesterday from an investment bank in London. They see an opportunity to make a profit here. Actually, I'm expecting others to follow with calls. At least, the reputation of ImplantSkills is good because of its many years of success. So you see, that's why I'm flying back to London tonight, in spite of arriving late yesterday. Oh … and I have this meeting with Mike. You remember him? The journalist who was here some time ago?'

'Mike, yes. I remember him. He's quite a nice fellow. If he had the money he'd probably buy an apartment here.'

'He sure would. But he's a journalist. Not a star-reporter.'

'What're you going to use him for this time?'

'I need to tell the world what's going on with ImplantSkills. Mike can give me the exposure I need to attract the correct investors.'

'Ah! That's clever.'

'I wouldn't call it clever. But necessary!'

'Hm. I guess in these cybertimes, it's better to hide the money under the pillow.'

'It's got to be a damn big one then!'

Mehdi Hanachi laughs. 'Good to see that nothing spoils your sense of humor.'

But then Mehdi Hanachi turns silent. Mason notices it. Before saying anything further, Mehdi Hanachi considers his next words very carefully.

'Mason! I've noticed something strange. It just dawned on me. Do you know Robert Martins and this other guy … uhh … James Hollister? They live on the other side of the Marina.'

'Our paths cross occasionally, but I've never talked to them.'

'Well, maybe you should. Their wives, or whatever they are, told me their husbands are in financial turmoil, too. And lately, at least according to the newspapers, a lot of rich people are having financial issues. This trend started some weeks ago.'

'What are you saying?'

'Mason! You know I'm not the type to spread rumors. But listening to some small talk from their wives, it sounds like the same problems you're having. Their financial troubles seem to have come out of the blue, too.'

'Did they get hacked?'

'Their wives didn't say. But there are parallels. Perhaps you ought to … Oh, there you are again Ms. I'll make your Cappuccino.'

'Thanks,' says Yulia, returning a beautiful smile.

'I think we'll take them to go,' suggests Mason Sanders. ' Can you make me another one?'

'Sure. It's on the house today. But Mason! There's something bothering me with this ImplantSkills situation. It's uhm … eh … well …' Mehdi Hanchi hesitates. 'It's not nice to say, but … and I cannot say it without sounding a little disrespectful. But reading about other people in the news who are also in your situation, then … Uhm …'

'Mehdi! Say what's on your mind.'

'You see, the common nominator is that … you're all extremely rich … but … also … uhm … a kind of rather overweight.'

CHAPTER 3

CUBAN ROAST. SLOW COOKED PORK, piled onto a baguette, with a layer of aioli cilantro and vegetables with caramelized onions, the morning sandwich from a bar in Ballard was as good as it could get. Chris Campbell, would never eat food like this in London. Well, perhaps an English breakfast, with bacon, beans, eggs champions, thick gravy, and whatever it takes to give him a bad conscience, but not this. At least he was strong enough to turn down a second repair beer to cure his hangover. But the reason for his stay is business. And business it is now.

'How far is it from here?' asks Chris.

'Downtown, close to your hotel. My boss, is already there, waiting for us.'

'What's his name again?'

'Mr. Andrews. Nobody knows his first name.'

'And your boss doesn't mind us looking like this?'

'He knows I grew up in Seattle.'

'Aha.'

The bus is packed with people. As they enter to buy tickets, fellow riders are kind enough to move aside and away from the two big men. Chris compares the bus with a Tube-ride in London. This mode of transportation is not his favorite. At least this time, it is *his* alcohol fumes and lack of a shower after a warm and sweaty night that seems to bother people and not the opposite.

'Here, Andy! There are two seats at the rear door. Let's take them.'

'You sit down. I don't think there's enough space on them for both of us.'

'You can sit on my lap,' offers Chris.

'That's okay. What will the others think.'

Chris Campbell sits down. Only a few seconds later, he turns his head to the window, watching the Seattle landscape move slowly by. People must have been awake for hours on this beautiful and sunny Saturday afternoon. He turns his head to an old lady. He noticed that she was staring at them and plugging her nose when they got on the bus. Now she is standing with her back to them.

He sighs. If people like her only knew, they would learn to appreciate and respect people of their size and stop treating them as outcasts. Everyone has a story to tell. Unfortunately, the story Andy Green and he have is one that they will have to take with them in their graves. The privilege of becoming an asset for The Special Council is the highest honour anyone can ever achieve. But privileges they cannot share with anyone else not even their wives, family or friends. In many jobs it can be difficult to see the results of the hard work which is put in every day. But working for The Special Council, you can see and feel the results of your hard work every time you walk out on the streets and you can be reassured that the time you put into an assignment makes a difference in the world. Why the Special Council selected him is, to this day, a mystery which he may never have the answer to. But he knows that if The Special Council is interested in some skill you possess, then you will be picked and if not, you will never know there is something called The Special Council. They are so good at investigating people, that you would not even realize you are being scanned and analyzed. In his case they certainly did not make it easy. He almost lost his job back then along with his family, friends and savings. But he kept a cool head and kept going by fighting his way back to life. He is a survivor, a fighter, obviously something that The Special Council appreciates in the people they hire. It was a hard time, but he passed their tests, and now, for the rest of his life, his future secured and he will never have to worry financially. The Old Man is a very good employer. But also one who sets high standards for his employees.

Where other intelligence agencies care about national interests and not the well-being of the world, the world can thank the Old Man for its work to keep it stabilized by doing all the crap that the United Nations does not have a mandate to do. He agrees with Andy when the man says that too many people take the democracy they live in for granted. A democracy is something that must be protected because the foundation of any democracy is naive and largly based on its self-interest. The vast research they perform, the thorough analysis and preparation that goes into making FDARs, or the so-called Future Directory Assessment Reports, is astonishing. They do not have FDARs often, but when they do, then they know that a high-ranking person is getting out of sync with rest of the world, endangering a democracy somewhere. To execute an FDAR and even be allowed to carry it out is up to the Continent Teams within The Special Council. One nation has one vote and there are a total of 193 votes world-wide. Although, depending on who you ask, there may be 196 nations. Also on this matter neither the world nor the United Nations seem to be able to agree on the exact count. All employees inside The Special Council, know how to keep a secret and work in silence to accomplish their objectives. Silence and secrecy are the ultimate ingredients for The Special Council success and its survival. Being fat and lazy and smelling like they do right now may make them very unpopular on the bus, but it is the best alibi for what they are doing for a professional living. Even his wife believes he pushes paper for a company somewhere in the financial district of London.

'We should have showered first,' comments Chris.

'I know,' answers Andy. 'But my boss is waiting. We slept late. No time.'

'The old woman standing with her back to us …' whispers Chris, doesn't seem to like us.'

'I noticed her too when we got in.'

'By God … my head … my hangover …' complains Chris.

'Just wait till tonight.'

'What happens tonight?'

'I have big plans for us.'

Oh no, thinks Chris. If tonight becomes a continuation of last night at Wilma's Junkyard, he is honestly looking forward to the plane ride back to London tomorrow evening. Then he has had enough partying for the rest of the year.

THE DAY after his departure from Piran, Mason Sanders returns to his home in London. The journalist questioning him carefully observes Mason Sanders body language. He senses the man's eyes are focused like an eagle's, the man's body posture relaxed and soft and that he only answers questions after carefully thinking them over. The man is an expert in sending messages via the media to people he wants to hear what he has to say.

Mike Hornett has followed ImplantSkills' progress closely for some years and has followed the skyrocketing career of its founder, the heavy-set man, now sitting in front of him. ImplantSkills' founder was not always this obese but with the company's rapid increase in success, it looks like its' founder has increased in size accordingly. Mike is quite surprised at the background story he has just been told and the numbers it entails.

'It's a lot of money you have at stake, Mason. I mean … 155 million. What happens if you fail to find the capital you need … what then?'

'This is something we can't fully agree on.'

'I think it's the first time you've shared how much money you actually have at stake privately with the public.'

'It *is* the first time.'

'What I find odd is' continues Mike, '… what are the odds of ImplantSkills banks getting hacked simultaneously all at the same time?'

'It's rather suspicious, isn't it?'

'I'd say so! But Mason, you say you don't think it's unfair for the banks to not support ImplantSkills by bridge-financing?'

'You need to see it from the banks' point-of-view. I assume they expect me to go to investors for help until the hacking issues have been settled. This is how banks work, you know?'

'How do you feel about it?'

'Deal with the situation; get on with it; don't fall into self-pity; get the work done. Then you'll survive.'

'I can't let go of this thing with the hacking of the banks and bank accounts. It does sound a little like a targeted job. Do you have any investors lined up?'

'Not yet. Well, perhaps one. But that's still pretty open. Okay, there are others, too. But one at a time. Later this week, I'm meeting with an investment house. In principle the situation is so delicate that I practically need to take the first one coming along. They'll be able to do a formidable deal.' And this was the message Mason wanted to make public. 'For the bank it doesn't matter who took the money. They'll take their time investigating what happened. It can take a week or two years. Without a line of temporary credit, the company could go bankrupt putting 2.500 employees worldwide on the streets for no apparent reason. ImplantSkills is in its' roots a healthy company.'

'Who would benefit from damaging ImplantSkills?'

'I have no idea.'

'A competitor?'

'No. They have as little interest in hurting us than we in hurting them. Competition is always good for innovation.'

'What kind of investor or investors do you need?'

'We need a loan for a quick-fix.' Also that needed to get out publicly.

'Mason. I'm going to ask you a completely typical idiotic journalistic question. Do you have any idea who did the hacking?'

'Ha ha, Mike. That's really a typical question from a journalist. I haven't got a clue.'

'Have you talked to the police?'

'We had to report it. Their cyberspace department is working on it.'

'I see on your face that you're holding back information, Mason. I think you do have an idea.'

'I honestly don't.'

'At least off the record?'

'Well ...' Once again, Mason considers his words carefully. He certainly trusts the man in front of him. Mike Hornett would never misuse the confidence they have built up over the years. But nevertheless, Mike is from the press and their relationship must be purely professional.

'I don't want to sound like a conspiracy theorist, Mike. But yes, I do actually have a hunch.'

'Like I said, it's off the record. It's for my understanding.'

'Okay.' Mason leans closer to Mike who does the same. 'It makes no sense for the banks to let ImplantSkills go bankrupt. On the other hand, it's not the banks' fault they were hacked. There's a lot of cybercrime out there with seventeen year old students breaking every rule in the textbooks. A distant friend of mine, who you probably remember from Piran, this guy from Libya who served us coffee ...'

'I remember him.'

'... has a theory based on things he's been seeing in the news lately that other people like me who are ... you know a little overweight ... have gotten themselves into the same situation as I have. He claims this thing with ImplantSkills, might have been a deliberate hit because I'm overweight.'

Mike moves back in his chair in surprise.

'Ha ha. That sounds silly!'

'I thought so too. And now that I've been paying more attention to the news, it might just be that Mehdi Hanachi could not be fully wrong.'

'You're kidding!'

'No, I'm not.'

'Hm.'

'That's why I want to ask you a favor, Mike. Can you make a more detailed analysis of what's coming into your news desk? I'd appreciate it.'

'I can run an analysis, sure. If there's anything to it, it might turn out to be an interesting story.'

'Great.'

'But just to complete our interview, I still have a bunch questions. I'm sure our readers would appreciate a comment about Ms. Seymour and her political performance.'

'By now, even skinny people ought to recognize how power has gone to her head?'

'Would she win if there's an election tomorrow?'

'There are too many ignorant, naysayers and conservatives on this little island for her not to. Many by now have probably regret voting for her. But I'm sure people would vote for her again to keep Brexit going. I think it all comes down to whether or not she changes anything. In my opinion, she won't change a thing. She'll only split the United Kingdom further with her obesity insanity. And I'm quite sure it'll be the rather large people like me who'll be blamed for Brexit if it doesn't work out.'

'That'd be another one for the history books.'

'I hope common sense prevails and she's defeated, but I doubt it.'

'Do we have to fear Victoria Seymour and The Party?'

'She's in it for her own interest, not for the United Kingdom's. But no, I don't think we need to fear either her or The Party.'

'Okay Mason, let's stop here. I think I have enough for another great article about ImplantSkills and you.'

'You don't like her either, do you?'

'None of us at the editorial do. Actually, I don't know how she won the election, because so far, I haven't met a single person who admits to voting for her. Unfortunately, the name Victoria Seymour is a damn good page turner. In the upcoming weekend edition, I'm writing an article that focuses on details of her childhood and private life.'

'You shouldn't give the woman so much attention.'

'We definitely should! We've come to learn the hard way that this woman is extremely conceited. When we write anything even a little negative about her and The Party, she comes on to us like a bulldog. The Party has already had people coming to our offices requesting that we ought to be more moderate in our criticism of her and The Party.'

'You're kidding!'

'We're almost certain she'll try to silence us after this weekend-edition.'

'Why do you print it, then?'

'My editor wants to make her look bad. He doesn't like what she doing to overweight people. If The Party has an issue with what we write, they have the right to pull us into court.'

'Is he looney?'

'Who?'

'Your editor.'

'No. He's a decent person who believes in justice. If Victoria Seymour drags us into court, it might make people wake up and see what kind of Prime Minister she really is.'

'Oh, that's good.'

'But Mason! If your Libyan friend's claim pans out, it'll be a big story! I'll keep you posted on my findings.'

ANDY GREEN and Chris Campbell, spend their Saturday afternoon informing Andy Green's Chief in Command, Mr. Andrews, about Victoria Seymour. He carefully analyses the contents of the Future Directive Assessment Report and transfers it to a secure memory stick.

'Killing a Head-of-State does not happen every day,' says Mr. Andrews. 'It seems our six Continent Teams have very little doubt about Ms. Seymour. Five Ayes. One Nay. There isn't much preventing this FDAR from turning into reality.'

'Well,' comments Andy. 'I guess we'll have to discuss how to carry out the FDAR then.'

'In about six months, Victoria Seymour will attend The Speakers Association on Political Domestic Collaboration in Tallahassee, Florida,' Chris informs them.

'This means we need reliable intelligence concerning the security around her and our own president. Are there scapegoats we can use, any stories we can use to cover up the assassination?'

'We'll have to look into it,' says Andy.

'If we only have six months, then we need to move fast on this one.'

'It's a reasonable window.'

'And Chris. I assume this is your first FDAR?'

'I'll return to London tomorrow. I just had to deliver the message.'

He notices how the two men are laughing.

'What?'

'No,' says Andy. 'You might return to London. Being the carrier is just another way of saying that you are now involved. That's how we all start our first FDAR.'

'Oh.'

'It would be good to have an extra set of hands,' growls their Chief. 'Assignments like these are extremely difficult to plan. In this case coordination between our two continents are required.'

'I'll be glad to assist. I'm currently without a mission.'

'I heard your boss at ImplantSkills has problems,' says Mr. Andrews.

'Yes. There's a cash-flow problem.'

'I'll call your London Chief on Monday. He'll first have to approve you working with us.'

Andy winks at Chris. Looks like they'll be working together again. It's going to be fun.

'Sooo ... ' draws out Mr. Andrews. 'According to the TSC Employer Manual, page 254 relevant for FDAR execution ... uhm ... measures to be taken ... eh ... I'm required to inform you about the FDAR contents on page five, saying that ...

In witness of:

The Continent Leaders and their Voters agree that Victoria Seymour is not in a position to handle power. Eighty-two percent of all Voters, based on the Six Continent Teams, define her capabilities, based on her psychological profile as not compatible with politics. Sixty-five percent has agreed that she is a general threat to the stability of the European Continent. Her evaluation on the world-stage is evaluated as low-to-average for invoking danger to the current geopolitical stability by seventy-one percent and critical-to-dangerous by fifteen percent. The concern is that what she is doing, and how she is doing it, will spread to other European countries and eventually to the US where obesity is also at reasonable concern.

Mr. Andrews pauses and looks across his desk at Chris and Andy. 'Don't take this as an insult, brothers.'

'None taken.'

Mr. Andrews continues:

In witness of:

Hundred-and-twenty-three pages in the FDAR, starting on page fifty-one, are allocated to describing three possible outcome scenarios designed by the Future Team after her assassination. The three scenarios fit with the Present Team's view on how the world could turn out if she is not assassinated. The Present Teams evaluation of her not getting assassinated and the Future Team's view on what happens if she is assassinated has generated a delta among the Present Team and the Future Team of eighty-three percent. The delta equates for a head's up for Victoria Seymour's assassination.

Mr. Andrews looks up from the screen.

'That's a gigantic delta,' exclaims Andy, surprised. 'I guess the chance of her not getting assassinated is rather low. With this result, we need to assassinate her at least two times before nailing her in her coffin.'

'Well, I guess it's settled then,' concludes Mr. Andrews. 'You're now witnesses to the fact that I'm familiar with the contents stated in the FDAR and agree to its execution. Please sign here.'

'Shall I sign too?' asks Chris.

'Yes. As mentioned, I'll arrange for your transfer and security clearance with your London supervisor on Monday. And Andy! Please start the process of selecting people for the preps on Monday, too. You're now officially in charge of preparing the shit-show. So, do me a favor and get off the bottle for a while, will you?'

'Sure thing, boss. But in six months, I'll be on it again.'

THE INTERVIEW with Mike Hornett, the journalist, makes Mason Sanders reflect a little on the last ten days. He was quick to offer the business jet, all the houses and assets here and there, to get an estimate on how much cash-flow he has available – if it becomes necessary. Unfortunately, the availability shows only enough to cover two weeks of operational costs for ImplantSkills and at least twelve weeks are the minimum necessary. And even more daunting is the fact that it takes way too long to get the cash liquid making it almost impossible to use his own resources. For the first time in ImplantSkills history, an external investor is required and that is something he does not want.

For a moment he turns melancholy. How do you describe to people, how it is to be in a situation where you stand to lose all you have because of a hacker attack? A hacker attack which is technically not possible. This is not the first time he has been in trouble. When he was twenty-five he ran his first company against the wall for the simple reason of not listening to others. The second time he went bust was when he was thirty-five, with a similar story, but there he listened to others. You can be as good as you want. You can listen, or not listen, shit simply just happens and there is nothing you can do about it. It happens to companies and to people all the time. It is very human to believe that you have things under control. But at the end you still get hit with a stroke of fate. Success is mainly based on having good luck and being at the right place at the right time. If anybody says anything else, they are nothing but arrogant people, not worth spending time on. A few failures on your CV or resume are not necessarily a bad thing, but many CEOs see any failure as a weakness. When he turned thirty-seven, he founded ImplantSkills and, in the process, selected people for his management team who were honest enough to admit their career failures. ImplantSkills has gone through the learning curve the hard way, especially in its early phase when capital was sparse. But had it not been for his criteria for selecting his management team – men who all were well skilled at navigating past the usual failure because they already tried to fail – then ImplantSkills would probably not have been the success it is today.

To maintain success is even worse than achieving it. Each time a new business is started, it is a little more complicated because the stakes are usually higher. As the numbers of the business increase, the entrepreneur feels the need for higher profits and consequently more freedom. But a third bankruptcy, and that being with ImplantSkills, would be a disaster and a painful experience. One with a recovery percentage close to zero. In his age and with his history and experience, luck would turn on him, just as it does at the moment. Though, if the unavoidable happens and he goes bust, he will only have himself to blame. The extreme success of ImplantSkills made him ignore the most important rule for every entrepreneur: Never go into private debt based on shareholder value when the market still hasn't paid you out. And do not make purchases financed on debt, because it's just plain stupid – especially when you end up in situations like this one. He could hit himself on the head for being so careless. Because if ImplantSkills becomes insolvent it will be very painful in the outside world. There are plenty of people who would love to see him fall and get screwed.

So, it is now time to show even more perseverance. He will have to roll his sleeves up a bit higher and get to work. It's time to work even harder. The banks' unwillingness to provide bridge financing or investors taking advantage of the situation will thwart neither ImplantSkills nor him. He will not allow this to happen. Tomorrow he has a first meeting in Canary Wharf with this investment house who called him while in Piran. If he can strike a deal, a fair one, then things will as always turn out just fine. He hopes it works out with them because he is not really in the mood to talk with too many investors. It is simply a waste of precious time.

FROM HIS bed, Chris Campbell looks at the table in the middle of the hotel room. On it, a movie is looping over and over on his laptop's DVD player showing that last night was a very unusual night. He has never ever before cheated on his wife like he did last night.

He should have known it was a set-up. The beautiful young woman on the DVD is obviously not in his league, but rather part of a plan. She seduced him completely and they made love all night. It was intense! It was amazing, or at least that's what it looks like on the DVD, though, Chris Campbell does not recall a single moment of banging this beautiful young girls brains out.

It is a strange feeling knowing you did something but not being able to recall it. He loves his wife and family very much and would never do such a thing, no matter how exciting the temptation is. Knowing that this is a set-up but not being able to figure out why in the world anyone would put him in this position or what anyone would want from him is aggravating. His wife would forgive him. And trust his explanation because she knows he loves her. So trying to blackmail him with this won't work.

But how did he end up with the DVD playing on his laptop? How would they know which hotel he is staying at and how did they get in? And someone had to have access to his room to install the three cameras that filmed the night's events and got edited very professionally.

He tries to replay last night. Andy was, of course, dead drunk when they met. The man drinks too much and too often. He is known for his heavy drinking and their Chief had said to leave the bottle alone beginning on Monday. But, as usual, after a good meal, there was that first drink and it should have stopped there because he had to fly the next day and that's no fun with a hangover. The plan was to leave the bar and get a good night's sleep but hell is paved with honourable intentions. The atmosphere at the bar was great and the cocktails were excellent. The warm evening meant that the girls were showing their legs and although the second drink was to be their last, somehow the plan was delayed and the rest was history.

He remembered that two very lovely young ladies asked if the neighboring bar stools were empty and then one of the girls spilt a Pina Colada over Andy's shirt. When she then offered to make up for her clumsiness by buying them a drink, the third drink turned into a fourth and so on. And so it probably was that he now finds himself the next morning in his hotel room watching a DVD of him and a beautiful but unknown woman romping in the sheets.

So, what do they want from him? He is neither rich nor important. And he lives in a country eleven-thousand kilometers away. He finds it difficult not to laugh when watching what is happening on the DVD. If the truth be known, he hates to admit it and would never let his wife know … he kind of regrets not remembering having sex with that lovely nymph who obviously enjoyed his tongue performing its magic between her beautiful spread legs.

Chris takes the DVD out of its drive and shuts down his laptop. Needless to say, some kind of tranquilizer must have been in one of those final Mojitos. But what about Andy? Did they set him up too? When did she leave with him to go to his hotel room? How did they get to the hotel? Did they walk or take a cab? Perhaps Andy knows something about the time between that fourth Mojito and right now.

CHRIS Campbell packs his luggage and heads down to the hotel lobby to check-out. Remembering what happened, he looks around in the lobby area with suspicion, observing people and trying to get a fix on the kind of people in the hotel. When he realizes his mania he continues to the reception.

'Say,' he says to the receptionist. 'I had an unexpected guest in my room last night. It was room 1104. Did you by any chance see me walk past here with a young girl yesterday evening, or early this morning, to pick up my key card?

'I was on duty last night, sir. And I recall how she was supporting you on the way to the elevators. You were … let's say … rather drunk.'

'I'm not proud of last night … but you see my intention was never to … well … please do believe me. I think I was set-up. And I don't recall a single moment from last night.'

'Oh.'

The surprise of the receptionist makes Chris smile. In a way he is sorry too. Then he looks at the man's badge. 'Mr. Popescu … I believe an extortion attempt was executed in your hotel. There's a DVD on my laptop showing my role in this event. My question is of course: Who put it there? Who had access to my room to install cameras? Do you understand where I'm heading?'

'We might be able to give you copies from the surveillance cameras, sir. Is there any way I can get in contact with you? We can also report the incidence to the police.'

'I'm quite sure none of us want any of that. Will you be on duty at the same time tomorrow?'

'Yes sir.'

'Then someone will drop by tomorrow and pick up the copies.' Chris nods to the man and goes toward the door, but on the way, he stops and returns to reception. 'You know, I don't know what was in those drinks, but being unfaithful and not remembering sleeping with such a perfect body, is almost a bigger crime than being unfaithful.'

The receptionist laughs. 'I hear you, sir!'

Before leaving the hotel, Chris goes to a near-by phone booth to make a call. 'Hey Andy!' he says when the man picks up his telephone. 'Guess what? I think I'll be staying a couple of extra nights. Something unusual happened last night.'

'Really? Why? What happened?'

'We need to meet somewhere safe. I'm not sure if I'm being followed or if I or my cell phone have been compromised. Shall we meet at Proximity One?'

'Sure. Whatever you say. Half an hour?'

'Suits me,' says Chris and hangs up. Perhaps Andy knows what happened after the fourth Mojito.

After hailing a taxi, he pulls out his cell phone and turns it off. He also takes out the battery as a precaution and puts it in one of the jacket pockets.

Only one thing is for sure.

Last night he had sex, which according to the DVD, was really good sex.

And he is not at all happy about this.

CHAPTER 4

IT IS A NEW DAY IN THE CENTRAL district of London. The sun is shining from a cloudless sky, turning a rather overcast last couple of days into a warm and promising day. In his large, ten room apartment with a terrace and view of the green part of London, Mason Sanders is going over the interview with Mike Hornett, the journalist. Neither did Mehdi Hanachi's idea and his theory about obese people nor Mike Hornett's questions about who might be behind such a hacker attack and what is going on pass by unnoticed. If there is any relevancy to what his Libyan friend says, then it fits quite well with the awful rhetoric of Victoria Seymour and The Party. He is obese. He is rich. He has the resources to fight her. Many other obese people also have the resources to fight her.

So what this is about? Disarming her potential and upcoming enemies?

It is worth following up on the other two rich businessmen from Piran that Hanachi had mentioned too. Robert Martins and James Hollister are also a rather obese bunch. As he remembers, their companies are registered in London too. It would be interesting to talk to them and see if their situations are the same as his. If this turns out to be the case, then it is obvious something is going on that specifically targets people of their size.

But who would prosper from such an act of insanity? A competitor? So far, ImplantSkills' competitors have not had a reason to start a competitive war against them. How about Victoria Seymour? How would she benefit? The effect of a large company like ImplantSkills going bankrupt is not only that obese people are on the streets and the country loses a large taxpayer, but also regular-sized employees who work for the company either directly or indirectly. It would be political suicide and it would make no sense whatsoever for the new Prime Minister to engage in such game. More and more questions seem to pop up by the hour. Hopefully, Mike Hornett will find a few leads they can follow up on, because at this moment, events seem rather blurry and don't make any sense at all.

Mason pulls out his cell phone and sends Yulia, his girlfriend, a text message. They always text each other when they are apart to let each other know that they're okay and that everything is running according to plan. He thinks about their last kiss. It was more intense than usual and he wonders if it could have been their last.

He dismiss the thought.

Yes, there is definitely a problem with ImplantSkills. Hopefully the matter will be resolved today with the woman who called him when he was in Piran. Her name is Christina Goldstein. The investment house she works for is called Cliff Brad Brokerage Partners and she is one of its' founding partners. He has never heard of her nor the investment house but she said they are willing to strike a fair deal for an interim investment in ImplantSkills. Since her call, though, other brokerages have also called which he anticipated, wanting to take advantage of ImplantSkills' unfortunate situation. At least it seems the article written by Mike Hornett and run yesterday has helped draw even further attention to ImplantSkills' situation.

'Excuse me,' Mason says to the bellboy in the lobby. 'What should I do today? Tube or Taxi to the Docklands?'

'Oh no, Mason. The morning traffic is awful.'

'So you suggest Tube?'

'You can borrow my bike.'

Mason laughs. 'Do you think your bike would survive?'

'Uhm. I don't want to jeopardize my tip so I'll just keep my mouth shut. Go to Victoria Station. Take Victoria Line to Green Park. Then Jubilee Line. It's a five minute walk from here.' The bellboy points in the direction of the Underground station.

'I thank you, sir,' jokes Mason, tipping the kid a couple of quid. He actually knows very well how to get from the apartment to Canary Wharf with the Tube but he loves the little quick morning chat with the kid. He seems so normal compared to the many people he meets every day whose wallets are loaded with money. Many years ago, before his second bankruptcy, he worked in one of the skyscrapers at Canary Wharf. With the money he put aside back then, he founded ImplantSkills. He knew from the first bankruptcy how important it is to put aside some cash to be able to get out of situations like these, should they arise. The world would be a better place to be if everyone had experienced to go bankrupt at least once. There would be more empathy and less ignorance about the subject. A bankruptcy makes you appreciate what you have. The private jet, the cool houses, the women and good food are all very nice to have but not really necessary in life. The first time he went bust, he lived on a daily budget no larger than the price of a pack of Marlboros. In truth, the gigantic success of ImplantSkills is based on years of catastrophic failures and disasters striking out again and again, where the only reasonable thing to do is to get up, brush off the dust and navigate through the difficult times. But who anticipates bank accounts at different banks to get hacked and cleaned out?

Well, he certainly didn't. At least he knows from experience that situations eventually improve, although, putting too much confidence in others to solve your problems is a very, very bad idea.

The distance to Green Park turns out to be much longer than five minutes. When he arrives at the entrance to the Underground, he realizes from the map that he must have walked at least 2.000 meters. He should have used a driver after all, but at rush-hour in this city you are much better off using the Underground. On the way down with the escalator, he hears a familiar noise. It is his stomach making rumbling noises. He had not taken the time to eat breakfast. So when he gets to the Docklands, he will go to his favorite bakery and buy breakfast.

After getting out at Canary Wharf, he walks the short distance from the station to the connecting underground shopping center. The bakery he usually uses is still there after so many years of his absence. It has always been his favorite because of its' high quality products, just like the sushi-bar a little further down the passage. That one also is still there. Good to know for a later return. Mason enters the bakery. It will be interesting to see if its' quality has remained the same.

'Good morning,' says Mason joyfully to a young black man with a pimpled face standing behind the counter. 'I'd like a box of mixed doughnuts.'

'Are you sure you shouldn't just stay with one?'

'I beg your pardon?'

'Do you need to eat them all?'

Mason stands there, completely speechless.

'Have you ever thought about joining the WeightForLife, program? That will certainly help you. Then you might be able to find a job somewhere.'

'What's that to you?' stutters Mason.

'Nothing. But you'd be happier to get out of that big body of yours, don't you think?'

He leaves the bakery at the speed of light and completely forgets about the doughnuts. Nobody has ever insulted him before so impolitely. It baffles him completely. Had it not been for the shock, he would have shown that immature shithead what he thinks of Victoria Seymour and her WeightForLife program. Taking the escalator at a fast pace or as fast as anyone of his size can walk, he goes to a bakery he knows in one of the other skyscrapers. On the way, he wonders why he hadn't made some joke about black people. He should have called him a gorilla, monkey or just smacked him. Why is it that the good come-backs come to you after the fact? And what on earth made him vote for that damn lady who runs the United Kingdom? He cannot recall what those reasons were – apart from her good Sarah Palin looks.

At the next bakery he is luckier. A thin young woman serves him, packing six doughnuts into a take-out box with no comment. Upon returning to the street, he walks to a vacant bench in the Oasis Park, sits down and lets one doughnut after the other dissolve into thin air.

After such an unpleasant incident, he certainly deserves them!

What should he do with the box now? Because of the new laws to prohibit terrorism, there are no trash cans in London. He tosses the wrapping on top of a mountain of trash behind the bench, then, with great effort, gets to his feet and walks on.

YESTERDAY should have been the end of the short business trip with the talks with Andy Green and his Chief in Command, Mr. Andrews. Though, with the blackmail affair, the trip must now be extended by a couple of days. According to the TSC Employer Manual, page 187, concerning blackmail and extortion attempts, he is obligated to report any such attempts so an investigation can get launched. The Special Council has a great deal of interest in protecting its employees, thereby protecting itself and its' existence. So contacting the authorities on matters like these never comes into question. It would mean a lot of unnecessary paperwork with names plastered all over it – which definitely should be prevented.

Chris Campbell gets into the taxi he has hailed, after quickly calling Andy from the public telephone in the hotel lobby area. Getting into the taxi, he almost loses his balance. The damn car doors these days are so small. He closes it and asks the driver to drive him to the Space Needle. When the cab starts moving he leans back into the soft seat, staring out his window. He sees huge white Cumulus clouds followed by a dark gray cover of Nimbostratus gathering over Mount Rainier before the Cascade mountain range. It is an awesome sight for someone who is not used to mountains. The summer weather has taken a shift. It is now so humid that he feels like taking a short nap. He looks out at Puget Sound and the people along the piers who live here also seen the warning that it is time to find shelter.

The taxi continues to Capitol Hill. Another five minutes and he will be at the Space Needle, or Proximity One, as they call it. Seeing the Seattle high-rise landscape pass by, it is obvious why the people of Seattle are so proud of their city. One must admit that Seattle is as livable as London.

Well, not quite. Recently, London has become a little too overrated and unaffordable. On top of the rising inflation due to this Brexit thing, the economy and political relationship to mainland Europe have gone more or less sour. And with Victoria Seymour as the new Prime Minister the situation worsens on a monthly basis. Were he young and without family, he would certainly return to Seattle and continue the fun Andy and he have always had.

On the other hand. An occasional business trip here is sufficient, too. Turning fifty-three next year has meant that the energy is definitely not the same as it used to be. Between forty and fifty-two he has slowly gained weight without really noticing it. And additionally, a lot has changed with the sudden change of the situation with ImplantSkills, making a part of his life more or less uncertain. It was not in the plan that he was to return to The Special Council's headquarters in London. At least, it was not so planned for the first couple of years, but to let him remain placed in ImplantSkills to follow its exceptional and highly advanced microchip hardware and software products and to keep an eye on the direction the technology and the company is heading. The Special Council has moles everywhere. No one had expected ImplantSkills to become such an important player in Artificial Intelligence. A whole world held it for impossible that ImplantSkills could do what it does today. Something others totally failed to envisage the company's vision – apart from the Old Man.

It's really clever what the company has developed. It is an organic microprocessor that is implanted into the body measuring heartbeat, fat-percentage, electrolysis and many other functions that sense whether the human body is healthy or not. With the advanced artificial intelligence software, the system sets off a warning, if a client requires medical attention. Insurance companies and healthcare services love the product and so do nursing homes and nursing services, who use the implant to check long-distance on patients by using The Internet of Things. For the military, information about its troops, are relayed real-time for training and battlefield purposes.

ImplantSkills has indeed a powerful product. The only real downside of its product is that the database at ImplantSkills knows a lot about their clients. One could argue that the implants are very efficient identity tags, which, if they fall into the hands of hackers or unfriendly governments, are an efficient way of tracking someone down. Or giving sensitive information about a person's health. Back when he was hired as a technician, it was soon obvious that he had the ability to understand the smallest of details of the technology. It did not take long for him to advance to Senior Manager of Technology, a job he can claim he has performed with great perfection and satisfaction. Being on-board and seeing ImplantSkills grow and seeing how software creates better software through the knowledge of software in the field is a once-in-a-lifetime experience. In the long run, the algorithms will eventually come to replace doctors and experts – at least within some fields. Even further down the line, may completely replace them in a kind of what Google does to truck- and taxi drivers with their autonomous vehicles.

This may lead to social unrest among those who are affected, though, it is a future that no one can prevent. That is why The Special Council is interested in keeping an eye on companies such as ImplantSkills, at best from the inside, as these huge technology players might unintended change the course of Democracy.

Had it not been for ImplantSkills sudden situation, he would have been close to sending a request to the Old Man to leave the The Special Council on behalf of ImplantSkills. Though, to leave may not have been so easy and the chances of rejection could had been rather high. As defined in the TSC Employer Manual on page 53, it is not foreseen that someone quits The Special Council due to the confidentiality and safety degree of their activities. When hired by The Special Council it is for life. That is what people sign up to. Everybody inside the organization are familiar with page 53. And everybody knows the consequences of a dishonest leave. At least, in return for the eternal confidence, salaries, employee benefits and retirement compensation are so much better than those found on the outside world. It is for sure he is proud to work for The Special Council. It's great to be part of something big which only a few people world-wide are a part of. It is as well great to contribute to a cause that is in everyone's best interests. But ImplantSkills is somewhat of a unique opportunity. He never expected to get promoted as fast as he did and raise to the position he is in today. Before the infiltration job, he worked as a senior coordinator, coordinating decisions from the Continent Teams and analyzing information that goes into the Future Directive Assessment Reports. It was quite interesting but also hard work to set-up the parameters for the Present Team and Future Team and to manage their decisions properly. ImplantSkills is somewhat different. It's more technology driven. Something where he can still change the world while simultanously assist in maintaining its' stability by acting as mole.

Chris gets out of the taxi. The first raindrops hang like thick fog in the air. Watching the taxi return up Capital Hill, he thinks about what Andy Green is going to tell him. After what happened last night, he may have become a security threat for The Special Council. That is page 187 in the TSC Employer Manual. Every employee knows that page too. Walking to the entrance of the Space Needle, he notices the little yellow Japanese car is already there, parked at the sidewalk with its huge front lights staring at him. The little car looks so innocent and so rusty. Had it been brown it would look new. Living five minutes from Bill Gates, it seems that a more decent car in the driveway would look better. But it will never happen. Andy loves that piece of Japanese autumn color. Chris leaves the elevator and gets out on the walk-way and sees Andy looking out at Puget Sound with a coffee in his hand.

'Your call surprised me,' says Andy while they move out to the barrier. They don't even bother shake their hands. 'Won't you miss your plane back to London?'

'I will for sure. But there's a reason for it …'

'You wanted to have a last drink, right?'

Chris laughs. 'As long as we don't end up at Wilma's Junkyard, its fine with me.' But then he becomes honest. 'Andy! Yesterday turned out differently than anticipated and according to the TSC Employer Manual, page 187, I'm obligated to report that I've been exposed to an extortion attempt.'

'In what way?'

'That's what I hoped you'd be able to tell me.'

'Tell you what?'

'Was I drunk last night?'

'You certainly were. Ha ha.'

'How many Mojito's did it take?'

'Surprisingly few but after the fourth, you started talking nonsense'

'And how about the girls.'

'Oh! Excellent ones. And young, you know. Wow, dude! You don't remember? One of them was really hitting on you hard.'

'Did she have blond hair?'

'She certainly did. The other was a brunette.'

'I remember her.'

'If you had given her the opportunity, she'd have eaten you raw right there on the spot.'

'She did. She went with me to my hotel and stayed the night.'

'You went to bed with her? You pig! You've never been unfaithful. Was the temptation too big, this time? Ha ha.'

'No. She went to bed with me. Not the other way around. I first found out about it this morning when I discovered a DVD and what was on it.'

'You had sex with her? Wow!'

'Yes. But I don't recall a single thing.'

'Sounds like something got into one of your Mojito's.'

'Sure thing! And now someone is probably going to extort me.'

'Ah, I get your point. That has to get reported'

'According to the TSC Employer Manual, then yes.'

'You had sex with her? Awesome. But why? What's so important about you? And why didn't it happen to me?'

'That's what I wanted you to tell me. I've concluded that they must have gotten hold of the wrong guy.'

'Ha! Then she really screwed up, didn't she? And you don't remember anything about doing her? I'd give up sex with my wife for a couple of years, just to do one of those two. No, hold on, I don't even have to give anything up. The little wife is already gone, ha ha. Guess we've been married too long.'

'Same story here. At least I got an excellent porn out of it.'

'Are you going to tell her?'

'Who?'

'Your wife.'

'Of course not. Why? As soon I'm on the plane, it's over.'

'But we still need to report it. Shall I do it?'

'Yes please. In a way it did happen in your district. But hey, if you want to, you can watch the DVD before you hand it over to the team. I'm quite a stud!'

'I'd like to see that girl naked, that's for sure. We'll find her and take her in for investigation, so we can check up on the circumstances.'

'I've asked at the hotel to make a copy of what the security cameras caught on tape yesterday night.'

'That's good. Then we have something to work with.'

'I believe so, too.'

'But you know what? I'm going to see the DVD in strict privacy. That girl, I gotta see naked! I just can't help myself.'

A COUPLE of hours later Andy and Chris say good-bye to each other. The poor bastard had sex and couldn't even enjoy it. Andy Green considers whether to stay a little longer at the Space Needle for another cup of coffee or drive home and use the rest of the day preparing things for tomorrow. At home it is at least still quiet. His wife and children will not return till later in the evening.

He decides on the second option. At home he is well able to make a coffee too. Perhaps an even better one and much cheaper than the horrible prices they charge at the Space Needle. With the extortion attempt on his buddy, it is unsure if the FDAR can still be carried out. The extortion incidence requires investigation. At least that is what is stated in the TSC and the TSC is always right, especially if anyone involved in FDARs in any way becomes disclosed, extorted, manipulated or perishes in some unfortunate, unexplainable event. The assignment must be put on hold for now and can only be continued when the protocols have been fully updated and the required framework set up, securing that the FDAR has not been compromised. He remembers it says so page 398, Article 15 – 31 to page 415, Article 32 – 48 in the TSC Employer Manual.

Thinking about all the bureaucracy at The Special Council, he sometimes misses the good old days when the Berlin Wall was still standing. Back then, there was an enemy, a physical one, who could be blamed for practically everything. These days, vast resources are used to figure out the slightest details behind some dreadful event. In the old days if anyone was extorted, it was probably the Russians. If anyone was kidnapped or disappeared forever, it was probably the Russians. The Russians must have occasionally felt unfairly treated for everything that went wrong in the Western world. But with the fall of the Berlin Wall entire military industries collapsed. This meant that there was a massive worldwide build up of military know-how including analysts and developers, nuclear missile scientists, chemical weapons experts, hackers, professional soldiers and military strategic advisers who were all looking for new jobs. Russian experts were quick to find new partners which, unfortunately, proved to be extreme religious or aristocratic countries such as Iran, Iraq, Pakistan, India and China. And to this day, the Western world still hasn't figured out how to cope with all this happening.

Without an enemy, the United States of America ceased to function as a proper entity. An entire high-tech military industry was almost closed down and President Reagan's Starwars Project scrapped forever. Money was re-directed to education and healthcare and to rebuilding the American infrastructure. Republicans like himself were confused. Had it not been for 9/11 in 2001, his proud nation would have torn itself apart. The armaments industry received a new boost, millions of old jobs in weapons systems and the intelligence service were reinstated when twenty terrorists changed the world over a cup of morning coffee. In hindsight, the terrorists involved in 9/11, created jobs worth 40 billion dollars per head, a total of 800 billion, in Homeland Security, the CIA, the FBI and military operations and took away the money for schools, healthcare, new roads and bridges which are now collapsing. Fifteen percent of the United States GNP is allocated to the military, because you certainly need tanks, fighter planes and guns to kill the terrorists who fly into skyscrapers and because you need hand guns to protect your family from terrorists even if you live in a corn field in Oklahoma. An even higher percentage of the United States GNP is spent on intelligence and surveillance, spying on its' own citizens and foreign countries. Thank you, you twenty terrorists! You have succeeded in turning this dumb country into an even dumber country which is now without a proper school system and healthcare system. Every year more people die from collapsing bridges and medicine overdoses than terrorist attacks.

He is a Republican at heart. He really is. Though, with the current era of right-wing politics in the White House, the Good Old Party and the Tea Party and now that a black person got to become president of the United States, it has become difficult to carry out any form of politics in general. He still believes deeply in his Republican roots even though he has slowly become more or less a closet-Democrat. In reality, former President Obama had no chance of making any changes at all. And neither can the current Republican president – or whatever branch he belongs to.

Who keeps the intelligence agencies around the world on a tight leash? Who keeps democratic governments from abusing their power? Who keeps democracies from collapsing throughout the world? The United Nations has taken on this role. Getting a mandate which allows them to actually do anything only happens if it is in the interest of all members. But the Old Man, he acts when an FDAR says it's necessary to act. There should be more people like him out there caring for others, caring for the world and its population. It is an honour to work for a man who does not act out of self-interest but truly cares about others.

'Donald! You are sitting and daydreaming. Have you been watching pornos while we were gone?'

'Huh? What?' The sudden interruption makes him lose his bearings. It is his voluptuous wife standing at the door to the study room. He must have dosed off for a couple of minutes and failed to hear them come home early.

'Why do you think that?'

'Because there's a DVD in the player. Dena wanted to see something.'

'Oh, honey ... You won't believe it, but that DVD doesn't belong to me. It was …'

'You know we agreed not to have stuff like that in the house. The children …'

'No, you misunderstand. It was Chris …'

'Of course he's to blame!' she responds bitterly. 'As usual.'

'He wanted to show me …'

'You didn't keep your promise. We …'

'Before you start your morality crap, why don't you take a look at the star on the DVD? If you'd bothered to let go of your prejudices before attacking me, you'd see it's Chris. As I was about to explain; he's in trouble for some unapparent reason, and was looking for advice. And … he … absolutely had to show me the cute lady he banged.'

'Now, stop it right there, Mr. Green! You have a lot of explaining to do.'

'It's easy Betty. Someone put something in his drink and wiped out his brains last night. He didn't know what he was doing. He was set-up.'

'Why would anyone set up Chris? He is just a decent hard-working person.'

'That's what we're trying to figure out.'

'Poor Chris. But could you at least remove the DVD?'

'Of course. But I'm quite sure Dena already did. At least now she has something fun to tell her friends at school tomorrow.'

CHRIS Campbell knows he is now officially prohibited from working for The Special Council. It is the end of his mission in Seattle and it is also the end of his role within The Special Council until things can be clarified. And what now when ImplantSkills is only running on half power? The only reasonable thing to do would be to return to his job there and try to solve the urgent matters. But at least Andy has the DVD. He picked up the surveillance tapes from the hotel this morning, he informed. This ought to be enough to identify the girl and find her.

Chris laughs. By choosing him as their victim, they haven't done themselves any favor because, in one way or another, The Special Council will find those who are attempting to extort him. It is of course not the first time that something like this has happened inside their organization. The worse-case scenario is when a member cheats on his wife and she hires a private investigator. The Special Council absolutely forbids marital cheating because it has no interest in outsiders sniffing around its' staff. Unfortunately, it is human nature that even the best and most loyal employees get horny. Not even an organization like The Special Council has the power to prevent this from happening. It would save a lot of security concerns if the dicks of those working inside the organization were cut off and holes filled with thick concrete. The Special Council, does not allow them to do anything without first looking into the TSC Employer Manual.

To serve and protect humanity, it says on page three. A couple of pages later, on page twenty-seven it says: Please read the TSC Employer Manual's regulations on personal behavior on Page 245 for detailed info regarding Smartphones and visits to toilets while on duty inside the TSC. The best and most frequently visited article is found on page 167. Sexual intercourse between a man and a woman is not allowed in rest-rooms, in offices or rooms used for accommodating personnel. Most employees have figured out that for the 800 employees working for The Special Council world-wide, the TSC Employer Manual does not mention a single thing about doing it in the basement or on car hoods.

But, of course, he would never be unfaithful. He loves his wife. One hard slam on his huge butt and they both can ride the wave to eternal heaven.

But right now, the ride is to Tacoma Airport and then back to London.

CHAPTER 5

CLIFF BRAD BROKERAGE PARTNERS offices are a one minute walk from the Canary Wharf station. It is amazing how Docklands has evolved into the place it is today. When he was a child, there was absolutely nothing here apart from ruins and crumbling buildings where people lived in poverty. Today, the richest banks and brokerage firms have their headquarters and offices here. He stops to look up at the 36 storey structure where he used to work. More than 200 billion pounds are pushed through the United Kingdom's financial systems every day. It's a lot of capital. He enters the building beside the one he used to work in and takes the elevator to the 23rd floor as the woman who called him in Piran had instructed him to do. Getting out on the floor, he wonders why so little money is spent on elevator doors, why they are so small instead of making them large. At the reception a beautiful young girl is doing her nails while trying to look busy. She is almost a copy of Yulia, his own girlfriend, thinks Mason. But the girl here, doing her nails, probably doesn't have the brains and intelligence he so much appreciates in his girlfriend.

Oh boy! He hates places like this. What do hedge funds and investment houses contribute to society other than enriching themselves? Absolutely nothing. The truth is they are willing to take chances and earn money although there are those who sit in their skyscrapers and take advantage of the naivety of their customers. It is up here that the vultures circle. Another truth is these are the people he so urgently needs to save ImplantSkills and his financial future.

He introduces himself to the girl at reception. 'Hello there. My name is Mason Sanders. Is Christina Goldstein there?'

'Do you have an appointment?'

'Yes.'

'I think she's in a meeting. It's taking a little longer than expected. I'll see when she'll be available.'

'I'd appreciate it.'

'Please be seated and help yourself to tea and cakes.'

'Tea is perfect.' After those doughnuts his throat is dry. Unfortunately, they were not as good as his preferred bakery's. Pouring himself some hot water, the receptionist returns with the news that Mrs. Goldstein, has been informed of his arrival.

'She'll be out in a moment.'

'Thank you!'

But the moment turns into five minutes. The five minutes into ten minutes. After twenty minutes he thinks it is about time to leave. There are other investors who have called him, but then he reminds himself of now he is the one to be humble.

'Ah, Mr. Sanders!' he hears someone say. 'How nice of you to drop by. My calendar is a bit full today. Sorry you had to wait.'

'Oh, not a problem.'

'Come this way, please. I've read about what's happening at ImplantSkills. That's why I called. It's awful.'

'It certainly is.'

'Mr. Sanders. We want to do a deal with you.'

'What an amazing view from up here,' exclaims Mason, looking out the huge panorama windows. 'London appears to be showing it's good side today. No rain. No clouds. And lovely temperature,' he says.

'Indeed. I never get tired of the view. Please, come and sit down.'

Mason moves in front of her desk and sits down.

He then asks, 'I need a bridging loan for 90 days. How much interest would a 50 million loan cost me?'

'I 've spent some time scrolling through ImplantSkills budget, the one your secretary send me yesterday. You really have a cash-cow going there.'

'We certainly do.'

'And when we talked, I understood that you expect the bank dispute to last for at least some months? In my opinion and experience, you'll probably end up in court.'

'Highly probable,' agrees Mason.

'We've discussed it and in spite of the dispute, we'd like to invest. You say 50 million?'

'Yes.'

'Okay.' She pauses. 'There's something you need to know about the investment you'll receive.'

'And that would be?'

'The investment will be allocated as government aid.'

'Government aid? Why?'

'Well, the hacker attacks were part of a military program of the British government which somehow got out of control. As it's a military program, I can, of course, not tell you any more and I personally don't know much about it. But a fund has been set up to repair the damage caused for companies like yours. The military has provided us with a list of those who have been affected. Your company is on it. We're the ones who are administering the list, cleaning up the mess the military has left behind.'

'So that's the reason you contacted me?'

'Yes.'

'Right now, I'm a little stunned. I don't know what to say …'

'… which we appreciate. One condition for this deal is absolutely non-disclosure not even to your associates.'

'I'm sure this isn't a problem. And I'm very pleased that the government is responding so quickly to our situation … may I … maybe … have a look at the list?'

'Of course. The list is no secret. You might have read about some of the companies on it in the news.' She opens a drawer and takes out a report and hands it over to Mason. When he gets it, he sees there are already company names crossed out all over it.

'I guess the military somehow screwed up, didn't they?' he asks.

'Indeed. But this has nothing to do with the deal we're going to make.'

It takes Mason less than fifteen seconds to find what he is searching for; the names of his two fellow businessmen from Piran. They are on the list, too but with their names still haven't been crossed out.

'These two here,' he says and shows her their names, 'are they also affected?'

'Yes. But I haven't had the opportunity to talk with them. I have so many people to contact and I'm doing this alone.'

'It's only you and your secretary here?'

'Exactly.'

Mason hands back the list.

'The deal we provide is better than what you'd get from any other investor,' she informs him. 'You'll receive the investment including a stipend that covers the losses the military has caused for your business. In return you'll not talk to others about the screw up. And you will not tell others about the conditions contained in the deal.'

'I accept that.'

'Good.'

'And what's the next step?'

'This is how it works: You'll need to go to our subsidiary in Germany to conclude the deal.'

'In Germany? May I ask why?'

'I guess the government wants to cover its back. The transactions are less transparent when the money comes from abroad.'

'I understand.'

Christina Goldstein provides Mason Sanders with a paper containing a telephone number and some practical information.

'You'll need to call this number to arrange a meeting. I'll inform them that you've agreed to our terms and they'll prepare the paperwork. Try to book a hotel for three days. When you receive the paperwork, you have two days to have it validated. But as I've said, the contract is not to fall into the hands of others – as we're dealing with the taxpayers money here.'

'I understand.'

Christina Goldstein gets up.

'On behalf of the military and our government, I'd like to apologize for the inconvenience we have caused you.'

'Well, at least you people react quickly. I guess once in a while weird things happen.' Mason stands. When they reach the door, they shake hands. But when he is about to leave, he turns and looks at the beautiful slim middle-aged woman.

'One quick, last question.'

'And that would be?' she asks.

'So, this is all happening because I and other rich blokes are obese?'

The comment catches Christina Goldstein completely off guard.

'The two I found on the list are pretty much same size as I am.'

'Mr. Sanders. We're fixing the problem.'

'So, my understanding is not completely a long-shot?'

'Not fully, Mr. Sanders. The military is in full swing trying to figure out what went wrong and who the hell is behind this crazy incidence. But as you understand, I can't say anything more about it.'

'What do you think of her?'

'Who?'

'Victoria Seymour and The Party.'

'Oh! I find what's going on rather bizarre. My mother is a heavy woman. And this Victoria Seymour really has a bizarre sense of humor with her rhetoric. I know influential people who have followed her career for a long time and are wondering why an intelligent woman like her would suddenly do a one-eighty like this. Who's next? People with small breasts like me?'

'I've noticed that Victoria Seymour's breasts are rather small, too. So I can only speculate. But yours match your body perfectly. Let them stay just like they are. Good day Ms. Goldstein. And thank you.'

'Oh, Mr. Sanders!'

'Yes.'

'Can you please do me a favor?'

'I might.'

'Why don't you inform your two friends about what we've been talking about? It would relieve my workload a lot. Then I can cross them off the list.'

'I can certainly do this. It would be no problem.'

'Thank you, Mr. Sanders.'

Returning to the elevators, Mason spends some time thinking about what he has just learned. What a deal he just got presented. Talk about going from bad to good. Come to think of it it's a once-in-a-lifetime deal. One he would never would have been able to negotiate with conventional investors. He kindly nods to the girl at reception who has finally finished doing her nails. Now she is reading a magazine and hardly notices him walk by. Cliff Brad Brokerage Partners. Now he understands why he has never heard of them. Since the military is behind it, it is nothing but a smoke screen. He realizes that they have very little to do up here apart from distributing capital to the affected companies. What matters is that he has received a life-line for a quick capital injection. And since he only needs 35 million, then this deal is probably going to be the best deal he will ever get. He will contact the German subsidiary tomorrow morning and arrange a meeting. They probably have a queue of CEOs before him, so he has some time to get a hold of the two others from Piran.

Getting out of the elevator and onto the street, he looks at the business card she gave him. It says Hamburg. Germany's second largest and most prosperous city. After Brexit they were quick to take some financial services away from The City of London. But that is not really his problem. Or Christina Goldstein's. It is crazy what is going on at the moment in the United Kingdom. Could the military perhaps be turning on Victoria Seymour? Is that what this is about? Do they have some fat generals wanting to assemble and equip obese people as resources for a possible fight against her government? Maybe there are powers operating in the shadow of the government that nobody knows about, fighting for justice for obese people. Nothing the government does at the moment is clear. It is going to be interesting what Mike Hornett, the journalist, comes up with regarding his research on obese people like himself.

Mason sighs.

Once again he might have steered clear.

WHEN Chris Campbell returns to London, the promised good weather does not exactly materialize. He was told that the sun was shining and the weather nice and warm; at least, that was what his wife said. As it turns out, she received a package with a copy of the DVD, but still hasn't unwrapped it. The perpetrators know where he lives. And they have the capability to transport and send data to London, to have a DVD burned and shipped out with a carrier in less than 24 hours after the incidence. He did not expect this to happen. It is obviously not a local Seattle gang.

'Bugger!' exclaims Chris.

The seriousness of the situation has changed and is now critical. His wife can yell as much as she likes if she wants to see what is on the DVD. The biggest danger is not carrying out the FDAR but him becoming a risk for The Special Council and its' anonymity. He needs to contact Andy on a safe phone. Because the less than 72 hour stay in Seattle now certainly means all kinds of trouble.

EPISODE 2

PEOPLE AT HIGH POSITIONS

CHAPTER 6

VICTORIA SEYMOUR'S CAMPAIGN MASTERPLAN for the upcoming election was to focus on the distribution of financial resources for education and social projects – such as improving the overloaded National Healthcare System – and provide better retirement benefits for senior citizens. Financial resources would come from huge cuts in military and intelligence budgets to prevent inflation from rising after Brexit. As part of the political manifesto, she has spend weeks writing, the plan to provide industry with better competitive conditions and being able to compete on World Trade Organization terms now that Britain is on its way out of the European Union and no longer dependent on the trade deals that the United Kingdom and the European Union have been using for the last forty some years, are now materializing. The political manifesto is excellent and well-thought out, but has not made as big an impact as they had anticipated on voters at the first weeks of the campaign.

BREXIT has changed the political landscape of the United Kingdom. To some extent it has destabilized the economy and the political landscape. It has made the so called 'political elite' unsure of how to shape the future and re-establish people's confidence in the democracy they live in. Brexit has shaken the morality and common values in England and completely distanced the United Kingdom from influence in the region it lives in. Lies were told on both sides of the Brexit argument. Xenophobia and hatred against foreigners and fellow European citizens followed, leading to increase in the pride, arrogance, bigotry, and self-confidence to an extent never before seen in the United Kingdom. It caused a loss of the United Kingdom's image as a liberal nation to the world.

The so called 'Special Relationships' and 'Special Trade Deals' with countries that stand in line fighting, to do such deals with the United Kingdom, have changed to any country that wants to enter into a deal at all. The trade deals argument unicorn was rather far-fetched. So far nothing seems to have improved in people's well-being. And yet, there are still people prefering to stay with the lies. People who still seem not to get it. People who only want to take advantage of the situation and don't really care whether it goes in one direction or the other.

From early on it was clear to Victoria and her team that talking common sense to people was not what was going to bring her and the The Party to 10 Downing Street. Voters do not give a damn about taking measures to improve the United Kingdom's economic deficit which former governments have inflicted upon citizens. Nor do people realize that the deindustrialization of the Western World has not yet ended and is mainly to blame for the unemployment in backbone industries which in recent decades has lead to a measurable increase in social unrest. It is challenging enough to convince fellow politicians that the 4th industrial revolution is on the foremarch where it will result in even higher unemployment at all economic levels. Blue- as well as white collar workers will have to acquire new skills to qualify for the technological advances in the work place. It is the ever-increasing use of Artificial Intelligence and smart robots that are revolutionizing the labour market that is going to kick-start the next round of social unrest.

Germany thinks about this already. But why does the United Kingdom postpone again and again? What will be the effect when machines are mobile and begin replacing people from all over the employment spectrum because they are smarter and can think on their own? Automated trains. Aircraft flying and landing automated for decades. What now with service jobs and office staff that do repetitive work? Or taxi and truck drivers up next as victims of the technological cliff edge. How is society going to cope with these immense changes? How will people be able to make a living when technology has begun to replace more jobs than it creates? It is the largest political issue for governments in the 21st century and in spite of this an issue that seems to bother no voter or politician.

But Victoria Seymour does with her political agenda because this means drastic changes for the government. One of the more serious problems is how tax will be generated in the future. How will the future of the welfare system get financed? Many voters believe they know politics, but they do not. And most are even too dumb to comprehend that most politicians actually do know what they are talking about. Not only has it been a big disappointment to recognize that most people do not care about The Party's political manifesto and its contents, but that people only care about feelings in politics, rather than facts. The hard and necessary decisions and reforms are not made and urgent matters postponed into eternity. It cannot continue like this. It was a startling wake-up call for Victoria after Brexit to realize that people do not care about the long-term dynamics of politics or the impact technology may inflict on their lives. People are too busy and overwhelmed in their daily lives and time has become a precious thing in which there is no room for being concerned with politics. It truly seems the times when politics were understood are over. Today it is only the headlines that catch the average person's attention and then only the headlines that promote scandal or entertainment. People are easily manipulated with easy-to-digest news. Brexit promised Unicorns on both sides and when the fairy tales didn't come true, no one asked the difficult question of what went wrong. How could the Remain and Leave camps play so much to people's feelings instead of to their common senses? It plagues a whole Kingdom.

Actually, it plaques most of the Western world.

Brexit demonstrated the true dynamics of politics and how uninteresting politics actually are for the majority of people. True politics are for the few. Something that only the political elite understands. Unfortunately, elections cannot be won with the elite alone. That was another lesson Victoria learned from Brexit. But appealing to the voters' common sense, by playing to their feelings, pride, arrogance and fears, that is how elections are won these days, confirming that winning elections has absolutely nothing to do with politics, but assuming that voters are only in it for own benefits. So, aligning topics with theirs fairy tales get easier sold to assure votes. And when the fairy tales fail to materialize, place the blame on someone else.

So, Victoria and her team started inventing unicorns. If they had played the election as they had in the election two years before Brexit when they had lost big time because they addressed the issues honestly, not lying as their political opponents had, they would have lost again. No, this time they decided to play to people's emotions, not their intelligence, by keeping facts and figures out of the equation. They lied more than any political party before them. And the result showed that they were right in doing so.

But how did they do it? How did they get to 10 Downing Street?

How did they get in power?

IT IS almost noon in the area around Westminster Abbey. After reading the last depressing polls, Victoria needs to get out of the office, out among strangers and have a coffee. She walks the five minutes to a cafe she found a few weeks ago. It has a nice atmosphere and has turned out to be a good place to mingle with the common people without actually being noticed. At the counter, two Indian waiters cope with the crowd of people coming in. She notices that most customers come for a coffee to-go and maybe a sandwich, but do not stay. There are a lot of empty seats and it becomes quite clear that here, in the middle of London, people don't have time to stop and eat at a table. A third employee looks busy repeating the same stuff over and over. If she had her way, then this stupid fat Pakistani idiot would be thrown to the lions for not properly supporting his colleagues. It is the same all over the world but some people simply cannot seem to get even the simplest things right.

'Is this place taken?' asks a voice.

Victoria looks up, slightly surprised. She recognizes Henry Montclair – her election campaign manager and political advisor who has been with her for some years now.

'Hi, Henry. As you might notice, you don't need to sit beside me. There are lots of free tables. But if you're nice, you may do so.'

The rude comment makes Henry Montclair laugh. 'I thought I was the only one who knows about this place.'

'I found it a couple of weeks ago. It's a nice place,' she says.

'Why didn't you say you were going here? I'd have joined you.'

'I'm sorry, Henry. I just needed some fresh air and to be alone for a minute. Don't take it personally. Have you seen our latest ratings?'

'I've seen them. They don't look too encouraging.'

'Oh, Henry! What are we doing wrong? What is it in my political manifesto and in our message to the people that they don't understand? I'm so sure we'll be able to change a lot in the country for the better – if people would just let us come to power.'

'Which, unfortunately, it seems they don't want.'

'What can we change? Tell me, please!'

'Hm,' mumbles Henry Montclair. 'It's an excellent political manifesto that you've written, Victoria. Pretty future secured. But you know how politics work as good as I.'

'What would it take to make people stop and listen?'

'I don't know. But I think we had better find out soon. Why not look to the United States and see how they do it?'

'I'm not sure if the world is dumb enough to fall for the rhetoric again. We need to think a little outside the box.'

'How about starting a war?

'A war?' she repeats, laughing.

'Yes! A war. Wars, scandals, terrorism, some huge crisis. Those things bind people together.'

'Wouldn't it be better to start with a scapegoat?'

'And who should this be?'

'I've no idea. What do you suggest?'

'You see it?' he asks.

'No. What?'

'Look.' Henry Montclair points to between his legs.

'Are you getting hard?'

'It's been a while since I was on top of you last time.'

'You're never on top of me. You always take me off the bed.'

'Just hearing you say that makes me horny.'

'Stop changing the subject. We need to find a new strategy. I don't want us to lose this election like we lost the last one. It was embarrassing.'

'Only wars make nations and its people true innovators. Don't you think Artificial Intelligence and robots should be much further advanced than they are today? Wars help on technological progress.'

'Why do you keep returning to the subject of war?'

'For no apparent reason. But think about the spin-offs from World War I and World War II. Our civilization thrives on challenges and progress. We only have what we have today because our ancestors had the courage to take chances. It's like our Western world has stopped this way of thinking because of the love to money. It has become out of fashion to take chances.'

'What exactly are you suggesting, Henry?'

'If we want The Party to succeed, we need to do something out of the extra-ordinary.'

'So, you say, we need to drop a bomb to get people gathered around my political manifesto? Great idea, Oppenheimer.'

'No. I'm saying we need to think differently, just to quote Apple Computers from the 80ties. Why are other European countries doing so much better than we are?'

'They're probably not as stupid as we are to leave the European Union, turning our backs on the world's biggest trade bloc. Our neighbors don't dwell on the past as many of us do and, like you as an example, believing we're still a superpower with colonies or that the Commonwealth is going to save our asses in the next war. Even East-bloc countries inside the European Union avoid us and now grow faster than us.'

'Ha ha,' laughs Henry Montclair. 'You'd make a good Prime Minister.'

'Having followed the United States and the United Kingdom's politics all my life, I sure hope we'll be able to navigate beyond the nationalism that Brexit has caused.'

'I won my bet. I'm happy that we're leaving the European Union.'

'I'm not going to discuss that with you. We've had that discussion too often. I want us to figure out how we're going to win this damn election.'

'That's right. But say, I totally forgot that you used to live in the United States.'

'I guess we make love more than we talk. I'm not sure if I've told you my mother comes from Leeds. My father was the American. They moved to the United States when I was twelve. I hated to move.'

'It's not to hear in your beautiful English accent.'

'I manage quite well to cover it up.'

'You certainly do.'

Victoria sighs. 'Maybe I should have stayed and gone into American politics.'

'Good that you didn't! Because with me at your side, you'll go to the top in this country.'

'Is that a promise?'

'Promise,' he says … 'You will need to work with me, then.'

Victoria sends Henry Montclair one of her attractive and seductive smiles. He notices the smile wrinkles appearing around her beautiful eyes and sees how her hands move up to her hair, putting it in a tight bun. She is one hot girl, he must admit, feeling his dick grow for the second time in a few minutes.

She, on the other hand, is wondering what Henry is thinking. He is her age, mid-fifties, all white hair, a masculine face and a nice slim body. If she weren't a career woman in the fast lane and her partner of many years might be sensing something was going on, she would let Henry take her right now. Right here on the table. It was only a few weeks ago that she let him screw her brains out and keep her on edge for days afterward. But she is so stressed at the moment trying to achieve her political goal of becoming the United Kingdom's next Prime Minister that the adventures must wait until later.

'You look a little like you're thinking about something?' she says.

He looks at her like a little boy.

'Something that does not have to do with you taking me on the table.'

'Hm. Mind-reader, aren't we?'

'I sense you didn't come here to drink coffee and gossip.'

'No, you're right.'

'What then?'

'We've both learned from Brexit. Maybe we should find a better way to sell our message. You know, a kind of repackaging of your manifesto's contents.'

'That's good for starters. What are you proposing?'

'By not selling the contents, but rather something that really matters to people. Like I meant with this war-stuff, we need to find a cause that unifies people. Something they understand and care about. When we've obtained power, we'll then re-wrap your manifesto and implement it.'

After seeing the polls, I'm quite open for suggestions.'

'Victoria! Focus on what's important.'

'What would make people care about what we're doing?' she asks. 'Immigration? The inadequate healthcare system? That we need to return to the Commonwealth? Those issues have already been exploited with Brexit.'

'There's a vacuum,' says Henry.

'A vacuum?'

'Yes, a vacuum. Now that the European Union is gone, who's to blame for all the problems in the Kingdom?'

'I'm quite sure the answer to this is: us, the politicians.'

'That's nothing new. That won't change. People are used to bitching about how awful we are and that they can do it better themselves. But what would make the majority of the voters get excited about our platform?'

'A terrorist attack? Some crazy lunatic shooting into the masses?'

'How about something that's right and wrong at the same time.'

'What do mean?'

'I've spent the last couple of days thinking about a thought I've had. You know as well as I do that one of our problems in this election is that we need the support of the middle-class as well as the working-class.'

That's obvious, Henry. Are you going to share your thoughts?'

'I just wanted to pave the way.'

'So, what are you suggesting?'

'Fat,' says Henry.

'I beg your pardon?'

'Obesity is a major problem in our society. And it's getting worse by the day. Did you know that the United Kingdom is the fattiest place in Europe?'

She starts laughing out loud. She should perhaps have slept with him before he lost his mind. 'You're so funny sometimes!' she says, removing a small tear from her face. 'Now I know we're really in trouble. How can you suggest such a thing? It's ridiculous.'

'No, Victoria. Listen to me. If people hear something often enough, they start believing it. We ought to talk about obesity and how it affects our daily lives, how it is becoming a burden to society.'

'Come on, Henry!'

'People will think it's strange at first; they will start talking about us. It will give us free advertising! I'm quite sure the media will pick-up on it as well and discuss the subject. And then, slowly, we'll add more and more to our case.'

Victoria realizes that Henry Montclair actually means what he is saying. 'You're serious, aren't you?'

'Yes I am.'

'So, now we want to discriminate against fat people because of our own failures in explaining our politics?'

'I didn't say anything about fat people. I specifically said that FAT is a problem. Not fat people. It's called planting a seed, Victoria. We all think fat people are a KIND of a problem. We know they are a burden on the healthcare and social system. Many stink because they don't take care of their hygiene. In buses, trains, aircraft and cinemas they need a double seat. People despise fat people because being fat is a sign of lack of personal discipline. You don't want to sit beside one or be friends with one. The boy in class who is mobbed is probably fat. And just to follow up on your statement, we, as a political party, will not talk about fat people. I'm sure the press and the tabloids will do that for us automatically.'

'I don't know what to say, Henry. It's disgusting. I'm a little baffled …'

'The good thing about fat people is; fat people can be of any skin color, nationality, age, gender, sexual direction. It's not racism. It's not antisemitism or xenophobia. It is discrimination. Look at the guy up there at the counter.' Henry points to the Pakistani waiter behind the desk who is trying unsuccessfully to get a grip on a mug of coffee.

'Fat, you say.' Victoria contemplates the subject and the consequences it might have for those they will be attacking. 'It's an evil thing to do,' she concludes. 'I'm sure the issue will go from fat to fat people. You don't know it, but I used to be one of them in my younger days, those individuals you want to harass. I can completely sympathize how painful it is to be fat. Stop the rubbish and come up with something usable.' She claps him on his thigh.

'Think about it,' asks Henry.

'About what?'

'About fat. Everyone needs a someone they can mock. That's your scapegoat. I truly believe you have written the best manifesto in the political history of the United Kingdom and that we can turn it into something much better. But first we need to get in power.'

'But fat, Henry. It's ridiculous.'

'Let's wrap up the manifesto for now. We can make use of the populist and nationalistic forces currently in society after Brexit to present our case. Just a little seed, Victoria. It's simple psychology. There are enough idiots out there to pick up on it. And when we're in, we let the subject fall and focus on what's important.'

'I guess, with good arguments, it could work,' agrees Victoria. 'Fat is a problem for society, true. There are many arguments against fat. Heart attacks, for instance. The National Health Services could save money …'

Victoria pauses for a moment.

'Hm,' she finally says. 'It's a sensitive subject with a lot of truths. I guess people on both sides of the topic would hop on-board, just like with Brexit.'

'Imagine the dialog,' suggests Henry Montclair. 'Consider the money that can be saved on obesity-related diseases, such as diabetes. The savings could be used to reduce taxes and kick-start innovative projects. Even without checking the facts, people will go for it, because it appeals to the their common sense. Now that's the direction we ought to be heading for.'

'An interesting approach, Henry. But the dialog must be kept clean. Not a single word about fat people. I do understand your point. It's clear that everybody wants to pay less taxes and reduce tax waste. I guess we will have people from the entire political spectrum who will be emotionally concerned.'

'I sense you're starting to follow me?'

'Your plan is getting interesting.'

'As one of the best speakers I've ever met, I'm sure you'll be able to sell the message without getting us into trouble.'

'If the timing is correct.'

Victoria spends some time considering Henry's words. 'But we need to play this one extremely carefully,' she finally says. Knowing the physical, social and psychological downsides of being fat, she knows they have to be very careful how the issue is presented so that it doesn't backfire. She feels a thrill go through her body, but it isn't a particularly nice one. She recalls the shame she felt when people looked at her. As is the case for many, she was addicted to sugar and fat and didn't care what she ate nor did she worry about the consequences of what she was doing to herself. During her studies, and up to her early thirties, she was extremely overweight. Then one day she saw her reflection in a window. She stood there for minutes, not moving but taking it all in and couldn't believe what she saw. It was difficult to see her image and accept the fact that something had gone awfully wrong. The shock of her appearance hit her so hard, that from one day to the next she completely overhauled her life. She started eating properly, exercising, and continued for six years until she returned to her former self.

For her it paid off. After becoming fat-free, her life improved ten-fold. In time, she realized that good looking people do eventually have better chances in life than ugly, fat ones. For years now, she has maintained a

Body Mass Index of 22. Well, actually, at the moment, it is 21. But that comes from the stress of the election campaign and the traveling. She feels comfortable at this weight which gives her legs an extra sexy look in skirts and dresses. Since she had her surplus skin removed, she enjoys sex as never before because she is no longer ashamed of her body. Being fat is now history for her.

So she is well aware of fat people's problems. The emotions, the feelings, the difficulties of extracting themselves from the eternal sugar and fat cycle and doing something about it. It demands so much self-discipline that most people eventually give up. But it isn't only people's fault for being overweight. Some are sucked into the sugar-fat-cycle because they do not have the money to afford healthy food. The food industry is almost forced to produce cheap, unhealthy products in order to compete and keep their customers. Fat and sugar, which are addictive, have become standard ingredients because they make food taste good. Although they may be better than artificial additives, they result in food products of low nutritional quality.

But who can blame anyone for picking up a chocolate bar instead of an apple? She has diligently done her research well on this subject. It has been an amazing journey to discover how the food industry manipulates and tricks us to save money and how it plays most people's ignorance on the subject. Enzymes make bread last longer although some are suspected of causing cancer. To keep the properties of many organic ingredients stable during production, chemicals are added to make them homogeneous and remain stable throughout the production process. Flour is a good example. Additives and aromas are added to food to enhance its taste which makes us forget how it originality tasted. Some flavors make children hyperactive. Others cause allergies and an increase in heartbeat, some even promote heart attacks. These are all legal additives but open to question. She personally has a problem with artificial sweeteners. When she consumes them by mistake the result is diarrhea and stomach trouble. Her sister had once suffered from food poisoning and it was after that that Victoria began her research on what is really in the food we consume.

'Hm.' What Henry says is not that far-fetched, she reconsiders. Reducing fat overall could ease the stress on the healthcare system and in other areas as well. People ought to pay more attention to what is in the food they consume. It could even make people more fit for the labour market. Maybe it is about time to address the subject.

She will need to sleep on it.

Once again, Victoria leads both hands to her head, grabbing the long dark hair and removing the knot she had just made in it. She feels good today. And the subject of fat could actually make her day end well.

'Fat you say? If fat will give us an edge, we should exploit it. Sixty-two per cent of the adults in the United Kingdom have a weight problem. Sixty-two per cent, Henry!'

'So, you understand?' asks Henry.

'I certainly do. As you say, people don't give a damn about economics when it's not their own. Nor do they care about politics. I think you're about to teach me an important lesson here. Let's see where this fat issue leads us. With our low poll rating, we don't have much to lose anyway. Like you said, let's put my political agenda on hold for a while. The priority must be first to get to power.'

'You're a fast learner, Victoria.'

'But how do we sell to the voters the fact that fat is society's enemy number one?'

'Do you want me to come up with a few sound bites?'

'Oh believe me, Henry! If you think that's the only thing I want you to come up with right now, then think again.'

Her seductive smile tells Henry Montclair that he's just about to get her again.

IT IS a pleasure to see how hours of hard work pays off when a strategy turns out well. No one at the campaign team expected The Party to win, but they did and it was childhood dream come true. She was elected Prime Minister and First Lord of the Treasure and Minister of Civil Service, as Henry Montclair, had promised her all the time. Continuous repetition of propaganda slogans containing absolutely no real information convinced the voters that this was a matter that was important in their daily lives. Henry knew it would happen and he was also right when assuming they would win some sixty-five percent of the vote.

For Victoria Seymour, it was a shocking experience to learn how little it takes to play to people's feelings. The tabloids quickly picked up on the subject and filled their pages with innuendos about how fat has led to obesity and obesity has led to an increase in unemployment and that has all led to a burden on the social system. So now that the European Union can no longer be blamed for the United Kingdom's problems, it is the overweight who have contributed to them. The message became clear that The Party will now be the one to roll up its sleeves and do what previously was not done. They will attack obesity and make the United Kingdom great again.

Luckily the majority of people have enough sense to know that obese people are not to blame for the United Kingdom's downfall. But some are. And they took over the dialogue enough that their shouts were heard. The media coverage with dubious facts, misinterpretation of statistics and emotional nonsense added to the dissatisfaction of the voters, gave The Party the impetus they needed to forge ahead in the polls and come out on top.

Most people agree with the fact that fat *is* a concern for society. But who had honestly thought a tiny little seed like the word fat, could move the minds of a whole island? It certainly did come as a surprise for Victoria, but for Henry it was less so. It had surprised her that after twenty years in the United States, she had found, upon returning to the United Kingdom, that the British had turned into lazy, overweight and ignorant people. It was even more shocking to see the naivety of the British. There were still many who believe the United Kingdom is a superpower that still controls half of the world, that the Commonwealth still gives a damn about the Royal Crown, and more shocking, that the Kingdom is better off outside the European Union. So playing to the emotions of a people who still believe that they are a superpower in possession of myriad colonies, a people who voted for Brexit without really knowing what it would entail, made it easy to see how the planting of a seed called 'fat' could sway them to whole heartedly vote for The Party.

There was, however, just one problem. Something that neither Victoria nor Henry had considered. Now that the snowball was rolling, how could it be stopped? Decent politicians would have stepped back when the debate about obese people began and nipped it in the bud. And although the opposing parties did just that, The Party did not. On the contrary. They used, or abused, the momentum the tabloids had provided and went along with the rhetoric that the United Kingdom has lost its empire and international standing and placed the blame on the three percent of its' porcine citizens. The blaming game, one of most important ingredient of politics, had begun. It seemed the tabloids had found Victoria a scapegoat.

The scapegoat Henry Montclair anticipated. Campaigning that the food processing industry is killing us all and especially killing the efficiency of society due to their poisoned products was seen by the media as the rallying cry that it is the obese people who are to blame. The Party did nothing to correct this and, to their regret, it turned into something that would split the United Kingdom even further than Brexit already had. At the time, the only thing that had mattered was obtaining power. And so they did. They as the smart ones. They were the ones now running the show. Fat had been a clever move. And a large part of the United Kingdom had been duped because they were too busy to bother investigating what the election really was about.

IT TURNS out that politics is much tougher when you are on the inside. The tax on fat, for example, the first law The Party passed in keeping with their campaign promises, faced resistance before it was actually in force. It was an honest attempt to reduce fat in products, the same as taxing cigarettes to cover the medical costs of smokers. But as is so often the case in politics, it is difficult to satisfy everyone and since Victoria's inauguration six months ago, her popularity as Prime Minister has fallen progressively. At Westminster, the resistance is turning against her, too. She knows it has to do with her skills, her ability to deal with complex matters in an instant, as a manager, troubleshooter and problem solver. It is her preparedness, her ability to answer questions randomly tossed at her that make the other politicians wary. That is the main reason why she has become so disliked among many fellow incompetent political colleagues, because, contrary to them, she is someone who gets the job done in days instead of months, and she stands by her promises. Had it been up to her, there would be no opposition parties while a government is at power. It would make it easier to rule, to get things done and instead of constantly being blocked by some ridiculous opposition argument that only wants attention rather than getting on with governing. Lately, the press has unfairly labeled her as the most despised person in British political history. She has stopped reading the news and though she knows this comes with the territory, it does hurt a little because the only thing she wants is the best for the United Kingdom.

It has been a childhood dream to enter the corridors of power. All the years that she had her head in the books while her fellow students partied, have finally paid off and her lifelong goal of reaching Westminster and Downing

Street. The pain of being an outsider, the sacrifice of hard work was all worth it, she thought, the moment she walked through that door of 10 Downing Street. At least here, she has a sense of being in control. And now being here, she is not keen on giving up any of the power and certainly doesn't like others dictating to her. What saved her often is her experience that prevents intelligent people from verbally abusing her. Something she learned quickly at the European Union and prepared her well for where she is today. There she was a kind of failing in striving to be one who takes the decisions. It was first when back in the United Kingdom she picked-up on how to also become verbally acute that others listens to her.

Shaking her head, Victoria's hair falls down into its full length, almost like how they do it in a television commercial. At the moment, she and The Party must be the most misunderstood political party in the United Kingdom as well as not getting the respect they deserve from abroad. The Fat Tax is an incentive to reduce fat consumption, not to punish people because they are fat. Neither has the law been pushed through to discriminate against fat people who have been suffering since the campaign began, as the tabloids would like the public to believe. The law is simply meant to motivate the food industry to produce better and healthier products. She will explain to her public, in her usual way, why they ought to stop being hostile to the Fat Tax. It is one of many initiatives to prepare the United Kingdom for a world outside the European Union. There are those who feel betrayed by The Party, even inside The Party. She isn't sure if it is jealousy or her personality or what, but there is one thing she wants to assure them ... she is determined to make the United Kingdom a great country once more and she will do everything in her power to do so. Anyone standing in her way will be run over because she is convinced that her's is the only way that Britain will be able to survive in the long run after Brexit.

CHAPTER 7

MASON SANDERS IS NOT THE usual early morning person. After a couple of hard slaps on the alarm clock, he realizes the noise is coming from his cell phone lying on the table beside his bed.

'Mason, its Mike.'

'... Mike ...'

'Awake?'

'... Let me have a second ...'

'Can we meet? It seems your Libyan friend isn't completely wrong.'

'About what?'

'About this thing with obese people and hacked bank accounts. It would make one hell of a story and piss-off Victoria Seymour if we print it!'

'Oh well, Mike. I'm not so sure you have such a great story after all. I've got news for you too. Where do you want to meet?'

'Where we always meet.'

'Covent Garden. See you in an hour.'

Mason hangs up.

He looks at the alarm clock. It shows 07:15. He climbs out of bed and goes to the bathroom. A quick shower and he will be fine.

HALF AN hour later, Mason is at street level and the usual morning traffic doesn't look at all good this morning. As usual, he salutes the bellboy as he walks by.

'No driver today, Mr. Sanders?'

'Underground will do just fine. Look at all the cars. I 'm not going far this morning. Covent Garden.' Mason moves aside to make room for a middle-aged woman passing by. To his surprise, she stops suddenly and looks rather rudely up and down his body, then walks away.

Mason is completely baffled as he watches her walk on. What was that? he asks himself. It is not the first time someone has stared at him because of his size, but it is the first time it has been done so deliberately and impolitely. He feels a cold breeze shiver through his body. It is the second time since the doughnut episode yesterday at Canary Wharf that someone has harassed him for his weight. At least the incidence yesterday at his favorite bakery did not get to him. But this incidence from such a cold hearted middle-aged woman, that actually hurts!

'By God,' he mumbles and starts his walk to the Underground. People may have their own thoughts and, to some extent, they might be justified he admits, but he is human too! He was not always this portly and his problem is his own fault. And now every time this woman Victoria Seymour opens her mouth, she gives him a bad conscience. She is changing the xenophobia of Brexit to something else. Now even black people, Muslims, or whatever join the Xenophobia because obesity does not have a color, a religion, a nationality and so on. With her agenda, she is manipulating the mood of London where after Brexit and the election of her, it is like society has become even more poisoned. He should have said something to that evil middle-aged woman. Because, she wasn't the most beautiful woman in the world herself.

Mason arrives at the Underground entrance. As always, the Tube is packed with people of all kind of colors, sizes, heights, nationalities, noses and various defects. People do not seem to take notice of him. The ride from Chester Square to Covent Garden takes only a few minutes. Out on the platform and up at street level, he walks the last two minutes to the Cafe where Mike Hornett and he regularly meet when he is in London. Mike has already arrived.

'I should've walked instead of taking the Underground, sorry.'

'You took the Tube for those two kilometers?'

'It's two point five – if I may so. Your girlfriend lives somewhere around here, right?'

'You remember! In six months she'll be my wife. She's pregnant, so we 'll tie the knot.'

'That's news! Congratulations. When's the due date?'

'She told me yesterday.'

'Ah, ha ha.'

Mike smiles all over his face. 'Look at this.' He pulls out scans from his wallet and shows Mason the sonic image of his child.

'Do you know what it's going to be?'

'No. As long as it's healthy and a boy. When a man goes in, a man must come out again.'

'Ha ha.'

'And how've you been since last time?' asks Mike.

'People stare at me.'

'I see. Ha ha ... why … I don't get it. Was it a joke?'

'They obviously stare at me because I'm obese. It's a new trend here in town. But I'm more interested in hearing what you have to say.'

'Oh Mason! I'm worried about the weekend edition. When our new Prime Minister reads the article. I've written about her youth and my views, she'll freak out. So you see, my editor is getting tenser and tenser by the hour.'

'I can imagine.'

Mike pulls out a bunch of papers from his briefcase. It seems he has been investigating the conspiracy theory from the café owner in Piran, Mehdi Hanachi.

'Now, you're not going to like this, Mason. I've searched the news feeds and databases to get as much data as possible. These papers,' he hands Mason two A4 pages, 'are a summary of what I've been able to find so far. On this paper …' he hands over a third A4, '… are all the companies affected by hacker attacks. Here are the pictures of their owners.' Mike hands over another five pages to Mason.

'They're all obese,' concludes Mason Sanders and sighs without actually looking at the pages. He assumed they would be, based on the list from Cliff Brad Brokerage Partners, where he found his two business friends from Piran.

'They are, aren't they,' replies Mike excitedly. 'How did they plan for this?'

'Who?'

'The Party.'

'What makes you so certain The Party is involved?'

'We've voted a demagogue into Downing Street. Isn't that obvious? What else would the objectives be of harassing people like you? I still don't get it.'

'I really can't tell. You might not have noticed, Mike. But so far, she hasn't harassed obese people. She talks about fat and its impact on society.'

Mike looks in surprise at Mason.

'You're not taking her side, are you?'

'No, of course I'm not! The woman has to go, that's for sure. But it's the tabloids and the damn right-wing politics and its stupid radio hosts and social media that are causing this mess. It wouldn't surprise me if they're all paid by the Russians to fragment our society, even further after Brexit.'

'Hm. I never saw it like this. I guess you could be right. The conflicts to her agenda aren't helping her very much. A lot of people who are not obese, stand to be unemployed if ImplantSkills and other companies go bankrupt. What does she have to gain?'

'She doesn't gain a thing,' says Mason. 'That's why I believe she isn't the one behind the bullshit. Of course, her rhetoric does seem to change the minds of some people out there.'

'Do we want to order coffee or what? I didn't have time for breakfast this morning. Coffee? Black?' asks Mike.

'Right,' agrees Mason Sanders. 'And a sandwich.'

'The usual one?'

'Yes, please.'

Mason scrolls through the bunch of papers on the table. It seems Mike has delved rather deeply into the topic he had asked him to. There has been a lot written about obesity these days. People seem to be getting obsessed with fat and there is no end to the stories. Fat has turned into a pretty good page turner with many stories about the negative effects of fat. This could be a good thing if it were only to inform readers, but now it seems that obese people and the impact they have on the society are taking the brunt of the attack that some disgusting journalists are spinning. It is as if a new frontier has been created for the press. They now always have something new to write about, a topic that was previously considered morally taboo. And in a way it has become increasingly dangerous and depressing what some tabloids are writing about.

At least both sides of the stories are represented. There are articles relating to obese people's fight for their rights to eat however they want vs. their hopeless fight to lose weight. His favorite story was about a woman who wanted to pay for her purchases but demanded another clerk because she felt that the one serving her was too fat. The story went viral within hours and even today, some tabloids still continue spinning the subject. It is no wonder that obese people are starting to protest against Victoria Seymour and The Party. It was not nice to implement the new Fat Tax which states that anyone with a Body Mass Index over 35 must lose weight by joining WeightForLife.

Reading the newspapers these days, one gets the impression that nothing really matters any more, apart from fat. At least Mike's employer, the Daily Evening Mail, is a reputable newspaper that has remained serious about politics and economics. But even they have sometimes fallen onto this insane populist wave with a few ridiculous articles.

He should have cancelled his meeting with Mike but still not come up with a good reason for doing so. He can't tell him that the bank hacking was a military operation gone wrong. It's clear that if Victoria Seymour was out to get obese people, her government would not try to cover up the military's mistake but simply let events take their turns. In his opinion, it is for sure nothing but a deflection maneuver by The Party all that is going on. It's the oldest trick on the books of politics to give citizens something to think about other than the real issues. There is so much division after Brexit; so much that has to be repaired; so many different views and opinions. So being a politician these days is not at all easy. For a while, obese people will be easier to cope with than the real problems facing the country. But attacking a minority *will* eventually backfire, when it finds the strength to resist. Seven months into her new job as Prime Minister, opinions among the more intelligent citizens are divided on her performance and how she is handling the government. And political analysts seem to have no idea what she is trying to achieve other than talking about fat and have lately also joined in the harassment of obese people.

'By God,' exclaims Mason, letting out air in a slow blow. What happened to her otherwise so fantastic political manifesto? To her agenda? Why has this smoke-screen been set up? Is it a cover for what is to come for the United Kingdom after fully leaving the European Union? Brexit has turned everything completely on its head. And now, with the European Union gone, who will keep an eye on a power-hungry politician like Victoria Seymour and her gang of vultures? It is going to be interesting to see what will happen to The Party when this obesity thing starts imploding on itself.

CHRIS CAMPBELL leaves his home to find something as seldom as a public telephone box. They have become a rather scarce since cell phones were introduced. So the question is: Where could he find a telephone box?

Chris gets into his car and drives to a near-by shopping center. In a public space like this, there must be telephones. The three-storey parking lot is full, so he drives up and up to the third floor until he finally sees a free spot in a dark corner. He quickly executes an impulsive high-speed turn into the gap, hitting the parking brake hard. Trying to get out of the car, he recognizes that the cars beside him are parked so close and that a man his size has no chance of getting out of the car on either side.

'Damn!' he exclaims, 'Everything is so small these days.'

He slams the door, turns the ignition key once again, puts the car into reverse and spins out of the parking place. He drives further down the lot until he sees two empty spots. This time he parks in the middle of the two spaces, right on the marking, so he can maneuver himself out of his car with plenty of room. Then he makes his way to the elevators.

But both are out of order so he has to use the stairs which isn't one of his favorite forms of exercise. He is elated to find a public telephone, right there, at the entrance of the shopping mall. It is even a modern one which takes credit cards. He picks up the receiver and inserts his credit card, but there is no dial tone. He hangs up, takes out the credit card and tries again. The result is the same. The damn telephone doesn't work.

He continues into the Mall, thinking that perhaps today is not his day. He has to call Andy in Seattle and it has to be on a secure line that can't be traced. Finally, in a far corner of the Mall, he finds what he's been looking for; an entire wall full of pay phones. At the first one, he picks up the receiver and is pleasantly surprised to hear a healthy dial tone. All at once, his stomach sinks as he realizes that Andy's phone number is in his cell phone – which he has left at home.

LESS THAN half an hour later, Chris returns to the row of public telephones thinking how astounding it is that we have become so dependent on cell phones. They provide such wonderful flexibility by being able to call anyone from anywhere, anytime. How did we ever live without them?

Although before cell phones the blackmailers would not have had the capability to transfer data, burn a DVD and ship it as fast as they did. What do they want from him? So far, he has not been able to figure out this simple question. He hasn't seen anyone around who is acting suspicious or trying to follow him. If they are professional people, which he assumes they are, they would have bugged his clothing or shoes while he was asleep at the hotel in Seattle, but so far he hasn't found anything in his personal items. When he told his wife about the incident, she took it rather calmly. Actually, at first she didn't believe him. But when she finally understood what was going on, she dealt with the DVD in her own good fashion.

He dials Andy Green's number. It must be early morning in Seattle.

'Hey Andy. Is your cell phone secure?'

'Chris? Is that you?'

'Is your cell phone secure?'

'My what? Just give me a second to wake up.'

'Your cell phone. Is it secure?'

'Yes, it's secure. What's up, Chris? I didn't expect to hear your voice so soon after your visit. You've been decommissioned, you know?'

'I know. But this is not a courtesy call. Something has come up.'

'He he, did you have sex with her again, Chris?'

'Please listen and stop joking around.'

'Oh. Okay. So what's on your mind.'

'The extortion attempt has taken a negative turn. Mary received a copy of the DVD before I even got back to London.'

'Oh. That excludes the assumption that it's a gang of …'

' … local criminals, I know. They know where I live and that means they probably know we met.'

'Oops, that's not good Chris. That will definitely decommission you for a while. The Old Man is going to see this as a threat to the existence of The Special Council.'

'That's why I'm calling. You need to take precautions. What I'm still trying to figure out is; why in Seattle? Why orchestrate a blackmail attempt in Seattle and not in London?'

'I figure there could be two possible scenarios. Either you were just unlucky here in Seattle or there is someone who knows you work for The Special Council and wants something from you.'

'This would be bad. But what?'

'Uhm. I don't know. Perhaps we should stop speculating. The evidence will come as we proceed.'

'It's really a bad time for me to be decommissioned. There's so much work to do on the FDAR.'

'True. But that's how life works sometimes, isn't it. I'll get in touch with the Old Man and inform him that we might have gotten ourselves compromised.'

'Okay, Andy. What shall I do in the meantime?'

'First of all, stay calm. Stay away from any activities relating to The Special Council. We're checking out the DVD and the hotel surveillance tapes. By the way, how's ImplantSkills coming along?'

'Not so good. My boss is working at full steam to find capital. It's a difficult situation. What about the FDAR? How's it coming along?'

'The Continent Teams meet in a couple of hours. Unless this matter is resolved quickly, expect, a postponement.'

'Ugh! Time is going to run fast on this one.'

There is a short pause.

'Ehm,' utters Andy Green. 'I'm actually glad that you called. I need to know more about the parliamentary system in the United Kingdom. I'm more a specialist on America.'

'What do you want to know?'

'In one of the FDAR scenarios, it says Victoria Seymour will use the absence of the European Union acting as a watchdog over its member nations. Who will then check up on the politicians in the United Kingdom?'

'That's done by Parliament and the Courts. They need to approve laws before they're implemented.'

'Uhm. Okay. Can you give me more details, please?'

'As you told me yourself, we don't have a constitution as you do in the United States. If you want to pass new laws, you need to make what's called a Green Paper. Anyone can do this. The contents are then reviewed by policy makers and cabinet ministers. A Green Paper turns into a White Paper which is presented to Members of Parliament in the House of Commons. Here, bills get scrutinized by the opposition, the government, and the House of Lords. When they're satisfied with its' contents, the bill is scrutinized again before being passed into legislation. The bills, though, must not only be approved by the Courts, but also by Her Majesty, which is just a formal matter, and then turned into an Act of Parliament.'

'I see.'

'Why? What does the FDAR scenario say?'

'It says that Brexit and the trouble with the European Union will enable bills to be passed in Parliament without the scrutiny process.'

'I know we talked about it when I was in Seattle. But that's not possible.'

'The Great Repeal Bill required for Brexit. Remember?' reminds Andy.

'What about it?'

'The 16.000 laws from the European Union. You said they require review before being amended to the legislation of the United Kingdom. The FDAR concludes it will be easy to slip in a couple of her own laws.'

'I honestly don't see how. Our lawmakers are already in a nightmare. I read there are around 130.000 paragraphs up for review inside those 16.000 laws.'

'So, it's possible to slip in laws unnoticed?'

'You still have the Lords and Courts. They are there to make sure this does not happen. They must still be approved by them. I don't know if you've heard about it, but we now have this new law, the Fat Tax.'

'I read about it.'

'Actually, a paragraph slipped through that shouldn't be there.'

'Which one?' ask Andy Green.

'The one saying that; if you possess a Body Mass Index of more than 35, you must lose weight and pay half your earnings to The Party?'

'Wow! That sounds a bit sick.'

'You need to understand that our political system is a little overwhelmed with this Brexit thing. A lot of errors are happening at the moment. I guess that would be a way to make things slip through. Laws made inside the United Kingdom are based on litigation from the Supreme Court and Acts of Parliament. It means that civil rights laws, for example, can be reinstated at any time. So constitutional laws can be made simply by passing new Acts of Parliament which overrule the previous ones. We've used this principle for four-hundred years.'

'Okay. I see.'

'Say, can you call me at this number at 8pm tomorrow? I need to buy a new cell phone. In spite of being decommissioned, I'd really like to stay in the loop. You need to send me the encrypted software.'

'Create an email address somewhere. I'll send you the App.'

'I will.'

'Uhm,' moans Andy. 'I'd like to mention that it's against the TSC Employer Manual, page 254, to stay in contact with you … but … why not?'

'Ha ha. You and your procedures! I have to hang up now. This call is costing me a fortune. You have my number on your display?'

'No. Give it to me.'

Chris reads out the number. 'The last digit is scratched off. You'll have to call me to figure it out. Let's do it right now.'

'Sure.'

While waiting for Andy to return the call Chris sees that the display says twenty-five quid. Twenty-five quid for twenty minutes! He ignores the fact that the money will never be refunded. To get his mind off the pain of the cost of the call, he looks around at his surroundings. It is actually quite a nice shopping mall. He isn't here as often as his wife and children are.

When the phone rings, he picks up the receiver and says, 'What number was it?'

'Nine.'

'Ha ha! No wonder it took so long to call back.'

'You have a nice day, Chris.'

'You too, Andy.'

'Talk to you tomorrow at exactly 8pm.'

MASON SANDERS spends a lot of time on his cell phone getting the numbers for his two fellow rich neighbors in Piran. When he finds them, he will do as instructed and forward the message from Christina Goldstein from Cliff Brad Brokerage Partners. It is perhaps to no one's surprise that both men are in London to iron out issues just as he is. From the numbers, he got from their secretaries, he dials the first from the little paper block. Because he forgot to write down the names beside the numbers, he isn't sure who his first call is going to. Waiting for the recipient to pick up the phone, he counts the dial tones. An old habit of his.

It is Robert Martens.

'Hey, Robert! Mason Sanders here.'

'Mason! What a pleasant surprise. What can I do for you?'

'I need to ask you a couple of questions. You've probably read that I've run into trouble.'

Yes, I have.'

'That's why I want to talk with you.'

'Oh, okay. What about?'

Mason hesitates for a few seconds. 'Well Robert, ImplantSkills' bank accounts have been hacked. There isn't a single penny left.'

'You don't say? That happened to my company as well.'

'So, it's not just my fantasy that something strange is going on.'

'What do you mean?' asks Robert.

'You probably need an investor as urgently as I do, right?'

'If you have any, I'm all ears. Do you want to invest?'

Mason laughs. 'Difficult. But I had a meeting with a woman who's able to help us.'

'Really! So what do you suggest?'

'I think we should meet. We'll be meeting with James Hollister, too. Its highly probable that he's in the same situation as we are. You know him, right?'

'I know who he is. Let's say as good as I know you. But I think it's our wives who really know each other.'

'Ah, okay. Well, they have nothing to do all day anyway.'

Now its Robert's turn to laugh. 'Can you brief me in advance?'

'I'd actually prefer to meet. I had a meeting with a woman from a brokerage house called Cliff Brad Brokerage Partners. She says our situations have been caused by an experiment gone wrong. The woman is there to clean up the mess her client has caused.'

'But why us?'

'I know this sounds strange, but it's because we're obese.'

There is total silence at the other end of the phone.

'Robert? Are you still there?'

'Uhm. I didn't quite catch what you meant.'

'Because we're obese. It was a hacker experiment that got out of control. The woman is there to assist us.'

'It sounds a kind crazy. But if it helps our companies I'm all ears.'

'Exactly. She's giving us an opportunity to access fresh capital. She knows it's difficult to find it on the financial market.'

'It sounds too good to be true. But count me in. I've had a few meetings with investors and capital houses and they're all squeezing the lemon a little too hard. I don't like their greed.'

'I was afraid of exactly that. That's why I want to prevent you from talking to investors.'

'So, when and where do you want to meet?'

'Let's meet at Covent Garden. There's a cafe across from the Transportation Museum.'

'I know it. Let's meet in three hours.' Robert hangs up.

Mason looks at his cell phone in surprise. Robert forgot that James Hollister still has to be informed of their meeting. Now he needs to call Robert and convince him to drop everything and join them in three hours.

THREE HOURS ahead and Mason returns to Covent Garden for the second time in less than five days. Robert Martens is already there, sitting under one of the sun umbrellas. James Hollister is not to be seen anywhere although he had promised to drop everything and join them.

'Thanks for coming on such short notice,' says Mason to Robert, shaking hands. Considering the fact that they are almost neighbors in Piran and their paths cross now and then, it is rather amazing that they have never really talked to each other.

'So, we finally meet,' says Robert Martens. 'Circumstances could have been better.'

'You can say that again.'

'But Mason, can you tell me how is it possible to hack bank accounts at different banks? If the criminals' intentions are to damage my business, they've certainly found the right way to do it.'

'As I mentioned during our short conversation, it was an experiment that got out of control. I'll tell you more when James arrives. You said you've been in contact with investors?'

'I am all the time. It's not something I like doing and I only play their game because I need a capital injection urgently.'

'When you're down and out everybody wants to screw you! That's rule number one in the business world. Have you ever heard of Cliff Brad

Brokerage Partners?'

'No.'

'I had an interesting conversation with a woman named Christina Goldstein. I promised her to inform you two about what she told me.'

'Okay.'

'Cliff Brad Brokerage Partners are willing to invest in …'

'Hey lads. Sorry for the delay.' It is James Hollister approaching their table.

'Hi James,' greets Mason. 'Good that you could come.'

'So, we finally meet. But the circumstances could have been better.'

'That's what I said a moment ago,' agrees Robert.

'When this matter is resolved,' Mason suggests, 'we should meet in Piran for coffee.'

'You mean Mehdi Hanchi's place in Piran? Cafe Casa, the best gossip stop in town?'

Mason laugh. 'That's it!'

'Mason says our obesity has something to do with our situations,' says Robert. 'You kind of painted this picture for me when we talked.'

'Actually, it was Medhi Hanchi who came up with the theory. Mehdi reads lots of newspapers. We're obese, rich, powerful and influential and he suggested that The Party wants us out of the way.'

'Why?'

'Because we're influential.'

'That sounds bizarre,' remarks James.

'Mason. It's somewhat rude of you to formulate it like that,' remarks Robert. 'Overweight is nicer than obese. I hate it when the Prime Minister uses the word 'fat' when referring to us. She could be more politically correct and at least call us 'portly' or something like that. She seems to forget that we three create lots of jobs, salaries and taxes.'

'We do, don't we?'

'But it can't be a coincidence that we've all been hit. James, you were hacked too?' asks Robert.

'You mean my company's bank accounts?

'Yes.'

'They were.'

'Hm.'

'Why does anyone want to harass us like this?'

'Gentlemen, stop speculating, please. I have the answers. That's why I have asked you to come,' explains Mason. 'We're powerful people. If we wanted to, we'd be able to fight Victoria Seymour and her agenda anytime. But that's not what this is about. It's about a military experiment that has run out of control. I guess, just like the Russians and Chinese, our government wanted to test how vulnerable our nation is against hacker attacks. The government is in the process of cleaning up the military's blunder and this is our chance to get back on our feet.'

'All this cybercrime,' exclaims Robert. 'No matter how good you protect yourself these days, you get hacked anyway.'

'So true,' confirms Mason.

'Before you came,' continues Robert, 'Mason was telling me about a woman who can help us. Could you go on with that, Mason?'

'James, have you heard about an investment house named Cliff Brad Brokerage Partners and a woman named Christina Goldstein?'

'No.'

'She represents the government and is the one who is cleaning up the military's blunder. I spoke with her yesterday. And she's there to assist us at extremely fair conditions.'

'What does 'extremely fair conditions' mean?'

'Our losses are recovered. The only thing we need to do is to shut up.'

'What about fees, hidden costs?'

'They aren't charging us anything! The money is in the form of government subventions.'

'Wow! That sounds like a blank cheque.'

'It solves our problems.'

No one says anything for a while.

'So, what's the plan? How do we proceed?' asks James.

'I contacted the German subsidiary this morning.'

'In Germany? Why Germany?' asks Robert.

'That should be obvious,' answers James. 'The money isn't part of the government's budget.'

'Where in Germany?'

'In Hamburg.'

'Ah.'

'I believe we're stronger together,' suggests Mason. 'We need to work together on this one.'

'Thank you, Mason,' says James. 'Thank you for contacting us. I think this is the lifeline we all have been waiting for.'

'Indeed it is,' agrees Robert.

Mason continues, 'They're expecting us to drop by either tomorrow or end of this week. In the meanwhile they'll prepare the paperwork for all three of us.'

'Great job, Mason. Really great job.'

'I went to Hamburg a couple of times,' says Robert. 'It's a very beautiful city. And very wealthy indeed. They've stolen quite a lot of jobs from London since Brexit.'

'So we're heading to Hamburg,' confirms James.

'Yes we are. Who still flies privately?' asks Mason.

'Uhm, I can still afford to …' confirms Robert, '… but in my aircraft there's only space for four passengers and I think we three together amounts to at least six persons.'

'Damn! Let's just rent a bigger aircraft and split the bill.'

'Perhaps one should attend this WeightForLife program that Victoria Seymour wants us to attend', jokes James.

'And pay half our earnings to The Party? I think not!'

'Have you ever considered WeightWatchers?'

'Didn't The Party close them down?'

'Oh, that's true, two weeks ago I think. It put a lot of people on the streets.'

'No wonder! What a shitty thing to do.'

'I can agree with that although I'll probably never use it anyway.'

'Well,' Mason concludes the discussion, pulling out his cell phone to order the jet. 'I guess we're going to Hamburg. I think that when we return we should probably start deciding what to do about this crazy bat who is clinging to her power like some old rockstar.'

CHAPTER 8

THE TWO SLIM AND BEAUTIFUL women head to one of the restaurants available for staff at the Right Honourable the Lords Spiritual and Temporal of the United Kingdom of Great Britain and Northern Ireland in Parliament, also called by people working there simply Palace of Westminster. It is noon and time to grab some food. The Palace of Westminster which include the Houses of Parliament, the House of Lords and Big Ben, consist of a wonderful mix of architectural structures dominated by neo-Gothic buttresses, towers and arches. The place is, however, not as old as it looks. The Parliament buildings were designed by Charles Barry and rebuilt in 1860, replacing the original Houses of Parliament which were destroyed by the fire of 1834. The Palace of Westminster contains 1.000 rooms and 11 courtyards, eight bars and six restaurants which staff and guests can use – plus a cafeteria for visitors. Victoria Seymour and her Minister for State Communication and Promotion, Lisa Ferguson, chat while walking to the third restaurant.

Victoria Seymour wonders why citizens question whether it is a good thing to put a tax on fat. The thought strikes her in the same moment as a fat colleague from an opposition party walks by. It is an obvious choice to put a tax on fat – if only to make people reduce their fat intake. The public, though, is upset and they may have good reasons to be so. It turns out there is a flaw with the law on the Fat Tax. There is a paragraph that neither she nor anyone else was aware of; one that was neither approved by her, by Parliament, the Lords nor the Courts but that had slipped through unnoticed although it made no sense. What the paragraph should have stated was that people with a Body Mass Index of 35 and upwards may attend The Party's WeightForLife program on a voluntary basis and also voluntarily pay half their earnings in support of others losing weight. The implemented paragraph states; people with a Body Mass Index of 35 and upwards must attend WeightForLife and also pay half their earnings to The Party with no mention of the word 'voluntary'. The tabloids had a field-day. They were quick to recognize the screw-up and are now taking the side of fat people.

'Do you see them anywhere?' asks Victoria Seymour.

'Over there,' points Lisa Ferguson. 'They've already served themselves.'

'We're a little late. I told Henry and Gregg they could start without us. First I first had to digest the contents of a paragraph in the Fat Tax law. How could such a mistake happen? Strange.'

'It's a pretty tough paragraph, I'd say,' confirms Lisa Ferguson. 'I read it too and cannot imagine it to be anything other than a mistake. I understand from Henry that Gregg is working on a fix.'

'Oh no! Do we really want to eat here?' asks Victory. 'This is not my kind of food. The salad bar is an absolute joke.'

'I know. But they wanted to eat burgers.'

'Fine with me. But look at the salad. It's not even fresh.'

Passing the salad bar, Victoria, looks at it one more time. She is a part time vegetarian. It's not that she doesn't like meat, but when she does eat meat, she only eats beef and only if it comes from a local farm, is organic and freshly slaughtered. In recent years, she has turned against industrialized meat where animals are treated without any kind of dignity. She knows from statistics that one out of ten cows are not fully anesthetized when they are slaughtered. It is awful. And either people simply just ignore the facts, do not know or simply do not care.

They greet their two colleagues, Henry Montclair, now First Secretary of State and Minister for the Cabinet Office and Victoria's spin-doctor and Gregg White, Chancellor and Secretary of State for Justice and go to the buffet. Lisa heads to the burgers. Victoria returns to the salad bar and, on the way there, she notices a chubby little Indian man standing behind the cash register, watching her. He did the same thing the last time she was here. And, to be honest, with all people coming to eat lunch here every day, he should be serving, not staring at her.

She grabs a bowl and begins putting lettuce, tomatoes, olives, onions and cucumber slices into it. She then chooses the Italian dressing, shooting it out in a little swift spray, reminding herself of what happened when Henry took her on her office desk yesterday. As she pays, she notices the Indian guy whispering to a colleague. Then they swap places. Oh God, a deliberate avoidance. It is not the first time she's experienced discrimination like this. When fat people feel harassed, they have absolutely no idea how she feels. She is the one who should feel harassed with all the things people say about her and The Party. She was not the one who started this thing with fat people. That came from the tabloids and now the overweight are blaming her.

But that will eventually change. When The Party starts implementing her political agenda, then people will wake up and understand how brilliant she is. She cashes out at the other cash register where slimmer cashier is working and returns to her three colleagues.

At the table Henry seems not to be able to keep the mayonnaise in his burger. Some keeps dropping onto the tray. For almost a year and throughout the entire election he has acted as her spin-doctor – and somewhat more. His role today has changed a bit and he is now, as Chancellor, in charge of the Great Appeal Bill whose job it is to reverse and scrutinize all the European Union laws that are to be integrated into the British Statue Book.

Again, a little mayonnaise drops onto the tray. She herself doesn't eat mayonnaise because it contains eggs from hens who have very little space to live their short lives in. Additionally, it makes her sick to think of the male hens who are sent to the shredder machines after hatching because they serve no purpose for the food industry.

'Henry,' she says, putting on one of her sweet smiles and knowing he doesn't have a chance to answer as long as the burger is in his mouth. He ought to be the right person to explain what went wrong with the paragraph for Fat Tax.

'Something was added to the Fat Tax that shouldn't be there. Did you check the tabloids this morning? Do you know what happened?' she asks, carefully watching his body language. The man is a snake, both career-wise and privately. He knows politics and how to work it just as she does. Waiting for him to swallow, she turns her attention to her own plate, pricking at a tomato which looks more or less lifeless with her fork. She kills it by sticking her fork into it.

'I don't know where it came from,' answers Henry. 'But with the Great Repeal Bill and 16.000 European laws to be implemented, stuff like this slips though once in a while. It's a typing error.'

Victoria Seymour laughs out loud. 'A typing error?! Are you aware how pissed the people and the press are at us?'

'So what? We'll tell people it's an error and it will be corrected. That they don't have to pay nor will they be forced to join up WeightForLife.'

'It will cost us votes in the next election. People are going to remember mistakes like this one.'

'Argh, don't be so melodramatic, Victoria. People eventually forget.'

'The tabloids won't. When will the paragraph be revoked?'

'Not at this time. We have too much to do with the Great Repeal Bill. It's going to take a while before we're that far.'

'That's not good enough, Henry!'

She watches Henry take a bite of his burger. Once again, mayonnaise squeezes out from between the buns and the beef pellet drops onto the tray. Contrary to her three colleagues she has just lost her appetite. It is a mystery that food can be of such low quality in a place where they demand that people lose weight. She throws her fork back into the bowl, watching Henry happily eat on. His burger is at least twelve centimeters high, and contains at least a full two days' ration of calories. The saturation degree is probably close to zero meaning that in two hours Henry, Gregg and Lisa will have the urge to eat again. That's what makes people fat. Doing it once in a while is fine. But some people do it every day with so much poor quality food that it is no wonder that people are fat.

'Sure it will cost us votes,' says Henry finally. 'But we'll gain them all back later when we start implementing your agenda.'

'I'm still waiting for that moment, Henry. We must discontinue this fat nonsense. People actually think I believe in what I'm saying. It's ridiculous.'

'Relax,' intervenes Gregg White.

'Don't tell me to relax.'

Let it all come with time. It's too early to pull back now,' says Gregg White, 'We still haven't completely secured our position in power. We still need time to implement our plan and, in the meantime, we have to distract the issues with something else.'

'That might be. But the intention was not to split the Kingdom even further after Brexit. I find this fat thing is getting out of control.'

'Come on, Victoria,' says Henry. 'I've put you in power for the next four years. But you need at least eight to accomblish your agenda. The Great Repeal Bill is our chance of doing so. We've had the discussion so often lately. I don't know what's gotten into you. Be patience, for God's sake. A couple more months and then we start focusing on what's important.'

'But haven't you noticed? We're releasing things we can't control. People out there are now finding it morally okay to harass fat people. This was never what we intended to do. It must stop, Henry.'

'We have nothing to do with what's going on out there,' says Lisa. 'Its the tabloids. The coverage of this woman Patty Griffith and her suicide is what has stuck with the public.'

'Honestly. What does her suicide, have to do with us?' asks Gregg.

'Who?' asks Victoria.

'Patty Griffith. Don't you remember?'

'No.'

'The woman you picked on last week on the Early Morning Show? She committed suicide a couple of days later.'

'Oh. No, I haven't heard. Why would she commit suicide?'

'Say? Don't you read newspapers?'

'Not so often. I don't like what they write about me.'

'The woman obviously had some problems with herself,' says Gregg.

'But it's awful. I never intended to ...'

'You think too much, Victoria,' concludes Henry. 'A couple more months and the law on Fat Tax will be revoked and this thing with fat phased out.'

'Who actually wrote the paragraph?' asks Victoria.

'I guess it was a civil servant who got it wrong,' explains Gregg. 'We don't actually write most laws ourselves. They're written by law-consultancy companies. We provide the guidelines and they fill in the contents. I guess the syntax slipped at this one.'

'But you know what,' says Henry. 'Meanwhile, and as long as the law is active, it motivates fat people to finally do something about their problem. I don't see why we need to rush to have this law revoked. Why does it bother you so much? As soon as they're below the required BMI, they don't need to pay the extra tax – or use WeightForLife. It's good for them and it's good for our society.'

'Our objective was to use fat as an issue to get to power. We are now at power.'

'At the moment, we are delivering what the majority of people wants us to deliver.'

'That is absolutely gibberish. The majority of the population finds this fat thing ridiculous. Don't you care what happens? Generations will read about us in the history books.'

'As your spin-doctor, I advise you to ride out the wave, at least until we've secured our power base – as Gregg mentioned. We need time to implement your agenda, but the priority must be to strengthen and secure your position as Prime Minister beyond the first four years. Don't worry Victoria, you'll soon be able to do what you intend.'

'And how far away are we?'

'Patience, girl. Patience! As I said; a couple of months. We're currently implementing the package.'

'What package?'

'The one securing yours and The Party's power in Parliament,' tells Gregg.

'I'm not familiar with that package. What's in it?'

'You've said you'd give me full authority to secure your position as Prime Minister, remember?'

'Yes but …'

'With The Great Repeal Bill, we'll be able to bypass the Lords and the Courts.'

'That's not possible. How?'

'We're going to replace a few paragraphs in the doctrine of Parliamentary Sovereignty, just to make it a little easier on your behalf.'

'I don't like you going behind my back like this! We've got the power with our majority in Parliament.'

'That's true. But not forever. And not with the Lords and Courts.'

'But …' intervenes Lisa. 'How is it possible to get laws through that have not been vetted or approved by the Lords and Courts?'

'There's a law from the 16th century. It's the law of Henry the VIII. With Brexit, there are at least 130.000 paragraphs to vet. Experts calculate it will take as long as 15 years and cost a fortune. But according to the 500 year old law which is still fully valid, a person can be appointed to accept and implement the laws without the scrutiny of Parliament, the Lords or the courts – if it is approved by Parliament. The laws are simply implemented in the name of the appointed person thus speeding up the process by light-years.'

'And this person will be …?'

'Me,' says Henry.

'You guys are smart!' expels Lisa.

'Isn't this going one step too far, Henry?' comments Victoria. 'It sounds a little like we're turning the United Kingdom into a banana republic.'

'You wanted to be Prime Minister. I gave it to you. You want to implement your political ideas. I pave the way for you to do so. Now let me do my work and you'll get the United Kingdom you've always dreamt of,' settles Henry.

'We should talk about this somewhere else,' whispers Lisa. 'This place has many ears.'

'You worry too much, Victoria,' says Gregg.

'As I've always said, we'll unwrap your agenda after we've secured your position in power,' Henry repeats.

'I hear you,' answers Victoria, resigned and giving in to the two gentlemen she so much appreciates. 'But, my question is; will we be able to reunite the Kingdom after what we've done with fat?'

'Something will eventually come up that will reunite the Kingdom; something that will capture the people's imagination and make them forget all about fat and fat people.'

'Is that a promise?'

'Have I ever let you down?' asks Henry.

'No.'

'Well, then let us do what we're paid to do.'

'HI MASON.' says Mike Hornett, the journalist. 'Good that you had the time to come. I recall you like doughnuts. I just ordered some for us.'

'They got doughnuts here?'

'Yep.'

'Tell me then, why I've then always only ordered a ham sandwich.'

'Because you probably wouldn't want to order from anywhere else than at your bakery at Canary Wharf.'

Mason Sanders laugh. 'Well, I guess those times are now also gone.'

'How shall we handle this going on, Mason? I got enough material for at least seven articles.'

'I read your article about Victoria Seymour, by the way. Uh, what happened afterwards? Did she sue your newspaper?'

'No. Something else happened. Something quite interesting. We got a visit to the editorial by two unpleasant men.'

'You did what?'

'They told us that we should ease up some of our criticism on her, and The Party.'

'No way.'

'Yes way. First time they came it was okay. But this time, and with this article, I've never experienced anything like it. They in a way told us to implement self-censure on topics relating to The Party. What amazes me is how those two assholes were smiling while talking. Real slick assholes.'

'Hm.'

'Anyway, how did your meeting go with your two soulmates you were to talk to?'

'You mean the two from Piran? Actually quite nicely. You remembered?'

'Of course.'

'They've been exposed to the same plot as I have. Hacked bank accounts at different banks.'

'So, I guess your Cafe owner from Piran could be right after all.'

'Well, yes and no. The situation has actually changed a bit since our last meeting. I was holding back information last time we met.'

'You were withholding information from me? Impossible!' laughs Mike.

'The problem is that I'm under a kind of oath so you can't write about what I'm going to tell you.'

'Well, why are you telling me then?'

Mike's flippancy surprises Mason. 'You're a journalist. I'd never have expected you to come up with such a remark.'

'Can I write about it some other time?'

'Some other time, yes, but not now. And if you write about it, you'll hurt a lot of healthy companies. But I want to share this piece of information with you.'

'Okay, got it.'

Mason updates Mike on Cliff Brad Brokerage Partners and Christina Goldstein and the meeting they had. The update lasts some twenty minutes. Mike listens carefully. There is silence as Mike takes time to digest what he's just heard. After a couple of minutes, he asks, 'So, you say it's a government project gone wrong. But how does that explain why most of the affected companies are owned by obese people?'

Mason stops to think. 'I don't know.'

'But can't you see the dilemma? On one hand, my research shows that it is only influential obese people who are affected, as your Cafe owner from Piran says. Now you tell me that the government is ironing out the military's mistake. It somehow doesn't make sense to me.'

'Maybe I'm not seeing the whole picture,' confirms Mason. 'That's why I wanted to share it with you. For me, the most important priority is to save ImplantSkills and get on with business as usual.'

'I fully understand. What's your next move?'

'The three of us are going to Hamburg.'

'Hamburg. You mean in Germany? Why?'

'Well, that's where the government has decided to do business with us. I understand from this woman at Cliff Brad Brokerage Partners that they want to keep things in the dark.'

'You mean, away from other politicians, the opposition and the press who might want to publicize with this rather embarrassing situation?'

'That's probably what she means. A lot of business has gone from London to Hamburg after Brexit.'

'I know. And I guess it could be a hot potato to make a mistake of such proportions. I wonder how high the total bill will be for us taxpayers. You say there was a list with names?'

'Yes. But I think you've done pretty well with your research. Apart from my two friends, I did recognize some other names on it.'

'But I still find it strange,' says Mike. 'And I must honestly say, Mason, I don't buy what she's told you. I understand the government screws up once in a while, but all the people affected are influential, successful and obese. That's a strange coincidence. How would the hackers know who is obese or not? This is what surprises me. It can't just be a coincidence. For coincidences like this, I'm too much of a journalist.'

'Hm.'

'There's more going on than this woman from Cliff Brad ... whatever they are called, is telling you.'

'If the military is behind it, then ...'

'She says the military is behind the screw-up, but how would you know?

She could be lying.'

'Don't you think it's worth traveling to Germany to find out?'

'Of course it is. That's not why I may sound so negative. Contrary to you trying to save your company, I'm trying to figure out what this is all about.'

'I wanted to ask if you could look into Cliff Brad Brokerage Partners a bit deeper. It would be great if you could find out more. And that's why I want to share this with you.'

'No problem. But, if it is or was a military operation gone wrong, I might not be able to find any information whatsoever. Still, projects and people, leave traces everywhere, so I'll give it a shot. But listen, Mason! I've been talking to people, too.'

'I'm listening.'

'The thing with obesity. Are you still with me on that one?'

'Of course! If I can, in any way help thwart Victoria, then let's go for it.'

'You're exactly the kind of person who has the resources to do so.'

'I know where you're heading. Yesterday, I actually read The Party's political manifesto again. It's a good manifesto, really well-thought out. So, it simply conflicts with what is going on.'

'I find the agenda quite reasonable, too. But why don't they start carrying out their politics instead of this fat nonsense?'

'I don't know, Mike. You're giving me a headache.'

Mike laughs. 'Okay, Mason. You go to Hamburg with your two mates and solve your financial matters. I'll dig deeper into what's going on. I'm just skeptical about the willingness of our government …' Mike looks down at the table. 'But Mason, you haven't touched your doughnut!'

'No. I'm trying to lose weight. It's difficult to enjoy doughnuts when everyone gives you a hard time about eating them. I guess, with the latest events and harassment, I'm beginning to feel guilty too about being so fat.'

RETURNING TO Downing Street in their black limousine, Lisa Ferguson notices that Victoria has fallen into a deep silence. She knows it was the debate with Henry and Gregg. It always is.

'What's the matter, Victoria,' she asks, just to ease the silence.

'Nothing,' replies Victoria.

'You don't look like it's nothing.'

'I'm not comfortable with what Henry and Gregg are doing.'

'Henry has brought you to power and now you're unhappy about it?'

'I'm not unhappy, I'm simply trying to figure out if we aren't, perhaps, stabbing ourselves in the back with these policies. And I can't seem to find the answer.'

'So, what's the problem?'

'I know what Harry is doing is necessary if we want to make a difference. I'm just afraid that we are dividing the Kingdom even further.

'That's rubbish. None of us are dividing the Kingdom.'

'I'm not really sure that's true.'

'You're reading too much into this fat thing. You heard them say that if we're to fully implement your visions, then we need to buy some time. And by the way, your politics are such a radical change that it can only be done if we get full control of the political situation, the opposition, the Lords and Courts.'

'Lisa! You're young. You're rather new to politics. Henry and Gregg, they're old, they're tough players who know exactly how to turn anything to their advantage. I don't know if you've sensed it, and it's probably my womanly intuition that I feel that Henry feeds on the increase in power The Party has accumulated. I've never seen him like this before and honestly believe the power is going to his head. Since Henry started this thing about fat, the world has been changing rapidly. We, as politicians, should stop it from accelerating, but we keep doing the exact opposite. We're fragmenting a whole population because of how much they weight. It has taken me completely by surprise that Henry wants to make changes to the fundamental rules of our democracy to secure mine and The Party's position. We never agreed to this when he and I established The Party. It should be clear that rewriting legislation for the doctrine of Parliamentary Sovereignty without scrutiny by Parliament, the Lords, or the Courts is a major threat to our political principles.'

'If it helps the United Kingdom out of its difficulties, I don't see why not.'

'You don't see the problem, do you?'

'Yes, I do see the problem, but from another viewpoint. You're the counterbalance that prevents Henry and Gregg from exceeding their limits. That's why I don't feel there's a problem.'

'They're wolves in sheep's clothing. I feel it.'

'I must admit I was a bit surprised myself at how easily the Fat Tax slipped through unnoticed. To be honest, I think Henry is lying. He knew very well about the paragraph. I think he changed that paragraph on purpose to test the Lords and Courts and see how quickly they'd discover it.'

'Currently, The Fat Tax is the most discussed political subject in the country. It shouldn't surprise you that the press picks up on it like hawks.'

'That's not really what I meant. The press is now busy with the Fat Tax while Henry is pushing his special package through without anyone noticing it.'

'You're a smart girl, Lisa. That's probably exactly what he's doing.'

They are lost in thought as they arrive at 10 Downing Street and go into Victoria's office. Lisa is the one to break the silence.

'Something else is bothering you, Victoria. I can see it on your face.'

'Yes, there is.'

'What?'

'This thing with Patty Griffith.'

'What about her?'

'It's what happened to her. I'm astounded that anybody would take their own life because of a couple of hard words. I mean, it's true what I said and if she hadn't been so overweight, it wouldn't have happened. I had no idea that things had taken such an unpleasant turn and that's what bothers me.'

'I think, Patty Griffith is a one-time incident. I read somewhere she had huge personal deficits as well as a rotten family life, a dead child and so on.'

'Ah, okay. I haven't followed the story. There are so many other pressing things at the moment. It just shocked me that things have gone so far.'

'Don't put too much into it. It's the media that blows it out of proportion … hm … But you know what, Victoria? I just had this idea! Why don't we use the incidence for something useful? Then at least she will have done something of value.'

'What are you thinking of?'

'Give me a couple of days. I'll get back to you.'

'Okay.'

'Ah, Victoria! We've all worked so hard to get here. It would be a shame if it fell apart now. One lesson we've learned is that it's difficult to achieve something good without sacrifice.'

'That's certainly true.'

'If people are dissatisfied with what we do, they shouldn't have put their vote for us.'

'Indeed!' agrees Victory.

'I might still be young, but I think I've learned to play the game rather quickly. Not everyone agrees with your politics and, I must say, I sometimes have my doubts too, but I think we're basically sticking to our agenda and I'm confident we'll be able to do what we've planned. Henry and Gregg will support you at any price. And then you have me as your press secretary to keep the pressure from the public in check. We're strong team.'

'I do appreciate having you around me, believe me!'

'Do we want some tea?' asks Victoria.

'A cuppa is always good.'

'Oh well,' sighs Victoria, 'As Henry said, this thing with fat will blow over in time and something will come along that will unite the Kingdom again. By then we'll have changed the United Kingdom into something we all can be proud of and turned our back on the European Union for once and all, though, I actually do like Europe.'

Lisa laughs. 'That would be nice, wouldn't it?'

THE PRIVATE jet is ready for departure. Mason feels an urge for a Coke and gets one from the onboard bar before making himself comfortable in the cozy leather seat of the leased aircraft. The plane has a payload capacity large enough to carry all three of them.

'Where exactly are we going?' asks Robert.

'Cliff Brad Brokerage Partners has their subsidiary in one of the more exclusive areas in Hamburg,' Mason informs them.

'I can imagine,' responds James, unsurprisingly. 'I've checked on the name Christina Goldstein and, of course, wasn't able to find anything on her or for that matter, the company she represents. If the military is involved it's kind of obvious, isn't it?'

'I couldn't care less if her name is Christina Goldstein or something else,' states Mason. 'The primary thing is to save our companies.'

'Affirmative,' replies Robert.

'Did you lads hear about this new law?' asks James.

'You mean the tax on fat?' asks Robert. 'Where we must give fifty per cent of all our earnings to The Party and have to go to WeightForLife sessions?'

'If I could show The Party my asshole, I'd do it. Unfortunately, it's covered in too much buttocks,' remarks Robert.

They laugh.

'I like your humor,' says James. 'You should go to Westminster and show them how it looks.'

'The law is ridiculous,' comments Mason. 'I'd say the law will be revoked by the end of the month.'

'It has provoked a lot people, that's true.'

'Especially people with a Body Mass Index of over 35.'

'Hey wait a minute!' exclaims James. 'That's us!'

Again they laugh.

'But that wasn't the law I was referring to,' says James.

'It wasn't?'

'It's another law. One that has slipped through unnoticed. I think because the media has been busy with Fat Tax, they have failed to grasp the story. I read it in a foreign newspaper.'

'Which one?'

'A French one, Le Figaro.'

'The story about the Fat Tax takes up most of our news these days,' confirms Mason.

'Then tell us about this other law,' says James.

'It's even more grotesque than the Fat Tax law. It says that people with a Body Mass Index of more than 35 are to have all their assets frozen as long as this person owns a private enterprise.'

This time there are no laughs. A silence spreads through the cabin and is only surpassed by the engines and airframe noise. Was this a joke?

'I don't believe you,' exclaims Mason. 'That would be legalizing the hacker attacks on our bank accounts. Tell me it's a joke.'

'It's not.'

Then Robert asks, 'Are you saying that, by law, we're no longer allowed to have our companies?'

'That's what I'm saying.'

'It must be another mistake. Sometimes the law makers get it wrong. I can imagine something like this happening in Russia, but not here.'

'Is this perhaps the reason why Christina Goldstein wants us out of the United Kingdom?' wonders James.

Mason Sanders answers, 'In a way, that doesn't make sense. The government wants to help us, and then it works against us by making strange laws.'

'Perhaps the government is not agreed on what to do.'

'That could be the case.'

'Hm.'

'Mason, have you wondered if they want to make an offer for our companies?' ask James.

'No, I haven't,' replies Mason. 'And I'm damn well not in a mood to sell.'

'Things are so confusing right now. It would be interesting to know what kind of games they're playing at Westminster,' exclaims James. 'There must be some people who aren't falling for Victoria Seymour's rubbish.'

'True, and I remember the Chancellor was one of them. But that has changed,' says Mason.

'Now that you mention it, we don't hear much from him, do we?'

'No.'

'He's turned into another one of Victoria Seymour's puppets without any real power any longer. I guess his only job today is to count the money she spends on 'Fat' campaigns.'

'What about Henry Montclair?'

'I don't know much about him. Nobody does. Just like Victoria Seymour, and rest of her gang, he comes from the European Union. He wasn't particularly popular there.'

'I recall that Victoria Seymour worked there as well.'

'And now they're back in the United Kingdom and in power. Great!' says John.

'I read The Party's agenda and it's actually quite good,' explains Mason. 'It's obvious that with Brexit, the social benefits we have are no longer very economically sustainable. The Party's agenda does, to some extent, solve these challenges quite elegantly.'

'How?'

'By preparing the United Kingdom for the fourth industrial revolution. Imagine how large our public sector is, or the fact that more than 1.4 Million people work for our national healthcare system, making it practically the third largest employer in the World except for the Chinese People's Liberation Army and the Indian National Railway System. Try to calculate the expenses when …'

'Walmart has 1.3 Million employees,' Robert adds.

'But contrary to Walmart, our National Healthcare Service does not generate revenue.'

James laughs. 'That's kind of true, Robert.'

'But Victoria Seymour's idea about computerizing the government's public services is actually not a bad idea. She wants to implement a Universal Basic Income and a fixed tax for anyone – people as well as companies.'

'So, what is all this talk about obese people? I'd say there's a big difference between what she's saying and her agenda. Does it say anything about being allowed to have a Universal Basic Income when you have a Body Mass Index of 35 or less?'

'No.'

'Well, it would make sense, wouldn't it? All those lazy fat people on welfare should have to earn their Universal Fat Income.'

They laugh.

'Robert, why don't you set up a fund for overweight people?' asks Mason. 'It would make her happy.'

'Or at least we could start a group to oppose her. That wouldn't cost anything.'

'But Mason! If the law John is talking about is true, which I can't believe, then they'd be able to expropriate our companies.'

'If that's the case, I honestly don't care what she's written in her agenda'

'I agree.'

'She's not only smart, she's really quick!' admits Robert.

'In what way?'

'If it's true about the law, it must have been implemented at the same time as the law on the Fat Tax. A really slick politician's maneuver.'

'I think it's sick.'

'James, how did you hear about the law?'

'La Figaro, as I told you. But probably soon also my accounting people.'

'So you're not just talking nonsense.'

'Come on lads!' exclaims Mason. 'How would a law like this pass the Lords and the Courts? I'm sure the Queen would never sign such legislation. Where's the legal foundation for carrying out these ridiculous laws?'

'I don't know. Does she use the institutions she has accessible to her?'

'How would I know?'

'That's pretty scary. What if we have to give away our companies, just to save them?'

'You mean they want to buy us out?'

'Yes.'

'I know there have been talks for a long time about stopping the privatization of companies and let them return to government ownership.'

'So you say that's why the law has been implemented?'

'From a political view it would make sense.'

'Well, if it would make sense, why only for people with a Body Mass Index of 35 or more?

'I don't know.'

'Whew, Robert, you're making me sweat,' says James.

'My God, the United Kingdom is going down the drain. Why is it suddenly so 'in' to think regressively? exclaims Robert.

'What choices do we have – apart from going with the flow?' asks Robert.

'We're doing the right thing by going to Hamburg. We need to follow up on any opportunity that comes along. If this meeting turns out negative, then at least, there are many other investors out there.'

'True.'

'Right now, I honestly wish I had a BMI below 35. These days, it would make life so much easier.'

'Did anyone of you vote to leave Brexit?'

'Well, actually ... I did,' admits James. 'It sounded so good to be able to make our laws and not being controlled by Brussels.'

'Did you get smarter?'

'I certainly did. But I'd vote to leave again.'

'Aw man. For Christ sake! Why?'

'Because, I think Brexit is about getting our lost identity back.'

'Bullshit. Absolutely bullshit,' exclaims Mason. 'So, you mean in the process of finding our souls again, obese people have to pay for whatever is wrong with this godforsaken Kingdom?'

'We don't have the European Union to blame any longer. Somebody's has to be to blame.'

'I was quite satisfied with immigrants and Muslims.'

'It's true what James says,' confirms Mason. 'Politics always needs a scapegoat. In my view, all the fat-stuff is nothing but a distraction from the troubles with Brexit.'

'Yeah, but making us responsible for the economic situation after Brexit is pretty unfair. First the bankers and brokers were praised by the press and government for their great genius and business acumen, and then when the crisis came in 2008, they were blamed for almost everything. Now they want to put the blame on us for what happened in 2016. I don't get it.'

'I'm not sure if obese people ever will be praised for anything.'

'My God, the United Kingdom is going down the drain.'

'I think we heard you the first time.'

'Apart from our companies, we have nothing to lose anyway – except a couple of pounds.'

'Ha ha, that was funny. A couple of pounds! I really need to lose a lot of pounds.'

'Me too.'

'We really do live in times of contradiction.'

'I'd say so.'

'Yep, the United Kingdom is certainly going down the drain.'

'Stop saying that!'

'Why? It's true,' confirms Robert.

'I think Brexit was the last straw that broke our rule of the world,' comments Mason. 'The colonization by England and Great Britain has now followed that of the Spaniards.'

'At least we still have Northern Ireland and Scotland,' states James.

'Who gives a shit about them?' asks Robert.

'I have family there,' responds James.

'Now you're thinking like an Englishman, Robert.'

'I'm actually from Wales.'

'Nobody is perfect.'

'But, Mason, you say the United Kingdom is turning into a new Mallorca. We have nothing left except our beautiful landscapes and Big Ben.'

'That's a cruel thing to say isn't it? Especially in view of the fact the sun never shines in this godforsaken Kingdom.'

'No, honestly,' says Robert. 'I get Mason's point. History has a tendency to repeat itself. In every new generation, new mistakes are made, which mostly have already been made by the previous generation. It's like not wanting to listen, or wanting to be like our parents. But in the end, we end up acting like the previous generation and making the same mistakes over and over.'

'I'm not following you.'

'All empires eventually collapse and it wasn't so long ago that ours collapsed. Unfortunately, we still haven't gotten used to the fact, or at least, many of us haven't gotten used to it.'

'Hm.'

'But that fits pretty good with the politics we're seeing from Westminster. They're actually quite good at playing to these feelings.'

'They are, aren't they?'

'I just want to say, I'm not like my parents – that's for sure!' says James.

'We're all like our parents. You just don't want to admit to it.'

'That's not what I meant. As far as weight goes, both of them weigh about as much as I do.'

'Ha ha.'

'Well …' remarks Mason, we'll either solve our problems, or we'll need to move on and let our problems solve elsewhere. Believe me, I don't want my empire to end and I'm sure you don't want yours to end either.'

CHAPTER 9

THE CAR APPROACHES VICTORIA Seymour's limousine at extremely high speed. But as luck would have it, it misses by twenty centimeters, and plows on, into a group of people waiting at a bus-stop close to Downing Street. The incident happens in less than thirty seconds.

IT WAS an attempted attack on Victoria Seymour by some fat woman who was trying to assassinate the Prime Minister and First Lord of the Treasure and Minister for the Civil Service of the United Kingdom. It was, however, so poorly planned that it was obviously only an amateur attempt, one that eventually had to come. Getting the large perpetraitor out of her crumpled car turned out to be more complicated than anticipated and the pictures that were taken were seen around the world. The worst of them were released by The Party's press and media department again and again. One picture showed firemen cutting a car in half in their attempt to free the porcine corpse.

VICTORIA SEYMOUR, was quick to ask Lisa Ferguson, Minister for State Communication and Promotion, to have her press department take advantage of what had happened. Lisa Ferguson handed over a speech to the Prime Minister, not written by her press department, but prepared by Henry Montclair in own person. Victoria Seymour appeared in front of 10 Downing Street and extended her condolences on behalf of her government and herself to the families of the victims and delivered the speech:

A 12 year old girl and a man in his mid-forties have died, and 8 people have been brought to the hospital with severe injuries, in this terrible act of terror. We're now sure that it was a personal vendetta against me, and that this awful terror attempt, was intentionally carried out to inflict damage on me. The perpetrator's name is Julia Goodrich, a 31 year old woman who weighted 172 kilo. She died on her way to the hospital after rescue worker recovered her body. At 17:25, ambulance services were called with reports of a vehicle plowing into people at a bus stop on Whitehall. They arrived within four minutes and the police arrived at 17:29. Officers also arrived at the scene of a second incident at Piccadilly Theatre at 17:27, where it had been reported that a perpetrator, also a rather fat person, was attempting to stab a restaurant employee due to a dispute. It later turned out that these two incidences were not related. The terrorist, Julia Goodrich, was successfully removed from her car after it had to be cut in half. She was wearing what were thought to be explosive vests but were later determined to be only the padding caused by her body fat. At 18:05, the two incidents were declared unrelated by the Metropolitan Police. At 18:10, the police confirmed that two people were killed in the rampage and 8 people taken to hospital. A third incidence at Docklands, a stabbing, was first thought to be related but has been declared unrelated by Scotland Yard. Also here, the perpetrator was well above a Body Mass Index of 35.

Victoria pauses, and then scrolls through the papers in front of her, quickly skimming through the text, surprised. She can hardly believe what she is about to read-out next. She makes a mental note to always read Henry's speeches in advance in the future before giving them before an audience. She gets a grip on herself and continues:

In light of what has happened, it has been decided to temporarily limit some civil rights for people with a Body Mass Index over 35.

The statement makes Victoria's mouth go dry but she continues:

A curfew of 11pm until 07am will be implemented for people with a Body Mass Index of over 35 and continued until further notice. Furthermore, people possessing a Body Mass Index over 35 will have their civil rights limited when attending demonstrations to insure that streets are safe against further acts of terror. Anyone seeing infringements of this order, are encouraged to report the incident to the police. Press releases and other important material can be found on

The Party's website.

'Thank you.'

Victoria goes into 10 Downing Street as quickly as possible. She hears journalists in the background starting to ask questions. She should have read the speech before giving it and should have discussed it with Henry and Lisa. This was not so good. To her surprise, she finds that the speech has completely exhausted her, now feeling somewhat guilty for giving such a hate speech. Yes, she feels a bit ashamed. She knows that she will now go down in history as the most obnoxious xenophobic Prime Minister in the United Kingdom. Did Henry just stab her in the back? She's not sure. She had promised Henry as well as Gregg White, that she would let them do what is necessary for her to implement her agenda.

She takes off her shoes and throws herself onto the couch in her office. She looks around. Nothing has been done since the last Prime Minister. Maybe she should have the room redecorated to better suit her taste. Politics can be difficult sometimes and trade-offs must occasionally be made. And now that this has been put before the public, it will be up to the voters to decide whether or not to accept it. She is fairly certain that one part of the population will not be happy and that is those who it affects. But eventually something must be done to calm down feelings of rest of citizens. That there are people who actually want to assassinate her, because of their politics, is somewhat of an eye-opener. The suicide of the woman from the Early Morning Show was also rather alarming. All that she wants is to get her political manifesto implemented after Brexit. Although she has no intention of disparaging any minority, people *are* beginning to despise her and her government. But again, good politics can not satisfy everyone.

Again she sighs. If Henry doesn't get the special package made into law very soon by using this Henry VIII law, then she will be out of office by the end of the month.

'I feel awful,' she says to Lisa, as the young woman comes into the office, and puts some papers on the table, then drops down beside her. 'I don't like limiting the rights of some people because of what happened. We can't keep going on like this,' she complains.

'Henry has definitely used today's incidence to turn things to our advantage, I'll give him that much. I'm just glad I'm not the pig out there.'

The comment makes Victoria giggle. 'You know, Lisa? You have a way with words.'

'Thanks, but you know what I mean, right?'

'Of course I do. But your comment was a piece of nice, good, old English black humor. In view of what happened today, I'll ask Henry to ease up a little when he writes up new laws. We shouldn't turn our society into a two-class society.'

'I'm sure there are groups out there who will be pissed off after today's comments. I hope that our supporters won't take revenge on the assassination attempt. I wouldn't want to see fat people lynched from street lamps. It would cost a fortune to make the poles straight again.'

'Ouch, Lisa! You're on a role today. That was not a nice thought. Think of the people who would have to pull them down.'

'Think of the expense of replacing the bent poles!'

'Well …' mumbles Victoria. 'After my speech today, intelligent people have probably become aware of how stupid some people are. What's left of the opposition and the House of Lords will probably do anything to get us out. Henry is really testing the voters and their willingness to accept what he is doing.'

'He told me,' Lisa informs her, 'that the more often we stage such scandals, the more people will get used to them and finally ignore us.'

'What do you mean, staged? Did we stage the assassination attempt?'

'What? No, of course not. That one was authentic.'

'Hm. It's a kind of sad. I never expected that my rise to power would play out like this.'

'I'm sure everything will be just fine in the end. When your agenda is finally implemented, the United Kingdom will be the envy of the whole world.'

'Yes I know. But did you read the latest article about me?'

'The one last weekend in the weekend edition?'

'Yes, the one where The Daily Evening Mail completely defiles me. The journalist made me look like a complete fool. I'm not a fool. I'm just doing what's right for the United Kingdom. Why is it so difficult to understand for some people?'

'Because, they don't know the details yet Victoria.'

'You're a smart young woman, you really are Lisa.'

'Thank you.'

'But who is this journalist who is interviewing people from my past? And now this!' exclaims Victoria holding up this morning's newspaper. I'm beginning to hate this journalist! What does he mean when he writes that I sent two gorillas to his home, to make him shut up and be a little moderate when he writes about me and The Party?'

'I haven't read the article, but what do you say we exclude his newspaper from any future press releases?' suggests Lisa. 'That might quiet his editor down a little.'

THE FIRST article Mike Hornett wrote for the weekend edition about Victoria Seymour was based on known facts about her. How she, as a child, fought her obesity problems and fought her way back to a normal life. He did a great job researching her background, finding old friends from the United States, where she had lived in her youth and studied politics. He received private pictures of her as an obese child and unfiltered information about her youth. Surprisingly, when people were asked, they were totally uninhibited about divulging memories which were not always to Victoria Seymour's advantage. One story came from a university boyfriend who had been very much in love with her. He related how all she cared about were her studies and how she exploited those around her to get the things done that she felt were important thereby rising to a political star. That part, of course, he left out of the article.

For his previous article in the previous weekend edition, he researched even more thoroughly, spending many late nights to get the contents just right. Though he already had a good reputation and was well-known in the news industry, the article about Patty Griffith and her suicide, made him into a serious investigative journalist. The article started a wild-fire at competing newspapers that had failed to see the star-story and were now regretting it. The story evidently discredited Victoria Seymour, and resulted in her henchmen visiting him at his home and, fortunately, hurling vicious words instead of hard punches.

That brought him to his recent third article in which he wrote exactly about this incidence. Though her henchmen did not dare to use anything other than verbal threats to which he was immune, he and his editor agreed to push his provocation of Victoria one step further hoping it would force her to make the mistake of trying to shut them up with violence. If the plan worked, they would be able to open people's eyes to what is going on and realize that their new government is in the process of muting the press's freedom of speech. His third article did not at all find favor at 10 Downing Street. This time she had two handsome henchmen, dressed in very expensive suits, verbally harass his editor and excluded their newspaper from attending any future press briefings held at the Palace or Downing Street. Now finally there have been an attack on Victoria Seymour. An event that most of the press had been waiting for eventually would happen. Upon evaluation, it became obvious that anyone could have hit the limousine instead of plowing into bystanders. Hopefully this state of affairs will not last long, and people are encouraged to assemble in the streets and demonstrate; to fight back against this despicable and disgusting person who is the Prime Minister of the United Kingdom. The discrimination against obese people must stop. It was okay to legislate against fat in food, but obesity is something completely different. It is obvious that the press's ability to scrutinize the government is under attack. Why else would a government go so far as to use henchmen to squelch his editor and him?

MASON SANDER'S girlfriend is getting worried. For the last couple of days, she has heard nothing from her boyfriend which is very unusual. They are in contact once a day, or at latest every second day, so they can coordinate their activities and keep tabs on each other. She knows he was going to Hamburg with Inna Martens' and Ludmilla Hollister's husbands. By this time he would usually have called her and said he had arrived safely. But both his cell phones are off so she sends Inna and Ludmilla Short Messages to see if they have heard anything from their husbands.

They have not.

And that is what is worrying her.

She grabs her cell phone to call the Daily Evening Mail in London. She recalls the last person Mason was to talk to was a journalist there. His name is Mike she remembers but that is more or less it.

Unfortunately, the receptionist at the Daily Evening Mail cannot give her a telephone number for Mike. There are several Mikes at the editorials and neither of them knows which one it could be.

'Listen,' she says. 'This is rather important. Would it be possible to at least get the email addresses of all the Mikes working in editorials?'

'There are six Mikes working here. You should have chosen a less popular name. I guess, I can give you their email addresses.'

'I'd really appreciate it, thanks.'

MIKE IS fast to react to Mason Sanders girlfriend's email. He calls her on the landline number she provided in her email.

'This is Mike. You tried to reach me. What can I do for you?'

'Hi. I'm Mason Sanders fiancé.'

'Oh! Hi. What can I do for you?'

'I know you two know each other. I haven't heard anything from Mason in days – which is unusual. So, I just wanted to check if you've heard anything from him?'

'No, and that worries me, too. I need his approval for an article we're running tomorrow. Two days ago, he said he'd drop by yesterday. It's very unusual for him not to keep his promises.'

'His cell phones are all turned off. Why would he do that? He never turns off his cell phones. At least not his private one.'

'How many does he have?'

'A couple, but his private one is always on.'

'I guess that's how the rich communicate.'

'Indeed! You have no idea how creative people can be at contacting rich people to suck them off for a penny or two. It's amazing!'

Mike laughs. 'I don't have those problems. I'm a journalist.'

'Did Mason tell you about those two business people from Piran?' she asks.

'He did.'

'Did they go to Hamburg together?'

'As far as I know he had a business jet waiting. I spoke with him shortly before his departure.'

'I've been in contact with their wives. They haven't heard anything from their men either.'

'Hm.'

'Mike. What should I do?'

'Maybe we should wait it out. Mason and his two lads probably have reasons for not being accessible. Let's give them some time. And if Mason doesn't contact you by tomorrow, we'll figure something out.'

'I don't like the sound of it, Mike'

'Things will turn out just fine. Mason says you have your own company.'

'Yes, I do. I'm an entrepreneur in the fashion business. Mason is a great supporter, not only financially, but also with his knowledge about start-ups.'

'He's taken a couple of beatings in his own career.'

'At least my start-up is doing well. In case ImplantSkills doesn't make it, we can live on what I earn. It's not much but enough for a decent life.'

'He appreciates you a lot. But you probably know this.'

'I certainly do. I'm not like the others – if that's what you meant. Mason is a nice decent guy, through and through, and he deserves better than most. But how do we find him?'

'Uhm. We're silly people, aren't we?' says Mike.

'What do you mean?'

'Well, isn't it obvious? He owns ImplantSkills. So, I'm pretty sure he must have an implant.'

'My God! Why didn't I think of that myself? Of course he has an implant! If I give you access to his data, could you take it from there? At the moment I'm not able to come to London.'

'Sure thing. But I probably need a written consent. ImplantSkills' office is a stone's throw away from our building.'

'Great! I'll send you a written consent within the hour.'

'Perfect.'

'And please keep me up to date with any news.'

'I certainly will.'

'Thanks, Mike. I really appreciate your help.'

CHRIS CAMPBELL gets into his car. Now that he is banned from attending The Special Council, he has returned to his work at ImplantSkills. There is still a lot to do even though the company is in trouble and cannot fulfill its financial commitments. It doesn't look good for salaries at the moment. There is simply not enough capital, but in spite of this everyone including him all agree that the job still has to get done. Of course, he has one advantage that the others don't have. Not only does he get a salary from ImplantSkills, but also from The Special Council.

He turns the key to the ignition. As on all mornings the M1 from Milton Keynes is empty. The congestion comes before London. If he pretended that he was a wise man, which his wife claims he is, he would take the train like anyone else. It's faster. But he loves the privacy of driving on his own. This morning he is troubled though. Where is Mason Sanders, his boss? And then he can't stop thinking of the Future Team and Present Team at The Special Council differentiating so much in their rating of Victoria Seymour. It tells him that they think there is a chance that the woman and her government will actually turn the United Kingdom into a minimal democracy, which both Russia and Turkey have done lately, under Putin and Erdogan. Allowing this to happen in the United Kingdom is absolutely out of the question and non-negotiable. Had anyone told him a year ago that this was the direction the United Kingdom was heading, he would have laughed his behind off. But he no longer laughs. People have become so used to democracy that they think nothing can hinder it. At least that's what he thought until he read the news this morning, and heard Victoria Seymour's speech outside Downing Street yesterday. People cannot possibly still play along with this nonsense! And yet, the whole political right is doing it in the name of Democracy and; 'We the people!'

One can say a lot about The Special Council, but they are right to be concerned. For him personally, Victoria Seymour is starting to get on his nerves. Arguing about obese people like him and Andy was, in the beginning, only ridiculous chatter. But now, the ridicule has vaporized and the borderlines got drawn up quite clearly with that speech. She now differentiates between people like him and other citizens, and in a way given the five percent absolute brain-dead idiots, and real social outcasts who are probably more violent than peaceful, a purpose in life by strengthening them in their beliefs that they are the superior ones. The speech tore down the last morale fence that it is okay to harass the 3 per cent morbid obese and 22 per cent obese that live in society.

What is most surprising is how Victoria Seymour has been able to turn a simple subject into an efficient tool for political demigods. Some radio hosts, have turned into true hate preachers, abusing the situation on both sides of the obesity argument. Without doubt, he would feel better in a slimmer body, and probably also perform a bit better without the unnecessary kilos, but that is how things have turned out, and though not happy about it, it is a private matter to be obese. One thing he really misses is walking around the park sea. It is a walk less than four kilometers, but simply too far now that he has so little energy. It would also be nice to simply be able to see where he piss when he takes a leak. He hasn't seen his best buddy down there for years, although he knows it tries to look up at him once in a while. His knees are worn out due to the massive overload. His hygiene is probably not the best because he is not able to reach all places he ought to. And now with increasing age, his health seems to be deteriorating because of the extra weight. What is even more depressing is his 65 kilo, one meter seventy-five wife who is still as beautiful and fit as the day he met her. Only God knows why she's still at his side and has not left with some young lover-boy. They have certainly turned into an odd couple over the years. When they met, he was in as good a shape as she was, with the muscles in all the right places, and even a six-pack most women would only dream of in a man. Of course back then, he was an elite soldier, and today it almost seems as if he is protecting his six-pack by wrapping it in huge layers of wobbling fat.

Perhaps Victoria Seymour is the wake-up call people like him need. To encourage them to self-reflect and finally do something about it. Limiting obese people's civil rights though, is not a really effective way to send the message. Had he not had the confidence he has, he would probably have ended up believing Victoria Seymour's stupid doctrine and would have signed up for WeightWatchers, although it seems the new government has shut them down now because of their own WeightForLife.

One of these days he'll sign up on one of the internet sites that are popping up everywhere opposing The Party and Victoria Seymour. That's for sure!

Chris Campbell arrives at ImplantSkills and drives down the ramp to the underground parking lot. This is probably the real reason he doesn't take the train. A guaranteed place to park. There are people saying it was Victoria Seymour who planned the attack on herself, simply to obtain some sympathy and get her ratings up. So far though, or at least according to The Special Council's latest report, there is no evidence of this being the case. What the report does show, however, is how well The Party is using any opportunity to its own advantage. The Fat Tax is an unfortunate mistake, they say, and claim it will be revoked. But there is more to it than just this. They are testing the public to see where its acceptance level is. Each time something happens, with each word or false statement, The Party stirs up waters to see where the sharks are. Either the majority of the population does not have eyes and ears, or they prefer to stick their heads deep into the sand, but for how long? And will it by then be too late? True. It is an amazing once-in-a-lifetime opportunity to observe at close hand the dynamics of right-wing politics and its impact on a whole Kingdom. But if he is honest, he would prefer reading about it in the history books. Not experiencing it firsthand. The problem is; people may not recognize it, but Victoria is a performer, and an excellent one. This is exactly what makes her so dangerous.

MIKE HORNETT hangs up the phone. Mason Sanders' girlfriend sounds like a nice woman. He knows she looks a little like Ivanka Trump, so she must really have it going for her. One hour later, the consent is in his inbox. He prints it, folds the paper, and sticks it into an envelope. Then he makes his way to ImplantSkills' London office, which is right around the corner from his office.

At ImplantSkills, it is he notices that things are not running as they used to. As Mason had said, capital is running low and, in spite of this, people are still there doing whatever they need to do to keep the company operational. This is obviously not a place where people leave the sinking ship because, as Mason always says, his employees are the ship.

'Chris,' calls the receptionist to Chris's office, 'there's a journalist here. He says he knows Mason and asks if we know where he is.'

'Ah. It must be Mike, Mason's personal journalist. Ask him what he wants.'

'Can you please come down? He has a written consent from Mason's fiancé, saying he's allowed to look into his whereabouts.'

'That's worrying. I'm wondering myself where Mason is.'

'Just come down, will you?'

'I'm on my way.'

A few minutes later, Chris greets Mike. The guy surprises him a little. Mike is much smaller than he had anticipated. He has a beard, but is completely bald, like a boiled egg. The man looks like someone who was pulled out of his mother with a plunger when he was born and never really recovered. At least the man seems to be rather fit and extreme charming. Everything about him radiates confidence, but, by God, concludes Chris, he has huge flat feet and walks like a duck.

'I read your articles about Victoria Seymour and The Party,' says Chris on their way to one of the meeting rooms. 'I like them. They are very well researched and written.'

'Thank you.'

When they arrive, Chris leads Mike to a couch, facing the windows, providing an excellent view of London and the River Thames. Before he sits down, he pours coffee into two mugs from a near-by take-away.

'I assume you drink coffee' he asks.

Mike nods.

'Black, please.'

He gets down next to Mike handing him his coffee.

'So, how can I help you?' he asks.

'I'm looking for Mason. As you're now aware, I'm the journalist writing about ImplantSkills. Mason and I go some time back.'

'Indeed you do,' responds Chris. 'It's amazing that we haven't met before.'

'Well you're into technology. Mason is economy and business strategy.'

'That's true.'

'But you've climbed the ladder quickly,' says Mike.

'I certainly have.'

'And how are things around here?'

'Well, I guess they could be better. But as you see, people are working their way through the crisis. It's good to have good employees.'

'I think Mason appreciates that.'

'He certainly does. I understand from our receptionist that you have authority to check into Mason's whereabouts. You got the allowance from his girlfriend?'

'Yes. She's worried sick about him. He hasn't called for a couple of days which is very unusual in their relationship.'

'Hm.'

'And I'm worried for him, too. We had an appointment.'

'I see. How long time has it been?'

'Four days. That's unusual for Mason.'

'It is,' replies Chris, considering his options. 'Unfortunately, her authority is insufficient. I'm quite certain she's not listed in the legal documents.'

'That's not good.'

'Have you called him often?'

'Well, not as often as his girlfriend.'

'Well, maybe we should check on him. He missed two meetings yesterday which is very unusual. When I tried this morning, his phones were all off.'

'Exactly.'

'Okay. Let's look into his activity log. I don't think he'd mind. I can of course not bring you into the restricted area, but I'll let you know when I've checked.'

'I'd appreciate it very much.'

'I'll be back in half an hour.'

Chris goes to the restricted area where only a few employees have access to the clients data. He is actually not one of those who is allowed to look into other people's logs. According to procedure, three people must be present to protocol what is done, though in this case, they will have to make an exception.

Chris goes to a rather young, Chinese colleague.

'Li Jiu, we have a problem with Mason. He's gone missing. His girlfriend wants to know where he is.'

'Does she have clearance?'

'No, not really. I'm quite sure she's not on the list, but could you please check?'

Li Jiu sits in front of the computer. He opens a program and waits for a name.

'What's the problem?' asks Chris.

'I need her name.'

'Oh! I honestly don't know who she is this year. Could we just pretend she's on the list?'

'Just hold on,' says Li Jiu. Then he writes something.

He turns to Chris. 'You're on Mason's list.'

'Oh really? I didn't know that. Then get a third person for the protocol and let's have a look.'

'I'll get Ali. Charles is not in today.'

A few minutes later, the three stand in front of another computer. First Chris enters his personal code. Then Li Jiu and finally Ali.

'Okay, we're in. What period do you want to retrieve?'

'One week up to today.'

'Tuesday to Tuesday, you say.'

'Why is the system working so slowly?'

'Because the servers are spread throughout the world.'

'Oh! That's the new safety feature, right?'

'Right.'

The data display on the screen shows long lines of dates and numbers.

'Sooo,' says Li Jiu. 'Now we just need the converter to turn it into something visual … and … here we go …'

Li Jiu follows the red line with his index finger. For every ten meter there is a mark, making the line look like a string of pearls. By clicking on them, they are provided with the data they need.

'It looks like he went to Hamburg on Wednesday, but the day after he went from Hamburg to Nordhausen … Hm …'

'What's, hm?'

'The data is behaving strangely. Hold on for a moment, I need to look into the detailed time-stamps.' Li Jiu scrolls up and down a list on the screen. 'This is really strange,' he says. 'I don't understand the data.'

'What's the matter?' asks Ali.

'The data must be compromised. Or the microchip is broken.'

'Why?'

'Yes, why?' asks Chris.

'Because, according to the data …' Li Jiu flips back to the map, enlarging the area around the last dot on the red line and slowly zooms to an area in the middle of practically nothing. 'Mason is in an area where there is nothing. Out in the woods – at least according to the satellite image.'

'Oh shit! This isn't good,' exclaims Ali.

'Tell me what's going on,' demands Chris.

'According to this data, Mason hasn't moved for three days. What do we have today, Tuesday? Since he arrived in this area, he hasn't moved.'

'What are you saying? You're making me nervous.'

'I have to go into the data details. Just hold on …'

The wait is unbearable. Something is obviously not right.

'I'm saying that Mason is not moving. Either his microchip has been removed or he's playing dead. The pattern does not match the one of a living person. Most people need to go to the toilet once in a while.'

Chris is stunned into silence. This was not expected.

'Where in the world are we?' he asks.

'He is close to a town called Nordhausen. Look! The map shows it's a very small town with pretty much nothing in the area. 'There's nothing. Why would Mason go there? Okay, the landing strip is huge, but the town is only a few houses.'

'How did he get there?'

'Just a minute …'

'From Hamburg to Nordhausen, he took the German autobahn at 90 km per hour.'

'Isn't that slow for Autobahn? Don't they have no speed limits there?'

'Perhaps he took the bus? Or he had plenty of time.'

'Buses normally drive 100. Trucks go 90.'

'So … you're saying something has happened to Mason?'

'I can't know. But looking at the data, this might be the case.'

'And he's not in a hospital?'

'It's in the damn woods.'

This is not good, thinks Chris. He tries to think what to do. This not only means trouble for ImplantSkills but also for The Special Council. They need ImplantSkills to maintain surveillance on influential people. If something has happened to Mason, then finding the capital they need to survive will turn extremely complicated.

'Damn! What now?' he exclaims.

'Shall we send out a recovery team?' asks Li Jiu.

'Shall I request one?' asks Ali.

'No! Keep this between us. I don't want anyone to know about Mason's sudden disappearance. It's too early to speculate whether he's dead or laying injured somewhere.'

'No rescue team?' asks Li Jiu again.

'This requires a special rescue team. I'll assemble my own.'

And that rescue team will consist of Andy Green from Seattle, himself and a colleague from The Special Council in Germany.

'Okay.'

'Just to be certain,' asks Chris to reassure himself, 'Mason's implant hasn't just fallen out, right?'

'And how could that be possible?'asks Ali.

'I was just hoping for … Damn! This is certainly not good.'

CHRIS returns to Mike. Before going into the meeting room, he takes some time to get a grip on himself. There is no evidence that Mason Sanders is dead, or hurt, or whatever. He puts on a fake smile, all the way to his ears. Maybe it'll work.

'He's in Hamburg,' he informs Mike, happily.

'In Hamburg? He told me he was going to Hamburg. It's just very unusual that his phone is off or he doesn't return my calls.'

'I know. But I guess he has his reasons. You know how critical the situation is for ImplantSkills at the moment.'

'I do.'

'I suggest you tell his girlfriend that everything is fine. That there's nothing to worry about.'

'Okay, I'll do that. She'll be glad to hear it. Chris, thank you for your time and help, I really appreciate it.'

'I think Mason would think so too. Anyway, thanks for dropping by.'

Chris follows Mike to the reception area. They shake hands and say goodbye. On the way to the building's entrance, Mike turns around, and sees Chris wobbling back to the offices and taking out his cell phone to place a call. Chris Campbell is lying, he is certain. After he had returned from the restricted area, he had looked concerned and somewhat upset.

AFTER HAVING brought Mike to the door, Chris dials a number on the new cell phone he had bought a few days ago. It had gotten exhausting driving to the shopping center every evening at 8pm to call Seattle, but now the line is secure. It must be the middle of the night over there, but this matter must be dealt with immediately.

A groaning voice picks up the receiver. 'Who's calling at this hour?' Chris hears the voice ask.

'It's Chris. You awake?'

'What a dumb question. No.'

'An urgent matter has come up. I need help.'

'With what?'

'I'm at Implantskills. I've just learned that my boss has been gone for days. He had a microchip and it says that he hasn't moved for the last couple of days.'

'How am I to understand this? Are you talking about Mason Sanders?'

'Yes. And I'd rather not speculate. It could be that someone's removed his implant, though his mobility log shows things are not right. There isn't the slightest indication that he's even been alive for the last couple of days.'

'You mean like … not moving … like dead?'

'Could be dead, yes.'

'That's not good. How can I help?'

'He's in Germany outside a city called Nordhausen. Usually we send out recovery teams to find lost people, but, I'd rather that we do this together.'

'But Nordhausen?' says a rather surprised Andy Green. 'What would he be doing there? That's an old restricted military area from World War II. That's where the Nazi regime built the world's first rockets.'

'I'm not sure if my boss is interested in rockets.'

'No. And he wouldn't be able to get in if he was. It is an absolutely restricted area, so there's no reason for your boss to be there. You can go to Dora, an old concentration camp and take a look. But that's it. I assume he didn't go to Nordhausen to lay dead on the floor of a museum.'

'His position didn't indicate he was in a museum, rather in the middle of some forest.'

'Hm. I suggest, we start with some satellite images. Order some from the Old Man. He'll get you what you need. But Chris, please keep me updated on this. If the man is in trouble, we need to reconsider our strategy for ImplantSkills. His company is simply too important in our surveillance of influential people.'

'You don't have to tell me that,' moans Chris. 'But I'm not able to order satellite images. I'm decommissioned. Remember?'

'Damn, I forgot. Okay, I'll order the images and forward them when I've received them.'

'Thanks Andy.'

VICTORIA SEYMOUR is upset with Mike Hornett's latest article. Actually, she is upset with all of them. The last two articles have been unusually rough on her. The damn journalist has tried to blame her for the woman taking her own life just because she told the woman the truth a few weeks ago on the Early Morning Show. Then there were the article about her using henchmen to force the editorial of their newspaper to be less critical toward her and The Party. And now he is accusing her or the Party of planning the incident in front of Downing Street themselves. It is absolutely bullocks. It is about time a damper is put on that damn newspaper and their lies; the damn journalist is spreading fake news, doing everything in his power to discredit her. Banning the media and what they are writing about her is, of course, not an option and she knows this, but she would appreciate it if they would stop putting stones in her path. Why are they doing this to her? Why are they so evil? Other newspapers and the tabloids are calming down, but not the Daily Evening Mail. They keep at it all the time, treating her like some second-rate politician. She is trying to get the United Kingdom back on its feet, and it doesn't even seem to help that they have been banned from future press conferences.

This is why she has asked James Dunham from the Early Morning Show to invite her once again so she can protect her stance on this Patty Griffith thing.

'Ms. Seymour, thank you for joining our morning show and taking time out from your busy schedule.'

'Thank you for the invitation.'

'I think the last time you were here was three or four weeks ago? It seems a lot has happened since. Do you deny the stories about your being behind your own attack or that the food industry is trying to buy influence to allow using more fat in their products?'

'Of course I did not stage my own assassination. It's absolutely ridiculous! It's this journalist, Mike Hornett with his lively fantasy.'

'So, you say that you had nothing to do with what happened?'

'Of course I had nothing to do with it. All those poor people who were hurt. I find it ghastly for Mike Hornett to discredit us by saying we had anything to do with such an evil act.

'What about the stories he has written about the industry trying to convince you to cancel the Fat Law …'

'All the stories written by Mike Hornett are nothing but stories. It's true that we've had the industry knocking on our doors. All the decent, hard-working people out there know we don't give in to lobbying or bribery. The Fat Tax will be rescinded when the government is ready.'

'So, you're saying Mike Hornett is lying?'

'All the time! But at least the public isn't sensitive to his bull.'

'He also accuses you of being a demagogue.'

'Firstly, I don't see where anyone would get the impression that I'm a demagogue, just because I publicize the fact that society has a problem with fat. On the contrary, I'd say, a man like Mike Hornett, writing cheap gossip stories like these, brings shame to anyone who wants to make the United Kingdom great again. I don't think we should waste words on discussing such an unpopular person like him.'

'There are rumors circulating that The Party is responsible for the sudden disappearance of obese people.'

Victoria Seymour was not prepared for this. For a few seconds she does not know what to say. She has recently heard that some obese people have gone missing. People do tend to sometimes go missing. 'I'm astounded to hear this.' replies Victoria truthfully. 'Is that this Mike Hornett again? What does this have to do with us? There are more serious matters to be discussed than ridiculous gossip.'

'But Ms. Seymour, isn't it right, you lied in a public statement some time ago, about …'

'I certainly have never lied in any public statement. When? It's not our fault that people go missing or that other political parties have serious weaknesses, and try to compensate by spreading lies about us. We're well organized and know exactly what our objectives are.'

'And if you could clarify them for us.'

'Why don't you read my political manifesto?'

'I did. And so far, none of its contents have been implemented.'

'We're still in the preparation phase. We need time to prepare the United

Kingdom for the difficult time outside the European Union. There's a lot to do, especially in the light of a weak economy.'

'Wouldn't it be better to concentrate on these issues, instead of focusing on fat and obesity?'

'We do focus on these matters! I still stand on what I've been saying all along. Fat is a major contributor to inefficiency, making it difficult for many to find a job. Fat people are a wasted resource in our goal of returning to our role as global player. Sixty-five percent of the people in the United Kingdom are overweight. If you're fat, it's only natural that you contribute less because you have limited capabilities. Fat is as inefficient for our society, as the European Union was and fat must be fought at any cost. We're Europe's fat man, a self-inflicted problem, but this problem can be solved.'

'I tend to compare your agenda to the early 1930ies when the Jews were blamed for …'

'That's something completely different! When you're a Jew, you're a Jew and you can't change this. But if someone is fat, they can certainly do something about it.'

'How do you define fat?'

'Fat is what is put in our products to make us fat. I'd like to emphasize today that we were not the ones who mentioned anything about fat people. That's something the newspapers and social media came up with. And, as time has now shown, it's an issue that troubles many. That's why we've decided to back these decent, hard-working citizens by doing something about the problem.'

'I'm not sure if you understood me correctly. I was thinking about the technical definition of being fat.'

'A Body Mass Index between 28 to 35 is where people go from having an acceptable weight to being overweight. This is where the true problems associated with being fat begin and it also turns into a major problem for society.'

'I guess, it's easy for a skinny person like you to set the parameters for others. What is your BMI? 20?'

'No! I'm 22 – which is spot on for my height, age and stature, but I wasn't always this way.'

'Let's show our viewers a picture from your earlier days. I think this picture was published in a magazine some weeks ago.'

'Oh boy! That was 32 years ago. I spent four and a half years losing that 150 kg.'

'Was it hard?'

'No. It takes a lot of self-discipline. I could do it, so if others try hard enough, they can too. And believe me, my life, my quality of life, has become a hundred times better!'

'Ms. Seymour, you told me that the reason for joining our show today, was because of the incidence with Patty Griffith.'

'Yes, and I'm terribly sorry to hear what happened. I would like to say; if I in any way contributed to her decision, I'm indeed sorry. But I can't imagine. Patty Griffith was a grown woman, fully capable of taking care of herself. It was never in The Party's or in my interests for Patty Griffith to do what she did. People ending their lives is a private matter and certainly not a topic to be discussed on a TV show. All that The Party wants is a United Kingdom that can represent itself on the world stage as the superpower we always were. Patty Griffith chose the easy way out thus put her part of the burden on the shoulders of everyone else. Her suicide shows what an egocentric person she really was.'

'Well, I … I assume that depends how you see …'

'I feel sorry for her family, relatives and friends, of course. I truly do. It must be very difficult for them. And it must be a great loss for them. But we cannot let an egocentric woman like Patty Griffith, who chose the easy way out, prevent the rest of us from achieving our goals. We must think of our children and our future. In this spirit, The Party, has decided to provide Patty Griffith with a national funeral next week to show her the last respect. Her family has already accepted and voiced their appreciation.'

'I guess that's a gesture many of us will never experience. How about a hand to Victoria Seymour and The Party before we continue with a word from our sponsors. After the break, we'll return with a young woman, whose love life changed overnight when learned that her little sister had run away with her boyfriend with whom she had been together with for six years. She'll tell us about her fight to get her boyfriend back knowing that her relationship with her sister will forever be broken. It's a heartbreaking story.'

IT IS Andy Green calling Chris Campbell. This time it is personal news.

It's good news.

'Chris, it's Andy.'

'Hi Andy. Did you get the satellite images?'

'Not yet. Is everything okay in your part of the world? I forgot to ask last time we spoke.'

'Not much has changed since yesterday. Did you get the satellite images?'

'Not yet, I said. It takes a while. The Old Man needs to pull some strings and it's not cheap!'

'I'll be patient then.'

'Anyway, I have some good news. We found the girl who was trying to blackmail you in Seattle. She's been in our custody and we've just released her.'

'Really! That was fast. How did you manage that?'

'It was actually quite easy. The hotel surveillance cameras had some very good images of her. When we had those, it was just a matter of asking around. I hope you used a condom, because, she's very popular. And rather expensive.'

'Wow, isn't that something. Should I feel lucky?'

'During the interview, she gave us what we thought she'd give us. You were nothing but a random victim. She and her girlfriend have done it hundreds of times before. It mostly happens to naive tourists and business men cheating on their wives.'

'Hm, but actually, I didn't want to. They drugged me.'

'That's true. Anyway, the reason they knew your address was simply because she looked in your wallet when you were asleep.'

Chris laughs. 'Slept? I was out! She didn't steal my money.'

'In her salary class, it would be embarrassing to steal from a little dick like yours. The other news is: Your decommission has been canceled. And that's good because my Chief in Command here in Seattle says we have loads of data to investigate before we can execute the FDAR.'

'Well, I guess that calls for a small celebration with a glass of fine wine.'

'You remember that I promised my boss to stay away from the bottle until the FDAR has been carried out. You heard it yourself, didn't you?'

'I heard it alright, but when we're through with the FDAR we'll have to empty a bottle.'

'We have to do that, Chris, we really do.'

'To be honest with you; I actually can't wait drinking that bottle.'

'Ha ha. And how do you think I feel? Let's say I call you when I got the satellite images.'

'Sure thing. Take care, Andy.'

'You too, buddy.'

EPISODE 3

SIGNS OF TROUBLE

Chapter 10

HOW DID SHE END UP IN THIS awkward situation? Monica Griffith is not at all satisfied with the national funeral for her sister with The Party and Victoria Seymour coming as guests of honour. No, she is extremely upset with the political elite intruding on her and her family's privacy.

Nothing has turned out as expected since she put those two ticks on the ballot sheet some time ago. Had she known that the economy would get worse for people like her after Brexit and that Victoria Seymour would start this craziness about fat in products that led to the ostracism of the obese, then she would have voted differently. Brexit and Victoria Seymour were nothing but protest votes to show how she feels about the political elite, the political parties and the establishment and of their incapability to change the slightest simplest things. Today though, she feels embarrassed and used.

How on earth could she be so simple-minded as to let herself be seduced by a demagogue like Victoria Seymour? She had never expected the woman to turn on people like her sister and herself. She as well as her sister had had issues with their weight bouncing up-and-down around a Body Mass Index well above 35. It is good to have the fat content of foodstuffs reduced, but it is not good to discriminate because of body size. Her sister had tried to change something in her life and had already lost 55 kilos. She was in the process of completely changing her life-style and it was working well. She had felt some of her dignity and self-esteem return and then came Victoria Seymour who demeaned her sister completely in front of a whole nation.

She has, as well, been trying to live a healthier life, but it is difficult on her low wages. Housing has become expensive and so has heating. She hopes that the coming winter will be milder than the last, and she also hopes that with global warming, winters will always be milder so she doesn't have to worry about the extra heating costs. Then there is the Fat Tax which dictates that she must join WeightForLife and pay half her wages to The Party. It is simply not good because now there is much less money left for food and daily necessities. How can any politician come up with laws like these? It is not only cruel, but also discriminatory, even racist to some extent. If the government wanted to discriminate against a group of people, they have certainly succeeded. It is simply unfair to punish someone for their obesity. She is reminded every day about it although she never actually thought of herself in this way. She knows she is a little overweight, has big behind, big legs and, if she's honest with herself, she knows her size will eventually cause her problems.

The tabloids have contributed their part in making her feel unhappy. At least they have scrutinized the law on the Fat Tax thoroughly and voiced their opinions against it. However, fewer and fewer newspapers have been opposing what is going on and have lately come to terms with how things evolve. It is not only scary, but scandalous that the media as well as many people have come to accept the propaganda that obesity is such a serious problem for society. The media, however, did suggest that a Body Mass Index of 35 is perhaps too low because it affects too many people, so it ought to be raised to 39. But Westminster has, so far, not responded leading people to believe that they don't really care about people like her.

The way things are at the moment makes her feel helpless. There is no platform for her to voice her opinion. In public, she feels the eyes on her, judging her and even distancing themselves from her. She has banned tabloids in her home because it has become depressing to read how the public is swallowing what is going on. The media doesn't seem to want to write about the hardship WeightForLife imposes on people like her who are on a low, fixed income so no one sees the other side of the real effects of the Fat Tax.

When she had decided not to go along with The Party and not join WeightForLife, three men in suits and ties broke into her apartment and waited for her to come home. They forced her to sign the contract, threatening that if she didn't, something might happen to her friends or family. How did they know who she was or where she lived? Is a neighbor a whistle-blower? She was also told that if she contacts the police or press, there will be serious repercussions for her loved ones.

The Party is making her life miserable as it did for her sister. People everywhere have joined the movement, ostracizing those who are overweight. They say that people of color, immigrants, the disabled and those of different ethnic backgrounds can't help being who they are, but overweight people have a choice and can simply take the necessary measures to lose weight. If it would be this simple she'd be first to smile.

What a shame the assassination attempt on Victoria Seymour wasn't successful. It may have ended this craziness. There is, thankfully, a rising resistance to her and her wacky party and it is growing. The day will come when an uprising puts an end to the insanity.

She takes a last look at her sister's picture.

Then she gets into her car and drives the 350 meters to WeightForLife.

'MR. GREEN!' His secretary calls him for a third time. She is standing in the doorway of his office. There is a familiar face next to her.

'Eh?' Andy comes out from his deep thoughts.

'Andy? Are you with us?' she asks.

'I was concentrating on something.' he answers, although in reality he was taking a power nap.

'Mr. Adams wants to talk to you.'

'Right, come in Kevin. I guess it's important if you take the trouble to come down to my floor.'

'I got the satellite images you ordered,' Kevin Adams informs him, waving them around in the air. In his other hand, he is holding his daily mug of hot chocolate.

'That smells good,' comments Andy. 'And you didn't bother bringing one for me?'

'Two mugs and those stairs would only end in disaster.'

'I know. Why don't you take the elevator like everyone else around here?'

'Exercise is good for me.'

'That's all just a trend, my friend.'

'So …' Kevin begins. 'There is something interesting about the images you ordered. They could potentially turn into a hot potato.'

'Why? Where did you get them from?'

'From Russia.'

'From Russia? Why?'

'None of our own satellites over Germany were available, but a Russian one was. They come from one of our moles in the Russian intelligence. But he stood up to the Old Man at first, not wanting to give us the images.'

'He did? Wow, I've never heard of anyone doing this to the Old Man before.'

'He literally had to get down on his knees to get them.'

Andy laughs. 'And I wasn't there to see it! But why?'

'Because there's something on those images our contact wants us to know about, but isn't allowed to disclose. He's putting himself pretty much at risk here, if those images get out, that's what he said.'

'But they won't get out, he should know this. If we gave them to our own intelligence agencies or made them public, it would blow The Special Councils cover.'

'I know. That's why we've been looking at them ourselves. But so far, we simply have not been able to figure out what his problem is. We haven't found anything out of the ordinary.' Kevin Adams spreads the images on the desk to give Andy Green a full overview. 'The only thing we've noticed is how good the resolution is. See? The quality is exceptionally good.'

'So?'

'This pretty much discloses the satellite's orbit and its flight capabilities.'

'That's true.'

'The question is; what it is, he wants us to see. The only thing we've come up with so far is what we don't see. There are no active military installations, only an old one from World War II. There is a small town, a civil airport with a pretty long runway and a museum called Mittelberg, surrounded by a forest and green fields.'

'Yes, Chris said the town is called Nordhausen.'

'Anyway, you're our military expert, so … we thought …'

Andy picks up a random photo. 'True,' he says after a short while. 'Nothing military apart from some old remnants. Is our Russian colleague suggesting some kind of unauthorized military activities, maybe military aircraft flying in and out?'

'We've already checked. No military aircraft fly in and out of there any longer. According to radar surveillance, two to three times a week a civilian transporter arrives from the United Kingdom in the late evening and a flight plan has always been filed.'

'Do you know anything about Nordhausen?'

'Should I?' responds Kevin, rather surprised at the question.

'Haven't you heard about Werner von Braun? The scientist who developed the V1 and V2 rockets for Adolf Hitler and the Third Reich?'

'You mean the rockets that were dropped on London?'

'That's it. Werner von Braun is a legend. Some people call him a Nazi, others a brilliant genius whose ideas made history. Without him, there would have been no ICBM's or moon landing.'

'ICBM's?'

'Gee. What do you guys do there on the upper floors? Inter-Continental Ballistic Missiles, you know, the things that carry the nuclear warheads.'

'But it still doesn't explain what our colleague in Russia wants us to see on those images.'

'I assume the Old Man has already squeezed for an explanation?'

'And our colleague stood up to him and just kept saying that what's on those images is our headache, not theirs.'

'Cooperative as always, those Russians, huh!' Andy looks at the images for a moment. 'Actually, it's Chris Campbell in London, who wants to see the aerial photos. Perhaps we should just send the images to him.'

'Are you going to give it at shot?'

'As if I have nothing else to do, but I'll give it a shot.'

VICTORIA SEYMOUR had to admit that it certainly wasn't the saddest funeral she'd ever attended. Six years ago her father had died suddenly of a heart attack. The heart attack happened when her family needed it the least, but that was how her father was. A coronary artery had narrowed, causing fat cells to build-up, leading to a condition called coronary artery disease, the most common cause of heart attacks. His blood pressure was too high as well causing atherosclerosis and diabetes. He had refused to get treatment because it was below his dignity to do so and it would mean changing his lifestyle by eating healthier and exercising. Her father was a stubborn fool who didn't take care of himself. He didn't take care of his family or his surroundings either nor did he let anyone butt into his life and tell him it was time to be careful. A typical behavioral pattern surrounding her family. When her mother died nine years before him, it became even worse with her father. She believes his condition started when her sister, his favorite daughter, died from food poisoning at the age of thirty-one. Today all that is left of her family is a cousin in South Wales, and an uncle in Manchester who is as insane as her late father and with whom nobody wants to spend time with.

Victoria greets Patty Griffith's family, extending her condolences and taking the pre-arranged seats in the second row with Henry Montclair, Gregg White, Lisa Ferguson and the Chancellor of the Exchequer. The family in the first row is struggling to hold back their tears of grief. The Griffith family seems to be a small group, like her own family. It is noticeable that most people present at Patty Griffith's funeral are outsiders who probably are only attending in the hope of having a picture taken at this rather spectacular media show. Victoria Seymour estimates that about five-hundred or so very important and very popular people have gathered this afternoon to send Patty Griffith on her way into the afterlife. She sees a few people from the opposition sitting behind her. Outside the church, thousands of people have shown up to extend their last respect. The public interest in Patty Griffith's death has become an amazing page turner, because, who doesn't want to take advantage of the momentum an event of this type provides to make a few easy quid or to help the media entertain its followers?

The only ones who are shedding honest tears are the three oversized family members in the first row. Tears run down their faces from their big pear-shaped heads saying their last goodbye to the woman they all loved. The family may not acknowledge the truth that the woman was a coward who took her own life rather than fighting for a better tomorrow. All they can probably think about is Patty Griffith's embrace, the warmth in her eyes and even her love. At least it is good to see that the family is not ashamed that she took her own life. They do seem to have loved her, but now she is gone and a light in their hearts has been extinguished forever. It is something they will have to get used to.

The funeral ceremony proceeds very slowly. The clicks from cameras are louder than the voice of the minister. Family and friends all have memories to share and favourite hymns to sing. The agency that arranged the funeral must have obliged every request of The Party's advertising department and those of the family and friends. And now, with the minister's slow, boring speech, Patty Griffith's sister starts swaying in her seat and had it not been for her rather obese father's support, she would had fallen on the floor in front of the minister. The final words from the minister bring a fresh round of tears and sobbing from the first row. She must remember to thank Lisa Ferguson for this ridiculous event. The funeral of Patty Griffith is nothing but a tribute to The Party's ability to court attention at any costs.

The walk to the churchyard is followed by a trail of people. Lisa Ferguson, Henry Montclair and Gregg White walk reverently with her behind the coffin. The memory of her own father's funeral, her walking alongside the coffin, returns. A grave, much wider than deep, has been dug. The sun's rays on this fantastic summer day seem to shine harder than what one might expect for an event of this kind and the birds are singing oblivious to the sadness of the occasion. The sun's brightness and the cheerful colors of summer seem to be telling the funeral party that the world will go on without Patty Griffith. Nobody here cares for Patty Griffith, the Griffith family or her sister, Monica Griffith, because, they are only here for their own exposure and interests.

Victoria hates arrangements of this type but protocol demands that she attend such funerals and provide sympathy on demand. Skipping the funeral would have been unforgivable and the press would have had a field day. Until now she has kept an appropriate distant feeling that the whole set-up is a waste of her precious time. So now it is time to cry and show feelings of guilt, to play to the press and Mike Hornett who accuse her of being responsible for Patty Griffith's death. Funerals bring back memories and cause people to reflect. This is the moment to find those thoughts and let the memories come, hoping that they will help her to shed a few tears. Lisa Ferguson had advised her to do this when the coffin is lowered so that her tears will add a human touch and make it look as if she truly feels empathy towards others. At first it didn't work, but as her thoughts travelled to the man her father really was, the tears ran unchecked down her cheeks, managing to keep her look of despair until the coffin had been lowered. Her father had been a despicable man, everyone had known it, but no one had the courage to stop him. The scars she had carried all her life for what he had done to her in young age would take a long time to heal.

Patty Griffith had planned her week to end earlier than usual. She never saw it end, but got lost in her thoughts about how bad it would be to make changes to her life and become like any other decent hard working person in the United Kingdom. That morning Patty had had an English Breakfast, at least five cups of low-quality coffee, a lot of low-quality orange juice, and ate a big breakfast of pancakes before taking her own life. She had bought fresh rose petals and strewn them all over in her bathroom. As she slit her wrists and let the blood flow to the floor covered with rose petals, she had probably not thought about the people she loved and who cared for her or the people who had to clean up after her. She resisted change in a world that consists only of changes. Change was, for her, an awful thing, an unmanageable challenge, a challenge she decided to ignore instead of pursue. And now, lying in her coffin in a beautiful white dress that was at least one size too small, surrounded again by rose petals, she must have been pleased to see that so many had gathered to wish her farewell. The only problem was that most of her farewell bidders were only there to satisfy their curiosity, to take part in the spectacle, not out of sympathy or love.

Walking through the cemetery and back to her waiting car, Victoria could not shed the thought of how she could have been the one lying in that huge coffin. She had been as porcine as Patty in her youth. The shame she felt for what her father had done to her, the hate she felt for him had been the catalyst that led to her being so overweight. Finally being able to free herself from the hate, even the hate for herself, had made her into a different person. One who had the strength and discipline to be who she wanted to be and reach her goals. She was here to pay respect to the Griffith family because she knew the pain of helplessness, but the family had not wanted her to deliver any eulogy and had been hostile to her presence.

IN SEATTLE the next day, Andy Green, has remarkably figured out what is on the images he was provided with. The conclusion, a not particularly enlightening one, and it was probably found more by coincidence and good luck rather than years of experience and professionalism. He takes the stairs up to Kevin Adams office. The damn elevator is now out of order. Up here clues come together. Analysts evaluate, sort, prioritize and handle information required to keep track of what is going on in North America. Kevin Adams' department acts as an intelligence agency, just like the national ones found throughout the world, but it doesn't belong to a nation. When he gets to Kevin's office, he sees him in deep conversation with his secretary.

'Ah hum,' he says, standing in the doorway.

Kevin turns to him and puts on a serious face. 'Did you come up with anything?'

'Kinda,' responds a rather troubled Andy Green. 'One of the images does illustrate something very unusual. And it has nothing to do with the military.'

'Is that so? Then come in and show me.'

Andy goes to Kevin's desk and places a huge blueprint which shows the outline of a building on it. He then places the images he got yesterday on top of the blueprint. He notices how Kevin quickly grabs a near-by magnifying glass.

'Where do you want me to look?'

'Here.'

'Where?'

'Here. By the truck. You see it?'

'Uhm, see what?'

'You see the payload?'

'It's difficult to see, but it looks like pigs.'

'Not quite ... Look again.'

He moves the magnifying glass closer. 'That's not pigs.'

When it strikes Kevin what he is seeing, he flies up out of his chair, tipping it over.

'No!' he exclaims.

'Yes.'

'No way!'

'Yes!'

'It's humans!'

'But a special branch of humans.'

'Oh my God! It's obese people.' He uprights the chair and sits down again. For a while, the man is stunned to silence.

'You recall what I said about Nordhausen and its place in the history books? The rockets?' recalls Andy. 'Werner von Braun? There's a whole city inside those hills. They used the place to hide the assembly lines and facilities to build and test the rockets. To start with, they developed them in Peenemunde. But the English bombed the site to the ground. In Nordhausen, thousands ... no, twenty-thousands of Jews and political opponents to the Nazi regime died while being forced to build the rockets there. They were inmates of Dora.' Andy points at the map, showing Dora, which is today a museum, but back then a concentration camp located four kilometers from the town of Nordhausen.

'I had no idea.'

'When World War II ended, the Allies, and in this particular case, the Soviets, collected the rocket hardware and transported it back to the USSR to reverse engineer the rockets. But we here in the US got Werner von Braun and his rocket team. Had it not been for the post-war resistance to invest in rocket technology, then Werner von Braun and his team could have beaten the Soviets in sending up a satellite long before they did.'

'I see.'

'The catacombs got sealed off after the war but they were not destroyed. They tried to destroy them, but the explosions did not have the anticipated effect. So instead, they sealed off the catacombs. It's a mass-graveyard down there.'

What are you getting to with this? I don't like the sound of it.'

'Because of my military experience, I know the importance of Nordhausen. The blueprint on your desk shows the outline of the catacombs. It's a gigantic underground site. There are still thousands of corpses down there, impossible to bury in a decent and respectful way. People who died excavating the tunnels and who didn't survive the Nazi's brutal pace were simply buried in the tunnel-linings and sprayed with cement.' Andy removes the images covering the blueprint and points to an access point with his finger. With the other index finger, he points to the truck he had shown Kevin. 'You see where the truck is parked? And you see what this outline illustrates? That's one of the access points to the catacombs.'

'Are you trying to tell me …'

'Take a look at this.' Andy takes a pencil and draws a circle around a tree. Kevin takes the magnifying glass to the circled area and looks.

'Ohhh shit! No way! This means trouble, Andy. Why did this have to land on my desk? If someone tosses all those obese people down into those catacombs, what are we up against? It couldn't possibly be Victoria Seymour and The Party. History wouldn't allow it to repeat itself.'

'I don't know Kevin. But that's not all. Look beneath the tree line … right here. That's why I made the circle in the first place. But you missed what I wanted you to see.'

Kevin takes the magnifying once again, moving it to the tree line. After investigating inside the circle, he looks at Andy in shock. 'This is not what I think it is.'

'I'd say it is.'

'But it looks like a stack of arms and legs sticking out from those leaves.'

'That's exactly what it is,' confirms Andy. 'A pile of very dead and rather obese arms and legs. It could have been one of mine.'

'Maybe you should get in contact with the Old Man.'

'I believe, getting in contact with the Old Man is a very good idea.'

CHAPTER 11

THE NEXT MORNING AT DOWNING Street, Victoria Seymour calls Henry Montclair and Lisa Ferguson for a quick meeting. She slept quite well this night, something that has been rather rare in these times of concern, conflict and difficulty. The press, the tabloids and social networks have taken The Party's presence at Patty Griffith's funeral without further debate, showing that Lisa Ferguson's Public Relations stunt has paid off. Of course, one newspaper was critical of the funeral. It is again this journalist, Mike Hornett, from the Daily Evening Mail, writing that her attempt to look sad was a far cry from someone who possessed human compassion. She should drag this man, and his newspaper to court for slander. In her opinion, Patty Griffith is now out of the way and the nation has shed the tears it wanted to so business life can finally return to normal.

'Well done,' says Victoria to Lisa.

'Thank you.'

Henry seems to have no opinion about the funeral. Instead, he takes out some papers from a plastic cover he just pulled from his briefcase.

'There are matters to discuss,' he says, seriously. 'We need to clean up The Party and concentrate on the responsibility scheme.'

'We need to do what?' asks Victoria.'

'We need to make some changes and clean up the people inside The Party,' repeats Henry.

'Why?'

'Some colleagues saw Lisa's funeral as taking things too far. They're already a little disturbed by the fat-thing going on. We're beginning to experience a little internal revolt among ourselves. There are even colleagues who are beginning to question your integrity, your leadership style and your lack of results.'

'Lack of results?' screams out Victoria. 'What do they mean? I assume you explained that before we can begin to carry out our agenda, we first need to clean up the previous government's mess.'

'Many of those who are revolting, aren't quick enough to grasp this. That's why we need to do some cleaning up.'

'So, what are you suggesting?'

'I suggest we start a re-shuffling of our inner-circle ...'

'Wouldn't it be better to hold a general assembly first?' asks Lisa.

'I'm not for it,' replies Henry. 'We need to do this quickly and efficiently if we want to get results. We need people to be surprised when they no longer have an office. We cannot have any of our people questioning Victoria's integrity.'

'Who from the top must go?' asks a rather surprised Lisa.

'Odsburn, Niles Cougburne, Melissa, Janie Luison, Peter Corneston and Roger Benhouse.'

'That's a lot of competence.' remarks Victoria. 'And who'll be my new Chancellor of the Exchequer?'

'Put some random idiot on the job. The position doesn't have any authority anyway. Gregg has more or less taken over the role a long time ago.'

'Dismissing Odsburn, this is really ...'

'There are rumors saying he's going against you. It must be done.'

'Why would he do this? He's such a nice man.'

'And who will fill the roles of those who are thrown out?' asks Lisa.

'There are enough people in the pipeline who are waiting for their chance. I've assembled a list.' Henry hands the papers to Victoria. Lisa leans in to read what it says. Together they go through the names.

'I don't recognize many of these names,' comments Victoria. 'Who are these people?'

'Colleagues from different ministries. I've selected them in collaboration with Gregg. They're all in a position to fill the shoes of those who will be leaving us.'

'What do you think, Lisa?'

'Well ... if they're opposed to what we're trying to do. We don't want the internal battles other parties have. It would prevent us from moving forward and finally getting your political manifesto implemented.'

'Exactly,' Henry confirms.

'So, better to let them depart now than later?' concludes Victoria.

'Victoria, they've got to go,' says Henry. 'It's that easy. They're difficult to work with and have the wrong mindset. We need a basis that is in full compliance with us. Especially after the special package has been implemented in the doctrine of Parliamentary Sovereignty, giving both you, me and Gregg, and to some extent also Lisa, more authority over the rest. The problem is; I need to take the heat from below and that sometimes makes my job difficult in protecting you from all levels below me,' he explains.

'Whew, this rotation at our top level and then a replacement round to the electorate and civil servants, how am I going to sell that to the public?' remarks Lisa.

'Will you be able to do it?' asks Henry.

'If they're leaving us, we should use them to carry out some of the trash we need to get rid of. It would be the best way to sell such a rotation and a good way to polish our image a little. Lately, it has become a little bleak.'

'My thoughts were going in this direction, too,' confirms Henry.

'At least, then they will be able to make a positive contribution.'

'Do we want them to leave individually or sack them all at the same time?' asks Victoria.

'Preferably at the same time,' says Lisa. 'Then it's over and done with and the press only attacks us once.'

'It will improve The Party's position and your popularity as a strong leader, Victoria. I'll personally write the speech for this press conference,' offers Henry.

'If it can raise our popularity polls, we ought to do it,' agrees Victoria. 'Lisa, will you set up a public relations plan?'

'Yes. But my people need time to figure out what trash we want carried out if we want to make full use of the situation.'

'Okay,' concludes Henry. 'Then I'll begin preparing for the reshuffle and resignations.'

'What about Gregg White?' asks Victoria.

'What about him?' responds Henry.

'Are you going to shuffle him into the position as Chancellor of the Exchequer?'

'No. Why? He'll stay as Chancellor and Secretary of State for Justice.'

'Will he take care of the Great Repeal Bill?'

'Yes. There will be minor changes to my role as well. But I did replace

Gregg with someone else and placed him in a function that suited his skills much better. But that was some time ago.'

'You did what?' exclaims Victoria, quite surprised at the news. 'Why haven't you said anything to Lisa and me?'

'You two have so many other things on your minds. I didn't think it was that important. He still represents the law writers on behalf of me, but, as it turns out, his true potential lays out there in society, taking care of our external representation.'

'And what exactly is meant by "Our external representation"?' Lisa wants to know.

'Talking with people, representing The Party and its interests and so on.'

'Oh, I see,' says Victoria.

'I thought I was the one taking care of our external representation,' exclaims an annoyed Lisa.

'Of course you are, Lisa. Gregg is just representing those who don't fully adhere to our politics. Oh well, it's a long story. But basically he's still the Chancellor and Secretary of State and Justice.'

'I'd rather we talk about this story now,' states Lisa.

'No, Henry is right. We don't have the time right now. We're running late for our meeting,' says Victoria.

'So the question is,' concludes Henry indicating with a sweep of his hand that he also needs to continue with things, 'Can we agree on a rotation within The Party?'

'If that's what's required, I'll go along with it,' agrees Victory.

'I guess so,' says Lisa hesitantly, trying not to show how uncomfortable she is with the decision. Henry is in the process of purging any criticism within their own ranks. That's her thought. Purges are never good news, at least not according to the history books. And Victoria thinks he's doing it to give her an advantage. She's turning naive.

ON THE way out of Henry's office, Lisa is, for the first time worried on behalf of The Party and English Democracy. Knowing history well, she realizes that, with the attendance of this meeting, she might be observing an unspoken chapter in political history made at Palace of Westminster.

'Victoria?' she asks.

'Yes?'

Victoria turns to Lisa and when the answer takes too long, she notices that the young girl looks rather pale.

'What's the matter?' she asks. 'What happened?'

'Henry made me feel uncomfortable.'

'In what way, Lisa?'

'In my blind faith of our democracy. My instinct says that Henry is up to no good.'

'Rubbish. You should be happy we have him. He's taking care of all the difficult stuff.'

'Exactly. I think you have too much blind faith in Henry.'

'Why do you say that?'

'Why didn't he tell us that Gregg is now doing something different? Gregg was hired to take care of the Great Appeal Bill an behalf of Henry. Why didn't he tell at least you about this change of roles?'

Victoria fails to find an appropriate answer. It makes Lisa, who is starting to feel insecure and uncertain about herself, continue talking.

'Henry is building up a power base around himself. I'm sure of it.'

'What exactly do you mean?'

'He is selecting people who support and protect him. Gregg is becoming an important part of his own puzzle.'

'You worry too much, Lisa. The power base is built around me. I'm the Prime Minister. Not Henry.'

'But didn't you feel it?' exclaims Lisa. 'Didn't you feel his power or notice that he hardly bothered looking at us.'

'That's how Henry is.'

'But you heard what he said. He got his special package through. They've implemented it, Victoria! Have you read it?'

'No. I didn't even know it has been passed.'

'That's what I mean. He didn't even bother to tell you.'

'Hm.'

'Henry is building a tremendous power base, building up an army around himself, not around you. And what you have just done was to approve him continuing to do so by firing people who stand in his way.'

'Henry has always been a strong man. We've know each other for some years now. Gregg is strong too. But Henry wouldn't go behind my back. Without him The Party wouldn't have come this far, so I find it rather rude of you to accuse him of treason. He's the reason we'll be able to achieve what I've set out to do.'

'And what is it exactly you've set out to do?'

'Lisa! Now you're behaving like a spoiled child. The manifesto.'

'Up until now we haven't achieved a single thing,' exclaims Lisa, feeling provoked. 'Not a damn thing! Nothing except splitting the country even further after Brexit and harassing a lot of fat people.'

'That's not fair, Lisa! What's the matter with you?'

'What's your assurance of him not turning on you?'

'I have confidence in all of us, Lisa. Each of us carries a great deal of responsibility. And I'm in full agreement with Henry when he says that those who don't fit in must leave. Henry has always and still is building up our power base ...'

'Yes, he certainly is,' interrupts Lisa.

'The opposition is weak, and is getting weaker by the day thanks to him and Gregg. We have full control over Parliament, but can only keep control if we agree within ourselves what to do. This is our chance to show what we can make of the United Kingdom.'

'But ...'

'You do an excellent job representing The Party, Lisa. Keep up the good work because there are good times ahead. After the reshuffle, I'm confident it will be easier to push things forward. I understand your concerns. But you're young and new to politics and this is how the game is played. I can tell you one thing about Henry: He would never do anything to damage or hurt our nation.'

'I'm skeptical, Victoria. I just wanted you to know this. I'm not so sure you're right about him. It just feels so wrong when someone starts messing around with the doctrine of Parliamentary Sovereignty like he has.'

'As far as I remember, you called them both brilliant some time ago when we were having lunch with them at the Palace of Westminster. Remember?'

'As you said; this was some time ago. Since then, a lot of unexpected things have happened inside the government we both represent.'

'It's going to be alright. Now it is you worrying too much, Lisa.'

'Perhaps. But now you know how I feel.'

'Politics are not about feelings. It's about achieving results.'

'I just ...'

'Now, come, Lisa. We have a lot on the to-do list.'

STILL EMOTIONALLY devastated one week after the funeral of her sister, Monica Griffith, can still not grasp the shocking treatment she has been given by the three men who have intruded on her privacy. The truth about the death of her little sister probably has less to do with Victoria Seymour's rhetoric than with what other men did to her sister. While raping her they had taken pictures showing her sister's face, tits and pussy, threatening to publish them if she didn't comply with their demands of loyalty and eternal respect for The Party. She was never supposed to find out what had happened to her little sister. In spite of this, her little sister had told her anyway about it in an attempt to attract attention. She has never seen the pictures, but trusts her sister's assessment that they exist. Because of all she has recently experienced, she can be sure that her sister had told the truth. By signing the The Party's contract, she is now required to go to WeightForLife every day after work and to pay The Party a percentage of her income. Certainly she is not the only one who had been affected by this ludicrous new law. There must be many others. She had joined one of many groups on the Internet who was opposed to Victoria Seymour and the Party in the hope of getting some help and finding someone to talk to, but now the groups have suddenly disappeared. One week ago they were all there. But now they are gone.

Who would have thought that.

IT IS not only Monica Griffith who has trouble with the authorities. For the third time in two months, Mike Hornett has become acquainted with the very well dressed people in suites and ties. It can't be verified that it is The Party behind the vandalism in his home, but one can make an educated guess. It seems they did not like the coverage of the attempted assassination of Victoria Seymour and in general his opinions of Victoria Seymour. The vandalism included a destroyed computer and keyboard, plates and glasses, most of his furnishings being turned topsy-turvy, and a few plants which were thrown around. It happened on the night after the weekend edition. He is unsure if they wanted to get him or if they were just frustrated that he wasn't home, so left him a visiting card.

At least, up to this point, there has been no physical violence from The Party, if they are the ones behind the vandalism as he expects, or against people he holds dear. Unfortunately, the hard evidence is missing and difficult to find. The gentlemen have obviously moved from verbal abuse to using tangible destruction. His editor has deliberately given him and two of his colleagues, a long leash to experiment with upsetting The Party in the hope that it will do something extremely stupid. And destroying furniture at homes is really stupid. A governing political party that uses verbal violence, life threats, and tangible violence against the people it governs is unimaginable. Within the last few months, things have escalated step-by-step, from limiting the rights of obese people to irritating the free press. Even his colleagues and fellow journalists have received verbal life threats if they write articles criticizing The Party. His editor had exploded and written a damning article when he learned of a new law that had been passed at the same time as the Fat Tax limiting the rights of obese people to own their own company. This had gotten him in huge trouble with the very well-dressed people in suites and ties. The newspaper, and his editor, has stated that they do not bend to any type of dictatorship against private person, professionals, or them as a newspaper.

Unfortunately, the pressure is starting to show. Since they have decided on a hard course against The Party, and Victoria Seymour, the Daily Evening Mail is not being distributed according to how the newpapers should be distributed. On the Internet, their website is constantly getting attacked by hackers. But they will not give in to the endangerment of free speech. They will remain firm until The Party comes around even if it means the failure of their newspaper and threatening of their jobs.

Other newspapers have decided to be a little more cautious. The motto has become that if you try to silence The Party, they will certainly silence you or destroy your computers. It is certain that if they have this kind of trouble at the Daily Evening Mail, then the smaller newspapers and some of the less powerful tabloids have had their share of trouble too. Some have probably already been forced to give in. It is good to know that a few of their larger competitors who may have pulled back on the hard words and criticism secretly support the Daily Evening Mail to the extent that they share tips and newsworthy info with them. Today, the underground press, with its own distribution network, can become a reality at any time, making the printed news network stronger by the day.

But The Party has strength too and the press is learning what it is capable of with its unlimited resources. The United Kingdom of today is markedly different from the United Kingdom of six months ago. Summer starts green and ends up brown when autumn arrives. Those are the colors The Party has chosen for their identity. The brown color stands for what people hold of The Party. The green color for what happens when shit carries too much bacteria around. What was a fight against some strange laws about fat is now slowly turning into a fight for the maintaining of free speech and personal freedom. No one except the journalists who are on the front line seems to have noticed what is happening. People have just not had the time to digest this regression of their liberties. Only now they have begun to comprehend that the democracy that they so cherish is slowly being taken away from them. When people have democracy, they do nothing to take care of it, when it is gone, they can do nothing to repair it. They should hit the streets and fight back. Because if they don't, they will not only lose their democracy, but also their souls. And as it looks right now, it is The Party who is winning this game of cat-and-mouse. Those who have noticed what has been happening lately, they should stop concentrating on fat and obese people. Stop before it's too late.

CHAPTER 12

IT WAS A LONG-DISTANCE CALL from The Special Council's American headquarters in Seattle. Chris Campbell was not particularly excited about forwarding the news from Andy Green to his chief in command Mr. Conners at The Special Councils headquarters in London.

'So, the Germans are up to it again,' comments Mr. Conners sarcastically in his lovely British English. 'How nice that we're out of the European Union. Now they can do whatever they want without the UK interfering.'

'I do believe the situation is the opposite. We need more detailed information on what's going on in Nordhausen,' says Chris. 'And by the way, we still haven't left the European Union – at least not fully.'

'That's true. We need hard facts. Have you and Andy agreed to get over here? I think you both should go to Nordhausen to search information that supports what we see on those images.'

'Shouldn't we first coordinate with our German subsidiary? They should do some scouting. Then we could send in a team afterwards. Actually, I'd very much like to have this journalist, Mike Hornett, on it too. If he reports what is happening in Germany, it might be an eye-opener for people on what's going on.'

'No. I think that's a bad idea. I think we should keep quiet about what is happening in Germany for now. First we need to find out what we're up against.'

'I insist on him joining Andy and me.'

Mr. Andrews is silent for a moment. 'The world is a cruel place, isn't it?' he says.

'That's why The Special Council exists. How does the Old Man evaluate what's going on?'

'He's cancelled the FDAR report and the Continental Teams supports him in his decision. It's the general opinion that what's going on, goes beyond Victoria Seymour. We've missed seeing the game that is being played out in the background.'

'So, The Special Council is starting to have doubts about her? That's interesting.'

'Well. We've always known she'd be the trigger for something uncomfortable, but a mass murder doesn't fit her psychological profile. Luckily, more and more obese people are getting together and demonstrating in the streets in front of Palace of Westminster. But, unfortunately, there are also the anti-groups who think that what The Party does is correct. I don't mind saying that so far there's not a single thread of evidence connecting what has happened in Nordhausen with what's going on in the United Kingdom. And by the way; if someone wants to dispose of people, why take the effort to send them to Germany?'

'Perhaps so they can deny the crime if they get caught?'

'It's a wary situation,' warns Mr. Conners. 'There's no link to The Party. We don't know who's behind it and we still don't know what we're dealing with.'

'I spoke with Andy about the catacombs. They're the perfect place to dispose of corpses. He says that within a year the flesh will have completely deteriorated and the bones will have mixed into the thousands of skeletons from World War II. It's a perfect place to hide evidence, right before people's noses.'

'... good that we found the place at this early stage.'

'And thank God for that!'

'Get Andy over here, right now,' demands Mr. Conners. 'Ask him to book a flight to Hamburg tomorrow, and you go there, too. If you feel it's the right thing to have this journalist join you, then the call is yours. I'll talk with the Old Man and ask him to get you a German guide.'

'How about Marcus?'

'Good choice! He can do the scouting as well.'

There is a moment of silence. Then Mr. Conners sighs and looks at Chris. 'Damn!' he exclaims. 'How are we going to proceed on this one? Oh, and just one more thing, Chris. You guys had better get the best evidence possible. DNA samples, a lot of pictures, GPS recordings ... everything we need for a case at the International Court of Justice.'

'I won't let you down, I promise. It could've been me on those images. And you know what? That really disturbs me.'

IT SEEMS it is not only Victoria Seymour's own fellow colleagues, but also foreign heads of state, presidents and leaders around the world, who are losing their enthusiasm for the Prime Minister. The tone is getting harsher as are the accusations about what is currently going on in the United Kingdom. With Victoria Seymour at the rudder, world-wide collaboration is becoming as unproductive as never before. The new government simply does not seem to listen. Old allies in the Commonwealth are not keen on being drawn into the uncertain game the United Kingdom is playing. There is a lot of whispering going on in political circles throughout the world about her government failing to meet even its simplest domestic and international obligations.

Inside the European Union, confusion is spreading on what future strategy the United Kingdom may follow for Brexit. After so many years in the process, it is still unclear if Scotland and Northern Ireland will agree with what Westminster decides and what that plan may be. Industry in the United Kingdom is becoming rather dissatisfied with the insanely slow progress. Brexit has turned into tons of red tape between the European Union and the United Kingdom the likes of which were last seen in the 60ties and 70ties.

But there is also trouble between the United Kingdom and rest of the world. New regulatory rules concerning the rules and regulations required to trade with rest of the world have not been legally bound into the British statue book, making it practically illegal to trade with anyone. One-hundred-and-fifty-two trade agreements, trade agreements that the United Kingdom shared with the European Union, haven't been enacted, making it difficult to even trade on World Trade Organization conditions. The great conditions that Brexiteers talked about all the time have not materialized and the efficiency of trade markedly reduced. The City of London has lost terrain to Frankfurt, Hamburg, Paris, Switzerland, New York and Singapore.

As if this is not enough, the government is now reorganizing itself, firing civil servants in huge numbers. When the world had just become familiar with the new people in government to be dealt with. In Brussels, the European Council is concerned about its oversized citizens and what is happening to their civil rights. So far, the government in Westminster has refused to discuss the subject. Rumors are making the rounds in the corridors of the European Union, about a law which had quietly been slipped-in, unscrutinized, past the Courts which harasses obese people even further. It is the Bank Regulatory & Investment Act, stating that anyone with a BMI over 35 will no longer be the true owner of his company. The new law has shocked many in Brussels.

Neither Victoria nor Lisa was aware of this new law. Victoria first learned of it when she was informed by her own government's representative to the European Union in Brussels. The telephone call with her representative was a short one and afterwards she hung up in unbelievable astonishment.

She turns to her laptop on her desk in her Downing Street office, then opens the email she had just received from the representative and presses 'enter' to print it.

'Why didn't I know about this?' she asks Lisa. 'Did you know about this law?'

'I did not.'

'Why haven't we been told by Henry?'

'I have no idea, Victoria.'

'What surprises me most is why the press hasn't pick up on it. This should be a law that the press would crack-down hard on.'

'I honestly have no idea. Who told you about it?'

'I just talked with our Brussels representative to the European Union.'

'This is unbelievable,' exclaims Lisa. 'So, now Henry wants to limit fat people's rights to have their own company. That's great, Victoria. That's just great!' remarks Lisa with a lot of irony in her voice. 'Is this also a part of Henry's Parliamentary Sovereignty special package, to secure our power base, you think?'

'No.'

'Is that all you have to say?' asks Lisa. She sighs, making an effort not to explode in fury. Her head is red and it feels even hotter. 'Now when we're on the subject, haven't you noticed how the press has become less critical about what's going on?'

'I'm actually starting to read the newspapers again. It's easier to read them when they're not so nasty toward me.'

Lisa does not know how to respond. For a minute she just stands there looking at her Prime Minister. That Victoria has such a fear of confrontation with the press and what they have written about her, surprises her. Either the woman is starting to fall apart because of the pressure on her shoulders, or she is losing sight of the situation and her role in it.'

'Who authorized this law?' asks Victoria. 'When did it pass, do you know? And why are we hearing about it first from abroad?'

'I don't know,' sighs Lisa once again, fighting herself to keep calm. 'But I'm starting to feel rather uncomfortable. I can't possibly imagine what people abroad must think of us.'

'I think you're right, Lisa. We cannot expropriate people's companies just because they're fat. It's ridiculous?'

'Why didn't the Lords catch it in the making?' ask Lisa.

'The Lords? They have nothing to say because of the Great Repeal Bill. Henry the VIII's law seems to be working quite nicely.'

'You need to do something, Victoria. Henry and Gregg are taking all this way too far.'

'I'm going to have a serious talk with Henry about this,' mumbles Victoria getting up from her desk and packing the email from Brussels into her briefcase. 'Yes. He's going to hear my opinion about this. That's for sure!'

IT TAKES less than two minutes to reach Henry Montclair in his office. She leaves 10 Downing Street and walks to the building beside hers, to the Cabinet Office.

He is in full swing reading something from a thick book.

'Henry,' shouts Victoria, signaling those around him that it is time to leave. Following her orders, the last one politely closes the door.

'Victoria ... What can I do for you?' he says quite surprised at the sudden unannounced intrusion. 'It was actually an important meeting.'

'The Bank Regulatory & Investment Act; who suggested this? Who put it on paper? And did Gregg authorize its implementation?'

'Wow, that's a lot of questions, Victoria. I don't know. It doesn't have anything to do with me. I don't even think it has anything to do with us.'

'What do you mean? It must have been implemented by someone. I just read it and it makes no sense! The whole damn world in Brussels is getting on my back.'

'Victoria, we have so much to do. There are Acts of Parliament from the previous government still in the pipeline, which are nearing publication. This is stuff that requires approval before other parts of the Brexit process can proceed.'

'It's an insane law! And it has nothing to do with Brexit. Don't patronize me! The contents conflict with just about everything in my agenda. We're already losing public support. Have you seen the latest polls?'

'No, and I don't really care. My doctrine of Parliamentary Sovereignty has been passed and it's just a matter of time before we have full control of the power in the United Kingdom.'

'Oh,' exclaims Victoria, quite surprised at the news. 'But that's good news. Then we can start implementing my Manifesto.' Then she returns to the subject she came to discuss. 'But it doesn't change the fact that the law is completely insane! We cannot do this to fat people. It's taking things one step too far.'

'If the law upsets you, why don't you get it revoked?'

'When was it implemented?'

'The same time as the Fat Tax.'

'Aha. So you knew after all. You just admitted it.'

'Damn it, Victoria!' cries Henry. 'Haven't you noticed how lately the fat part of our society is making life difficult for us? So we need to act accordingly. Have you already forgotten?'

'Forgotten what?'

'The fat lady who wanted to assassinate you?'

'Of course not. But we cannot confiscated our citizens' property. It will only accelerate the current situation of unrest.'

'We're talking about fat people here. Get over it! They're compensated financially for giving up their companies. We need efficient managers to run our most successful companies in the United Kingdom, not fat blokes who think they know what they're doing. You want the United Kingdom to survive this crisis, right?'

'I … I just don't know what's happening to you, Henry. 'It's taking a direction toward oppression. We're turning into …'

'Stop it, Victoria! You're losing the big picture here! Your political agenda is perfect. There's just one little detail which you have totally missed out on.'

'What's that supposed to mean? Are you criticizing my work?'

'I can write an excellent strategy for the United Kingdom as well. But your manifesto says absolutely nothing about where the money should come from or the how to implement your excellent visions and that's all they are: Visions.'

Victoria gasps. This is the first time Henry has ever been negative about her agenda, the one she worked so hard on before the election. She could have chosen some easy solutions to make people understand her grand plan, but in general, everyone, including some from the opposition, agrees with her visions.

'It will take some time to revoke the Bank Regulatory & Investment Act,' continues Henry. 'There are so many other priorities …'

'Tell me what you have in mind with this Bank and Investment law.'

'Fat people with money also have networks, influence and resources. They could easily become a threat to you and The Party in the long term. You have been telling the nation how inefficient fat people are, that they are bad managers, so now it is logical to replace them. Our supporters will believe it will strengthen the United Kingdom's economy.'

'So the owners are paid off?'

'Yes, they get a golden handshake.'

'But if you pay them off, aren't you afraid they will turn on us when they have the hard cash to fight us?'

'No, that's not going to happen. I can completely guarantee it. Why should they? With the money they receive, they'd rather live it up and eat themselves to death … ha ha.'

'I don't find that funny, Henry.'

'Come on, Victoria. You shouldn't lose your sense of humor. Why do you seem so tense lately? What's the matter? Is it something in your private life? Haven't I been good to you lately? We can meet tonight if you want to.'

'Why haven't I heard a single word about this Bank Regulatory & Investment Act?'

'But that's the beauty of it, isn't it?' It is difficult for Henry not to put on his biggest smile. 'The laws we push through are suddenly there should anyone like our opponents or the Courts, that we still don't fully control, ask. It puts us in a position to act before they can react. With the implementation of my Parliamentary Sovereignty special package, you now have plenty of time to implement your visions.'

'I do?'

'I didn't want to discredit your excellent work, but I'm the one who takes care of practicality in establishing foundations for your visions. Next time you write such an excellent political agenda, you should include a chapter on how to turn theory into practice. It would make my work easier. But don't worry, for that you've always got me.'

'Henry, I'm so sorry I yelled at you. It's just so …'

'You don't have to apologize. I'm fully aware of the stress and pressure we all suffer. It comes with the territory and the responsibility we've put on our shoulders. In a few months, people will forgive us for what we've done and begin to understand what we're doing. They'll realize that we're taking the Kingdom forward in giant steps.'

'Ah yes, sighs Victory. 'Now we're finally getting to the point I want us to be.' She sees Henry get up from his desk and walk to the office door and lock it. She is glad that she chose to wear a skirt this morning.

CHAPTER 13

MIKE HORNETT PICKS UP HIS CELL phone and answers the call. To his surprise, it is the voice of Chris Campbell from ImplantSkills.

'Chris, how are you?' he asks.

'Oh, I'm fine,' answers Chris. 'But it seems our friend, Mason, isn't so fine.'

'What happened?'

'Well, could you perhaps drop by my office this afternoon?'

'I guess I can. When do you want me to come by?'

'How about now?'

'This fast?'

'Yes. This fast. Please drop by now.'

Some twenty minutes later, Mike arrives at ImplantSkills headquarters for the second time this week. The receptionist, immediately recognizes him from his first visit and also as the journalist who wrote the article about Victoria Seymour and the one about Patty Griffith. She looks at him pleasantly.

'I really liked your article about Patty Griffith,' she tells him.

'Thank you, but there were others who didn't.'

'Aren't you afraid of getting fired?'

'Well, if that's the worst thing that could happen, then it would fine with me.'

'Mr. Campbell is waiting in his office. Shall I show you the way up or can I just give you directions?'

'As you prefer.'

'Go past the meeting rooms where you met him last time, then take the elevator to the 10th floor. Go around the dome to the left and then down the long corridor. His office is at the end, you can't miss it. The door is usually open.'

'Okay. Thanks.'

Mike goes through the glass door, passes the meeting room they were in last time and continues to the elevators. He takes the waiting elevator to the 10th floor. When he gets out, he sees the dome. She was not kidding. He looks up and sees there is actually a dome covering a relatively huge open space. Before proceeding, he moves to a banister and looks down into the open space. Several floors of the skyscraper receive natural light from up here. On the ground floor, there are plants and soft furniture and a little cafe with enough coffee machines to send the fresh smell of ground coffee beans up to his nostrils.

He claps once on the banister and walks to the other side, counting the floors to the bottom level. There are five floors in all. It must be sad to work on the lower floors where the light is only artificial.

Passing the open space, he walks down the corridor and sees the open door of Chris's office. He knocks gently on the door.

'Mr. Campbell,' he addresses the rather overweight man.

'Ah, Mike! Come in.' Chris Campbell gets up from his office chair and walks toward his guest. 'You found me without our beautiful receptionist accompanying you!'

'Your receptionist gave me excellent instructions.'

'Well, come in and sit down.'

Mike goes to a couch strategically placed at the large windows to provide an excellent view of London. He looks out.

'So, what was it? Coffee black?'

'Very well remembered!'

'It was only a couple of days ago '

'Ha ha. True.'

Chris goes to the mini bar on the other side of his desk and pours two cups of coffee and puts some cookies on a plate.

'Please be seated, offers Chris. He sits down next to Mike in the cosy couch and puts the coffee and cookies on the beside coffee table.

Mike notices that Chris is sweating like a pig. Every move seems to be a challenge for the big man. With the last of summer in full swing, it has become very warm.

'So ...' begins Chris. 'We have an unpleasant situation and what I'm about to tell you, may not be shared with anyone. That means that you may not write about it – at least not yet.'

The request makes Mike laugh, 'It seems at the moment, a lot of people want to confide in me, but don't want me to write about it. If this goes on, I don't know how to earn money.'

'Mason is probably dead.'

The directness surprises Mike. This was unexpected.

'I … don't know how to respond.' Says Mike, shocked. Now it has become really really warm.

'You know what? Let's forget the coffee,' says Chris, going to the door and closing it. He then proceeds to a shelf and takes down a bottle of whisky and two fine crystal glasses, and returns to the couch. With some effort, he again sits down.

'This cannot be true,' stutters Mike.

'Mike, I was lying to you the last time you were here.' admits Chris, pouring the whisky. 'We'd already figured out something was not right, but I couldn't tell you. We …' Chris pauses. He has to be careful not to disclose the fact that he is in a double role. 'We can see on the data received from his implant that something is not right.'

'All this stuff with ImplantSkills,' says Mike. 'Is it only happening because he's obese? I might as well tell you what he told me the last time I talked to him. The military made a mistake. And they were going to fix it. Do you know about it?'

'He hasn't told me.'

Mike takes a long sip of his whisky. He feels it burn all way down, making him even warmer. 'He told me that the military was executing a cyberexperiment that went wrong. I'm not allowed to write about it – at least not yet, because it can damage companies like ImplantSkills. I understand that the military has contracted a unit to cover up their mistake, and they are to compensate people like Mason for the trouble they have caused their companies.'

'And that's why he had to go to Hamburg?'

'Yes. The business setup cannot be executed on our soil.'

Chris feels every muscle in his body tighten. This is not good, he thinks. Not good at all. With the information in his possession, a grim picture is starting to materialize in his head. 'Listen,' he says to Mike. 'I'm assembling a team. We're going to Hamburg. We need to find out more. And I want you to join us.'

'What will you be doing there?'

'We know the whereabouts of Mason, and are going to follow his lead. It's still too soon to say he's dead, but it may be the best way to handle the situation for now.'

'When do we leave?'

'Hopefully tomorrow but no later than Wednesday. What you will learn is going to change your life forever. Forgive me asking you to join us on this, but this is important.'

'Well … I am a journalist. I do experience strange things once in a while.'

'Not of this character, my friend. Do I have your full confidence?'

'Yes.'

'Bring your best camera and a lot of memory cards.'

'Okay.

Chris sighs shortly.

Then he gathers himself. 'Are you ready to get briefed?' he asks Mike.

'I assume so.'

'Well, I'm not really sure if I'm ready to tell what I'm about to tell you. But something has taken place in Germany. Something very, very awful. It's for your eyes only. Do you accept?'

'Yes.'

'Okay.'

Chris gets off the couch. The weather is killing him today. He moves to his desk and extracts a key from the top drawer. Opening another drawer, he removes the copies of the satellite images he received from Andy Green yesterday afternoon and returns to Mike.

WITH THE political environment in the United Kingdom turning nasty, it is becoming difficult to be obese. Monica Griffith is working harder than ever to get below a Body Mass Index of 35, simply to get rid of the authorities breathing down her neck. And true enough, it does feel better to be thinner, although that is not what this is about.

No. It is about the government interfering in the daily lives of its citizens and their private affairs.

The Internet seems to be no longer of any use. The forums she signed up for to talk to other obese people, no longer exist. In fact, in the world of bits and bytes, there is not a single site where she is able to vent her anger and get advice on what is going on. It has become so obvious that the government is censuring the Internet. Doing a search for 'Fat' returns up long lists of websites, articles, news and documents referring to how awful obesity is and how it must be fought. There are even websites against obese people with terribly unpleasant contents. It all makes her feel like crying or moving to another country.

But there was a time before the Internet. So she decided to get out in the real world and try to track down a group or groups who have the same frustrations and hate as she got after the funeral of her sister and the visits by the unknown well-dressed men. But also out in the real world, the government has a good grip on what is going on. There, well-dressed men are everywhere, too. She feels them following her. Their breathing and presence on every street corner. It is difficult not to feel haunted and a little frantic about what the future might hold for people like her.

But there is one thing The Party hadn't thought through. At WeightForLife, she meets a lot of fellow citizens. And it is there that she has found the group she'd been looking for. The meetings are held in the basement of the WeightForLife building, and after they are through with their training, they still have a half hour before the curfew begins. She figured out that her shadows follow her to WeightForLife only, probably to be sure she attends the meetings, but they don't follow her home, leaving other agents to enforce the curfew. So every three days there is time for the group to meet. A day will come, and they, uprise when they have organized efficiently how to fight The Party and its sick officials, civil servants, employees and the herd of people who blindly follow their politics. She knows though, that she and the group are taking a huge risk by attending these meetings and that there might be repercussions if caught. The curfew forbids people with a Body Mass Index of above 35, to meet in groups larger than three people. And The Party's shadows are very good at enforcing this rule, by observing people from a distance to see exactly how many people congregate. Those who meet illegally will be punished, the well-dressed men say. But she doesn't know how and doesn't care. The enforcers have turned out to be swines with low moral standards and no empathy for their fellow human beings. It is awful to experience their indifference about whether they destroy people's lives or not and it has made her reflect a lot about life lately.

I MIGHT BE FAT. BUT YOU ARE UGLY!
I CAN CHANGE. BUT WHAT CAN YOU DO?

That has become their groups slogan. When she heard it it made her laugh hard and has given her hopes and aspirations for a better future when all this nonsense finally ends. Her sister's funeral was the turning point bringing her over the cliff. She began to stop seeing herself as the center of her world through WeightForLife and with the subsequent group meetings afterwards, she has come to recognize that being part of something much bigger than herself is the best way to make her sister's death mean something. The Party can go screw itself. So can Victoria Seymour and her crooks and all the people who turn an eye away from what is going on. They are not going to get away with taking away their civil rights just because they are obese. She thought she would never have the courage to stick a knife into someone, but she is wrong. She had no idea that she can hate so much that she would be prepared to use a knife, if this is what it takes to protect her and other obese people's rights. She has become ready to sacrifice her life for her fellow obese citizens. Before her sister died, she had been the type of person to simply enjoy each day and go about her own business. But now she is taking a deeper look into the function of society as a whole and wonders if things were really so bad before Brexit. They are the ones who must fight for democracy, not all the damn traitors who are blind to what is going on. Victoria Seymour and The Party must be removed from power.

It's a damn shame that that terror attack failed on her.

CHAPTER 14

AROUND NOON IN THE MIDDLE of her difficult day, Victoria Seymour decides to leave her desk at Downing Street for a while, to grab a coffee in her favorite coffee shop at the Palace of Westminster. At least there, she is rarely bothered by random spectators, like she is outside, where people are getting nastier and nastier to her. She calls her bodyguards and asks them to get the limousine ready. Although it is a short ride of less than five minutes, Gregg White, the Chancellor and Secretary of State and Justice, has notched up the safety around her.

After the short ride, she arrives at Palace of Westminster and enters the cafe to order a coffee. She sits down in one of the cosy seats. Being a celebrity in the media does impact a person's life. She has withdrawn somewhat from public life on the rare occasions that she is not working and she has been avoiding her colleagues as well since she has noticed that they are not as friendly as they used to be. So it works fine for her when even people she knows walk by and ignore her when she is sitting alone in her favorite cafe.

Today not a single person seems to take notice of her. Once in a while, it does happen that a visitor to the Palace of Westminster stops to talk or to get an autograph. She always cordially accepts although she feels it is a waste of her time. After all, her job does require some Public Relations. She takes the first sip of her coffee and looks into the cup. The coffee here is really good. It was Henry who found the place some time ago and they both come here when they have time. Gregg White comes here too when he can get away from his office at Petty France. On the other hand, coffee is not Lisa's thing. She prefers either fresh-pressed orange juice or green tea, something Victoria has stopped drinking many years ago. She discovered that she needs the caffeine to get her going in the morning and for long negotiations that last into the night.

For a moment, Victoria Seymour sits, enjoying her coffee and the silence. She sees a couple of military personnel walk by, which seems to happen more frequently since the attempted assassination on her. The sight of them makes her reflect on the past. There was Brexit, which had nothing to do with them and The Party and can be written off to the political party in power at the time. During the campaign, the biggest challenge they had were the military and intelligence service. She had absolutely no understanding why billions must be pumped into these institutions when the school system and healthcare system were suffering from many years of budget cuts. This view was obviously not shared by the military and the intelligence service. Their lobbies played to the feelings of the old United Kingdom, claiming that the Kingdom could once again become the military power it was many years ago, if just a couple billions were invested. She hated their empty arguments, but they provided the opposition parties with enough fuel to overthrow her arguments. One of the established political parties saw the opportunity to attack The Party using its earlier success in playing to the voters' fears about how awful the world had become. The topic forced The Party into a discussion it was not prepared to have and into an area in which they had little knowledge. They knew they had to stick to what they earlier had said because any sway in their opinions could hurt them on Election Day. And the voters actually rallied behind them, not fully accepting their platform, but merely because it made sense to use the money for improvements in education and healthcare.

But then something happened that neither Henry Montclair, she, nor anyone else could have anticipated. Troops had been sent to support the South of Turkey in the fight against the Islamic State in Syria but the military equipment was so out of date that most of it did not work. This led to a reversal of the voters' concerns and increasing the military budget was suddenly the more urgent investment that needed to be made. It was an embarrassing moment and an eye opener for many about how deteriorated the United Kingdom's power position had actually become. What had happened in Syria did not help The Party's to be elected to 10 Downing Street.

In live television interview a day after the Syrian incident, the question was presented about security on terrorism and if a revamp of the United Kingdom and its military and intelligence still would be appropriate. Her arguments about decreasing military budgets and reallocating the money to the school and health system totally fell off the cliff. Actually, it was a rather discomforting moment for Victoria Seymour. She had completely missed out on the events on the international stage, holding it for less important. Perhaps she had also waited too long for Henry and his advisors' opinion as it seemed the lobby turned out to not be fully wrong on the subject after all. Voters were of course no longer of The Party's opinion. And she the following day slow in recognizing the change in political opinion. Unsure about how to answer and what to do to save face, but knew she had to reply quickly and compelling or she would be roasted by the interviewer because every political party needs a scapegoat, it looked as if The Party was going to be just that. People want simple answers when things go wrong. They want someone to blame. So, what better people are there to look down upon than … fat people.

Fat people she responded to the question. *Fat people will pick up the bill. Most haven't had military service*, she said.

The interviewer was a little baffled, and so was the audience. But while they spent time trying to figure out exactly what she meant, she bought herself time and prepared for the following questions.

Victoria Seymour looks into her cup. It is empty. She tries to decide whether to order another coffee or simply stay put and spend a couple of minutes just sitting there doing nothing. She decides on the latter and thinks back to the interview. It is not really that long time ago, although, it feels like a lifetime has gone by. So much has happened since those words slipped out her mouth. When she thinks back, it was not the tabloids who started the campaign against fat people, but actually her. It must have been the first time in history that anyone had used the word fat in such a way as she did. Parrots started flocking around her simple sound-bites almost like vultures, repeating again and again what she had said. It was something nobody really understood, something that was built upon. She had planted Henry Montclair's seed by a mistake, but the moment looked right. The press, the newspapers and radio stations kept on trying to make people understand what she had meant. When they asked her, she just shook on her shoulders and let their questions stand open. The Party led their political opponents for weeks with the free advertising. And even the opposition played along by trying to figure out if there was a way to use what she had said to put The Party in a bad light.

What a ride it has been so far. Had she known what it would lead to back then, she would probably have kept her mouth shut and simply accepted defeat. But hindsight is always easy. Soon they will be in a position to finally carry out the politics they had planned. People want progress and it is time to phase out this fat thing. Not tomorrow or the day after, but now, if

The Party is to not disappoint voters any further.

Fat has turned into a balancing act between what is sane and what is insane. Laws are now pushed through that actually are insane. What she and Henry have started, was never intended to take over like it has. And unfortunately sometimes Henry's methods to reach goals may get a little out of hand. In truth, there is no excuse for what they have done. But reality is that fat has turned out to be an efficient tool in distracting from the real issue troubling the United Kingdom … them grasping for power. Fat has had its fifteen minutes of fame. And now it must stop.

There is just one problem and she is unsure how to cope with it. It seems Henry does not have the slightest intention of stopping what is going on. He might be right that it is too late to return to common sense, but it would be better now than later. In spite of that, he keeps putting gasoline on the fire. He even says that they are no longer in a position to stop the forces they have started. She does not agree with this, but can follow his thinking. The Party has not been the only political party to take advantage of the momentum fat and fat people have provided. There is no doubt though that the current situation is what she feared back then. Fat has caused division between those who are indifferent and those who are less intelligent or brain dead and have absorbed the rhetoric and digested the easy-written online social media and the tabloids' propaganda. They have found a minority they can mock by discriminating legally, making them feel superior. What she and Henry have begun was not meant to happen. It has simply taken over.

Fat is starting to backfire. But a solution on how to end it is, at the moment, not a question she is able to fully answer. The only good news is that the negative aspects felt throughout society; the strains from the heated debates on television and the radio have mostly turned out to The Party's advantage.

IN THE EARLY evening, Andy Green, arrives at the Hamburg airport. With his luggage as his only companion, he walks the short distance from Arrivals to the five-star hotel across the street. Mike Hornett, from the Daily Evening Mail, is already waiting at the bar in the lobby.

'So, you must be Mike?' concludes Andy. 'Chris said you'd be joining us.'

'I am. It's nice to meet you, Andy. Would you like something to drink?'

'Well … I … I think I'll pass for now.'

'I must say, those images, have really gotten to me,' Mike admits. 'Chris showed me the pictures yesterday. I still need some time for it to sink in. It's not every day you see evil like this.'

'Not nice, huh? But Mike ...' says Andy throwing down his luggage and taking a seat. '... take some good advice. I know you're not used to this type of field work like Chris and I are, but don't let what you see distract you from your ability to think. Do not try to make any conclusions yet. Focus on the mission.'

'I'll keep that in mind.'

'I've understood from Chris that he has chosen you because you write about Victoria Seymour and The Party and know Mason Sanders as well as he does.'

'On a professional level, we know each other very well, yes.'

'You can probably figure out that this type of fieldwork is different from your usual paper pushing.'

'I promise to get a grip on myself.'

'Ha ha. We'll see about that.'

'But I do appreciate your concerns.'

'How about Chris? Has he arrived?'

'No. I checked at the reception half an hour ago. He's still not in.'

'Okay. Listen! I think I need that drink after all. Would you want another?' Andy winks to the waitress to come and orders two Mojitos.

'I assume you drink Mojitos.' he asks after having ordered.

'I guess I do now.'

'Well, get used to it! On this roadtrip, you'll be drinking a lot of Mojitos.'

'Hi lads,' they hear someone say.' It's Chris. 'I saw you just ordered. Did you order something for me too?'

'Aw man! You're one minute late.'

'Hey Mike. Good that you're with us. This will inspire you to write a couple of great articles about Victoria Seymour, that's for sure!'

'And, hopefully, be able to drink a beer with Mason.'

'I think you'll have to cross that from your list – unfortunately.' Chris sits beside the others. He grabs the waitress passing by. 'One for me as well, please.'

'So,' Andy begins. 'I told Mike what to expect from the next couple of days.'

'Uhm yes, definitely,' mumbles Chris. 'But Mike, you have to keep it impersonal. This will not be easy for any of us.'

'I won't take it personally. Andy just told me. But seeing those images …'

'So, how's your wife, Andy?' interrupts Chris.

'Oh well,' answers Andy. 'I never told you the follow up story, did I?

'About what?' asks Chris.

'About the DVD and Betty. My youngest child found it.'

'Oh no.'

'I forgot to remove it from the DVD player.'

'You did what?'

'Yep. She was watching until Betty turned it off. Boy, was she angry.'

'Your youngest saw me bang that girl?'

'Ah, only for a moment. It's true, Mike. My wife and I have a mutual agreement about not watching porn because of our children. You know, she thinks children don't have access to porn on the Internet.'

'But why was Chris on the DVD?'

'Ha ha, good question, Mike. But we'll get into that later.'

'Man! What must she think of me, next time I come to Seattle.'

'Who? Betty or my daughter?'

'Both, for Christ sake!'

'Ah, don't worry. I gave Betty the limited edition on what happened.'

'And your daughter?'

'She wouldn't know the difference between you and a teddy bear.'

'What happened?' asks Mike.

'Well, I got caught up in a mystery,' replies Chris. 'There was an attempt to blackmail me when I was in Seattle visiting Andy some time ago. The police found the perpetrators quite fast.'

'Anyway, what's with those Mojitos? How long can it take to fix a couple of Mojitos?' remarks Andy Green.

Chris agrees, 'It is taking a long time, isn't it?'

'Well, this means we'll have to order the next couple when she brings us the first round.'

'Your plan make sense.'

'You blokes are used to drinking Mojitos'?' Mike asks.

'Hee hee. In a way we are.' confirms Andy.

'How was the flight?' asks Chris.

'Oh! It was excellent. A well-trained crew. The food was good too. And it was a nice aircraft.'

'Which one was it?'

'An Airbus A380 from Lufthansa. From Frankfurt to Hamburg, an Airbus A320. The A380 is one hell of a big bird! It's like a memory of how the United States has lost technological ground to Europe – and for that matter, the rest of the world. As a buddy of mine once said; 'The only thing that doesn't differentiate Europe from the United States are projects like the Space Shuttle and Airbus A380 that then end up being a burden for the taxpayers.'

'Ha ha, that's about it,' giggles Chris. 'I've read the A380 will never reach its Return on Investment.'

'How do you lads know each other?' asks Mike.

'Oh, we go way back,' answers Chris. 'We both served in the military during the cold war. Andy is with the American military,' he lies.

'It's been a couple of years, that's true,' confirms Andy.'

'And you?' asks Chris. 'How long have you been a journalist?'

'A couple of decades, I think, maybe two and a half. It's funny that we two have never met at ImplantSkills, in view of the fact that Mason is your boss and mine too, kind of.'

'He kept you to himself. As you know, he's a pretty private person. And you probably don't know this, but you are actually one of the persons he has come to appreciate very much.'

'Thank you.'

'Let's just get practical for a moment,' Andy Green changes the subject. 'Our fourth team member arrives tomorrow. He couldn't make it today.'

'Markus arrives tomorrow? Damn!' exclaims Chris. 'I was looking forward to drinking a Mojito with him tonight. I haven't seen him in ages. I think, last time was at the congress in Nairobi. Do you remember?'

Andy laughs. 'How can I forget? Back then, I was half the weight I am today. Imagine that! Stairs were no problem, I could see my dick. What happened to us, Chris?'

'We didn't enter Victoria Seymour's WeightForLife program. I'm not even sure if my dick is still down there.'

All three laugh.

'You'll be sad when you see how small it is.'

They laugh again.

'Contrary to yours, mine is still a master at what it does. And I have that on a DVD!'

'God! You're so funny, Chris.'

'Ha ha.'

'Say, when was the last time you had sex, Andy?'

'I think it was on the same day I bought my little Japanese car.'

Chris whispers to Mike. 'That was in 1998.'

'Actually, its shit to be obese, isn't it?' mumbles Andy.

'But not as bad as ending up in some catacombs in Germany for the wrong reasons,' comments Mike.

That comment completely silences the discussion.

'Wow, I thought I was the only with black humor,' says Andy.

'You just found someone who beats you,' laughs Chris.

'That one was perhaps a little misplaced,' admits Mike.

'It was actually excellent,' confirms Chris. 'At least for today. Tomorrow morning, before we leave, you'll feel a mood change. So, if you have more to post, then post it right now.'

'Ha ha,' laughs Andy.

'Don't forget, I'm actually a virgin,' says Mike

'You'll get used to it. Chris and I just have a weird way of communicating.'

'Where are we actually going tomorrow?' asks Mike.

'To the middle of Germany. To the East.'

'Ahhh, finally …' exclaims Andy. 'Our drinks! What took so long?'

'What's the story on that area?'

'Who cares. Just drink.'

'I'll say cheers to that.'

SHE IS just about to leave the little cafe inside Palace of Westminster, when a beautiful well-trained elderly man with half-dark skin approaches her, carefully asking if he can sit beside her. Victoria Seymour tries to recognize if it is someone she has seen in the corridors of Palace of Westminster.

'Well, I was actually on my way back to my office. But, be seated.'

'May I have your autograph?'

'Of course you may, sir. I hear out on your dialect, you come from somewhere in the Arabic world. It sounds like Persian. Tourist? Vacation?'

'Actually, it's Persian. Though, currently, I live in Seattle. And no, I'm at Westminster due to official reasons.'

'Oh! Seattle. What a beautiful city. In a months time, I'm meeting your President in Florida. But listen! I really got to go.'

She makes a gesture with her arm, showing in what direction she will be leaving, while getting up from the furniture. But right as she about to walk, she feels the man's hand grab softly around her arm.

'I got a message for you,' the stranger says, still seated, but looking up at her.

'Please, let go of my arm.'

'Henry Montclair, isn't your companion. He's a real psychopath. He's gonna lead the United Kingdom into disaster.'

'Could you please let go of my arm, sir?'

The man lets go of her arm.

'He's the reason why people disappear.'

The stranger gets up and leaves almost as fast as he came.

Victoria Seymour stands completely perplexed. What did he mean with that? She lets herself fall back into the cosy furniture. What was the man suggesting?

'Mr. Seymour? Would you like another coffee?' asks the young barista girl.

She almost gets a chock when she sees her. 'Why not? I've only had one. Have you ever seen the man who just left?' she asks.

'I don't think so.'

Why do things now suddenly stand so clear to her? Why did they not stand this clear to her only thirty seconds ago? By God! Sometimes she's really more body than brains! In spite of all the things Henry Montclair say and comforts her with, Lisa is right when saying they have actually achieved absolutely nothing up. *They* are the ones who have initiated the damn mess.

Not Brexit! And not the former government. People are actually uniting against *her* and The Party. Amazingly as it may sound, at least right in this moment, but she can not believe that there are actually people agreeing to the politics they so far have been executing. Those are the ones she has been listening to. The ones clinging to in her little private bubble. Not to the ones who starts hating her for reasons that now stand quite apparently.

What are they actually turning the United Kingdom into?

It starts dim on her. There are too many open ends. There always were. To much confusion around what they promise the people and what Henry Montclair and Gregg White promise her. She read some days ago that forty percent of all Americans believe the earth is less than 6.000 years old. How does half a continent come to believe in such bigotry? Three percent even believe the Earth is flat. Perhaps, when all comes to all, she has been relying a little too much on Henry because of her addiction to her political manifesto, and simply failed to see his true intentions. Power corrupts, as the old saying claims, and like Henry and Gregg she has got sucked deeply into the saying. Every time she is told something by Henry she constantly ends up somewhere else. She has failed on Lisa in listening to what she tried to tell. Observations that she in a lifetime never would had hold for possible in a place like the United Kingdom.

'Can you be so kind and bring me another coffee?' she asks the girl, returning with the one she just ordered.

'Then you've had three? Mostly you only drink one.'

'If you have something stronger than coffee, I'll take that too.'

'We only got coffee.'

'Then you know what to do.'

'Yes, Ms. Seymour.'

She looks down at her hands. They vibrate. Then she lets them to her purse, cluttering around, trying to find her cell phone to place a call to her partner through many years. She needs someone she can talk confident with and get support from.

'Hi, darling! What a surprise,' says the voice at the other end.

'What are you doing this weekend?' she asks.

'You sound sad. What happened?'

'I've just had a bad morning. What are you doing this weekend?'

'Unfortunately, not good. I promised my daughter to tour to the theater. What about next week, Wednesday or Thursday? It would fit perfectly in.'

'Wait … I'll just have to check my calendar. Mm … Seems fine with me.'

'Evening?'

'Only evening!'

'Okay, I had hoped to see you sooner. But that's how life is.'

'But what's the matter Victoria? You seem rather tense.'

'Something did actually happen, five minutes ago,' she explains. 'Someone opened my eyes. He said I shall be careful with Henry and that he's not my friend.'

'Victoria, I've said it all the time! The man is up to no good. There's a reason why he was thrown out of the European Parliament.'

'I know. You keep reminding me of that.'

'If something bothers you, let's talk about it on Wednesday.'

'Okay. We should do that. I look forward being in your arms.'

'And below me.'

'Actually, at the moment, that's probably the only place I'd feel safe.'

'Okay. Kiss you. Bye bye.'

They hang up.

A new thought strikes Victoria Seymour. She can not fully get a grasp on its contents, but a part of the thought materializes. What have they been doing lately apart from turning the United Kingdom into a place for xenophobic and a Wild West for stupid and unintelligent people? Since Brexit, time again and again has shown what happens when less intelligent and intellectual people get the chance to air their opinions. Is Henry Montclair playing her? Using her as an useful idiot for some purpose that she is simply not capable of figuring out? Is she the bitch at the rudder everybody wants to hate?

She needs to get back to office to dig out dirt. She might find information worth leaking out. Something that will overthrow her and her government. Considering that all this has happened in the wave of Henry Montclair's simple suggestion of using fat as a method to get to power, who would had thought it worked so well?

Yes, who would had thought of it?

CHAPTER 15

SOME FAMILY TIES HAVE been split, some friendships and marriages broken. Who would have thought it possible to twist a society such as the English and Welsh into disagreement on whether it is right to treat obese people with a Body Mass Index above 35 as second class citizens? In the north things are at least calmer with some people pulling up roots and moving to Scotland or Northern Ireland. But in an environment where fear is replacing basic sound reasoning, this might not last long.

In London, in the City of Westminster Abbey, the latest protest march in support of civil rights for obese people worsens by the hour and so have the number of casualties. What should have been a peaceful demonstration, turned into one of the most horrifying demonstrations to ever take place in the United Kingdom. Thousands came to show their sympathy with obese people. Obese people came too. But when a group of anti-obese protesters joined in, they not only attacked obese people, but also their supporters and brutally attacked the police and TV news crews, smashing their cameras. Then the vans arrived. When gunfire from automatic weapons spread, Monica Griffith knew it was time to run for her life. The crowd panicked just like she did, children stumbled and were trampled to death by the overweight who were present. She does not know who shot first, as more anti-protesters joined in with additional shotguns, rifles and pistols, but it was certainly not her and the other peaceful protesters, nor was it the police. More police assembled on the front line, where she was at the time, and on their way she felt their truncheons and clubs. The water sprayed from big police trucks did settle part of the uprising, but did nothing to improve the chaotic situation. Whatever happened in the minutes thereafter caused the police to turn brutal. Someone told her that nine policemen had been executed at close range.

The well-dressed men were waiting for her and they were waiting for many of her kind. When she had the chance and finally got her feet back on the ground, she ran and she ran. With protesters now spreading in all directions, she once again noticed the well-dressed men who had been following her earlier that day. They came to get her as they were coming to get others. She ran as fast as she could and it suddenly struck her how much she regrets being overweight. This time when she was beaten, it was not from the police, she is sure about this, but forgot everything from the minute her face got smashed to the ground.

LIKE MANY others from the demonstration, Monica Griffith wakes up in a cell on a hard mattress laying on a cold concrete floor. Up to this point, no one has come to her to read her her rights and she is very hungry, having no idea when she ate the last time. She thinks of the rumors she heard two weeks ago about people who oppose the system and are brought to places that have absolutely nothing to do with the regular prison system.

She hears a key turn and sees the steel door open. It is a little skinny ugly man in his twenties, maybe beginning thirties who enters her cell.

'Get up,' he says.

Monica Griffith obeys. 'Why am I here?' she asks.

The man does not respond.

'Why am I here?' she asks again.

This time the man responds with his truncheon. The beatings are painful and cause her to fall onto the hard concrete floor.

'Get up,' the young man repeats.

She gets up with great effort, looking at him more or less in shock.

'Now, follow me,' he commands.

She obeys. Her head wants to disobey but the thought of more beatings makes her give in. Walking in front of the man, she takes in her surroundings which, as anticipated, do not seem to relate to a prison, but are more like a warehouse that has been refurbished to hold people. Not all cells are solid like hers. There are also fenced spaces full of inmates who stare at her as she walks by. They all look beaten, dirty, tired, and obese.

'Get in here,' the little piece of shit man commands.

She enters a door and sees one of the henchmen responsible for her at a desk. He smiles and politely asks her to sit down.

'So, Ms. Griffith,' he begins. 'We've been a bad girl, haven't we?' He smiles in a way that discomforts her.

'What are we going to do with you?' he asks, shaking his head. 'As if we don't know what was going on.'

Her discomfort is replaced by raw fear. She feels every muscle in her broken body intensify. This is not a good situation. But even a moron can figure this out. Perhaps they might knew after all what was going on in the basement of WeightForLife.

'MS. FERGUSON, thanks for joining our show this morning. It's so kind of you to take out time for us.'

'Thank you for the invitation.'

'I believe it's the first time you have been on our show. As you might know, we've had Ms. Seymour on a couple of times.'

'Yes. I should send her regards. She's very busy at the moment with Brexit negotiations in Brussels.'

'I can imagine. I understand you're from Spain?'

'Madrid to be more precise.'

'Madrid is a wonderful city. How many years have you lived in the United Kingdom?'

'I think we moved to London when I was six or so. My father is from England and my mother from Catalonia.'

'How's your Spanish?'

'Excellent. And yours?'

The audience laughs.

'Somewhat rusty, but I manage quite well on the tourist level, thank you.'

'I'm glad to hear this.'

'So, Ms. Ferguson, how are Ms. Seymour's Brexit negotiations going?'

'Well, the International Monetary Fund just released its quarterly World Economic Outlook, showing that, because of the sterling's collapse, the economy in the United Kingdom has been overtaken by France's. And if you look at India's Gross Domestic Product, it's now right behind that of the United Kingdom, so it's really a matter of months before they overtake us too. Isn't that ironic! Because of Brexit, the United Kingdom has gone from a 5th to 7th place as an economic power in less than a couple of months! The Centre for Economics & Business Research predicted that, before Brexit, and by 2030, the economy of the United Kingdom would overtake both Germany and Japan. But with the new figures from the International

Monetary Fund, Brazil, Russia, Indonesia, and Mexico, will likely overtake the United Kingdom as well within the next 5 to 10 years, and probably also Turkey, Nigeria and Italy. So in all honestly, no matter how the negotiations end up with the European Union, the only really amazing thing we've achieved is to use the same bullet to shoot ourselves in the head and the foot at the same time.'

'So … the negotiations aren't going too well.'

'You're a bright person, Mr. Dunham. Anyone who thinks the United Kingdom is a great world power is deluded. It's a country with poor skills, failing education and low productivity. For decades now, we've used the European Union as a scapegoat to hide our own weaknesses and have failed to do anything about it. So, to all of you people out there, you should be glad we have a Prime Minister like Victoria Seymour who is reuniting our spirits. Thanks to her, progress is in the making. We're now heading towards good times again and are on our way to becoming a superpower again.'

'That sounds very promising Ms. Ferguson. What's your opinion about the demonstration in London, yesterday?'

'What about it?'

'How do you feel about what happened?'

'I was briefed by the police commissioner himself. He says everything went smoothly. Apart from a few riots here and there caused by obese people, it went peacefully.'

'There are rumors that people from the demonstration have disappeared. Do you know anything about this?'

'No. How should I?'

'The police have been receiving missing person reports like never before.'

'But what does have to do with The Party? If this is the case, we should allocate the police additional resources, so that they're able to work more efficiently.'

'And where will the money come from?'

'Money is not a problem. If we need more, we simply print more.'

'How do you mean, print more?'

'We print more money. Why is it so difficult to understand that?'

'What about inflation, rising costs, static salaries?'

'What about it?'

'You cannot just print more money without it having an effect on inflation.'

'That's true. But as you might recall, inflation is on the rise because of Brexit. So, a couple of percentage points on top won't tip the total balance.'

'Uhm. This thing about people disappearing ...'

'You know, if you're so worried about people disappearing, why don't you go search for them?'

Again the audience laughs.

'Oh! I see we just received a Twitter message from one of our viewers. He asks, when will the Fat Tax be revoked?'

Lisa Ferguson, rather annoyed that the Fat Tax issue never seems to die, answers, 'Regardless of what people say and think, we at Westminster are a little surprised that it hasn't already been revoked. The now famous paragraph is fully rubbish and will eventually be taken out of the law.'

'When?'

'I can't say with certainty. When a law has been implemented, it requires a lot of work to get it undone.'

'You did not answer my question. Can you give me a date?'

'I did answer your question. To my knowledge, it's in progress. We're aware that the law has put us and The Party in a bad light. But what this journalist Mike Hornett keeps writing about us is simply not true. We're not using the Brexit situation to push through unscrutinized legislation.'

'What about the law of Henry the VIII?'

'What about it?'

'The law gives one person the power to bypass Parliament and the Lords to allow laws to be implemented without scrutiny.'

'So? What's your point?'

'Well, this means that laws can be implemented into the system by your government, that neither Parliament, the Lords, nor the Courts have approved or, for that matter, even seen.'

'And why would our government do that? The law of Henry the VIII, only covers European Union laws. I don't see any danger in bypassing Parliament, the Lords or the Courts, as these European Union laws are already in use in our daily lives. The real danger starts when journalists like Mike Hornett try discredit our country when the rest us are trying to make the United Kingdom a better place to live.'

'And how does he discredit the United Kingdom?'

'We have the impression that he's accusing us of turning the United Kingdom into an aristocracy. It's absolutely nonsense and nothing could be less true. Why would we do this? Our democratic process and our European history wouldn't allow it to happen. I would say that the intentions of Mike Hornett, are to promote his own career and gain fame. The man brings shame upon anyone who honestly tries to solve the issues we're struggling with because of Brexit.'

'Ms. Ferguson, isn't it right that Ms. Seymour said some time ago that The Party had a whistle-blower? That a deal has been cut with the military to provide money for updating their expired hardware? At least that's what Mike Hornett has written.'

'I'm not aware of a deal with the military.'

'It was a decision made to compensate for our embarrassing retreat in Syria against Islamic State.'

'I remember the incident, but not that a deal has been struck with the military.'

'Ms. Ferguson. Thank you for joining us today.'

'On behalf of Victoria Seymour and The Party, thank you for having me.'

'And now a word from our sponsors.'

'SO …' says Monica Griffith's henchman. 'I see you've made some progress on your weight.' He looks at some papers in front of him and picks up the one on top. '19 kilo's in two months. That's below average. What went wrong?'

Monica Griffith doesn't know how to answer. 'I …' she starts to stutter. 'I …'

'Does it have anything to do with your other activities? But let's not talk about those right now. How are you Ms. Griffith?'

'I … I'm fine.'

'Are we treating you alright?'

'I …'

'Go ahead, say what you want; you're safe here with me. At this place, we can exchange opinions honestly. Are we treating you alright?' he asks again.

'Yes, I guess I can't complain.'

'And how's the food?'

'So far, I haven't had anything to eat.'

'Oh … Could that perhaps have to do with your not losing enough weight ?'

'I …'

'Of course it isn't. I can inform you, you've slept for quite a while. We didn't want to wake you up. You seemed to need the sleep after this horrible demonstration yesterday. As we were unsure of your identity, we brought you here. There's absolutely no reason to be worried or be afraid.'

With that, Monica Griffith, at least to some extent, feels her muscles relax a little.

'Does it mean I can go after this?'

'It certainly does.' The man puts down his papers, but then picks up others. 'Of course, in return, we would like you to do us a little favor.'

'What favor do you want from me?' she asks.

'Oh, just a little one. We know you've been meeting with others, in the basement of your local WeightForLife, arranging these demonstrations. We'd like to know the names of those who are not fat like you are, but have supported the demonstration. Could you perhaps give us some names?'

'I don't know …' she hardly has time to end the sentence before the first blow falls. It hits her behind the left shoulder. Her body cannot take anymore beatings. She had not noticed the person behind her. Actually, she now sees that there are two persons behind her chair.

'So … I'll just ask again. Any names of persons we might be interested in?'

'No …'

The next blow. This one makes her feel completely exposed and empowered. She does not know what to say or do. Whoever is doing this to her has now begun to use physical violence. She had been honest. She does not know any regular sized people who sympathize with her. 'I don't know, I honestly don't,' she says. 'I don't know any decent, normal, hard working people who support us.' She immediately recognizes from whom that phrase came.

The pain is unbearable. This time both people behind her are using their clubs. The beatings with their nightsticks hit spot on every time. They know where it hurts, and they seem to like it.

'Stop it! Stop it,' she screams. 'Okay, I'll give you names.'

She starts giving names of people she knows. People she holds for very dear. Unfortunately, it is names of people who have absolutely nothing to do with the mission she is on. But it just hurts so much.

IN HAMBURG the next morning, Mike Hornett, is getting dressed. With one eye, he tries to get his clothes on, with the other he watches Euronews. His head hurts after last night's Mojitos at the bar. One must say, Andy Green and Chris Campbell really know how to drink – or he simply is not in as good shape as they are.

At once he stops what he is doing and turns his attention to the television. Something happened yesterday in London. The commentator says that not much information has been made available, but there was another demonstration and many protesters were wounded with at least two dozen dead. How many exactly, the reporter does not know.

He goes to the bed and sits down, watching the cell phone pictures rolling over the flat-screen. They are horrifying. There is extreme violence by unidentifiable people, who obviously have mingled in with the demonstrators and police. The picture quality is not the best, but the videos show people lying motionless on the ground. There are children among the dead too. Why has he not heard anything about the demonstration from his girlfriend? They talked this morning while he was brushing his teeth?

The female voice continues talking. She says that after this demonstration, with so much civil disobedience, Ms. Seymour had signed executive orders last night to use military force to arrest rioters who oppose resistance, and imprison them indefinitely without conviction. This has put the United Kingdom in direct opposition to European Union policies and caused a rift between the two entities.

The socks fall out of Mike's hands. This is a disaster, not only for obese people but for the United Kingdom as well! The government is really pushing hard this time. It is a slow disintegration of the civil rights for people with a Body Mass Index of over 35 and for the people who support them.

'... with tensions increasing on both sides of the channel between the United Kingdom and the European Union,' the female newsreader continues, 'the President of the European Council has confirmed Ms. Seymour is in a position to declare martial law in peace time, if it is required.' He picks up his socks and pulls them on. What is going on in England and Wales is turning into a downright nightmare.

THE TWO big men are already in the restaurant eating breakfast. He did not expect to see them so soon. Marcus Schneider, Andy Green's German colleague, has arrived too. Then the team is assembled. Chris is the first to see him come to the table.

'Mike! You've slept late.'

He doesn't immediately respond, but pulls out a chair at the table and sits down beside Andy Green.

'Mike? What's wrong?' asks Andy. 'Do you have a hangover?'

Chris laughs.

'Have you seen the news this morning?', asks Mike.

'This is Marcus, by the way.' says Andy, introducing Marcus.

'Hi,' Mike says, shaking hands. 'Sorry for my mental absence. I had an awful morning watching the news,' excusing himself.

'No problem.'

'He'll be our guide in Nordhausen,' Andy informs him.

But Mike fails to appreciate the information. 'Have you people seen the news?' he asks.

'About what happened yesterday in London?' answers Chris.

'Yes.'

'We were about to discuss it when you came out of the elevator.'

'We need to stop it.'

'Stop what?' ask Marcus.

'You didn't hear about what happened in London?' asks Chris.

'Something about a demonstration. I heard there are supposed to be a lot of dead and injured people.'

'Frankly, this thing with Victoria Seymour and The Party is starting to get under my skin,' tells Mike. 'I talked with my girlfriend this morning, and she wasn't even aware there were casualties. At least if she had known, she'd certainly have told me. I'm a journalist. As I told Andy and Chris yesterday, there are people who are threatening to stop me from writing.'

'Well, Mike ...' says Andy, 'I think the times for journalists and opponents of the government being safe are reaching the end-phase. I'm sure with this demonstration that modern political history of the United Kingdom is changing forever.'

'And not only that,' continues Chris, 'this is the moment where your role will change forever, too.'

'What do you mean?' ask Mike.

'You'll see soon enough.'

'You're not going to tell me?'

'Mike, if I were in your place, I'd eat a good breakfast. The next time you eat, it might come up again.'

WITH THE rented car, they depart from Hamburg and make their way to Nordhausen. According to the BMW's navigation system, it is a three hour drive. Mason Sanders' implant is still where it was when Chris discovered something was not as it should be. Yesterday's mood is slowly changing to one of thought and concentration – which ought not to be a surprise for people who have seen what's on the satellite images and who will, perhaps, soon be standing there themselves. It is not totally wrong what Andy said at the hotel; that what they might find, could change their lives and maybe the course of history as well.

Marcus is driving. To break the deafening silence, he tries a joke. But it falls on deaf ears. Then he tries something more informative. 'So, do you people know anything about this part of Germany we're going to?'

'What about it?' asks Mike, sitting with a notebook, preparing his work, not really interested in a history lesson.

'Well, the area we're heading to is part of the old East Germany. When the Berlin Wall was still standing, the region was becoming very decayed because the Communists didn't have any money for maintenance. But, to the disappointment of many East-Germans, it continued to decay after the reunification of Germany because the government in Bonn was focused on infrastructure like this Autobahn, and cities like Berlin, Dresden, Leipzig and so on. There was no money for the smaller cities. However, fifteen years after the reunification, things started to pick up speed. All of Germany now had access to the Baltic Sea, not just the North-Sea, so the Baltic coastline received a major overhaul.'

'Marcus, that's good know, thanks man.'

He is silent. It is an awful silence that he really does not want to be in with the thoughts he has in his head.

'Today it's packed with exclusive hotels, restaurants, outdoor activities and loved by everyone – especially those with money. The area along the coastline has become so trendy that Germans now come from as far as the South. It seem that they would rather go there instead of flying to Spain. But I can tell you guys, Dora, the internment camp and these catacombs … believe me, Mike, that's really …'

'Thank you,' exclaims Mike. 'I already have the pictures – Literally.'

'I'm not sure if we want to go into that subject, now,' confirms Chris.

'Sorry,' says Marcus. 'I guess we all prepare in our own way.'

'Exactly. If we could just continue saying nothing?' suggests Andy.

'I just wanted to …'

'We know. But just keep it zipped, Marcus. It's better so.'

FOR THE last two hours of the trip there is silence. The weather is getting worse. The meteorologists had promised rain for rest of the evening and into the night too. And they were certainly right. The rain is splashing down on the windshield as hard as a shower at full blast. Marcus reduces his speed from 180km per hours to less than 80km per hour for the last few kilometers before they turn off the Autobahn, less than six kilometers from Dora, the old concentration camp which is now a museum.

They finally arrive to their first destination. During a dry spell, they get out to stretch their legs. It is less than two kilometers from Mason Sanders' implant, which still shows he is in the middle of nowhere.

'This is where the restricted area starts,' says Andy, putting a detailed military map on top of the wet car's hood. 'First, we need find a way to get into those catacombs.' He takes out the satellite images and selects the one showing the truck carrying the dead people which also shows one of the few possible entrances into the catacombs.

'The truck probably used this road, so we'll have to follow it too.' He points with his index finger and moves it along to a fence where the access point is, approximately five and a half kilometer from their current position. 'They only use this entrance.'

'The others entrances aren't accessible. We checked.' says Marcus.

'So, it looks like we'll need to use the one they use?' asks Mike.

'Correct. But there's a barrier. And it's occupied with personnel,' Marcus informs him. 'There are always two people. I've had all access points under observation. And, as Andy says; the others are inaccessible, so this is the one we need to use, too. Unfortunately, it's rather frequently used.'

'That's not good. We wouldn't like to meet those people – at least, not Andy and I,' says Chris.

'No, certainly not,' agrees Andy.

'The street leading to the entrance is in pretty bad shape. Look at this.' Marcus shows them the street on the military map. 'They need to go slow with their trucks, I wouldn't even call it a road anymore, although it's still on the maps.'

'We should probably not use the road they use.'

'That would be dumb, I agree. We haven't seen any, but I'm sure they have some kind of surveillance. That's why we need to follow the old railroad tracks here. It passes the old concentration camp and leads to the sealed part of the area.'

'You mean the restricted area?'

'Yes.'

'How do we get inside?'

'We'll cut a hole in the fence some 250 meters from the barrier. Then it's a 150 meter run to the catacomb. The entrance is nothing but a tunnel. You can just walk in.'

'Do we do this at night or in daylight?' asks Chris.

'We need to do it at night. From the barrier, they have visual contact of the entrance. We'll never have the chance to get by.'

'I understood they off-load at night,' asks Mike.

'Not always.'

'What's the surveillance status?' ask Chris.

'My scout team hasn't picked up any infrared or similar equipment that can discover us.'

'Okay,' confirms Andy. 'Then we take the 150 meters from the hole in the fence to the entrance.' He points on the map. 'Here, in this belt of trees we're invisible. And here ...' he continues, 'we need to watch the road, to warn if trucks or other vehicles approach.'

'How far is it from the border? Four hundred meters?'

'About 400. Due to the road's condition, they can't drive fast, so that gives us approximately 3 to 4 minutes to get out of the catacombs. From the entrance, I figure you need one minute to get back on the other side of the fence,' calculates Marcus.

'Sounds about right,' confirms Andy.

'You two,' Marcus points at Andy and Chris, 'do the watch. Then Mike and I go in and retrieve as much information as we can.'

'And Mike?' asks Andy. 'Are you ready for this?'

'Yes.'

The other three laugh.

'No, you're not.' says Chris. 'You'll never be ready for a mission like this. None of us will.'

THIS TIME she realizes Henry has taken things one step too far. Victoria Seymour is fuming with anger. She looks for him in his new office on Petty France, but he seems to have vanished. Instead, she bumps into Lisa who is there for reasons she does not ask about. The young, good looking girl with completely black hair, big brown eyes who is thin and with beautiful breasts, sees that Victoria looks more upset and concerned than she normally does.

'What's the matter?' she asks Victoria.

'That was some performance you gave at the interview this morning,' she grunts.

'I was a bitch, I know.'

'Yes, the cameras change your personality sometimes. It's a show.'

'How did it go with the Brexit negotiations?'

'What Brexit negotiations?'

'I thought you were in Brussels to negotiate?'

'Who told you that?'

'Henry. He said you had to go to Brussels. That's why I did the interview with James Dunham, instead of you.'

'Oh he did, did he? He's a son of a bitch. I'm not sure he wants me to do more interviews. He's getting suspicious of me.'

'Suspicious about what?'

'Have you seen the news this morning?' she asks.

'No. Why?'

'I now have the power to throw people in prison, regardless of whether they are guilty or not. That's why I want to get hold of Henry. Again he's taken things a step too far.'

'Since when can you do this?'

'Since yesterday evening. You didn't know about it?'

'No.'

'Have you seen Henry, around here? Or for that matter Gregg?'

'No. I think they went to the coffee shop.'

'At Westminster? Why didn't you say so? Which one?'

'I think your favorite one.'

'Henry is ruining my name and reputation. He's pushing a lot of things through in my name. Things, I don't want to have associated with me. Did I understand correctly that you said he asked you to do the interview in my place because I was in Brussels?'

'Yes.'

'When I get hold of that …' she mumbles, getting out her phone, and having her bodyguards pick her up. She go to them at her favorite coffee shop at the Palace of Westminster.

SHE FINDS them where Lisa thought they would be, relaxing in a cosy corner, sipping their coffee.

'My jaw dropped to my breasts when I watched the news this morning,' she says in a voice full of bitterness.

'Hi, Victoria?' says Gregg.

'How can it be?' comments Henry. 'They're too small.'

The comment makes Gregg giggle.

'That's not funny!' screams Victoria Seymour. 'They're fine as they are thank you!' The subject 'bosom' is a sensitive topic for her. Back then under the knife, a lot of surplus skin had been removed.

'What are you doing?' she wants to know. 'Military authority … Indefinite imprisonment without conviction … have you completely lost your mind?'

'Relax, Victoria …' says Gregg.

'Don't tell me to relax,' she yells so loudly that other people turn and look. 'Have you two gone completely insane?'

'Now, calm down, Victoria,' tries Henry. 'There's a reason for it. You've seen yourself how bad it's gotten out there. We need to take counter-measures. If we don't, this thing, might bring the Kingdom to the brink of a civil war.'

'That's absolutely bullshit! Civil war my ass! Why did you lie to Lisa about me being in Brussels?'

'Victoria, relax now,' says Henry firmly. 'I had the feeling from our last meeting that you're a little overloaded with work. I thought you went to Brussels. I somehow got it mixed up. And for that, I'd like to apologize.'

Victoria looks at him in frustration. She cannot find the words to tell him what she thinks of him at the moment. He is so slick and well-spoken, he is even worse than she is. Then she asks, 'What deal exactly you have struck with the military?'

'What do you mean?' he asks.

'The military must have gotten something in return for their loyalty to us.'

'Ah, that's right,' says Gregg. 'Remember, Victoria? During the election you promised the military a revamped budget?'

'That was during the election. That has nothing to do with now. Where do you think the money should come from?' she asks.

'But isn't it obvious?' Henry asks. 'You said it yourself: From fat people.'

'I never said that.'

'Yes, you did, Victoria. And the entire United Kingdom heard it.'

'You're confusing me, Henry.'

'The latest new laws state that rich, fat business people no longer have ownership of their companies. We sell them to investors. That's how the big hole in the military budget is financed, enabling us to provide additional financial resources to the school and healthcare system as well, and in accordance with your agenda.'

'But I never signed that legislation.'

'Yes, you did. Four months ago.'

'It's pretty smart, don't you think, Victoria?' continues Gregg. 'We've satisfied the military, our greatest opposition as well as the educational system, and the healthcare system.'

Victoria is speechless. She tries to formulate what she thinks and feels, but she does not know how to let it out, so she lets it go. Those two have turned into a disgrace for the United Kingdom. They are destroying what so many decent and hard working people have spent centuries building up. She now understands that Lisa's earlier observations were absolutely correct. Henry has been building up his own army of loyal followers, and now she realizes that Gregg is the one who is backing the man's wishes. The power is slipping out of her hands – if she was ever the one in power. At this stage, there is no chance of her beating Henry at his own game. Now, she either plays by his rules or she resigns as Prime Minister and lets him take her place. Henry and Gregg have used her name and reputation to get through, the filthiest politics ever seen in the United Kingdom, to establish their own strong political base. She, though, will be the one people remember as the bitch at the rudder. She looks at them again.

Then she walks away.

'MONICA,' says the voice emphatically, while six eyes stare at her. 'Why didn't you tell us the names of your accomplices earlier? Then we wouldn't have beaten you up like this. We forgive you for your misdeeds and the rampage you have caused, and want to make you an offer.'

'An offer,' she repeats.

'Yes. An offer.'

'What kind of an offer?'

'You can get out of the situation you have caused and continue your life as if nothing happened.'

She fails to show any gratitude to their offer. If they expect her to be grateful, then they must be crazier than she thought. How can they possibly believe she will think everything is all right after this ordeal, when what has happened is so wrong? She is not a person who forgives easily and threatening her doesn't help either. How can any of these idiots believe nothing has happened? Does anyone outside these four walls, these dark painted walls where it is cold and unpleasant, know what is going on? This is the United Kingdom and what she is experiencing should not happen here.

But blaming her for what has happened in the last two years, saying that it is her fault and her fault alone because she is fat, is pathetic. Not with her! They will eventually be punished for their dirty deeds and get what they deserve for the insanity they have perpetrated. They are weak people who for the first time in their lives feel important through the empowerment of others. Unfortunately, the self- importance they feel, she feels as physical and mental pain. She will do anything in her power to get out of here so she can fight them.

'What do you want me to do?' she asks resignedly.

'We'll give you the chance to leave the country, to emigrate to another country forever. We'll even provide you with the financial resources you need to start over.'

'Why would I leave my country? I like it here.'

'Oh? You like it here? But we don't like you. You see, that's the problem.'

'Ah, okay. Then I'll just leave.'

'So, we have an agreement?'

'I guess so.'

Her appointed henchman nods to the two men behind her chair. They pull her up by the arms and turn her flabby body around, pointing her to the door.

'See to it that she gets on the cargo plane tonight.'

IT WAS a warning from the Old Man that he went to Westminster Palace to visit Victoria Seymour. Although her policy concerning obese people is not a smart thing to do, the Continental Teams have decided it isn't reason enough to assassinate her. At least not anymore. He went to Palace of Westminster to warn her and look her in the eye. He always wants to look people in the eye when he knows their time is running out and Victoria Seymour's time is certainly running out because time always runs out for politicians in one way or another.

In the case of The Party, it seems less true at the moment thanks to this Henry Montclair, a player who The Special Council has not at all had on their radar, but they are looking very closely at him now.

The Old Man sighs. It has been a long way for him and The Special Council. It has also been a long way for heads of states, aristocrats, dictators, and the sudden rise of Victoria Seymour, who is relatively new to the political stage after having served many years in the European Council in Brussels. People like her are dangerous. They think they know how the game is played, but get surprised when the game is played completely differently. It is like common people, talking about democracy. People are foolish when they talk about democracy. Especially people on the right wing of politics falling for the typical rhetoric of 'We the People' democracy. There is a lot of misconception about democracy and what it represents and stands for and the responsibilities necessary to maintain it are rarely understood by the majority. Free speech, civil rights and politicians being obligated to their citizens are not specifically guaranteed in a democracy. These are things that have resulted from the on-going democratic process. So, if you are overweight according to the new laws in the United Kingdom, you might think that your rights are being violated because you suddenly find yourself in the minority. But this is not the case. The Party has changed the rules by changing the Constitution thanks to a ridiculous, almost 500 year old law, a law that has made it possible to bypass the courts and alter the English non-existing Constitution, making it a crime to have a BMI of over 35. Those who these new laws affect may be shocked to learn that it is completely legal and there is nothing either they or the rest of the world can do about it.

Aristocratic tendencies come in small increments and are not placed upon the majority but only the minorities. Some people who are aware enough to see what is going on would think of the events in Germany before World War II. And then again, many would not because they are not aware of history and politics. Before World War II, famous people like Albert Einstein, the parents of Henry Kissinger, Karl Marx and Clara Zetkin, just to mention a few, understood when it was about time to get out. Clara Zetkin was a key leader in the German Communist movement who fled from Nazi Germany in 1932 to seek asylum in the Soviet Union (which probably was not the smartest thing to do. But who would had known back then). Others, the optimists, those without financial resources and the less intellectual and intelligent people, stayed, either because they ignored the signs of what was going on or hoped that things would eventually improve. In the end, many of them ended up in ovens, gassed and burned. Those who weren't affected try not to think this far or cannot think this far, which is something they cannot be blamed for. It makes it easier to get through life when simply close the eyes and cover the ears while the bulldog is pissing up your pants. You have seen pictures of the dog. You have heard about it; it is big and angry and by letting it continue its business, you survive the wet pants which is preferable because you never really expect to meet the dog. That only happens to others. The majority fail to appreciate what they have because of their disinterest and ignorance in the subject of dogs … at least, until the point when they realize that they now too stand before the dog.

Unfortunately, at this point, there is no time left to make a quick change and put on shorts instead of pants.

Seen from a suppressor's point of view, there are seven meals between peace and a civil war. It is a good trick to feed the majority and only disrupt the minority. The Party plays this game very well – either deliberately or not. Sometimes, heads of states, aristocrats and dictators simply need to get hit by a truck or a train or have their aircraft fall out of the sky. Leaders who disrupt the world's democratic balance too much or grow too strong need to go. What The Special Council does not interfere in is poverty, war crimes, or political decisions about going to war, unless, of course, it is a dictator who pushes his luck by expanding into other countries he thinks belong to him. Then he or she will eventually be assassinated. In the democratic part of the world, it is not so often that some nut ball politician makes a power-grab. However if he steps too far away from his authority or does something completely in his own interests, then this person might be caught with a hooker in a hotel and maybe with some drugs or there may suddenly be too much money in his private bank account. It is the small cute scandals that wake up the wrath of the public, and if that doesn't help, then there are always the sudden, unforeseen accidents.

The rules and procedures that The Special Council follows are strict. They know that the power they have corrupts. And they know that anyone can be corrupted. The Special Council is good at acting as whistle-blowers, as judges and they are especially good at executing self-justice that isn't dependent on diplomacy, political or religious conviction. They are good at putting a damper on some of the injustices throughout the world. The Special Council is involved deeply in everybody's daily life throughout the world. They are not seen. They are not heard but they hear everything. The consequences of their work is felt practically everywhere but not noticed. It has been this way for now almost fifty-five years.

Had it not been for the rape and the brutal torture of his wife, and her being thrown out like a piece of trash by the government of the country he used to call home, The Special Council would never have come into existence. When they were through with his wife and children, they cut off a couple of his fingers and toes, cutting so deep it almost killed him. One person had done the cutting while two others held him. He was very much awake when they performed their disgusting, inhuman acts. Imagine what was going through his conscious mind seeing his body parts being cut off and at the same time seeing his wife being raped and monstrous things being done to his children. Most humans would pass out under such intense pressure, but he decided not to. No, on the contrary. He saved the impressions, the hate; he bundled them together to keep for later and turned his hatred of the pigs to forgiveness. His damned government had done this to him, not those who had carried out the task they were assigned, fearing for their own life and the lives of their beloved ones.

How he had ended up in the situation then was because he had helped a woman, whose husband had nearly beat her to death because she did not let his brother have a go at her. It was against her will and her husband had not accepted this. The Special Council found out later that her husband had better connections than he did so the husband never landed in jail. After the ordeal he had two choices. He could continue being the anti-hero he had always been and accept what had happened, and accept the evil taking place every day, minute by minute, all the time, all over the world, again and again. The other choice was to do something about this. The money he had and the time now available to him after being thrown on the street would make this possible. But it turned out that neither acceptance nor revenge was a viable solution. The solution was another. He had enough money stowed away in foreign accounts to hire people to take care of his problems, or rather, to take care of the world's problems. With his money and that of other millionaires who joined him, his organization grew on a continual basis. He could reverse the evil actions of people in power by simply killing one indecent, powerful person after the other. People who themselves had never held a knife but were not afraid to have others carry out their devious deeds. He eventually got his revenge and could avenge the deaths of his wife and children. And as world-history shows, there is plenty of work to get done in an ever-changing world.

VICTORIA Seymour returns to her office at Downing Street. She feels betrayed and maligned at the same time. Standing there in front of Henry and Gregg, she had felt the way Lisa had felt earlier: They've grown too powerful. At her desk, she can't keep her tears back any longer. She covers her face from the harsh world and the realities out there. The tears keep rolling down her cheeks, her grand plan, her visions for the United Kingdom will never come to fruition.

She takes a Kleenex from a near-by drawer and dries her tears. She cannot work here much longer, at least not before she has had some rest. That damn journalist! Had she taken his articles seriously, then she might not have ended up in this difficult situation and could have fired Henry and Gregg much earlier and prevented the dangerous course The Party has taken. She has become weak, without influence, she is mentally now completely finished, her career is over and done with.

How could she have been so blind? The signs were there from early on. Not many, but when added up, one could predict what was going to happen. Henry's talks about war all the time. Once he had said to her: 'If we don't have enemies or set new goals, then there will be no payback. The industries won't be able to make new products. There will be no new innovations. If we don't set new challenges that inspire our youth, they will have no motivation to improve society. Everything we have today, we can thank our ancestors who had the courage to leave the world they knew and go out and build new worlds. So, the choice is simple: either we grow or we decay. I suggest we should let the United Kingdom grow by giving it its next crisis. Every generation needs something to fight for so they can thrive afterward and appreciate what they have.'

'That's pretty philosophic,' was her answer.

'Yes it is,' was his answer.

'So, you say we should start a war to keep people on their toes?'

'Yes. That's what I'm saying.'

'You mean a war with weapons, like killing people?'

'No. Physical wars ended with the Vietnam War. Today, wars have been replaced with minor conflicts and a few civil wars. You should rather consider a trade or business war. They contribute to keeping people busy and on their toes. Scared people or those under enormous pressure are the ones who really contribute. They're the ones we want in our society. Not all those under-performers.'

'That makes sense in a way.'

'So, you see Victoria, a war, is the best way to make a nation move forward. At the moment, the United Kingdom is doing the exact opposite, as you mentioned earlier. It's falling asleep, feeding on the remnants of a long-gone past. A past that never was, an imaginary past.'

The conversation with Henry is still clear in her mind. It was before he mentioned this thing about using fat as an objective.

She leans back in her soft office chair and grabs the latest edition of the Daily Evening Mail on her desk that one of her servants had put there. Perhaps if she had read newspapers regularly instead of being so vain, she would have grasped that Henry and Gregg were doing a great job in silencing the media. She must admit that they are a great duo, they really are. When she resigns, Henry will be the one to take her throne. The only question she has left is: how does she get out of this mess without losing her reputation, her pride and her neck completely?

She needs to sleep on it for at least one night.

'A war,' she mumbles out loud to herself.'

He will get his war.

Let people think what they want of her. She will find a way to get out of the spotlight. Eventually Henry will screw up, they all do, and when he does, she will be there to pick up the pieces. Meanwhile, she will use the time to revamp her position and find a new political alliance.

'You're so absolutely right, Victoria,' she says to herself. One does not always reach the goal in a straight line. Sometimes it bends and curls many times and in many directions. Fat people cannot be blamed forever for what is going on in the United Kingdom. And that is where Henry will eventually make the biggest mistake in his professional career.

CHAPTER 16

CLOSE TO DINNER TIME, VICTORIA Seymour wakes up. She has been sleeping for four hours. She gets out of bed and puts on a fresh shirt. The first thoughts going through her mind feel a little uncomfortable and confusing, but she ignores them and focuses on what matters. It is time to find some dirt on Henry and Gregg and prepare her upcoming exit from politics.

She picks up her cell phone and speed dials Lisa.

'Hi, it's me. I know it's kind of late, but I need you to meet with me.'

'Where do you want to meet?'

'Here.'

'Where is here?'

'Downing Street.'

'Okay, I'll be there in half an hour.'

LISA FERGUSON arrives at Downing Street thirty-five minutes later. She is shown to Victoria Seymour's private living quarters. She has not been in these rooms very often. They usually meet in her office or at the cafe at Westminster or in the meeting rooms and ministries spread throughout Westminster Abbey.

'Good that you could come on such short notice,' says Victoria. 'Do you want something to eat?'

'No, it's okay. I ate right before you called.'

'I need a vacation,' says Victoria.

'You need what?' remarks Lisa, rather surprised at the comment.

'Recent events have shown that my role as Prime Minister is ending – if I ever had one. You were right in your observations about Henry, Lisa. Henry and Gregg are up to no good.'

'Oh! Thank you, Victoria!' replies Lisa. 'I thought you wouldn't come to your senses. Henry passed the red line many months ago. I don't know what to say or do anymore – apart from playing along.'

'I know. This replacement round of ministers and servants has opened my eyes. I should have taken the opportunity to get rid of those two fools long ago. I guess Henry's fortress is nearing completion, I know this now too. After I met him and Gregg last time, they thwarted me and didn't take a single word I said seriously.'

'I don't know what to say.'

'They're replacing me, Lisa. Henry and Gregg are replacing me.'

'With whom?'

'Themselves.'

'But they can't unless you resign.'

'And that's exactly what I'm about to do.'

'What? You can't do that! How will you fight them, then? Fighting them from the inside is much better than fighting them from the outside. I don't recommend it.'

'They might not be able to replace me right now, but I'm quite sure they'll find a way to do it; like sneaking in another law.'

'They could, I guess. Or ask the opposition to … I don't know.'

For a moment they are silent.

'So, what do you recommend that I do?' asks Lisa.

'I need you to get me onto the Late Morning Show tomorrow morning. I want an interview with James Dunham.'

'That's pretty short notice. I'm not sure if they'll be able to do it.'

'Oh yes they will, because I'm going to resign on open camera.'

'I can't t believe you're actually saying this.'

'I am.'

'I'll see if I can get in contact with him tonight.'

'Thanks Lisa. I'd really appreciate it.'

'But what exactly do you intend to do?'

'Not much. I'll let Henry and Gregg believe I'm backing down. I'll tell the voters that my government is stepping down.'

'You will what?'

'Tell the public that I and my government are resigning.'

'Don't do it, Victoria! There must be a better way. A way to publicly discredit Henry and Gregg.'

'I'm not sure if that's possible at the moment. The shit hangs on me. But if I go on air and proclaim that I'm not in sync with what is going on and Henry takes over power, then they're eventually going to recognize who's responsible for the shit show.'

'Well ...' laughs Lisa. 'I get your point. That could actually work.'

'You laugh, but you know what, Lisa? The truth is; the United Kingdom has always been a great nation and a nice place to live. How dare Henry, Gregg, you, me, we, or the people on the street say otherwise?'

THAT NIGHT, Victoria actually slept well – at least for a couple of hours before she woke up and started to prepare her last interview on television as Prime Minister of the United Kingdom. As she is about to leave, she does what she usually does and called her bodyguards to pick her up. She puts her long hair in a tight bun while thinking about how she is going to explain to the United Kingdom and its inhabitants that everything that is going on will now stop when she and her government step down. She gets into the black limousine. She will miss Downing Street, oh yes, she certainly will. And she will miss the excitement and the high of politics. The limousine turns onto Whitehall, driving past Westminster Palace and the Ministry of Justice on Petty France where Gregg has his office. The drive to the British Broadcasting Corporation lasts half an hour; the traffic is awful as it usually is at morning time. She would have preferred to walk on this beautiful day, but as one of the country's most despised women and as Prime Minister, she is required to always be accompanied by her five bodyguards and driven where ever she goes no matter how short the distance to her destination is.

She gets out of the limousine, followed closely by her five bodyguards, jumping out of the cars in front of and behind her. At the entrance to the broadcasting facilities, the head of the British Broadcasting Corporation receives her and brings her to the news studio where the Early Morning Show is recorded. She passes the production rooms and takes her seat on the set. James Dunham, the host, approaches her.

'Ms. Seymour. This is all so unexpected. Don't forget, we broadcast live and this is totally unprepared. May I, perhaps, be so rude as to ask how long you need and what the objective of our interview is and why this sudden, unannounced appearance?'

'Didn't my press secretary tell you?'

'The only thing she briefed us on was that you would be coming this morning to give a statement.'

'I see. Well, I'm resigning as Prime Minister.'

James Dunham and the others around Victoria are completely silent. It is difficult for her not to suppress a feeling of joy.

They keep look at her, stunned.

'You are what?' exclaims James Dunham.

'I'm resigning. I've had enough of this madness. I want to inform our nation that their government is corrupt and if it stays in power, we might end up in a dictatorship and in a much worse position than the one we were in before Brexit.'

'I'm … a kind of stunned Ms. Seymour. What … can I say? How about the other news channels? Have they been informed too … do they know?'

Victoria starts laughing. It is sincere laughter.

'No. And actually, neither does my government. The only other one who knows is Lisa Ferguson.' She observes James Dunham closely. The man really does look surprised and his producer, Felix Raymond, who is responsible for the Early Morning Show, smiles a broad smile and is probably thinking that after this he will certainly get a pay raise.

'Okay. We'll take it from here,' says James Dunham. 'You take the time you need to deliver your message. Don't think about anything else. We'll adapt the show according to your requirements.'

But it never comes to this.

Before the show starts, five very obese people with masks storm the television studio, shooting Victoria's five bodyguards at close range. Surprised at what is going on, James Dunham grabs Victoria, pushes her on the floor and throws himself on top of her. This doesn't help much. Four of the obese perpetrators herd the other employees into a corner of the studio while one goes to Victoria and James Dunham who are lying on the floor.

'Get off her,' the very obese person says.

But James Dunham doesn't move.

'I said; get off her.'

'Don't,' he says, 'She's about to announce that she's resigning as Prime Minister.'

But little does it help.

'Get off her.'

He finally moves off her.

'You shot my bodyguards,' cries Victoria.

'Don't worry, it's only a tranquilizer. For you, though, we have a special cocktail.' The man lifts his weapon and takes aim and shoots Victoria in the leg.

She feels a light sting in her right leg. When the pain gets too big, she grabs her leg with her right hand, trying to scratch the feeling away. But little does it help.

'I hope you'll burn in hell.'

The man turns around, making a sign to the others that it is time to leave. As he is about to depart, the man suddenly turns around and looks at James Dunham for a while. He raises his weapon and shoots.

'For an awful show full of shit.'

Victoria feels a sneaking dizziness come over her. She looks at James, lying to her right. Both of them can now hardly move anything except their lips.

'What did you do?' she asks James Dunham.

'I think I've been following your government's guideline a little too progressively in harassing fat people.'

'It's called overweight people, Mr. Dunham. Not fat people. That's rather rude.'

This was the last sentence Victoria managed before the dizziness was overtaken by a sensation of choking. Now only half of the air she breathes reaches her lungs. It is just enough air to stay conscious of what is going on. She recognizes it is painful to think, that this is the end, that she's going to die. She can feel it all over her body. Then the stroke comes and her heart stops beating. She senses her back and chest shooting up because of the cramps running through her central nerve system. She has never before had a heart attack. Many before her have had one and survived, but she knows her perpetrators have no intention of letting her survive. She doesn't deserve this. At least not before she has repaired the damage she and others around her have caused for the United Kingdom and many of its citizens. She is too young to die. Henry and Gregg should know this. What an evil thing they have done. They are going to exploit her death to carry out trash and then tighten up things even further. Henry will now become the new Prime

Minister, the first aristocrat of the United Kingdom in centuries.

What a son of a bitch he has turned out to be.

EPISODE 4

PERPETRAITORS

CHAPTER 17

FIVE YEARS BEFORE BREXIT something happened in Henry Montclair's life that would change it forever. A woman came into his boring life, turning everything up-side-down. She was a beautiful woman, with long brown hair and a tendency to constantly put it into a bun, then remove it and let it fall, waving it from side to side as if she was some famous actress. She would do it over and over, either just for the fun of it, or when she was nervous or when she simply had nothing better to do. Apart from her hair, her body was nearly perfect too. She had beautiful curves and a nice set of tight tits like a twenty-five year old; long, strong legs and fingers only few women can dream about. And to top it all off, her smile could seduce anyone who came in contact with her.

The first time Henry met Victoria Seymour, she was wearing a red dress. He had never seen her before but after that first encounter, he couldn't get her out of his mind. He began going into the European Union building for no apparent reason other than to catch a glimpse of her, hoping that she would notice him. She worked as an assistant to Denda Escudos, the President of the European Council and Henry felt that the risk of meeting his enemy was well worth a chance encounter with Victoria.

Henry had, at the time, been married to his wife of eighteen years. Eighteen fine and stable years, with two children, and only a few occasional lovers – not important ones and not at all like Victoria who was so full of life, so quantum solace, so dangerous to fall in love with. Oh yes, so dangerous, because when their eyes met that very first time, he knew he had to have her. What he did not know at the time, was if she was thinking the same thing. So he took it upon himself to take the risk of being caught in the corridors where he had no business being, in the corridors that belonged to Denda Escudos and his gang of criminals, as Henry referred to the President of the European Council. He simply needed to find out more about this remarkable woman.

One day he saw her leaving for home and followed her to a supermarket. He waited outside for her and when he saw her at the checkout, he wanted to go in and ask her if he could help her put her groceries into her bags. He realized, however, it might be better to first find out if she had a boyfriend like most women her age do. She looked neither happy, sad, nor satisfied. And from what he could make out of what she had bought, she probably didn't have a family or a boyfriend. She looked like someone who had found an anchor in life in her work; someone who had eventually created an X out of her husband and threw him out on the street. Would she be the kind of woman mature enough for a little comfort from another man in her life? Would she allow a stranger to penetrate her for some satisfaction in a life that has grown colorless? While he was thinking about all those questions, she went to the parking area and got into a red Toyota Corolla and put the groceries on the passenger seat. That the car was somewhat old and in need of repair, answered the question of whether she had a rich husband or boyfriend.

Following her to the supermarket had been an innocent attempt to find out more about her. Henry had never done anything like that before, but it was the lust he had for this woman that drove him to do it again and again. Not for a minute did he think about the consequences it could have for him if his wife found out. So far he had never been caught and had developed a particular talent for avoiding discovery. In his quest to find out more about Victoria- how she ticks, her habits, how she tastes- he found himself being swept off his feet every time he saw her. And that was happening more and more often now that he was frequenting the cafeteria where he now saw her almost every day. She had awoken feelings he had not had for years or perhaps had never had. He wanted his tongue to satisfy her, to be present the moment she comes. He wanted to climax at the same time as her, to open the gates of lust and fly to seventh heaven. For those reasons, Henry kept stalking her a little longer than he had planned. A day turned into two weeks, including evenings. He told his wife again and again over the telephone how beautiful some city was which he was supposedly visiting on business. It was not because he had nothing else to do but by following her day and night, he wanted to see whether or not she had a boyfriend in her life. He figured out that she wasn't living with anyone and if there was a boyfriend, he only visited three times in the time she was being stalked.

Now that Henry knew more about what was going on in her life, he started searching for that space in her life, a hole big enough to squeeze through, to become a part of her world. He knew she was already aware of him, but not enough to make her interested. Now was the question how he could make her aware of his true intentions without hurting his pride. He knew she was responsible for the coordination of activities between the European Council and the European Commission, but he wasn't exactly sure what she did. It didn't really matter to him since it wasn't his objective to find out how she earned her money.

He decided it was time to enter the empire of Denda Escudos. He would make an official visit and visit her office. So one day he simply walked in and sat down by her secretary and waited until Victoria returned from some ridiculous meeting. When she finally arrived, her eyes got big and she flashed that beautiful smile as only she could. They shook hands, their first physical contact, making him want her more than ever before. She showed him into her office and inquired what she could do for him. She closed the door after them, went to her desk and indicated where he could sit. For the first time, he saw her raise her hands to her hair and release her bun, letting her hair fall. She then tucked it behind her ears and drew it into a ponytail and by doing so thrust her chest forward, showing her breasts. He could not take his eyes of them. He knew it is inappropriate to stare at a woman's breasts too long, so he moved his glance to her lips, her rose red lips, filled with warm hot blood. They barely said anything in the 45 seconds her show went on, and after she had completed it, they sat in silence knowing that they eventually were going to get to know each other better.

'What can I help you with, Mr. Montclair?' said Victoria breaking the silence.

'I've got a problem,' he responded. 'The girl down at reception said that you can help me.'

'Well, perhaps. In what way?'

He handed her a paper with a corporate logo on it. That was all the paper had on it; the logo of a big company – one that had been in the press for some time for abusing its position on the market as a single-player. While she looked at it, he observed her closely. Her movements were gentle but somehow swift. It was a riddle why a woman like this would be together with an ugly fart like her boyfriend.

'I see,' she said. 'No, this has nothing to do with me. You need to go to the Commission. This is the Council.'

'But the girl down at reception said I should talk to you.'

'She did? Well, I guess she doesn't know anything about what we do up here.'

'You mean, like the rest of Europe?'

A mild and sincere laughter came out of her.

'Well …' she said, 'the new girl at reception still has a lot to learn.'

'So, where do you suggest I go? Do you have a name?'

'Why not try at the other building?' she pointed out her window. 'That's where the anti-trust people are. You need to talk with Evangelina Katsifaras.'

'Oh no, not her!'

'Do you know her?'

'I've heard about her and that she can be a very difficult woman to work with,' he said. But he left out the story about how close she was to telling his wife that they had it going for a couple months. Her not blowing the whistle on him had had expensive financial repercussions. 'I've seen her a couple of times at the Parliament,' he continued. 'She seems to be one tough woman.'

'I've heard this, too,' agreed Victoria. 'But that's what we need around here.'

'We certainly do! But many underestimate her because of her good wrapping.'

'I must admit that, yes, she's very well wrapped. Even a woman can see that.'

Silence.

'No, no! Don't misunderstand me,' said Henry, feeling somewhat embarrassed, realizing it could be misunderstood. 'I find you very attractive too, that's not what I intended to say.' He put his hand on his jaw, to show that he regretted what he had just said. 'I didn't want to offend …' he continued.

'That was quite sweet,' responded Victoria Seymour. 'But it's her you need to speak to about the logo. Now, if you'll excuse me, I have to attend another meeting in ten minutes. Was I helpful to you?'

'You certainly were Ms. Seymour … Well … Actually no.'

She got up from her chair, bringing up her hands to her hair to unfasten her ponytail. She then returned her hair to the previous bun. He followed her routine, again noticing her breasts, but this time her nipples had turned hard. When she moved to his side of the desk, he got up as well and followed her to her secretary's office and then out to the corridor.

'I have to go this way, she said,' shaking his hand. He took her hand and felt the warmth of her body. She started walking, but suddenly stopped and turned to him, whispering something in his ear. 'But please don't tell anyone what we've just talked about. It's rude to talk behind other colleagues' backs.'

'Of course not. Promise.'

'Good. Then we'll see each other soon!'

She smiled and turned with a momentum that was so high-energy that there would have been enough power to make her hair crush the walls if it not been in a bun. Henry just stood there for a while, watching her walk down the corridor. So, his plan had worked! He knew she knew Evangelina Katsifaras. Then they had something to talk about. But the smart thing he had done was to plant a piece of information that he found her attractive. Women do not forget things like that. And that is how the next affair begins.

IT was only a few days before Henry Montclair came up with a new plan to meet her again. At least now the foundation had been established for her to recognize him again among all the other idiots working for the European Union. He kept stalking her, now for the third week in a row. He had found out that once or twice in a week she went to gymnastics. If there was enough time, she would drop by a coffee shop not far from the European Council's building to sit down and relax and have a coffee.

So, it was time for a visit to the coffee shop. He had never been much of a coffee drinker, but since that very first day when he met her, he had become addicted to the black gold, mixed with milk which was costing him more than 900 Euro annually.

During that time, his wife thought he was traveling a lot. For days in a row he had not seen his children. He sometimes called a hooker service to the hotels in Brussels he was staying at, just to get rid of the pressure. Then the day came when he saw her sitting in the cafe after her gymnastics class and coincidentally dropped by to get a coffee too. He walked up to her and acted innocent and surprised to see her sitting there, sipping her coffee.

'Oh, don't we know each other?' he asked. 'You're the beautiful woman who knows nothing about anti-trust matters.'

'Not as much as the beautiful woman across the street,' she smiled back.

'May I join you? It's my first coffee today.'

'Of course. But isn't it a little late for coffee?'

'But you're having coffee!'

'No, today I'm having hot chocolate so I won't have problems sleeping.'

'Oh yes. I have that problem too,' he lied. And then he said, 'I'm really sorry, I didn't want to embarrass you back at your office.'

'Actually ... I think you're the one who should be embarrassed.'

The comment and sudden change of roles made him look at her in astonishment. He saw her smile and the smile-wrinkles start appearing around her eyes, again making him feel completely helpless.

'Why should I be embarrassed?' he asked.

'Because, I asked the girls at reception and they don't remember anyone asking about me.'

'Oh ...' Henry brought his hand to his face, covering half of it in an attempt to feel ashamed. But before he had the chance to protect himself, she continued talking. 'I don't think we were properly introduced. My name is Victoria.' Once again she extended her hand. 'And I hope you found what you were looking for.'

'Well, in a matter of speaking, I must admit I did.'

'Do you think I'm that stupid to not know how much you want me?'

Total silence broke out between them.

'You've been following me now for at least a couple of days. If it's sex you want, fine with me! I don't remember how stuff like that works anymore.'

It is not that often Henry was speechless, but this was one of those moments. One of God's better creatures had just invited him into her most private and guarded place.

'How about if I first invite you out to a nice candlelight dinner and then we can make love later? How about that?' he said rather eagerly.

'You bring the food and I'll cook for us.'

'But your boyfriend?'

She got up from the couch. 'He's on a business trip and I could use a good fuck.' She came closer and whispered in his ear. 'You know. You're a good looker yourself; one that turns a woman's scanner on. We just don't show it as openly as you men do.'

She kissed him on the cheek and left. Henry sat back with his coffee and a feeling of being caught with his pants down. It was only a matter of days and they would have sex. He could hardly wait.

DINNER was excellent. One must give her that. She was certainly a good cook! At least, that is what he told Victoria. All those vegetables instead of meat on his plate, was a bit hard to digest (no pun intended!). As a general rule, he does not want to take away food from animals by eating theirs, so it is better to eat the animals. That's his theory anyway – do the animals a favor by leaving the veggies and grain for them. That she was such a veggie freak was a bit of a downer, but that was probably the price she paid for her beautiful appearances. On this night, though, no matter how much of a vegetarian she was, she got her fill of meat. Before the salad bowl had been emptied, he had laid her on the table, pushed up her dress, took off her panties and licked her with his tongue. When he saw her pussy, he knew he had hit the jackpot and penetrating her, he knew this was going to be a long affair. Her tight little hole, her perfect labia produced a suction force so hard it could hold his cock forever. It felt like he had never had sex before and she acted like he was the first real man she had ever had. They functioned perfectly together, climaxing together and with such intensity that he honestly considered at that moment to leave his wife and take this woman as his personal sex slave. He did not want to end this feeling of complete lust too soon and she certainly wasn't ready to end it either. She climaxed twice, if not three times to his one and lay limp in his arms, gasping.

SO HERE they were; two very different adults having a wonderful time in bed, driven like teenagers, but mostly driven by each other's good looks. The first evening they were together, there had been no time for talking. She told him a few things about her past and present and he told her about his company and going bankrupt. This seemed to impress her, making her wet again and again.

'But why did you do it?' was her question.

'I don't know. I wanted the freedom to do whatever I wanted to do.'

'And because you're a little offended by authorities?'

'Mm. You can say this, yes. I guess our parents left some old Woodstock in us. I just … you know … I got tired of working for others. They got all the benefits of your hard work, and then if anything ever went wrong, you were the one with your head on the block.'

'How long have you worked at the European Union?'

'Not long. Perhaps a year. And I must say I'm already getting tired of it.'

'I know that feeling.'

'And you?'

'I was at Westminster and some of the ministries. And now I've been at the European Union for about twelve years. I do like it here, but the feeling is a little like the one you described. It's very difficult to make a difference. You know, big companies and institutions tend to get their own way.'

'Everything could be so much easier.'

'I honestly sometimes think about returning to London and founding my own political party.'

'I'll certainly join you.'

'You will?'

'With this wonderful sex, I don't see any alternative.'

Victoria laughed. 'You're cute. What did your company do?'

'I was investing other people's money. But after the financial crisis, it got difficult to make a profit.'

'But I guess, back then, it was a good idea?'

'It certainly was. When I started my company, I had ten quid in my pocket. Then the crisis came. At least I was good at protecting my own investments. But in the end it was a wash-out, I neither lost nor won a single quid.'

'I used to know someone who went bankrupt, too. He said he'd never experienced anything like it. The humiliation, the powerlessness, the debt he ended up with and the aftermath of finding a job and defending having to admit to others that he had gone bankrupt were all things he never wanted to experience again.'

'I went through it all, believe me. I lived with friends and relatives to save money; with girlfriends too (he left out how many). Afterwards, when I started my own company, my salary was lower than that of a student with study grants. My wife was furious with me for years for starting all over again I'm still amazed that she didn't leave me.'

'She loves you.'

'She certainly does. Once I missed out on an investment round and had to find a job somewhere. I found one at Heathrow Airport, working evenings and weekends. When you start your own company, it's near to impossible to work somewhere else. You need time for entrepreneurial activities. Unfortunately, sometimes that collides with the fact that we humans need to eat and have a roof over our head. This costs money.'

'You said you missed out on an investment round?'

'A buddy of mine screwed up. He started spending capital on things that weren't approved by our investors.'

'So, what happened?'

'In the beginning everything went fine, but only because we continuously got money from new investors. Then we had enough to pay earlier investors their interest. But of course, at some point, the bottom went out of the financial market and then they all wanted to withdraw their money at the same time. That's when they discovered that a lot of money was missing and had been invested in things that shouldn't have been invested in.'

'It sounds nasty.'

'My buddy went to jail.'

'But not you?'

'No. I could prove my innocence.'

'How?'

'It was his name on the papers, not mine.'

'But didn't he work for you?'

'He did. But it was he who was responsible for the investments. I was just vetting and selecting them.'

IT WAS a shame that she never dared to throw herself to the lions and let go of the bourgeois because of her boyfriend. But had Victoria done so, then Henry's lust might have remitted. The show stopper had to come one day, and they both knew it would happen. Her lover and also his wife began to notice abnormal behavior in their partners' sexual habits. In those 783 days of the affair he had never had better sex. Afterward, the thoughts of her tight, wet pussy were still so clear that he always felt aroused when he saw her in the corridors. He could still taste her sweet salty pussy juice on his tongue, still felt the sensation of being inside her, was still driven by the lust to bang her brains out and take her over and over again and he was sure he could smell her pussy getting wet when she walked by. How many times had he seen the longing in her eyes? And how many times had he had his tongue between her legs, making her come with an intensity he had rarely experienced with other woman, even his wife. In his sexual fantasies, the game with Victoria was far from over. In daily life, a new chapter had begun. Now they only made love occasionally when there was a tremendous urge to do so.

'Are you two acquainted?' a colleague once asked when they both were attending a meeting.

He knew he was taking a risk when he sent her that look of longing.

'Sometimes our assignments cross,' he replied.

'So!' his colleague said, changing the subject. 'Have you come up with anything, Henry?'

'Kinda,' laughed Henry at his joke.

That day she was the last to leave the meeting room. He held the door for her, observing her perfect figure as she walked by. He carefully closed the door after her, carefully correcting his pants and then walked away from her. No scene today. No scenes in the past. No scenes in the future. Only the scent of a drug that hung in the air between them, never fully wanting to evaporate.

CHAPTER 18

THE IDEA THAT TWO PEOPLE IN A relationship must be able to give solace to each other and be there when a situation requires it, is nothing new. If it is not there, there is no respect left and the relationship is over. So, in a matter of speaking, Victoria and Henry needed to make love once in a while to maintain what they in reality failed to maintain on a personal level. But as time passed, it turned out that they actually had more in common than only sex. They had politics. Their sexual adventures never fully found an end over the years although the frequency became less and less. It was the comfort they gave each other that remained. It was politics that filled their sexual void, binding them closer and closer on a psychological level. They had not expected to remain employees of the European Union and Henry later ended up at the European Parliament as a Member of Parliament which was a surprise because in the beginning things had not looked all that good for him. Perhaps it had been too big a mouthful. He had always been a critic of the European Project and one year after his arrival, the contact between Henry and his colleague, Denda Escudos, President and dictator of the European Council, as Henry called him, began to run red-hot. Over the few years of working together, they came to despise each other. At meetings, they literally tore each other's heads off. Often, people would take the side of Escudos, making Henry feel misunderstood. This misunderstanding turned into hate toward his colleagues who never quite understood the clash between Henry and Escudos. When Henry Montliar, as they started calling him behind his back, left the European Union, they were happy and Henry never forgave them for it.

At least his time at the European Union, first at the European Commission and then some years later at the European Parliament, gave him new purpose in his professional career. Months later, back in London with his family, he began giving lectures and interviews on television shows about how awful the European Union is. It always made him angry to see the Eurocrats waste taxpayer money on the strangest things and the unfairness there was towards the United Kingdom which was one of the biggest contributors to the

European budget although they received nothing in return. From early on, Henry discovered how most civil servants working for the European Union simply just sat there doing nothing other than cashing in every month their salaries, fees, and allowances. In addition, they worked fewer hours per week than is standard within the industry. As an entrepreneur before he began working at the European Union, he had to work hard for every single penny. His job at the European Union, threw him completely off balance when he saw the billions and billions that were, in his opinion, wasted on infrastructure projects in Romania, Bulgaria, Slovenia and Croatia and other East-bloc countries that nobody really cared about. If he had had as much money that the EU wasted every day, every week, every year at his disposal back then, he could have changed the world into a better place for his investors and himself.

Then there are the strange decisions made by the Eurocrats, a name that upset him when others used it for him. The weird laws and rules, the over-regulation of practically every simple little thing the European Commission forced him to prepare for the European Council on strange things to harmonize such as traffic signs, regulations for vacuum cleaners and refrigerators. It was always some idiot from the European Commission who figured out that the environment could be improved if vacuum cleaners used half the energy they used to use. This would supposedly force the industry to design more efficient devices. However, on a flight home to London for the weekend, he had met an expert who told him that this would only benefit the German vacuum cleaner industry, not that of the United Kingdom. One regulation that he had to prepare for the European Council made him completely blow up. It was a regulation for the disposal of refrigerators. One used to just throw them in a hole at the landfill but now a foreign power should decide what is good and bad for the environment and not the United Kingdom itself. Suddenly, refrigerators had become hazardous and had to be disposed of in specially authorized treatment facilities, irritating a lot of householders who also had to pay a waste recycling tax that went directly into the pockets of the Eurocrats. And then there was the tax on recycling for households which forced people like his wife to separate waste. There were also regulations on light bulbs that restricted the use of traditional light bulbs with a warm light to low energy models that were the favorite of the German industry.

The light bulb regulations still make him angry. Actually, there were a lot of things that upset him when he worked for the European Union. At least, one thing his colleagues there never achieved was to change the UK's electric outlets. They were unsafe, yes, but unique to the United Kingdom and no one wanted to change to the new standardized electric outlets recommended by the European Union, which were based on the German technical norms. Working for the European Union was like accepting the invasion of his homeland. It was an invasion that all the traitors in his country who ignored what was going on in Brussels were complicit in. The European Union is nothing but an attempt by foreign nations to destroy the United Kingdom's proud traditions and political system, with Germany as its leader. They might have lost World War II, but it seemed as though through the European Union, Germany had found a way to slowly win the war by tearing the United Kingdom to pieces. He made it his life mission to save his homeland from this sneaking invasion. In the first place, people must learn to think differently about the European Union. Up till now he has not been able to understand why the people of the United Kingdom allowed it to happen in 1975. Why would they vote to let the European Union interfere in its affairs and politics?

A good example of this was that, before the EU, British citizens could simply show their passports at Customs when entering their own country. Now they have to line up with all other EU passengers and have even lost their loved, blue passports which have been replaced by the burgundy passports of the EU. Why would the United Kingdom be complicit in its own downfall? Much of the European Union's legislation has had a negative impact on the economy of his homeland, and has done nothing to reduce the red tape in its wake of membership. The European Union, with all its regulations, is the number one reason why the United Kingdom is not capable of really taking off and blooming as it did in colonial times with the Commonwealth when it was an industrial and global military power. Even the courts no longer have anything to say because the traitors in Westminster accepted the fact that European Union law overrules British law and all disputes are ultimately overseen by the European Court of Justice in Luxembourg instead of the courts in the United Kingdom. He did not know all this before coming to Brussels, but he now knew that he was right in being skeptical of the European Project, as well as the Lisbon Treaty which prevents the United Kingdom from being the sovereign nation it has always been.

Yes, 1975 was really an insanely sad year. It was the year when the United Kingdom ended up in this mess and surrendered to foreign powers. Instead of continuing down this disastrous path, they should have ended it in 1975 when they had the chance. But the population was too dumb to figure it out back then, that the European Union is nothing but a bunch of criminals filling their own pockets at the expense of the taxpayer. The European Commission is so ridiculously corrupt, being bribed by industry that it would be better for the United Kingdom to stay out. He realized this in his first job at the European Commission, and when he later was offered a job as Member of Parliament, he took it because it was a good pay raise and an opportunity to stop the madness of turning Europe into a self-serving pulp of uniformity. Had it been otherwise in 1975, remaining outside the Union would have meant that the United Kingdom would maintain the right to decide on its own sovereignty, be fully independent from others deciding its destiny and not be forced to go along with regulations from weird countries like Slovenia and Croatia. The United Kingdom would have been freed of having to follow regulations uninitiated by a Union that is almost as unlawful as a nation ruled by dictators.

And now there are talks about inviting even further nations into the European collaboration; countries from southeast Europe such as Turkey, Macedonia, Montenegro, Serbia and Albania; countries where people have sixteen children and only want to come to England to freewheel on its society and goods. Under EU regulations, the United Kingdom has nothing to say. It is obligated to open its borders and its wallet and let the scum flow in. The free movement within the European Union gives half a billion Europeans the right to come to the United Kingdom and steal and rape and mistreat women, to take away jobs and housing, abuse the school system and overload the National Health Care system, making it difficult for UK citizens to live a decent life. The expansion of the European Union will not improve the situation. It will only make it worse and this is why it has become so important for him to get the United Kingdom out of this madness and enable it to act on its own again. This is urgently needed after the disastrous decision to remain in the European Project, voted on by all the naive voters back in 1975.

VICTORIA SEYMOUR, on the other hand, had always been a true Eurocrat and did not mind being called one as she saw things from a completely different perspective than Henry. She thought that collaboration among nations was the only way to ensure continued security and prosperity in an ever faster moving world in which North-America and Asia were competing at large in areas such as technology, high-tech knowledge, high-tech products and, to some extent, also education. She was very well aware of the weaknesses the European Union had, but tried to come to terms with the hopeless bureaucracy, the inefficiencies, cultural conflicts and self-interests of the system. Working for the European Union was no different from working for a large global corporation.

She preferred to focus on the strengths that the European Union provided. Ten percent of the work force in the United Kingdom was either directly or indirectly dependent on trade with the European Union. Immigrants, not only from Europe, but also from outside, were needed to keep the economy going, where more work required more workers than were available in the UK. At least this is what the statistics said that Victoria so much loved to read before bedtime. If people would bother to look into statistics just once, they would find that there is a big difference between how immigration is reported by the tabloids and how it actually looks. Immigration is unavoidable, especially in a world where any point on the earth is reachable within 48 hours. People fleeing from wars and conflicts and people searching for a better life should be seen as a resource not as a problem. And again, when reading statistics, immigrants have always contributed more to the societies they live in than they take from them.

How trade, free from barriers and bureaucracy, moves within the European Union is what interests her. No Spanish, French, Dutch, or Greek authority has the power to say what you are allowed to export and import, whether you have exceeded your import quota or what products you are allowed to ban. It has become easy to sell, distribute and transport products as well as services, knowledge and labor. This can all be done without red tape due to a continuous unification and standardization of national laws, meaning that manufacturers all over the European Union do not have to adapt to 28 different national requirements but only to one, contributing to major savings in the development and sale of products. Products, services, knowledge and labor cross borders in no time, making the European Union's common market the biggest and freest multi-national trade zone in the world, representing 15 percent of global trade. The benefits for businesses in the United Kingdom and all the other European Union member nations, is easy access to 507 million customers in 28 countries. The region she lives in exports around 44 percent of its goods and services with financial services making up almost 80 percent of its total exports according to her statistics. What people still do not tend to fully grasp, is how easy their daily lives have become. They fail to comprehend that this easiness has become the cornerstone for all European Union member nations and for the stability of their economies.

The European Union is often blamed for being a protectorate. This is true. It protects technology, companies and jobs from being traded freely on the world market on behalf of European Union citizens. With this common market, a basis has been created for investors and foreign companies to invest and establish factories in the European Union, creating lots of technology and new jobs. The United Kingdom is a popular destination due to its language and acts as gateway to 27 other nations with the exact same standards as those in the United Kingdom. She knows there are doubts about the bureaucracy in the European Union which prevents it from working fully efficiently, but, in her opinion, this is a low price to pay for an institution that provides prosperity and geopolitical stability. It is true that the European Commission puts its nose into almost everything, and that if a fire was to be fuelled by regulations from the European Commission it would burn for weeks. But she would prefer this kind of fire to the import and export fires that burned in the 70s and 80s between neighboring nations. More than 40,000 laws make up four decades of European industrial and political standardization, resulting in 15,000 court verdicts and 62,000 international standards, all of which must be respected and obeyed by citizens and companies in the European Union and by industries outside the common market. The number of binding acts is higher than 134.500 if all are counted together. But also here people tend to forget that, compared to local laws, European Union laws only account for about one-eighth of total local legislation. As she always jokes, burning all the European Union regulations would be great, but unfortunately, they would all have to be rewritten the next day to keep the 28 nations functioning.

She finds it strange how many people don't appreciate what the European Union does for its citizens. They have become used to things working across borders, and become used to the free movement of practically everything, including themselves, forgetting how it once was when there were borders and customs and different regulations. People who complain about this have absolutely no idea what would happen if the European Union would suddenly cease to exist or if a right-wing politician came to power and destroyed what has been built up through decades of political collaboration and industrial integration. Free trade deals are, for instance, free from the World Trade Organization's totally non-compliant and insufficient world trade regulations. The European Union, with its 507 million inhabitants, can protect its interests, its consumers, its industries and environment much better that if the 28 member nations were to do it alone. People tend to read only the negative headlines, not the positive. One example of the many advantages of the EU is the European Union safety directives introduced in 1996 by Denmark. These standards represented the highest safety standards world-wide, reducing workplace fatalities in the United Kingdom by half. Today all over the EU, the little, white running man green fire exit sign, tells you wherever you are, whether in a movie theater in Greece or a restaurant in Finland, where the exit is. Another detail is the emergency number 112 or 110 for the police which is standard throughout Europe, making it easy for tourists to make a call when necessary. The United Kingdom, however, has chosen to keep 999 as their emergency number. There are the rights of expectant mothers that enable them to return to their jobs after maternity leave, and the bans on age, color, race religion or sexual orientation discrimination. The high roaming charges for cell phones have now been removed, making it possible to telephone at local rates all over the European Union as well as lower fees for ATM withdrawals outside the country of your bank. Airlines must also pay proper compensation when flights are delayed or cancelled and the Erasmus student exchange program allows students to study at any university within the European Union. All of these benefits are without cross border bureaucracy and the tons of paperwork that used to be necessary thanks to the European Union's attempts to simplify and harmonize matters that once were difficult. It has become so easy to be a European citizen today. But here are always people who do not seem to appreciate it, like her lover, Henry Montclair.

The most important aspect of the European Project is its history. It took a fierce and deadly war, ending in 1945, in which more than 60 million people died, to finally make Europe settle down and agree on peace. Since World War II, there has never been a longer period of peace and prosperity, apart from the conflict in Yugoslavia in the 1990ties. The economies of the European Union's member nations are now so intertwined that it would be almost impossible to repeat what happened at the beginning of the 20th century. It is odd that there are people who want the European Project to break up, knowing that the consequences would lead to the next big European conflict. The European Union voices common political standpoints with one strong voice instead of 28 smaller ones. Within the collaboration through the European Arrest Warrant Agreement program and Europol, the European police agency, allows member nations to access each other's databases to search for criminals all over the European Union. Collaboration on political levels like these matter, because they strengthen and create flexibility among nations in a world that is constantly changing and in which individual nations have little to say.

IN THEIR hefty discussion about politics, which they both understood quite well although they had different views and backgrounds, they never seemed to agree on anything. The only point that they could agree on was, that if they were in power, the United Kingdom would be a much better place to live in. They would always end up with this conclusion, simply to prevent the heated debates from hurting one another. This was occasionally followed by hot, heated sex to make sure that their relationship would remain as it was.

But then one day things changed. Victoria decided it was time to leave the European Union and return to London. She finally gave up on all the bureaucracy and the late nights that didn't in any way contribute to anything worthwhile either for her or for Europe. It came as a shock to Henry. They had often talked about founding their own political party, but it was nothing but an internal joke. What Henry never realized was that for her, it was less of a joke and more of a future. She was confident enough to believe that if she actually did establish her own party and won the confidence of some of the voters, she would be able to make a difference instead of just talking about it. Her political plan was simple; abolish mob and direct democracy; people do not know much about politics anyway. Even politicians seem to stumble most of the time. Institute a simplified version of parliamentary democracy; make the process so simple that politics and its implementation would be more efficient.

But there was a problem. Victoria had no money, no sponsors, and no resources available to actually get it going. Henry solved her problems in his own typical way, by earning money holding speeches about the rotten

European Union while still working for the European Union. This, of course, turned him into one of the most unpopular, despised and unwanted person to ever sit in the European Parliament as he was more involved with promoting his own ideas rather than those of his employer.

But Henry did not care. When they kicked him out, his criticism of the European Union turned out to be quite good business back in the United Kingdom, good enough for both of them to live on until they found sponsors for The Party. He was glad to be back in London, back to his family and also with Victoria.

Unfortunately, Henry had never been the one of three sons his parents would have called bright. Smart and a survivor, but not bright. And they certainly never expected him to become a politician. As toddler, as a young boy and as a teenager, their son always seemed to be behind all the others – or at least it felt that way, compared to his two older brothers. But one thing he had always been good at was convincing others that whatever he said was correct and right, no matter how often he changed his mind. As the old saying goes: there are two sides to every problem but only one common solution. We often tend to forget this in a battle. It's a natural thing, but unfortunately also devastating because of our tendency to see things from our own perspective. Ordinary people would probably recognize this relatively early in their lives, realizing that hindsight can be applied as an efficient tool to make us better persons. But when attempting to use empathy to understand others, it often makes us end up with the wrong conclusions insuring that the next conflict is just around the corner.

Henry, never came this far in his personal development because of his skills to manage words efficiently. How we humans tend to behave in conflicts, and the self-reflection that ought to follow, often is so blurred from our incapacity to admit that we might be wrong that justification of any kind is used to make our indiscretions right. Forgiveness is probably the only real tool that works for most situations. But to admit that we might be wrong is probably the most difficult skill anyone should learn because in doing so, we admit to our imperfections and leads to others seeing our vulnerabilities. Even worse; it means that we might have to change our behavior.

Henry's complete failure to self-reflect and recognize his imperfections always gets in the way of rectifying things. He tends to continue with his lies, thus turning his life into a messy affair. One of the few people, who can keep him and his lies in check, is not his wife, but Victoria Seymour.

Henry's biggest challenge with Victoria is preventing her from making easy things complicated and to complicate easy things. In other words; he understands women quite well.

The first people who voted for The Party turned out to be a rather mixed bunch and from all levels of society. The Party grew bigger and bigger, and with it, the re-awakening of Victoria's childhood ambition of one day getting into Parliament and becoming Prime Minister. It had looked rather good back then and more and more people climbed on board. This was when Gregg White showed up. Victoria was not thrilled about having him join their cause. His opinions were too extreme in opinions and his way of communicating with other people was not the best. But Henry insisted, arguing that she could not always have it her way. Lisa Ferguson on the other hand, was nothing but a young woman in her early thirties who appeared randomly and asked for an internship at The Party. During her internship, she figured out that public relations in politics was a closer call to her than doing public relations for industry.

CHAPTER 19

HENRY'S SUGGESTION to use fat as an agenda for election purposes was one of the most ridiculous things Victoria had ever heard from him. But, as always, Henry had a very fine way of manipulating words. When he convinced her to think it over that day when they were drinking coffee at the little cafe in Westminster, she decided to sleep on it. But she never got back to him on the subject and the next morning, she still had not given it any more thought. When Henry pulled her aside and asked if they should talk with the others about it, she recalled their conversation.

During the election after Brexit, there was enough to do to get The Party to power. For some weeks Victoria and Henry used fat as a standing joke to compensate for the unforgiving late hours and stress of being on the campaign trail. Back then, Victoria had spent a lot of time developing The Party's political manifesto. Henry liked its contents from day one, just as Gregg and Lisa did. But contrary to Victoria, they saw some issues in its realization as voters did. The Party had actually done quite well in polls. But Henry and Victoria's constant split views on the European Union exhausted some voters. And though Victoria and Henry never really solved the problem about whether they were for or against the European Union, Brexit solved the issue for them and Victoria decided to retreat on the question. But polls showed that The Party was not fully capable of sending a message that people understood loud and clear on how to implement Victoria's excellent political manifesto. The other parties, the old, established ones, were better trained through years of expertise in handling elections and voters. Victoria knew that Brexit and leaving the European Union would not improve the situation of the United Kingdom's rather honest economic deficit. Instead, it might lead to a downfall of its economy which would not make the United Kingdom great again. It would probably mean reduced healthcare for the poorest and part of the middle class and a lack of a good educational system because of stretched budgets. Industry would find it difficult to sell products in quantities that keeps them afloat, turning domestic products so expensive that people would hardly be able to afford them. Greg, Lisa and Victoria all knew that leaving the European

Union would not be a good idea, but the people had voted and Henry did not care about the practical details. It was not a message that The Party could use as a selling point.

At least they saw one benefit that the old and established political parties did not have. They could be used as a protest party for people to dump their votes. When chaos rules and people are frustrated, they tend to lose their common sense and sound reasoning. Henry's campaign about fat were, in a way, pretty much in alignment with the situation in the United Kingdom, and how stupid it had all become. When Henry kept coming up with his ridiculous fat suggestion, Gregg, Lisa and Victoria began to laugh less although they still didn't think much of it.

'Henry. Now we've heard your suggestion for the fifth time this week. It's not funny anymore,' said Victoria.

'I still find it funny,' said Gregg.

'That's what people expect from you, Gregg. I must say, I slowly find all these jokes rather insulting,' declared Lisa.

Gregg laughed. 'Come on, Lisa! Why now so honest?'

'Because instead of being funny, it's beginning to sound discriminating. That's why.'

'I'll bet you, Henry, it will never work anyway,' said Gregg.

'That's what I've been telling him all morning,' remarked Victoria.

'But how much 'fat person' are we talking about?' asked Gregg.

'I would say a Body Mass Index of above 35. That's quite oversized.'

'But how?' Gregg wanted to know.

'How what?'

'How do we get people to accept the fact that fat is not good for society?'

'I don't know. But Victoria is an excellent speaker. I'm sure she'll figure out a way to turn the topic to our advantage.'

'I will?' responded Victoria.

'I still find it a ridiculous topic,' remarked Lisa. 'It's a kind of despicable. My mother is a little obese.'

'Easy now, Lisa,' remarked Henry.

Then she continued, 'But I agree with Gregg. It won't work anyway.'

'But fat people *is* a problem for society.'

'I haven't really talked about fat people. I've just said that fat costs society a lot of money.'

'But how do you want to make people aware that there is a problem?' asked Victoria.

'You see, that's the problem, isn't it?' replied Henry. 'We need an event, something that pushes people's attention to fat.'

'You mean like fat people attacking a fast-food restaurant because there's a rumor burgers will be banned,' laughed Gregg.

'Listen to yourself,' remarked Lisa. 'Can you hear how dumb you sound?'

'No. But I fully understand what Henry is saying.'

'The first thing we ought to do is to talk a lot about the subject,' suggested Henry. 'Talk a lot about fat and how it affects our society. If people hear it often enough, they will start to believe it. Lisa, I know you have contacts in the media. This talk show host … uhm … what's the show called … Mm …'

'The Early Morning Show with James Dunham. Is that what you mean? I watch his show from time to time. It's designed to make me feel better and after watching all those low-lives with their ridiculous problems, I do actually feel better.'

'Most of those people are overweight,' remarked Gregg, thereby admitting that he too had seen the show.

'I find it an amazing waste of time watching stuff like that,' said Victoria. 'There are more important things; such as politics and winning elections …'

'Isn't this Dunham shacking the young blonde from Eastenders?'

'I thought he was married?'

'Yeah, he has four children and a beautiful wife.'

'I don't recall the young woman's name, but she's quite well-wrapped.'

'That's why he's on her,' said Henry. 'Any married man would do the same.' He notices Victoria's eyes clamping together for a split second. 'Could we stick to the subject of fat?' she asked.

'Look,' says Henry. 'I'm just saying that I believe fat can be used to draw attention to us. I mean, with Brexit there is so much going on that people simply don't want to talk about it anymore. They need something new, something that can draw their attention away from the current discussion.'

'Hm.'

'But fat. Honestly, Henry. I don't see how that would work.'

'Why don't we make a list of fat people, now when we're at it? Then put them into camps and gas them?' asked Lisa. 'That would make voters notice us.'

'Don't be so ridiculous, Lisa,' responded Victoria.

Henry continued, 'Contrary to you, I've actually done some research on the subject. Fat is a major concern to our society. I had this talk with Victoria two weeks ago and she told me, she's been there.'

'Henry, we don't have to talk about it here.'

'What do mean 'been there'?' asked Lisa.

'When I was young, I was pretty … chubby,' explained Victoria.

'I can't imagine. Not with your body!'

'It's amazing what knives can do. I know we've had fun about this, but in a way I'm beginning to understand Henry. Think how many people die from heart attacks due to health issues associated with fat or other related deceases. My father is an example of one of those victims. I could have been one too. It's a self-inflicted problem. And why should society and other people pay for this?'

'True,' said Henry. 'Actually, statistics from the World Health Organization says that …'

'Since when do you read statistics?' asked Victoria.

'I just wanted to check up on what the Body Mass Index for a healthy life is. Did you know that the average BMI in the United States is 27,5? They're the heaviest nation in the world. In Canada, it's only 26, compared to Ethiopia with an average of 21, although their women have a BMI of 28 and more.'

'Well, not my wife!'

'Yes, you've trained her well Gregg. I'll give you that. But she doesn't come from Ethiopia, does she?'

'No. She's from Russia.'

'I don't even know what a Body Mass Index is,' said Lisa.

It is Victoria who asks. 'What Body Mass Index did you figure out is good for a decent quality of life?'

'Around 27. I'd say the transition starts from 25 to 30. At 28 you end up on your doctor's observation list. And according to the World Health Organization, when you're over a Body Mass Index of 30, then you're pretty much in trouble. So, I'd suggest a Body Mass Index of 35, is a good limit for life-quality issues. Things start to seriously deteriorate beyond that point. You don't want to be in the swimming pool when one of those jumps into it.'

'Sounds like a mini-Tsunami to me,' joked Gregg.

Henry continued, 'People with a Body Mass Index of above 35 are in the minority. They're the ones that are the most expensive for the healthcare system. So it justifies my strategy that something should be done when someone is over this value.'

'What do you mean with; justifies my strategy?' asked Lisa. 'I'm not familiar with anything in our political manifesto discriminating against people just because they are fat.'

'Fat is not only a problem for fat people, but for society as such. Someone's got to pay the bill,' argued Henry.

'This is ridiculous! There are no valid arguments for discriminating against fat people. Why don't you go and discriminate against some Europeans or Muslims, like the rest the United Kingdom is doing?' exclaimed Lisa.

Henry laughed scornfully, 'No valid arguments? Then try with these: Fat people are not very well educated. They have difficulties finding jobs because they're fat, so most end up on welfare. They're tremendously costly for the healthcare sector. They sweat and stink because they hardly get a chance to do anything about their hygiene because they can't reach the places that need to be cleaned. Only very few decision makers are fat people. Fat people are a wasted resource in the global competition for resources and maintaining our healthcare system. They take up unnecessary space in cinemas, buses, and airplanes, making it annoying for others to be close to them. And they have a major effect on the environment because they eat too much, simply because they don't have the self-discipline to do anything about it and are always stuffing in their mouths.'

The group went silent for a long moment.

Gregg started laughing.

'Can you also say anything nice about fat people?' asked Lisa.

'Why?'

'Wow, Henry,' said Victoria. 'You did your homework on this one, didn't you? Why didn't you do the same with Brexit?'

'Why don't you make fat people wear an armband stating they are fat, just like the Nazi's did with the Jews?' asked Lisa turning red in the face.

'Why? Don't you think their size makes them noticeable?'

Again Gregg laughed.

The comment made Lisa almost explode. But she kept it together. 'That's not what I meant,' she said

'Then let people sympathizing with them wear one.' suggested Gregg.

'Mm, that's actually not a bad idea. Got any idea for a text?'

'I am a Fat Swine's supporter,' laughed Gregg.

'No, too long,' giggled Henry.

'Minister of pig riding?'

'Ha ha, that one is good. But we need to save space for a pig on it as well.'

'Yeah, that's good. A pig!'

'Both of you stop it!' shouted Victoria. 'Enough of this talk! We've had enough of the nonsense and the topic is not funny any longer. We have an election to win. So please come up with constructive ideas that make sense and convince people to vote for us.'

'I still find the idea with the yellow armband excellent,' commented Gregg.

'I said stop it!'

BUT HOW would Victoria know? How would she know, though she despised the conversation, just like Lisa did, that the seed Henry eventually succeeded in planting in her head, would grow; that she would finally use it when she was under pressure to find a simple answer to where the money should come from for the military after its failure in Syria, saying the words that now have become famous:

Fat people.
Fat people will pick up the bill.
Most haven't had military service.

None of the four people attending that fateful meeting could ever have imagined that the word 'fat', would actually slip out of Victoria's mouth.

At least … not in public.

EPISODE 5

EVIL NEVER DIES

CHAPTER 20

THE NEWS ABOUT A TERRIBLE TERROR attack at the British Broadcasting Corporation in London by five very obese people, spread through the United Kingdom and rest of the world as fast as ones and zeros can move through glass fibers. The sudden and dreadful death of Victoria Seymour has meant relief for some and for others, uncertainty and turmoil. Opinions spread like wildfire on social media, varying according to who writes them and Lisa Ferguson's department of State Communication and Promotion, on behalf of Henry Montclair, can simply not censor the rumors fast enough. The official and conventional media are more careful in how they approach the news. They know what happens if they go too far. In spite of Victoria Seymour's death, who knows what will come next.

The death of The Party's front figure has quickly put The Party into a vacuum. Who is going to take over the Prime Minister's role? Will there be new elections? Lisa Ferguson is about to provide the public with an official statement on what happened and how it happened. She skims through the three-pager, then stops in disbelief before walking out of 10 Downing Street. She is not really sure if she wants to announce what Henry Montclair has written for her. Due to the murder of Victoria Seymour and James Dunham there are now new consequences for people with a Body Mass Index above 35.

'Are you ready?' asks one of Lisa's colleagues.

'I'm certainly not, but I guess this is what I get paid to do.'

She gets her act together, sighs, then lets the servant open the door and walks to the podium. She sees that not only the local press is waiting but also the world press. She puts down the papers on the small desk and begins to read:

Today at 6:30am, our Prime Minister, Victoria Seymour, was assassinated by some mad people at the British Broadcasting Corporation while trying to do her job for the United Kingdom. In this act of unbelievable evil and terror, five obese terrorists assassinated

James Dunham, the host of the Late Morning Show, as well, without any reason. Five bodyguards and four employees of the British Broadcasting Corporation were also shot and were unable to assist Victory Seymour in her struggle to survive. At 6:35pm, the terrorists left the studio, shooting one security guard. The terrorists were wearing black masks and dressed in street clothes. Their common denominator is; they are very fat and therefore recognizable. The terrorists are still at large and all citizens are requested to report to the police, or military, or special units on the street if they saw suspicious fat people in the area of the British Broadcasting Corporation in the hours between 6am to 8am this morning. Rumors say that Victoria Seymour was considering resigning as Prime Minister. This is, however, not true.

To assure the safety of United Kingdom citizens, the military has been informed to assist the police and the authorities to track down these very obese terrorists. For the next four weeks, martial law is enforced under the direction of Gregg White, responsible for the Ministry of Justice. Henry Montclair will take over the position as interim Prime Minister until the government has re-arranged itself.

As a consequence of the terror attack on Victoria Seymour, laws will be implemented to prevent further assassination attempts of politicians and civil servants. Lately, several attempts have been carried out by fat people nation-wide, and enforcement is now required to bring back the United Kingdom to a safe and secure state. The curfew between 11pm and 07am for people with a Body Mass Index above thirty-five will remain as will the ban on attending demonstrations. The current ban on groups of three or more will be reduced to two persons. England is on the brink of a civil war because fat people are ruining the lives' of its citizens. Any acts disobeying these regulations will be punished with fines and imprisonment.

People ask when the Fat Tax will be revoked. The government has decided that in view of the latest incidences, the law will not be revoked. Statistics show that health in the United Kingdom is improving and the average weight has decreased a few percentage points. This is proof that the government's strategy of making the nation fit for after Brexit is working.

Furthermore, The Party, has decided to implement its biggest challenge so far. The government will call its project - Efficiency Through Joy – an initiative for people with a Body Mass Index of less than 35. These decent, hard-working citizens will be entitled to two weeks free vacation from The Party in Newquay in South England. An artificial lagoon with beaches and 20.000 hotel beds are in the planning. All rooms will have a view of the ocean; there will be cinemas and theatres, sports facilities, a healthcare center and a daycare center for children. The initiative has been introduced as a reward for the regular and decent, hard-working population who work hard and thereby contribute to our national pride by making the United Kingdom great again. Furthermore, there will be access to swimming pools, fitness centers, restaurants, a new amusement park, a surfing and sailing park and an expansion of the local zoological garden and aquarium. Press releases and further information about – Efficiency Through Joy are available on The Party's website.

'We're not answering questions today,' Lisa adds, while gathering her papers. She turns her back on the press and returns through the door of 10 Downing Street. She is numb and completely in shock about the ridiculous bullshit she has just read to the public.

INSIDE 10 Downing Street Lisa throws herself onto the couch so often used by Victoria Seymour and, occasionally, herself. One of the servants comes to her and asks if she would like something to drink.

'Yes, please. Bring me something strong. And make it big.'

'As you like, Ms.'

'Oh, by the way, have you seen Henry anywhere?'

'No Ms.'

That is good, she thinks, because, if he were here, she would probably kill him with her bare fists. She is not enthusiastic about Henry's speech or, for that matter, the man himself. The announcement, or the so called speech to the people, made a lot of promises but did not mention a single thing about the former Prime Minister's life. Nor did it express any regrets about what is going on. Standing there at the podium, reading the terrible speech, she recognized that this is far from ending. If she knows Henry Montclair, he is going to use her as a scapegoat and let the population get rid of steam on Victoria. It's amazing how The Party keeps putting the blame on someone else.

'Efficiency Through Joy,' she groans through two tight lips. For her, it sounds like a place where people gather and are indoctrinated with all kinds of party propaganda about how great the United Kingdom once was and will again become. Cinemas? What kind of movies are they going to play there? Old movies about the empire? Great Fake News bulletins about the future and all the good things that are happening? Free restaurants, sports, child care; what game is Henry playing? Training the youth for the next big war? For 1984? Or copying Germany in its early thirties? For her 'Efficiency Through Joy', sounds like a place where the next batch of loyal party scum are to be vetted and then selected. Good soldiers of The Party.

'ARE WE ready to rumble?' asks Chris Campbell.

'Yes.'

'Then turn on your walkie talkies.'

'Sound check.'

- Click, click, click -

'Try to keep radio silence for as long as possible,' says Marcus Schmidt. 'Transmit only if unwanted guests are detected – or in an emergency.'

'Got it.'

'Any questions?' he asks. 'No? That's good. The mission starts in 45 minutes. Synchronize your watches, gentlemen … aaaand … now!'

'Okay, let's move.'

Chris starts walking to his appointed stakeout. It is 800 meters from the parked car. After a long and sweaty 17 minute walk through corn fields and forest, he arrives at an opening where the bumpy and battered road passes through. The GPS unit indicates that he has arrived at his destination. He finds a place behind a bunch of bushes and pulls out a 10-pack of Snickers. They did not have time to eat. He thought they were going to spend the time in a hotel but that didn't happen. If anyone is to discover him, it will be because his growling stomach gives him away.

ANDY remains at the rented car. Due to his weight, there is no major role for him to play apart from driving the escape car – if this is required. He sees Marcus and Mike walking out of his sight and is a little envious. Had he been a little less overweight, he would have gone with them. However in the event of a retreat that required running, he would have absolutely no chance of survival.

MARCUS and Mike arrive at the fence, at the agreed GPS position. Marcus takes out a wire cutter and starts cutting a hole large enough for them both to pass through. Mike pushes the cut metal inward and bends it down to the ground.

'Okay,' says Marcus, 'That should do it, don't you think?'

'I believe so. But we'll still have to wait twenty-six minutes before the mission starts.'

'Sound check,' says Marcus into the walkie talkie.

'Road here.'

'Car here.'

'Sound check complete.'

Marcus and Mike stay at the fence and begin their wait. 'The waiting is always the worse,' says Marcus. 'But we can use the time to observe the two guards at the gate.' He points to the gate and the little guard house. One man is sitting inside; another is walking his rounds back and forth along the barrier to the entrance.'

'That one who is walking could become a problem,' remarks Marcus. 'He has full view of the entrance area every time he walks back to the guard house. How're we going to go from that point there,' he points at a couple of barrels providing visible protection, ' to the entrance?'

'Hm,' thinks Mike. 'That's not the only problem. The entrance is illuminated. If we get behind those barrels, we only have twenty seconds to get inside before the guard turns around.'

'Did you calculate the time?'

'Yes.'

'And it's illuminated inside as well.'

'Two trucks on their way,' they hear Chris whisper into the walkie talkie.

'Roger.'

Only minutes later, they hear something approaching. It is a deep buzzing sound, almost like an invasion. Both guards at the gate are outside, ready to receive the convoy. The one who was walking along the barrier, opens the gate and the trucks drive through.

Mike starts shooting pictures. 'That's probably why the place is illuminated,' suggests Marcus. 'Remember the satellite images? This is where they parked the truck. They don't drive into the catacombs.'

'The entrance is too small. But that's good. If they offload here, we don't need to go inside to take pictures. I'm fine with that. Believe me!'

The two trucks are painted in the German military's colors and make a 180 degree turn in the forecourt. They park parallel to each other less than 30 meters from the entrance. Then the drivers and passengers jump out to loosen the tarpaulins on the deck to access the payload. Mike takes a constant flow of pictures. When he sees a man jump onto the load of the first truck, pulling out bodies, he lowers the camera and cannot believe what he is seeing. One overweight person after another other is thrown brutally down onto the hard concrete. Dead, overweight people.

'Take pictures for Christ sake,' whispers Marcus, punching him hard on the shoulder.

Mike awakens from his trance and continues snapping.

Then something happens at the entrance to the catacombs. A crew of four comes out, dressed in white scrubs and pulling trolleys behind them. More bodies are thrown out of the trucks. Some corpses need three or four of the crew to pull them onto the trolleys. Mike counts fifty-three bodies through his camera lens. Then he notices something odd.

'It's not just obese people.'

'I've noticed.'

'But regular people as well.'

'I would suggest they're critics of the system.'

'Uh, this is not good!'

'Stop talking! Keep photographing.'

Mike keeps the photographs rolling. When the two trucks are empty, a man closes the tarpaulins on both military trucks. The men who pulled out the payload return to the driver cabins. Doors slam and engines ignite. The two guards at the guard house open the gate to let the trucks out. When they have passed, Mike sees the crew of four pull away with the trolleys. They keep returning to get all people stowed away. After maybe ten minutes, all lights are turned off.

The place fall silent.

Mike sits in the dark. His hands are shaking. He takes out two memory cards from his inner pocket and sticks the first one into the camera. 'I'll make you a copy. These pictures must be backed up,' he says to Marcus. He then makes a copy for himself. 'I cannot believe this,' he comments in disgust. 'This is a nightmare for the United Kingdom. Even with these pictures in our possession, nobody is going to believe us. What a disaster this will turn into.'

He turns off the camera and lets himself fall down beside the fence.

'How am I ever again going to have faith in humanity?'

'You're putting too much into it. It's a shit world, that's what it is.'

'But this is just not possible. Not in my part of the world.'

'You just saw it's possible.'

Mike puts his hand on his forehead. He suddenly realizes he is sweating like a beast.

'But we don't have enough. We need DNA evidence,' says Marcus.

'No fucking way!' whispers Mike. 'I'm not going in there.'

'We *need* DNA.'

'How's it going?' they hear Chris on the walkie talkie.

'We've got the pictures, but the DNA evidence is still missing. We're just talking about that right now.'

'And how does it look?'

'Difficult. There are people working in those catacombs who will keep the operation moving. It would not be very smart to go in there. We got pictures. Lots of pictures. That should be enough.'

They hear Andy's voice. 'Received. If we have the pictures, then let's abort the mission. That should be good enough to raise questions. All of you return to base immediately.'

'Road returning.'

'Fence returning.'

BACK AT the rented car, Marcus Schmidt and Mike Hornett arrive first. Andy gets out of the car.

'Mike, you look a little pale.'

Mike doesn't answer.

'He lost his virginity today. I think it hurt.'

The only one not laughing is Mike.

'Well, Mike. Welcome to the world of true brutality. It seems that what once happened in this place is repeating itself. Our perpetrators couldn't have chosen a better place to stick it out in front of people's noses.'

'That's true,' confirms Marcus. 'But Mike, you did well! You did very well. To be perfectly honest, I'm a little shaken too. We have a tendency to use sarcasm, to cover up for our true feelings. Sarcasm and humor are the best way to cope with reality.'

'Well, what now?' asks Mike.

'That's not up to us to decide.'

'Say,' notices Marcus. 'Where's Chris?'

'Hm. You're right. He should be here by now shouldn't he?' agrees Andy.

'Road?' he speaks into the walkie talkie. 'Road?'

But there is no answer.

'Damn! What do we do now?'

'I guess, we'll have to wait,' suggests Andy.

QUITE HONESTLY, it is not one of the saddest funerals that Henry has attended in his fifty-eight years. He will miss her and her nice tight pussy, this much is for certain. But now she is dead and might as well be used as an opportunity to get some of the skeletons The Party has in its closet buried along with her.

He has noticed a mood change in the public now that he has taken over the rudder. There are hopes of a bright future for the United Kingdom. Henry greets Victoria's closest family. An uncle from Manchester, a cousin from South Wales and a couple friends are all present. He expresses his condolences before taking his seat in the second row with Lisa and Gregg and the idiot Chancellor of the Exchequer who doesn't have any power anyway. The family members and friends are struggling to not show their grief but unable to hold back the tears that flow like rivers. The Seymour family seems to be small as is his family. Most people present at Victoria's funeral are representatives of heads of states who seem not to appreciate the government of the United Kingdom and what it does, but probably only come to prove whether this arrangement has been staged. Spies they all are. Outside of the church, thousands of people have shown up to also show their disgust of the protagonist of this tragic event. The public's interest in Victoria Seymour's death has become an amazing page turner with shocking and negative stories about her political life and strange private interests and awkward sex fantasies that are beyond imagination. The only ones shedding honest tears are those in row one.

The funeral ceremony proceeds slower than an old hunchback man can walk with a stick. There is no speech from the minister but only clicks from cameras. It seems that friends and family have no memories to share or a favourite hymn to sing. Whichever agency agreed to arrange this state funeral learned their lessons well from Patty Griffith's funeral and have adhered to the wishes of The Party's department for State Communication and Promotion. The final words from the minister bring a fresh round of tears and crying from the first row. His words have been well planned and spoken as directed by The Party's advertising department and Henry makes a mental note to thank Lisa for this ridiculous event. The funeral of Victoria Seymour is nothing but a tribute to The Party's ability to court attention at any costs.

The walk to the churchyard is followed by a crowd of people, with him, Lisa, Gregg and the idiot Chancellor of the Exchequer leading the way behind the coffin. It is like a vague memory of his mother's funeral, him walking alongside her coffin. A grave has been dug – seemingly much longer than deep. This autumn day is an unusually cold one, but its brown and green colors fit well with the colors of The Party. Henry hears the birds singing happily. The trees are losing their leaves as if they want to tell the crowd that the world will go on without Victoria and that something new is beginning. Nobody at this funeral cares about Victoria Seymour or her cousin and uncle.

But as much as he hates arrangements of this type, his etiquette demands that he attend to Victoria Seymour's family and provide sympathy on demand. In spite of what Victoria did or what the country thought she did it would have been unthinkable to not attend her funeral. Up until now, he has kept his acting in check and felt the entire funeral as success. It is a good way for The Party to get rid of some of those skeletons in the closet. Funerals always open old wounds; they bring back memories and give occasion for reflection. Lisa had told him that if he can conjure up old memories at the moment when Victoria is lowered into the ground, it will make it easier for him to cry and show his human side. He recognized the truth of what she had said and realized that it would be a bonus to his image now that he is the new leader and sign of hope. At first, it didn't really work but then he started thinking about his broken childhood. Then the tears came and it was impossible to hold them back. He managed to maintain a face of pain and despair until the end of the service by thinking of how others had always mocked him as a child and how difficult it had been. He had had to suffer a lot to reach the point where he is today. He has lied a great deal of his life, the biggest lie being about what he had done to his mother. This turned out to be the best way to get tears to run down those cheeks and show he cares for others. He has always been a sinner. He knows that. Everybody knows it. But no one has ever done anything to stop him, not even his mother from the time she carried him under her heart.

Those were all the things Henry was thinking about as he walked back to the waiting car. He couldn't shake the image in his mind that he was the one laying in the coffin. It was a narrow coffin that only took four people to lower it down into the pitch black. His mother's coffin had been smaller. Her family had not wanted him to deliver a eulogy because of the government's complicity in the policies Victoria had initiated. They knew she had screwed up. And he was here at the funeral only because no one really knew that it was he who was actually behind Victoria's new laws and policies. Her family has been very friendly toward him, something that makes him respect them and feel compassion for them at the same time.

TWENTY-FIVE minutes later, Chris has still not returned to the rented car. And there is no sign of either over his walkie talkie. Andy starts getting nervous.

'Road?' he transmits a last time.

Still no answer.

'Hush … Did you lads hear that?' asks Mike.

'No, what?'

'It sounded like dogs.'

'Dogs?'

They are silent and listen.

'Holy shit! It is dogs,' confirms Marcus. 'Get into the car right now. We've gotta get out of here.'

Marcus starts the motor and hits the gas when the other two get in the car. Andy looks at him from the passenger seat.

'Step on it,' he screams. 'Step on it, harder!'

The car wheels spin on the gravel road as the car picks up to speed. Just as Marcus lightens up on the accelerator, a truck appears out of the dark and stops, blocking the road. The BMW collides head on, releasing all airbags.

For a moment all go silent.

Mike, who is in the backseat, recognizes that he is still fully conscious after the collision. When he looks to the front, he sees that Marcus and Andy are both unconscious. He peers out of the windshield and side windows and sees several men on the left hand side with hand guns. He recognizes them as the men who were driving the trucks and removing the corpses.

Then he notices that the right hand door has opened on impact. There is a gap large enough to crawl through unnoticed. He looks again and reassures himself that the men are still standing to the left of the car. Taking his camera, he slips undetected out of the car and disappears into the dark.

Now he remembers the dogs and hears them barking. He's glad that he works out regularly and helps youth sport groups. He is fit and in good shape. He thinks of the other two for a moment but remembers what they trained him to do. *Focus on the mission, never on the results caused by others. That's what matters*. He runs and runs and runs all he can. But no matter how fast he runs, it seems those dogs can run much faster.

IT IS the first meeting Lisa and Henry have had on their own after the latest announcement to the people. They decide to meet at the late Victoria Seymour's favorite cafe, just to keep up the tradition. Lisa is still somewhat shaken by the events of the last few days, but she tries not to show Henry. He, on the other hand, seems to be taking things quite easily.

'Hey there, Lisa,' he almost sings – as if he is full of joy.

'Hi Henry. What are you drinking?'

'Cappuccino.'

She goes to the counter and orders two Cappuccino and returns to the cosy couch to sit down beside Henry. She notices that he always stares at her breasts. Hopefully, this is not what he has in mind for today, because, in all honestly, she is not in the mood for anything like that at the moment.

'That was some speech you had me give,' she remarks. 'Is The Party really going to start this huge program?'

'What program?'

'This: Efficiency Through Joy?'

'Definitely!'

'Why? Don't you think the state deficit is high enough?'

'In bad times, it's important to keep people working with infrastructure programs.'

'But this isn't bad times. The economy is not doing badly enough to start any infrastructure programs.'

'That's true, Lisa. But we need something to motivate people. When they work hard, they should also be rewarded. It's good for people to have a carrot in front of their noses, but also to feel appreciated.'

'But honestly, Henry, a lot of fat people are starting to run scared because of the negative rumors floating around out there about people disappearing. And they're upset about what happened last night. Didn't you hear? Hours after Victoria's funeral, a group of autonomous thugs targeted several fast-food chains all over England and Wales.'

'Of course I heard about it. But do you think it's important?'

'Well, why haven't we done anything to restore law and order?'

'The Party has never had so many free voluntary members as it has today. WeightForLife is a huge success and a great income source as well. Victoria didn't die in vain, you know?'

Lisa doesn't know whether or not to express her true opinion on the subject.

'So? Aren't you just a little impressed? I mean, don't you find what we do, brilliant?' Henry asks.

Lisa puts on one of her best smiles. 'Yes, I certainly do, Henry.' What else would she dare to answer?

'You're one hell of an iron lady, Lisa.'

'A what?'

'Iron lady. Have you never heard that expression before?'

'Of course I have. But please don't compare me with one of the greatest politicians in British history.'

'Ha ha. Who says Margaret Thatcher was a great politician? She destroyed our industries. She partly destroyed the European Union with her demands about liberalization. But you, on the contrary, you are a great politician and have a great and exiting future.'

'It's nice of you to build up my confidence, Henry. But I'm in Public Relations. The only thing I need is the names of the people you want out of your way. Then I'll ask my people to dig out dirt on them.'

Lately, she feels shivers blasting through her body when she talks to him. And something has changed about him since yesterday's funeral. It's better to give him what he expects to hear. He is growing powerful. Hopefully, when he gets too powerful and when this power grab is over, the abroad world will have more influence in the daily business of the United Kingdom. Because in this global and interconnected world, the place for people like Henry is getting narrower. And the idiot doesn't even seem to recognize it.

MIRACULOUSLY, a riverbed appeared in front of him. He jumped into the water and let the stream take him along. At least it made the dogs lose his track. Many, many kilometers later, he reached a town and decided it was time to get out of the cold water. Resting on the shores of the river, he thinks about what could possibly have gone wrong. Why didn't Chris return? Why did he not answer his walkie talkie? How did the perpetrators get hold of them? He will probably never know.

And it does not matter. Focus on the mission, never on the results caused by others as he was instructed. That's what matters he tells himself again and again to keep a clear head. What is important now is to get a memory card to London or, at this stage, to get the camera dried so he can make a third and a fourth copy in case Marcus has not gotten out alive. When he returns to London, he will write the end-article, finally wiping Victoria Seymour from the political stage and forever out of the United Kingdom.

At least it is a relatively warm autumn night. He decides to rest a couple of hours in the bushes, and then continue the journey in the morning. By then his clothes will be dry. Before doing so, he opens his camera and tries to get as much water as possible out of it. Hopefully, by tomorrow it will be dry too. When he gets to town, he will find a post office and mail one memory card to his mother and another to his girlfriend. Then his mother can get hold of his news editor in person.

BY THE next morning, Mike's clothes are only half dry. The sun is up and its autumn strength can still be felt. He picks up the camera, which seems to be dry – at least, on the outside. He presses the on-button and it powers up. Well, it's a Carl Zeiss, which, ironically, is produced in Jena, less than 50 kilometers from his current position. He takes out the empty memory cards from his pocket and starts copying data on to them.

Then he gets up. His legs hurt from floating around in the river, hitting stones and debris several times. It was, at least, better than being violently bitten by aggressive dogs and perhaps being hit in the head with a bullet. There are a lot of things he will never complain about again.

It is time to go to town and find a post office and he is getting hungry too. It must be at least 24 hours since the last time he ate. He quickly checks his surroundings before preparing his departure. The nature in this area is simply magnificent. On his left, the river he pulled himself out of is flowing forcefully by. To his right, there is a long, low hill leading up to a guard rail. He assumes it probably leads to a passing road. He goes up the hill to the road and tries his luck as a hitchhiker.

It takes a while, but a truck finally stops. The door to the passenger side opens. Getting in, the driver looks at him in surprise. 'Was ist denn mit dir passiert?' he asks.

'Sorry, my German is not so good.'

'Eh. What is with you happened?' the driver politely attempts.

'I had to take a leak,' lies Mike. 'And then I fell over the guard rail.'

The truck driver laughs loudly.

'Penis hang out, und dann … BUM … Ha ha … over edge.'

Mike tries to return the laughter although he realizes how false it sounds.

'Where are you going?' he tries to change the subject.

'Czech Republic. Praque.'

'Can you drive me to town or do we pass a bigger city before Praque?'

'Leipzig. One hour max.'

'Okay. That's perhaps not a bad idea.'

The hour goes by without many words exchanged. The impressions from the evening before run through Mike's head like a movie looping over and over. The thought of what might have happened to the others, disturbs him. At least the truck driver is one hell of a nice lad who offers him something to eat. They listen to the latest Czech music. The driver even offers that Mike might like to marry his eldest daughter who still lives home and costs a fortune in parental maintenance though she is only seventeen. When he gets out of the truck, the two shake hands profusely as if they are the best of friends and will never to see each other again – which in a way is true.

He stands on the Autobahn exit before Leipzig and realizes he does not know how to get to the Central Station. What now? He tries to turn on his cell phone which also had gotten wet. Yesterday, it didn't work, but, thankfully, it seems to be working now.

One Short Message after another pops up big time in his inbox. Some are from his wife and buddies, but most are from his editor at the Daily Evening Mail. He starts from the top. And then …

Victoria Seymour has been assassinated. Unbelievable. By five obese people. It makes him bend backwards and laugh out loud. He cannot stop laughing. What happens now? Is the nightmare over? He sticks his thumb out and starts hitchhiking again. Someone is quick to stop. This time it is a car with an old man in it.

'Wo wollen Sie hin?'

'Sorry, my German is not so good.'

'Oh. Hop in? Where do you want to go?'

'Well, where are you going?'

'Not so far from a street car, if you need one.'

'That would be perfect!'

Mike closes the door and they start driving.

'So,' the old man asks. 'Where are you from?'

'England.'

'Uh, sorry to hear what just happened.'

'Don't be sorry. I'm not. Not at all. On the contrary!' says Mike.

'No, you shouldn't be sad, that's right. We've had our troubles here too in the old days. I was in England, you know.'

'Oh, you were?'

'Yes, but it was mostly dark and at an altitude of thirty-thousand feet.'

'Oh really. My grandfather was in the Royal Air Force. You might have seen him up there,' jokes Mike.

'No, it was mostly dark.'

Okay, bummed out. People are obviously right when they say that Germans have no sense of humor. Don't mention the war, thinks Mike. Talk about John Cleese, someone people all over the United Kingdom have come to laugh about as Basil from Faulty Towers.

'Take some good advice,' says the old man rather honestly. 'You should get rid of that government. The sooner you do it, the better. Governments like this have a tendency of growing stronger than anyone ever anticipates and with things that are difficult to stop. What's happening over on your side, reminds me so much about how it started here. Especially we old ones who lived through it are starting to worry on your behalf.'

'Believe me; I'm certainly worried, too. How far is it to the street car stop?'

'Just a few more minutes.'

Good, thinks Mike. This is not the kind of memories he needs right now. If the poor bastard beside him knew what he knows about what is happening inside the mountains close by the man would go and hang himself. He will make the photographs accessible all over the world.

They arrive at the street car stop. Mike thanks the old man several times for the ride and also for the warning. He goes to the departures sign and looks at the time table. Even with his lack in German skills he understands that he must change trains two times before the central station. Once there, he will take the high-speed train to Hamburg and fly back to London.

CHAPTER 21

WHEN HENRY MONTCLAIR STARTED his new job as First Secretary of State and Minister for the Cabinet Office in Whitehall, less than 500 meters away from Palace of Westminster, he was as surprised as many of his former colleagues from the European Union. He had never expected to end up here, not after his many years at the European Parliament. He, as well, had never expected to get married and have two children.

Of course, it's life events such as these that make life so amazingly interesting and complicated.

Henry takes the time to reflect a little on life, while clutching his coffee cup. He has still not fully come to terms with what went wrong at the European Parliament and what they meant when they said he had done so many things wrong. At least on this side of the Channel, where he was born, people have received him well; especially his colleagues from The Party and its sponsors from Russia. Less than four years ago, when he had joined, The Party was small and unimportant. But due to his contacts, Victoria Seymour was able to finally establish the political party she, as well as he, had been dreaming about. He has been rather unknown in the United Kingdom until Victoria's assassination, but now he is coming out from backstage into the limelight and turning himself into a rock-star by using her unpopularity.

He finishes his coffee in less than thirty seconds and pours himself another cup which he downs equally fast. To compensate for his lack of sleep in the last couple of days, he quickly downs a third cup. He is fully aware it is he who will take over the role of Prime Minster and fill the vacuum. He isn't entirely comfortable with this thought, but now people will finally get to know him and all the good The Party has done for the United Kingdom.

Lisa's performance at the latest press conference was excellent. The girl is young; she has the good looks and sex appeal that Victoria had. She is ambitious, intelligent and works very hard. And now, after Victoria's funeral, he must figure out how to get the best out of Lisa – on the public stage as well as in the bedroom.

At least now there is some time to relax. The military got their money to upgrade their hardware, the intelligence service got theirs too which seemed to please many people in high positions. How he financed this huge black hole and still prevented an increase in the state budget deficit was by selling companies of obese people. Later, these sales will be rescinded and the foreign investors thrown out of the United Kingdom.

There is one company, though, that will remain in the government's hands and not be sold to investors. It is ImplantSkills. Their work of tracing people and managing their health is a good thing. His plan is to have everyone in the United Kingdom have an implant, making it easy for him to keep track of people and opponents. Gregg White has already initiated the legislation and is also in the process of initiating the first campaigns. Of course, not everyone will accept the chip implantation, but for them there are other solutions.

The death of Victoria is, of course, a tragedy and an unexpected turn in his career. He never really expected that he would become the Prime Minister one day. But now, with her gone, he is the one making the decisions as he always has, albeit behind the scenes. Now he will be doing it legally and helping to make Victoria's vision come true.

At first, Lisa was a little worried about what he has been doing lately and what he is going to do in the future. She may be young, but she is maturing and she is a fast learner. Now it seems she has come to terms with her new destiny and his plans. She knows the demonstrations and rioting are not forever, because Lisa is clever and wise enough to not ask too many hard questions. She understands the power that is slowly, but surely building up around her.

AFTER THREE and a half hours at 300 km per hour, the high-speed train arrives at Hamburg Central Station. Mike takes the subway for the half hour ride to the airport. He is unsure of what to do. Should he report what he knows to the German authorities, or should he wait until he is back in London? But who can he fully trust and rely on in London who are not loyalists? The old German guy had advised him to step carefully and he is certainly going to take his advice.

Mike gets out of the subway and goes with the escalators to the departure terminal. In the large hall, he proceeds to one of the airline counters to buy a ticket. Funny enough, without thinking, he has chosen Lufthansa instead of the obvious choice of British Airways. After he has checked-in, he continues to the security area. His passport is still wet, but at least the people at security did not ask him questions.

There is still an hour and a half before departure. He proceeds to the big panorama windows and looks out on an Airbus A320, an aircraft that seemed to impress Andy Green. This is how far Western Europe has come. Airbus is the role model for Pan-European integration. Four countries and suppliers from all over Europe build this wonderful machine. It had taken Boeing, another aircraft manufacturer, a while to realize that they had a serious competitor on their necks. The ESA or European Space Agency, is also giving the Americans a good fight for the buck. And the newly established high-speed train networks throughout the European Union carry people at speeds of up to 330 km per hour thereby reducing the connection time between major European cities to 2 to 3 hours. Moving around the European Union these days makes it feel so small. Most of his life, he had been against the European Project. Then one day, he went from London to Paris via the Eurotunnel and it changed his mind forever. It has become so easy to travel, so easy to move around, so easy to find jobs and live anywhere you want because all practical stuff has been harmonized between the countries in the European Union. In the last couple of decades the European Union has been getting stronger and creating a safe haven for its citizens by building an efficient infrastructure so countries within the Union can remain global partners.

When boarding starts, he looks out onto the apron. He has never missed his girlfriend and unborn child so much as right now. He notices how the machine is only half-full. It seems not many Germans want to go to London these days. The stewardess approaches him soon after takeoff and asks if he would like a cup of coffee. He looks up at her with big wet eyes.

'Yes,' he says. 'Coffee would be perfect. And please, make it a big cup with lots of cream and lots of sugar.'

ONE AND a half hours later, the aircraft lands at Heathrow Airport. The landing was a little hard and probably manually. Mike is the first to leave the cabin. Proceeding through the finger to the terminal, he stops and looks at a poster on the terminal wall, saying:

WELCOME TO LONDON. HOME OF THE FIT.

Efficiency is at our hearts

He tries not to laugh out loud, causing passersby to look at him strangely, wondering what to think. The slogan is over the edge! How can people be so blind as not to see what is going on? He continues on, blindly following the last part of the crowd to the immigration counters.

'Aw man!' he sighs when he sees the long queues. Before Brexit and the new immigration laws, people from the United Kingdom and Commonwealth went to the left, Euro trash to the right, and the rest of the world were held up for hours in other lines. The Party is obviously using Brexit to seal off the United Kingdom from itself and Europe and rest of the world. The queue he decides to take moves, of course, the slowest, but at least it moves. When he finally reaches passport control and puts his passport on the desk, the officer takes it, checks its validity and then takes a long look at Mike.

'Sorry. I can't let you in,' the officer says.

'I beg your pardon?'

'You're blacklisted.'

'For what?'

'It doesn't say. But it says that when you turn up, you're to be arrested. I suggest you go back into the terminal and figure out a way to get back to where you came from. Go my friend. Go write some articles about what's happening here.'

Mike turns around in shock. In his astonishment, he completely fails to thank the man, who has probably saved his life. With his passport in his hand, he walks back into the terminal moving against the masses of people wanting to get into the United Kingdom. He is no longer welcome in the country of his birth, the place he has lived all his life. There is an arrest warrant out for him. What's all this coming to? What about his girlfriend? His unborn child? Shouldn't it all have stopped now that Victoria Seymour is gone? He proceeds to a pay phone and inserts in it a quid and dials his girlfriend's cell phone number.

'Honey! It's me. Listen to me very carefully and don't interrupt. I want you to buy a ticket to Brussels right now, and meet me there. You need to get out of the United Kingdom, right now! And I mean, right now!'

THE FIRST official meeting Henry attended abroad after his inauguration as First Lord of the Treasure and Minister for the Civil Service, or simply Prime Minister, takes place with the President of the European Council. Denda Escudos and Henry Montclair have not seen each other for years now, and there is mutual feeling that when it comes to not ever seeing each other again, this would be fine. But that is not how politics work.

'Sooo,' says Denda Escudos to his assistant, watching Henry and his two bodyguards walk around the corridors of the huge European Union building, looking for his new office. 'Let's just wait here for a while and let him knock on a few doors.'

'You seem to not like the man'

'I certainly don't. Most of us in this building don't.'

'Why not?'

'Well, you haven't been around long enough to have felt his presence.' Denda Escudos scratches himself behind his ear and grey hair. 'The guy is a hate preacher and does it best behind your back. He's a real slick one. He's good at detecting the worse in people. He promises them the world to get them on his side and then uses them for his own purpose until they have outlived their use. Egoistical people and those with no empathy have a tendency to be drawn to him. If you don't know him well, he's a very charming and charismatic person.'

'How did he land here by us?'

'Like they all do. When they fail as politicians back home. If this weren't the case, the European Union would probably work a lot better and be less corrupt.'

'That's a harsh way to talk about our colleagues.'

'Is it? If you haven't noticed, one-fourth of all Members of the European Parliament are anti-EU people. Do you think this is good for progress? Or for member nations who actually want to solve problems together? Henry was good at reminding the world that we just sit there and accept grants while putting on wide smiles and thinking how stupid European citizens are, even though Henry is the worst of them all.'

'But that's not true ...'

'Oh, never mind,' sighs Denda Escudos. 'It's a common notion that everybody thinks we're corrupt. Let's take care of our disgusting guest.' Denda Escudos goes to his side of the door and bellows: 'Hey Henry, we're in here.'

Henry tries to figure out where the voice is coming from. Did he get the number of the meeting room wrong? Or is Denda Escudos the same as always? A lazy bureaucratic asshole, hiding in the corridors of the European Union, sucking off tax payers money until he retires.

'Ahh Denda! There you are,' he says.

'I'm sorry,' Denda Escudos apologizes. 'The meeting room I booked for us is occupied. Chalakowsky screwed up as always. He has an important meeting about this Nuclear Power Act stuff.'

'Oh God. They're still discussing that? They've been discussing it for years. Still no progress?'

'Oh yes! But slowly. You know as well as I do that things take time around here. Come in and sit down.'

'That's probably the only thing we'll ever come to agree upon.'

Denda Escudos laughs. 'Certainly. Anyway, we can use my office. I believe it's been a while since the last time you were here.'

'It's been exactly four years and thirty-two days.'

'Well, I guess only people who despise this place keep track of the days,' answers Denda Escudos, surprised that it's been that long.

Then he realizes he forgot to introduce his assistant.

'This is my assistant. He's relatively new to the European Council.'

'Nice to meet you,' says Henry without really meaning it.

'Nice meeting you, too.'

'So, Henry. Come and sit down.'

'Thank you.'

'I would first like to offer my condolences for Victoria. She was popular around here when she worked for us.'

'Thank you.'

'It must be hard for you now that she's gone.'

'It certainly is. But things have quieted down a bit with her passing away.'

'So, who's taking care of the Brexit negotiations?'

'Uh, Denda. That's a difficult one.'

'It seems Brexit isn't running so smoothly after all, huh?'

'In spite of how much I hate this institution, it was a dumb decision of the former Prime Minister to initiate such a referendum. The general voter is ignorant, not an expert.'

'That's a little hard. But I guess what you're saying is true. At least, I see you have achieved there what you couldn't achieve here.'

'Yes, I'm quite proud of myself, actually. But it hasn't been easy.'

'And that's what I want to talk with you about before you go to the European Council members.'

'Yes, I was a little surprised at your invitation.'

'I wanted to talk about this with you in privacy and off the record. I hope it's okay if my assistant remains here?'

'No problem.'

'You have a lot of explaining to do, Henry. What are you going to tell the Council? If the United Kingdom continues in its current direction and this harassment of some citizens doesn't come to a halt, the Council may implement a trade embargo against you.'

'I don't know why the Council would do such a thing. What are you referring to?'

'You and Victoria have turned the United Kingdom into a disaster. What's next? Are you going to hunt down thin people next?'

Henry laughs at the ridiculous comment. 'You are blaming me for something that has absolutely nothing to do with me. Victoria Seymour is the one you want to blame. It was her ambitions, her objectives that we were all obliged to follow. I told her often that what she is doing cannot end well. But she wouldn't listen.'

'So, what are you going to do now that she's no longer among us?'

'Well, I've only had one week as Prime Minister of the United Kingdom ...' Henry interrupts himself. He has never really recognized, at least not up to this point, but he is actually the Prime Minister of the United Kingdom. It makes him horny saying this to a retard like Denda Escudos. He gets a grip on himself and continues, 'My new government needs a turn around and after that we'll start cleaning up the trash from Victoria's rule.'

'And how about these laws which were implemented, what about those?'

'I had no idea she'd taken it this far. The changes have been integrated into our doctrine of Parliamentary Sovereignty. I'll get the changes revoked as soon as it's possible.'

'How soon?'

'I would say … between one and one and a half years.'

'Not good enough, Henry! There's no reason to take this long.'

'Well, she's made it difficult for us. The laws haven't been listed in the formal British statue book. She put them on a separate list, which we still haven't been able to find although we're searching hard for it. It forces us to go through all the current laws to find them. You know as well as I do, this takes time. And we don't even know what we're looking for.'

'That's story telling, and you know it, Henry.'

'Denda, now you disappoint me.'

'What about the military? When will you finally cancel the curfew for obese people and their supporters and rollback the Prime Minister's authority to impose Martial Law?'

'When the demonstrations have calmed down. The police are simply not in a position to cope with this type of violence. The military is better equipped and respected by the population, so it will remain in effect for some time.'

'I see.'

There is a moment of silence.

Then Denda gets up from his chair and, pointing at the door, indicates that the meeting is over.

'Well! It was good of you to drop by before your speech at the Council later this afternoon,' says Denda. 'I really appreciate hearing your version of what's going on in the United Kingdom.'

Yes, it was good to see you again, Denda. The delegation I've brought with me has 32 issues up for discussion. If we get just one through, we've been amazingly efficient.'

Denda laughs. 'This is true! But thanks for taking the time to come by and brief me in advance. We'll see each other later then.'

'We certainly will.'

Denda's assistant notices that no one shakes hands. He sees the fit and well-dressed UK Prime Minister return to the elevators.

Denda then closes the office door.

'So, I guess that went pretty good,' he says to Denda.

'You're kidding, right?'

'What do you mean?'

'He's lying and telling fairy tales. He hasn't changed a bit. And now he's Prime Minister of the United Kingdom. I'll tell you, it's going to end in a disaster. I know them both, but at least Victoria Seymour had some morals, which Henry doesn't seem to have.'

'That's bad.'

'I told you he's slick. If we had an army, we should invade the United Kingdom right now and pull the plug and let it sink into the ocean with all those arrogant English people that seem to be running the country now.'

'But doesn't he come from Wales?'

'Well, yes he does. But that doesn't change in the slightest as to how he thinks of himself and the United Kingdom.'

THIS MORNING Lisa flew in with Henry and a delegation of eleven heads. It is the first time she has ever flown on a private business jet and it felt nice. However, the sense of feeling important vanished immediately after getting out on the apron at Brussels Airport, knowing that journalists from all over Europe and rest of the world will ask her difficult questions after the announcement she is about to read in a few minutes. It will be difficult, because, here in Brussels, the press has not been muffled like at home where the press's critical voices have ceased.

Lisa has changed markedly after Victoria Seymour's death. Though still responsible for State Communication and Promotion, she is not a minister any longer. She is still responsible, but she has taken over Henry's old role as First Secretary of State and Minister for the Cabinet Office. Somehow, in this government, titles seem to play a less important role than the abilities people possess. But in spite of all the titles she now has, she cannot let go of the thought that she is turning into a Joseph Goebbels, Adolf Hitler's propaganda minister. She doesn't want to admit that she as well is to blame for the current state of affairs, but it seems the people below her have done an efficient job in achieving exactly this with the support of Gregg White and his team of well-dressed henchmen. Today when the media wants to write anything critical about The Party or those who oppose them, they do it indirectly so their audience has to read between the lines. This sensorship did not happen overnight. No, it happened slowly, steadily and not immediately recognized over a period of time. But common people learn to read better between the lines.

She is not particularly happy about what is happening in the United Kingdom, and especially England and Wales, but it is her job and this is what she gets paid to do. One thing she regrets is that she was the one who tipped off Henry that Victoria was going on the Early Morning Show to blow the whistle on the government and resign. She had no idea that Henry would arrange such a massacre and it shocked her. It has made her a little afraid of the power he has built up for himself in the last year. Occasionally, they still make love, but if it was not for her fear of his wrath, she would immediately end their affair and resign as First Secretary of State and Minister for the Cabinet Office and her responsibility for State Communication and Promotion. Unfortunately, she cannot quit because she must continue the affair so she can pump him for information in the same way he used Victoria and kept her on a short leash. She plays three roles at the moment and realizes that she has to be careful who she trusts.

She redirects her thoughts. The world wants answers about what direction the United Kingdom will be taking after Victoria's assassination. After her speech announcing the United Kingdom's plans for the future, it is quite obvious that none of the newsmen at the press conference seem to buy into her stories. Now comes the moment she has feared since stepping off the business jet at Brussels Airport.

'Yes, you down there,' she says to a journalist sitting with other journalists.

'Niles Benham, New York Times. There are rumors about people disappearing in the United Kingdom. So far it's approximately 1.500 missing cases. Why has the number of missing person in the United Kingdom suddenly exploded?'

'I know there are rumors, but, according to our statistics, there are no more people missing today than at any other time.'

'Most of them seem to be obese people,' continues the journalist.

'What rubbish! Among the 1.500 missing people, there are people who aren't overweight. I'll say this clearly and only once: It's rumors spread by people who want to discredit our government, nothing else.'

'But isn't it right that many of your so-called 'Fat People' have been brutally murdered and then buried in Nordhausen, Germany?' shouts another journalist.

The accusation shocks Lisa.

'I beg your pardon?' she responds. She sees that the person asking the question is Mike Hornett from the Daily Evening Mail. According to the list she receives every morning from Gregg's squad, he should be in custody by now. What is he doing here in Brussels?

'I went to Nordhausen in Germany,' continues Mike, addressing the journalists present. 'And I saw what the government is doing to its obese people and critics of The Party.'

Lisa stands there, stunned, not knowing how to respond. For a few seconds there is silence while eyes move from Mike Hornett to her, the crowd awaiting an answer.

'I … I have absolutely no idea what he's talking about. I honestly don't.' She realizes that what comes next will be very unpleasant.

'Well … take a look at these photographs.' Mike throws a pile of photographs up in the air. They settle among the journalists who begin picking them up one by one. What they see makes them mumble in shock, at first a little, then a lot.

There is a loud outcry as the crowd looks at Lisa in disgust. Some start taking photographs of her and Mike and at the photographs lying all over the floor. Lisa steps down from the podium and also begins picking up the pictures. She is aghast at what she sees. They show men pulling huge corpses from military trucks. She collects a handful of pictures and returns to the podium.

'Listen to me! All of you!' she screams. 'Listen to me! Please!' When the crowd finally calms down, she pulls herself together and starts to speak.

'Listen to me! This has nothing to do with my government. How dare you to believe that! Look at these trucks. They're German military trucks.'

The journalists are completely silent. Then things start to move in a direction she had never expected. They start booing her. A journalist picks up a coffee mug and throws it at her. Then another mug almost hits her. Bigger objects start flying at her. Lisa leaves her papers on the podium and decides it is time to return to the airport.

HENRY MONTCLAIR is also encountering some problems at the European Council. They are not as friendly to him as Denda Escudos was this morning. With the news of what has happened at the press center, the mood has turned even more poisonous than it was. Henry collects his papers and walks out. He pulls out his cell phone and calls Lisa.

'What happened?' he asks.

'For some unknown reason, Mike Hornett from the Daily Evening Mail, was present at the conference. He had pictures. Is it true, Henry?'

'I think it's better if we get back to the airport. Meet me at the jet in half an hour.'

'Okay.'

THIRTY MINUTES later they meet at the general aviation terminal of Brussels Airport. They hop into the transporter that drives them to the business jet standing on the apron. They sit in silence saying nothing. When they finally reach the aircraft, Lisa asks, 'What about the others from the delegation? How do they get back home?'

'They'll figure it out.'

Entering the aircraft, Henry goes directly to the mini-bar. He looks for something strong and, luckily, finds a bottle of good whisky.

'Would you like a glass as well?' he asks.

'I think so, yes.'

With two glasses in his hands, he sits down next to her and hands over a glass.

'Well, that didn't go as well as planned,' he concludes.

'Is it really true what those pictures show?'

'I haven't seen them.'

'I have a couple here.' She pulls them out of her briefcase and hands them to him.

'Uh, that doesn't look good. Oh my God! So, the rumors about people disappearing are true after all. Whew! Who'd have thought this of Victoria?'

'Yes, who would have thought that?'

'Times are very interesting, Lisa. It kind of excites me. And you?'

'Well … I guess so.'

When the jet passes through the thick cloud layer over Brussels, up where the sun always shines, they move to the back of the little cabin and start making love.

CHAPTER 22

AT THE SPECIAL COUNCIL IN SEATTLE, things are not exactly running according to plan. Mr. Andrews, Andy Green's Chief in Command, is lying in bed, worried about what is going on. Mr. Connors, Chris Campbell's Chief in Command in London is also concerned. It has been almost six days since their agents last signed in. And now it is becoming a major problem for the continuous safety of The Special Council.

'Where are our regular and two oversized agents? And who the hell shot Victoria Seymour?' asks Mr. Conners in a telephone call with Mr. Andrews.

'Have you had any interim reporting?' asks Mr. Andrews.

'Only that they arrived to Nordhausen. And you?'

'Nothing.'

'Berlin reports the same.'

'Damn! This is not good. Then we need to take measures to protect ourselves. If they have gotten themselves caught up in the middle, then the chance of us being exposed is rather high. Have you talked with the Old Man?'

'Not yet.'

'Well, I did. He's still on stand-by. According to the TSC Employeer Manual, if they do not sign in by tomorrow, then we'll need to reallocate.'

'Phew. That's going to be expensive.'

'It is.'

'But actually, this is not why I call you, in the middle of the night.'

'Then why?'

'There has been an incidence at the European Union in Brussels today.'

'What incidence?' asks Mr. Andrews.

'Haven't you seen the photographs Mike Hornett took?' asks Mr. Conners.

'What photographs? I'm still in bed. We're eight hours behind European time, you know! What happened?'

'Sorry. Of course you are. But, please go online. Then you'll see.'

Mr. Andrews gets out of bed. He goes down to his office to his computer.

'What do you want me to look for?'

'Type "Nordhausen".'

'How's it spelled?'

'November Oscar Romeo Delta Hotel Alpha Uniform Sierra Ekko November, in Germany.'

'Nord … hausen … in Germany … holy shit!' exclaims Mr. Andrews.

'Why did Mike Hornett publicize those photographs now?'

'This is what surprises me, too.'

'Wow! That's something for breakfast! Oh my God!'

'When you see the photographs, what do they remind you of?' asks Mr. Conners.

'Something I would prefer not to think about. Do you think our guys are down in the catacombs?'

'And perhaps Marcus Schmidt from Germany, too. Berlin says there is no sign of him as well.

'Damn! This is not good. If they have them down there, then the chance of The Special Council's cover being blown is very much at hand. I hope they've done the right thing.'

'They're disciplined. They'll do it,' says Mr. Conners. 'That's the price we all pay for working here. I can tell you that the Germans have reacted instantly. They 're in the process raiding the place.'

'That's good. At least with the photographs, we know that Mike Hornett made it out. He must be around somewhere. If he isn't, we should send out a team to look for him. When is the last time he was seen?'

'At a press conference at the European Union in Brussels.'

'And the Germans?'

'Oh, they're trying to explain themselves. It's obviously not them, everybody knows this. Lisa Ferguson was holding a press conference, trying to explain how innocent The Party is. Suddenly, she and the delegation she came with left in a big hurry.'

'I'd have done the same, just to keep my head. But Charles, there's something you don't know. Lisa Ferguson, works for us,' Mr. Andrews informs him

'Well, well. You always get surprised at The Special Council, don't you?'

'The woman lying beside you at night could be working for us too and you'd never know it.'

'The question is whether I should direct our German division to arrange a recovery team for our journalist' asks Mr. Conners.

'Aw man! Finding him will be like finding a needle in a haystack,' grunts Mr. Andrews. 'Does he have an implant?'

'Don't think so. He's a journalist. And even if he had one, now that Chris is gone we won't be able to access the databases at ImplantSkills.'

'Is that how important the company has become to us? Don't we have a mole or a backup or something?'

'You know how difficult it is to place moles.'

'What a mess all this has turned into. Do you guys in London have any idea who's behind the assassination of Victoria Seymour? I'm completely baffled, we all are. The initial report on my desk surprisingly excludes Henry Montclair.'

'Wow! That's a surprise. He would be the one to gain most from her death.'

'I'm not so sure about that. He's weak when he's in the spotlight. He's much better suited to working behind the scenes, at least that's what Lisa says.'

'Do you people in Seattle have any idea who else it could be?'

'Well, it's all circumstantial. A lot of people are working on it, trying to figure it out.'

'Why wouldn't he kill her?'

'Because it simply doesn't fit his profile. He needs to lean on other people, not be the one in command.'

'What about Gregg White?'

'Well, he fits in well … but … that's not what our experts say.'

'So, they do say something?'

'Like I said, it's all circumstantial. Some clues lead to the European Union.'

Mr. Conners is silent.

'It's circumstantial.'

'Hm. That would be hard to believe.'

'With all the power Henry and Gregg have accumulated, they are beginning to think that they are immortal. They're beginning to think they can do anything they please.'

'True,' agrees Mr. Conners. 'Henry has been able to push most of what happened in the past onto Victoria Seymour. But if you're saying what I think you are, I think the timing is wrong. He still does not have the military entirely under control. I mean, without the military's support, he won't be able to take full control.'

'What do you think the chances are of this?' asks Mr. Andrews.

'It probably won't come to this. After the murder of Victoria Seymour, I'm now in charge of a possible assassination of Henry Montclair. There's a new FDAR.'

'Wow! Seems to be a lot of them at the moment.'

'He's really a blunder on our part. All the time, we've been wrong about Victoria Seymour. We've somehow missed seeing that it was Henry Montclair pulling strings in the background.'

'Well, we're only human. We try to do our best, but it shows how fallible The Party is.'

'Yes, and that brings us to our next problem.'

'Which would be?'

'Lisa Ferguson. The team thinks she's getting scared. We're afraid she might be in the process of changing sides.'

'Oh no! Not one of our own,' exclaims Mr. Andrews.

'She wants the Old Man to pull her out, but the Old Man cannot pull her out. She needs to continue the charade because we need the information.'

'Poor girl, she's young. She must be under a lot of psychological strain.'

'You see, we've failed to figure out who's behind Henry Montclair's secret network. We're aware that Gregg White is in control, but simply haven't been able to infiltrate into the underneath network. If we want put an end to what is going on in the United Kingdom, we have to not only pull up grass, but also pull up the roots.'

'He's good at building up walls around himself.'

'Indeed he is! And Gregg functions as his firewall. Henry is very good at covering his tracks. They use very little paperwork so we cannot assassinate him unless there's enough evidence pointing at him, or at least, that's what the TSC Employeer Manual says.'

'We're turning into a mini United Nations, aren't we?'

'Yes, who would have thought that only a couple of years ago?' Mr.

Conners thinks for a moment. Then he continues. 'What about the journalist?'

'I'd appreciate it if you could take care of it. He's probably still is on your continent.'

'Okay, I will.'

'There must be a way we can track him down.'

'Try his cell phone.'

'He can't be that stupid.'

'He must be connected to a mast somewhere on the European mainland.'

'Charles, you're talking nonsense. I'm sure the government in Westminster has as much interest in finding him as we do. I'm certain they have scouts hunting him down.'

'What do we actually need him for?' ask Mr. Conners.

'He needs to be debriefed.'

'Hm.'

'And if we don't find him first, he'll be killed. Wouldn't it be good to clarify what happened in Nordhausen?'

'Pandora is out of her box with those pictures. In principle, it doesn't matter whether we debrief him or not, his role has expired.'

'Well, I guess we'll have to let him go then.' sighs Mr. Andrews.

'I guess so, too.'

Mr. Andrews and Mr. Conners finish their conversation. There isn't much they can do for Mike Hornett. They will not be able to find him if he has turned off his cell phone.

Mr. Andrews sits in front of his computer, reading about what happened in Brussels when his cell phone begins to vibrate. The display says it is Mr. Conners again.

'Say, Kelsey, according to Mike Hornett's file, he has a girlfriend in London. Why don't we give her a call? He'll surely have contacted her.'

'Holy macaroni! You know what Charles? You might just have saved the man from that pitiful and disgraceful country you come from.'

'I'll immediately get on it asap.'

'If you need me, I'm here 24/7.'

THERE HAS been a major turn in the mood of the United Kingdom and the world after yesterday's release of the photographs from Nordhausen. What should have changed the mood to one of hopefulness with Henry's climb to power now seems to have turned into a complete nightmare. Henry had hoped that Victoria's death would bring a wave of optimism with him at the helm, but that plan is now obviously turning on him. It was his only plan and he knew exactly where he was going with it.

Henry Montclair is not really sure why people are so angry with his government. At this point, the German authorities have not even confirmed that the victims are citizens of the United Kingdom. Even with only circumstantial evidence, there has been a surge in demonstrations against him and his government, urging him to step down. This of course is out of the question. Last night's demonstrations at Westminster, expanded rapidly to Downing Street where one guard was badly injured and another was nearly beaten to death. It is the first time he has feared for his own life. He ordered the police and military on the streets to separate the demonstrators and prevent more groups from assembling. Unfortunately, they quickly lost control of the situation. He had not thought of the fact that the military is not trained in psychological crowd control and the result was that the military cracked down on the rioters as if they were terrorists, wounding many and even killing a few. At a press conference this morning, he made it very clear that Martial Law will now be imposed for all citizens, not only fat ones, and that further civil disobedience will not be tolerated.

With yesterday's crackdown on the demonstration, he has send a clear signal to the public that his government is prepared to use force against civil disobedience to call order. Victoria Seymour's government had reacted by implementing more laws and laws incriminating people who aid the obese. But this approach seem now not to work any longer. Cell phone pictures and videos flashed through social media faster than the government could stop them by censuring data and turning off relay masts. Lisa's department for State Communication and Promotion tries to censor the Internet, it is impossible. There is too much data to handle. There are too many users on the Internet, too many digital gateways. They always seem to be one or two hours too late, making it difficult for information not to slip out. If he could have his way, he would turn off the Internet completely. At least, after the debacle in Brussels yesterday, and with the demonstrations that followed, they were fast to cut off the electrical grid and telephone services. In spite of this, information from Brussels came through anyway, making it apparent to Lisa's team that they still have a lot work to do if they are to control the information flow effectively.

It should by now be obvious that he demands law and order. In his office at Downing Street, the telephones didn't stop ringing all day. Calls from all over the world came in although callers didn't seem to understand that they had nothing to say about the domestic policy in the United Kingdom. Not only the public, but also First Ministers of Northern Ireland and Scotland, the European Union and the United Nations as well as the damn Internet, are all starting to get on his nerves. But especially Scotland and Northern Ireland start to oppose to his government.

CHAPTER 23

MASON SANDERS IS SURPRISED to see Chris Campbell and his friends among the mountains of obese people lying here and there. The lighting in the catacombs is intense, enabling the guards to see where people and things are located. Mason is careful not to show that he recognizes the three men who have just been marched into the catacomb. Mason sees four men in white scrubs return with another batch of trolleys full of obese as well as thinner people. It is now his duty to sort and pile the corpses according to size before they are sent into the forgotten and forbidden catacombs of World War II. This time he counts fifty-three corpses and the three prisoners, two of which are very obese and one is quite slim and dressed like a soldier. He approaches the trolley that the three are handcuffed to and begins to remove the first corpse.

'What're you doing here?' whispers Mason to Chris.

Chris can hardly believe his eyes. He tries to suppress the shock of seeing his boss so he doesn't give him away.

'Why aren't you dead, like the others?' whispers Chris. 'Your implant told us that you're dead.'

'No it didn't. It told you where I went. I bit it out and hid it before they found it. I knew you'd come and look for me,' he says, pulling down the next heavy body. 'They obviously have plans for me. I think they know that I own ImplantSkills, so they gave me this lovely job.' answers Mason.

'What happens to the corpses?'

'You remember the story about the Jews?'

'They all get gassed and burned?'

'Uhm, they're not that advanced. They use bullets. You don't need an oven for that.'

'You lost weight, Mason. It looks good on you.'

'Thank you. I'm sure my Yulia will be glad.'

'Where're the other guys you went to Hamburg with?'

'They went to the group of very obese corpses.' Mason turns his head to the pile and nods.

'Oh my God.'

'No. He's somewhere else. But be quiet before they see us talking. They're all psychopaths here with IQs lower than rats, but their fists are harder than steel.' Mason takes the corpse he pulled down first and tows it with great effort to one of the piles. Chris watches Mason doing his job. 'I wonder what goes through his head,' he says to Marcus.

'You can ask me, what's going through mine,' suggests Andy.

'This is insane. There must be at least five hundred bodies in those piles.'

'I don't care how many there are. What I care about is how we get out of this hell hole,' remarks Andy.

'You don't,' they hear a voice behind them. 'Now move on with the trolley in front of you to that tunnel over there.'

THE CATACOMBS curve in an arc from one wall to the other. They are sprayed with gray concrete nine meters across and approximately 6 meters in height. Part of the ceiling has been reinforced where overhead cranes were once found. Every twenty meters or so, there are cross-passages, connecting the three main parallel shafts with each other. The first tunnels were built in 1936 for the purpose of erecting an underground warehouse to store fuel and other important resources required for a possible war. With the English bombardment of Peenemuende in 1943, the original location the Nazi regime used to produce their retaliation rockets was moved underground to minimize any damage from air strikes. Inmates from concentration camps were used to expand the catacomb tunnel system in the 1940ies to include construction of test facilities for the rockets. This required the man power of 60.000 prisoners from concentrations camps such as Auschwitz and Chelmno. More than twenty-thousand inmates died of hunger, disease, exhaustion and the brutality of the Nazis while building the catacombs and the rockets. With the liberation of Nordhausen in March 1945, the Americans were the first to discover what had been going on and were met by only a few hundred prisoners who had survived the Nazi regime's terrible crimes. Three years later, the catacombs were blown up. Unfortunately, destroying the place turned out to be a costly affair due to the surrounding geographical conditions the tunnels had been built in. Instead, the facility was walled-up, preserving some remnants of the tunnel system relating to the Dora Concentration Camp. Today it is only accessible as a reminder of the horror, never to be forgotten by the next generations to come.

Knowing the history of Nordhausen, there is just one small nuisance about the catacombs, or Mittelbau, as the tunnels are called. When the facility was active, there were four entrances. Two were on the west side leading to the concentration camp Dora. Another two entrances were on the east side leading to the mountain and down to a river. The entrances to the west are where the museum is today. Here it is possible for tourists to enter and see a couple hundred meters into the now closed facility. But on the other side, of the mountain, to the east where the entrances were blocked, it was easy to re-build the destroyed part and make the tunnel system usable again. No one on this side of the mountain would ever realize that 9.000 square meters of the approximately 180.000 square meter old tunnel system were once again being used.

Beyond those 9.000 square meters is where Mason is heading with his little gas-driven forklift truck. The dark depths of the catacombs, the 171.000 square meters that are wet with humidity close to a 100 percent, are untouched by time and cursed by historians who had gone there to document the unfortunate dead. When they had finished with their work, they turned the sanctuary into a forbidden zone.

THE EMPTY trolley, pushed by its three passengers attached to its long railing, rolls into one of the tunnel systems cross-passages. The tunnel has been equipped with offices made of half-transparent, plastic lining attached to steel bars. There are piles of corpses everywhere along the short route. Andy concludes the bodies must be fresh because if not, the place would stink unbearably. On the way, he sees other prisoners, some fat, others slender, who are probably being kept alive to remove the corpses. Or perhaps they are waiting for a very unpleasant interview. It seems the world down here is a brutal, reckless, and an inhumane shit-hole.

'You,' someone shouts in Andy's ear. 'You two get over on the other side of the trolley.'

Chris and Marcus do as they are instructed.

Andy's right handcuff is opened and released from the trolley's railing. He gets a hard push in the back and is shown to one of the offices. He is followed by two relatively fit young men with automatic weapons. One follows him closely, the other at a distance, preventing him from escaping easily.

'In here,' commands the smaller of the two men. 'Sit down on the chair.'

Andy sits down on the chair. In front of him, a long table extends from one end of the plastic lining to the other. Behind it, a man in his forties is sitting, his hair completely white and his rough square face without a beard. He has the body of a photo model and is reading some papers.

'Take his handcuffs off,' the man says without looking up.

Andy's right handcuff is opened and removed. The hand cuffs are placed beside him on the table. The man still does not look up from his papers. It feels like an eternity. The waiting is always the worst. From his old days as a professional soldier, he knows what this is about. He is used to playing games like these. Once he was caught by the Russians and they were not always the most polite people to deal with. At least, they never killed anyone, because it would certainly cause diplomatic issues and they would be rewarded with a one-way ticket to Siberia.

This is different though. The cold war is over. His career as a professional soldier is over as well. And he is almost three times his optimal weight.

'So, you work for The Special Council,' the man says.

'BIIIIITE,' screams Andy as loud as he can, in the hope that his colleagues hear him. Andy bites hard in the cyanide capsule hidden in his gums, where he had put when it was clear that they had no chance to an escape. He feels his heart stop beating after only a few seconds. This followed by cramps coming one after the other. His last thoughts are of his wife and six children and life in general. But the efficiency of the cyanide capsule makes it impossible to think the thoughts to the end.

CHRIS and Marcus do not hear the warning from Andy because at that moment, Mason returns with his little gas-driven forklift truck, passing by where they are tied to the trolley. Andy's message is drowned by the engine noise. They see the two guards return from the offices heading in their direction. When they stop in front of them, nothing happens. They just stand there, waiting, waiting, and waiting. Suddenly Marcus and Chris feel someone grabbing them from behind, holding them tight stabilizing their bodies. They feel a tool being pressed between their front teeth, smashing them in the process. When their mouths are wide open, fingers start fumbling around, searching for something. Both are now aware of what it is and in an instant their cyanide capsules are fished out of their gums.

The tools are removed and the six men withdraw, leaving them alone. Marcus looks at his broken front teeth lying on the hard, concrete floor as does Chris.

'Aw, fuck, that hurt,' says Marcus.

'Well, I guess that's it then. Andy is dead.'

'I think he's the lucky one.'

'It makes me wonder what made him bite that capsule so fast.'

'We'll soon find out.'

'Do you have more capsules?'

'You know we only get one per mission.'

'Yes, I do.'

'How do we get out of this shit?'

'We might as well just run for it. We've got nothing to lose. I think a bullet in the back is better than what's awaiting us in there.'

'I agree. But what about the trolley? How?'

'Let's simply just take it along.'

'Where's the exit?'

'In that direction,' says Chris, turning his head to the wall opposite the cross-passage where the offices are. 'There are three main tunnels. This one must be the outer tunnel to the left of the entrance at the East side. So we need to run in that direction.'

'Okay. But how do we get through the barrier at the exit?'

'We don't. They'll shoot us long before.'

'Oh, just screw it! Let's go for it. It was nice seeing you again, Chris.'

'Yes, you too, Marcus. It has been a while. Sorry about the circumstances. The fun always ends some day. And that day seems to be today.'

'Okay. Ready? On your mark … 3 … 2 … 1 … go …'

They start running. It must look grotesque to the guards. A rather fat man, attempting to run in spite of a figure that doesn't allow him to do so, followed closely by a slender man with a trolley in tow. The trolley, of course, was never designed for this and it eventually loses equilibrium and crashes with a thud, getting the guards' attention. Lying there, tumbling around on the concrete floor, they see five guards scrambling around them, laughing. Marcus looks up and then closes his eyes. So, this is what will become of them. Feed for the worms in an old Nazi structure nobody knows is active again. Hopefully Mike got out with those pictures, so the world will finally know what is truly going on in the United Kingdom. What is going on the other side of the Channel is not really his problem but has become his problem. An now for the first time in his adult life, he knows the kind of fear his German grandmother and grandfather felt back then when Adolf Hitler was in power.

SURPRISINGLY, their attempt to escape is not punished. The result of their failed effort was that the trolley also was chained up.

'So, what now my superhero?' asks Marcus sarcastically.

'Don't know. That somehow didn't go according to plan.'

'No shit, Sherlock.'

'We're still alive.'

'Yes we are.'

'What now? Any new ideas?'

'Actually, yes. How about we sit it out and accept what's in store for us?'

'Very good idea. Why didn't I come up with this?'

It does not take long before two guards come to the trolley. One of them points at Marcus, ordering him in loud voice to move to the other side of the trolley, just as he had done when they picked up Andy. Marcus moves away so the two men can release Chris's handcuff.

Chris takes a long, final look at Marcus as the two guards walk away with him. From now on and for the rest of their time down here, their lives will be very, very lonely. Inside the plastic wrapping of the offices, Chris sits down on the chair where Andy sat, in front of a table almost as long as the office. It is an ugly table and it does not fit in the surroundings at all, Chris thinks. The man in his middle forties is sitting still there and doesn't even bother to look at him.

'Take his handcuffs off,' the man says, still not looking up.

Chris's left handcuff is opened. The handcuffs are put on the table. The man behind the table still fails to look up.

'So, you work for The Special Council?' the man asks.

So, that is why Andy bit that capsule so fast.

'How would you know?'

'We have spies everywhere.'

'You mean we've been infiltrated?'

'Yes and I assume, you know one of them.'

'And who may that be?'

'Lisa Ferguson, The Party's press secretary.'

'I actually did not know that. How should I? I wouldn't even know if my own wife works there. If you know so much about The Special Council, then you don't need to ask me questions. Why don't you ask Lisa Ferguson?'

'You're a double agent, aren't you?'

'What do you mean?'

'You also work for ImplantSkills?'

'If you already know, why do you ask?'

'You see, there's a way of getting out of this mess. You just need to do us a little favor.'

'Oh fuck you! You're very well aware that I'd rather take my own life.'

'But now that you don't have your little pill anymore, are you really prepared to go through what we have in store for you?'

Chris fails to come up with an answer. He knows exactly what is in store for him. As a soldier he had been through it twice and, strangely, his body has never gotten used to it. Therefore, it is better to tell the man what he wants to know or to start with some lies and then, if necessary, end with the truth. For him, the result will eventually be the same. Down here there are no human rights and they both know it.

'Okay,' starts Chris. 'What do you want to know?'

'Tell me how you came to join The Special Council.'

'Why? Can't you ask Lisa Ferguson how she came to join?'

'Please just answer my question.'

'I don't know. They wanted me and recruited me without me actually knowing it. To make a long story short, I passed their tests, whatever they were.'

'Aha. I see. And then they placed you at ImplantSkills?'

'Back then, ImplantSkills was only a small company. I guess The Special Council pulled some strings to get me in. And they were right in their assumption that the company would become influential.'

'You mean the Old Man got you in.'

'Yes, I mean the Old Man.'

'And where is the Old Man now?'

'I don't know. Nobody knows.'

The first blow comes. It hits below the right shoulder blade, connecting to the skeleton. He feels an intense tingling sensation pass from the upper part of his body down to his hand. Later it will hurt, really hurt.

'Shall we try one more time?'

'As I said, nobody knows.'

The next blow is to the left hand side below the shoulder blade producing the same intense tingling sensation. Now it truly hurts. The body can feel pain at only one spot at a time but if it is done right, several spots with pain can turn into an amplified on-going pain and that is what is happening now. The men behind him know all the tricks.

'Why don't you ask Lisa Ferguson?' grumbles Chris.

'She doesn't know.'

'That's what I said. Nobody knows.'

'But didn't you visit him in Seattle? Weren't you the carrier of the message about the FDAR assignment about Victoria Seymour?'

The question stops Chris's ability to think for a moment. It is certainly not good that they know he was in Seattle. They must have known it from very early on. 'And the hooker at my hotel?' he asks. 'What function did she have?'

'She put a trace unit under your skin. We were not sure where The Special Council is located in London and needed you to show us, so we could keep an eye out when the Old Man came by.'

Under the skin! The only place he would not have thought to look.

'Don't tell me it's one of ImplantSkills'?' Chris asks.

'Of course it is! You silly boy. They're the best on the market.'

'So, why all this with the DVD to my wife and so on?'

'Well, it worked didn't it? A pure deviation maneuver. Look at yourself. Up till now, you haven't had the slightest clue that we've been watching you all the time. And you still wouldn't if it hadn't been for you and your friends showing up here.'

Oh no! Now it 's obvious to Chris why they were suddenly there, pulling his ten-pack of Snickers out of his hands, handcuffing and dragging him along the road. It is the damn trace unit implanted in him that gave them away.

'You guys are really smart. I must give you that,' he says, meaning every word. 'So, what now? Now that you know where the headquarters of The Special Council in London is and, I presume, in Seattle as well, then you don't need me anymore.'

'My problem is that I want to find the Old Man.'

'As I said, nobody knows. He always moves around. I don't even know what he looks like. Not many do.'

'Is there an FDAR on Henry Montclair?'

'In all honesty, I don't know. My focus was Victoria Seymour …'

'Who is dead now. How did The Special Council do that?'

'According to my information, we didn't. The FDAR was put on hold because of what happened. Or, rather cancelled. Victoria Seymour's murder also puzzled the Old Man and us. It seems nobody knows who assassinated her.'

'Hm.'

There is a moment of silence. Chris is the first to interrupt seeing it as an chance to negotiate a little.

'I don't see that I'm in a position to help you any further. You seem to be well-informed about The Special Council from Lisa Ferguson. She must also have told you that what each individual knows is quite limited, and that security measures are always taken when agents do not report at the allotted time. Right now, I'm sure the Special Council is in the process of completely re-organizing itself because of my and my other two colleagues' silence.'

'Yes, your colleague didn't have much to inform.'

'So, what do you suggest?'

Gregg White thinks things over a bit. Meanwhile, Chris considers his situation but comes to the same conclusion he had earlier. Now, it is only a matter of getting it over as painlessly as possible.

'I don't know,' sighs Gregg White. 'This is becoming a difficult situation for us both, isn't it? You're an ex-soldier, aren't you?'

'Yes, I am.'

'Me too. I'm not active any longer, at least not in the sense of today's military tactics. Can you offer me something that's worth your life?'

'Even under torture?'

'Yes.'

'Not something that you don't know and not when it comes to the Old Man and his whereabouts.'

'And your colleague?'

'As well not.'

'Well …' Gregg White gets up from his chair. 'Let's go outside again to your friend. 'Please follow me.' He puts a hand on Chris's shoulder. 'Oops, sorry. That probably hurt, but, please … after you.'

Chris sees a surprised Marcus. It is obvious that he did not expect them to meet again. When Chris approaches the trolley, he whispers into Marcus' ear, 'Don't worry. We'll get out of this without it hurting.'

'Take off his handcuffs,' orders Gregg White to his men, taking off Marcus's handcuffs.

'Now gentlemen, if you would be so kind as to not cause trouble, and go to the wall over there, we'll do this in a respectful manner. Can we agree?'

'Yes,' agrees Chris

'Agreed,' says Marcus.

They go to the wall.

Six guards form a row in front of them.

Then the command is given.

Five minutes later, Mason comes along with his little forklift truck. After pulling the dead bodies onto the forks, he returns to the driver's seat and drives into the dark, humid and forbidden sanctuary with a colleague and two people he has never seen before in his life. And in all honesty, he does not care who they are, because down here, they're all the same.

CHAPTER 24

SOMETHING NOT SO GOOD IS BREWING in Scotland and Northern Ireland. Henry Montclair feels that they are pushing England and Westminster away even more so than when Brexit was the issue. There are so many things that he has never considered now that he is in power. Things like how important history and diplomacy are for cooperation within politics. Victoria Seymour was better at easing people's feelings, their objections and moods because of her knowledge about the past, present, and future. It was due to her diplomatic skill, the will to compromise and the understanding of the psychological make-up of people in general that she was good on all points in which he feels rather weak and awkward right now.

Perhaps he should have listened a little more to Victoria. Maybe he should have convinced her to stand at his side instead of pushing her out in the cold. He recalls her saying that there is no place for an aristocrat or dictator in a society that has been democratic for generations. They will only be successful if people are dissatisfied enough. But that is not the case with the United Kingdom. He does not see himself as an aristocrat or as a dictator. No, on the contrary. He sees himself as someone who is going to solve the crisis that the United Kingdom has gotten itself into with Brexit.

It is so difficult for a politician to satisfy all the people. He heard a rumor today that the population has begun calling the City of Westminster Abbey "The City of Great Worries". He was told it came from up North. At least he can count on Wales, contrary to Scotland and Northern Ireland, to praise him as their new savior in the hopes of crumbs falling onto their plates.

And crumbs they have certainly received. The new armaments to Wales and England have helped calm them down and stabilized the military after the purge he initiated under Victoria Seymour's rule. Of course, some military personnel have become worried with the photographs from Nordhausen circulating. He will probably have to arrange a new purge, which is not going to be as easy as the first time. Back then, two-thirds of the military had their stripes taken away and many older soldiers were put on the streets to prevent them from turning on him. The English and Welsh units under his command have remained loyal. The military has been tough in their crack-downs at demonstrations and at least now the majority of citizens are now behaving properly. Some are still causing civil disobedience on an unheard scale which is difficult to put down. But there are solutions for that too.

He must navigate carefully in order not to trigger internal riots in the military, which he needs to maintain his power. That is why additional money is constantly allocated to improve salaries and military equipment. Likewise, the intelligence service has had an increase in their budget to enable them to expand their surveillance of citizens which has led to a much more stable society. He's glad that during the purge, he didn't send new armaments to Scotland and Northern Ireland.

The military and intelligence only cover some of the challenges before him. It seems Gregg White's strategy about weakening the Scottish and North Irish have, to some extent, backfired. With the recurring problems in the public sector in which one-third of the people were laid off under the first reshuffle to the goverment, the purge has had an unexpected and unforeseen consequence of indirectly weakening the government's ability to keep up some civil services. Dissatisfaction is now spreading to all levels of society. Under the purge, Gregg should have remained by the military and intelligence service. But they agreed that purging out civil servants would decrease the chances of an internal revolt against them. Back then, it had sounded like a good idea although it went against what Victoria Seymour claimed: Let only the minorities be affected, not the majority, because, then society will eventually turn its back on you. It is something that he understands now.

Yes, there are so many problems. Scotland Yard has still not figured out who killed her. But one thing is for sure; if he wants to remain in power, he has to play his cards over a much longer period of time and get back the population's confidence by starting to rewind this thing about fat people. He now recognizes that the violence and unfairness against fat people was only a way to come to power, not a way to keep it. The implantation of microchips from ImplantSkills is proceeding, but much slower than anticipated. He is getting tired of some citizens behaving badly, tearing out implants again and again, and thereby contributing to an overload of the prison system. It means internment camps had to be built and that is very expensive.

Then now there is Nordhausen. If it really turns out that the victims from Nordhausen are citizens of the United Kingdom, then things might not turn out well for his government in the long run. Or for that matter turn out well for him. People have begun turning against him after seeing the photographs and especially after the hard crack-down at the latest demonstration. He has heard people saying in public that he should hang from a light pole and suffer a similar fate as Victory Seymour. He cannot accept people saying this about him, so now a law is in the making, preventing any such further annoyance. Since his rise to power, the threat for an uprising against him, has become a real problem. And in spite of the military on the streets, the curfew and Martial Law, people are continuing to demonstrate and the government keeps cracking-down. It seems some citizens do not care about the consequences for themselves, their families and loved ones.

The sudden change in the public mood and in what is going on, makes him see enemies everywhere. It is not only the population that is getting out of control, but also Northern Ireland, Scotland, the European Union, the United Nations and now the damn Amnesty International. They are all opposed to him and his government's rule. His refusal to step down as Prime Minister because of Nordhausen and his refusal to revoke the changes made under Victoria Seymour's rule to the doctrine of Parliamentary Sovereignty, seems to bother Scotland and Northern Ireland very much and they feel that their autonomy is being threatened. It upsets him that they and the rest of the world simply don't just shut up. The constant intervention from the rest of the world, such as the European Union and the United Nations, is worsening his ulcer. Hopefully by rewinding time and events back a little, he can buy some precious time. He will revoke the laws for fat people and give those with a Body Mass Index above 35 their civil rights back. If such a trade-off is negotiable with the world, it might accept that the changes to the doctrine of Parliamentary Sovereignty remain as they are.

Why did those fat bastards have to kill Victoria Seymour? All he wanted was to pave the way for her excellent political agenda. Admittedly, he may have gotten a little carried away after her death, seeing an opportunity to grasp power. But with the death of Victoria it is the first time Gregg has truly failed him. He should have protected her much better. Additionally, Greggs handling of fat people domestically was something not even he had anticipated. All the well-dressed henchmen costing a fortune. Fat people are, after all, citizens of the United Kingdom. The reality is that because of what Gregg has done, the situation in Great Britain seems to be getting worse by the day. But Henry knows that if he wants to stay in power, he has to hold on to Gregg.

CHAPTER 25

ONE DAY AFTER THE PHOTOGRAPHS from Nordhausen reach the press, the nightmare of shoveling dead people into deep and dark catacombs for what seems like forever, ends for Mason Sanders. At the German Defense Ministry in Berlin, all hell broke loose after the press conference at the European Union's headquarters in Brussels. Several military divisions were sent from the Karl-Guenther Barracks in Nordhausen, some ten kilometers away from Dora and Mittelbau, to immediately seal off the crime scene. From the General-Weber military installation in Paderborn, two technical delegations including forensic experts and psychologists who knew how to handle situations like these were also sent.

Mason hears footsteps. He is sitting beside a stack of dead obese people, staring into the air when he sees a soldier only a few meters from him. The soldier looks at him.

'Es gibt überlebende,' he hears a voice shout. He sees another soldier approaching him. They are both carrying weapons, but down here, he has become used to weapons.

'Wir brauchen ein Sanitäter,' the first soldiers screams and then asks, 'Ist alles in Ordnung? Sind Sie okay?'

'What?' answers Mason.

'Eh … are you alright?'

'Yes, I'm fine. Thank you. And you?'

'How many people are down here, do you know?'

'I think, I counted nine alive. They shot some before they left. The others hid somewhere inside the forbidden zone.'

The soldiers help Mason come to his feet. One of the soldiers takes off his backpack and leans down to open it, fumbling around inside.

'Here,' the soldier says. 'Water and some chocolate. Please eat, but stay put here, okay?'

'Sure, I love chocolate.'

The soldiers return to where they came from. More voices can be heard in the distance. It seems there are many coming to save them. Why couldn't they have arrived earlier, thinks Mason.

He hears people yelling in German and sees a commander arrive on the scene. Mason thinks to understand what they are saying. They all look rather surprised at their findings. *Die sind nicht Deutschen aber Engländern*, he hears someone say. *Was machen die denn hier unten? Der Krieg ist doch vorbei?* The last thing he understood was something about being English, not German, and something about the war having ended. A medic comes to his help and asks, 'Are you alright?'

'Why do people keep asking me that?'

'Are you able to walk?'

'Yes, why?'

'Come, let's get you out of here. This must have been a living hell.'

'Oh well, it's amazing how fast we humans get used to new things.'

'You're in shock. Come on, let's go. Do you remember your name?'

'Of course I remember my name. What a silly question. It's … it's … Eh ... actually … No. I don't remember.'

'Don't worry. We'll find out soon enough. You'll come to your senses later, I promise you and then you can tell me what your name is. There's absolutely nothing to worry about.'

'Oh! That's good to know. You seem to be a nice lad.'

'Let's get out in the sun.'

THE SUN'S rays blind Mason. He blinks a few times as his eyes adjust to the light. His nose instantly fills up with an intense smell of wet, humid earth. He recognizes the colors of autumn and hears birds twittering in a nearby tree.

'Oh my God,' he says. 'I thought I'd never see the sun again. What happened down there?'

'That's what we're trying to figure out. Are you from England?'

'No. I'm from the United Kingdom. All of us down there are. As well as the mountains of people in those piles. We're a product of Victoria Seymour's ambition.'

'You probably don't know, but she's dead.'

'Oh really? That's the best news I've had for weeks. What happened?'

'She was assassinated by people who probably weren't fully satisfied with her politics.'

'Ha ha. Was it some obese person?'

'It was actually five obese persons, yes.'

Mason is silent, then breaks out in laughter causing the soldiers and people standing nearby to look at him. He doesn't care. Nothing could make him happier at the moment than the news of Victoria Seymour's death. Justice happens after all! When he calms down, he addresses the medic, asking, 'So, I guess everything has returned to normal in the United Kingdom?'

'Well ... not quite. But this is not the time to worry about such unimportant matters. If you don't mind and if you have the energy, we'd like to ask you some questions. We can answer your questions later. How about it?'

'Sure. But you know what?'

'No.'

'Is it possible to get a cup of coffee around here?'

The medic laughs. 'It certainly is my friend.' He points at a tent on the horizon. 'Go there and drink and eat as much as you like. I'm sure the German taxpayers won't mind you eating a couple of sausages and drinking as much coffee as you prefer.'

ALL TOGETHER, there are nine survivors – eight men and one woman. Four are rather obese, one is of normal size, two are rather skinny and two still somewhat chubby, one of which is Mason. He has lost a great deal of weight in those catacombs. The work of tossing obese people from here to there has taken its toll on him. The surviving woman, whose name is Monica Griffith, has also lost quite a bit of weight. A criminal investigator goes to Mason and asks if he can sign some papers. Then he is free to go and do as he likes. Two officers dressed in casual clothing are at his service and offer to bring him anywhere in the world he would like to go.

Mason is still in deep shock. Anything else would be rather unusual. It will take a while for him to recover from the effects of seeing and experiencing so much death and evil and having been a part of it. It is clear that what happened will forever be rooted deeply inside of him. But it is not impossible to move on. Sometimes life punches you where it really hurts.

But surprisingly, he comes to the conclusion that the feelings and thoughts he has right now are not as destructive as he would have anticipated. As the psychologist said to him; it could be worse, he could be dead. Germans obviously are a little more direct when talking about scandals. She has also reassured him that he is not the cause of the conflict but a victim. He thought about this for a while, and realized that she is right and concluded that maybe in a year or so he might require psychological help, but not now.

He is well aware of the fact that it is very human nature to believe that things are under control, when they are not. Seen in this perspective, everyone must eventually go through the learning process the hard way to mature. Forecasting how the weather is going to turn out for the next two years and promise it will actually behave as forecasted, is perhaps not the best example to use, but many people do forecast how they expect life to turn out. Unfortunately, you can be as good as you want and sometimes things turn out the way you would like them to, but most of the time, however, you simply fail because you either misjudge yourself or make the wrong decisions or because external conditions are not in your favor.

To put it mildly: Shit happens. People get hit by cars and die. Airplanes crash, trains wreck, ships sink, or some drunk drives his car into you while crossing the street. It is part of life to die or to sometimes get caught in impossible situations like sweeping dead people off the floor in some unpleasant place. It is a very human thing to believe that we have our lives under control, even though we do not. But believing this, we feel safe which is necessary for our survival and a way for us to ignore the fact that life actually is dangerous.

What insurance policy is worth the paper it is written on if the earth is destroyed by a meteor? Or what insurance policy today, does not provide as an extra feature, terrorism, to sell more polices, even though 0,00000005 percent of the world's population will ever end up in a terrorist attack? The chances of meeting someone dangerous are probably higher than ending up somewhere in Germany shoveling dead corpses for some insane government. He and 2.387 other people were simply just unlucky. But he was lucky to have been given this chance to survive and get on with his life. He was surprised and shocked to hear that the situation has worsened even further after Victoria's death in the country he was born and raised in and used to be so proud of. Now this Henry Montclair has become Prime Minister. The name rings a small bell in relation to a position he had at the Cabinet Office.

Mason gets into the backseat of the Mercedes with the two civilian dressed officers. He asks them if it is possible for them to drive him to the Berlin Airport where a German military jet is waiting for him. He wants to return to Slovenia, to Piran, his summer residence and apply for asylum there. For the rest of his days, and may they be many, he would like to spend his time doing absolutely nothing, just sitting in a sun-lounger, looking out over the town square and its harbour and think about what to do next. He will visit Café Piran every morning, chat with Mehdi Hanachi, tune in on the latest gossip and perhaps, once in a while, assist his girlfriend in building up her enterprise. At least he is lucky because he can afford it, whereas Monica Griffith has nothing left. She wants to return to England where she will track down the underground resistance and support it in eradicating the government. He, on the contrary, finds that if people are so dumb and careless about the democracy they live in, it is their own damn fucking fault. He has promised to support her fight against the government with financial aid and with connections he has on the European mainland and throughout the world.

YULIA, Mason's girlfriend, has permission to go out on the apron and wait for the military business jet, instead of inside the small terminal. She sees the plane in the clear sky turning onto final approach. She was thrilled to hear Mason's voice after so many weeks of worrying herself sick. She thought the worse had happened and because she couldn't contact Mike Hornett, it all seemed so frustrating and sad.

In such situations her thoughts were rolling. Coming from Romania, she is old enough to have experienced her first years under the rule of an evil and brutal dictator. Her parents and grand-parents used to tell stories about those times and with all that is happening now, she is worried about the situation in the United Kingdom. Ceaușescu, the Romanian dictator, was a popular figure with the West because he had a tendency to challenge authorities of the Soviet Union. At home though, it was a different story. Here he was hated by his people. Her father was a respected politician with a high position who eventually turned on Ceaușescu openly, disapproving the worsening conditions to the Romanian population from the 1980ies and onwards and the state's brutal crack-down on its citizens. He had tried to change things from the inside and was eventually unwilling to support the further Ceaușescu regime, finally forcing him to flee the country with his family.

Some ten years ago she started visiting her country of birth on a regular basis again. Much has changed since Romania joined European Union. Most of the old, almost non-existing infrastructure is new. Industry is becoming more productive and efficient, and the economy is slowly turning in the right direction. Salaries are still low, but increasing and not only the rich are becoming more prosperous, but also the new middle-class and even the poorest. Today Romania has environmental standards on the same level as other nations in the European Union. It is amazing how much has changed since she has been returning more regularly to her country.

Yulia sees the wheels of the business jet touch the runway. A light cloud of smoke from the wheels follows the plane down the runway. When the jet turns onto the taxi way and continues to the apron, a follow-me car takes over and brings the aircraft to its parking position. She cannot wait to see Mason. It has been five long weeks of uncertainty, and because he did not tell her over the telephone what has been going on or where he has been, she is going to inform him that such behavior is not acceptable. The business aircraft turns off its engines. A moment later, the door opens and falls slowly to the ground, stretching out its stairs in the back. One of the pilots comes out first and talks to the ground-personal followed by her big lover-boy.

Yulia hardly recognizes him. She is shocked to see it is Mason. He is much slimmer than the last time she saw him. What has been going on? She throws her arms around him, exclaiming, 'Oh my God! What happened to you?'

'You don't want to know. Believe me. You don't!'

They embrace and kiss without saying anything for a long time.

'Wow Mason, I love the new you! But I think I'm going to have difficulties having you to myself.'

'I'm thinking about having the surplus skin surgically removed.'

'Dear Mason! What you don't understand is that people care for you because you're a nice person with your heart in the right place.'

'And now with a smaller body.'

'At least you seem to still have your good mood, so what you've been through can't be that bad.'

'It's in the past. I've heard it's gotten worse in the United Kingdom and I need to help do something about it.'

'You ought to. We all ought to. You know my background very well – or my parent's background. Those photographs. It can't be true.'

'Believe me! It is. And if anyone tries to tell you otherwise, you bring them to me, and I'll tell them about it.'

'Come, Mason, let's go inside the terminal. I think we need a cup of coffee.'

'And do our normal arrival routine?'

'Of course. It's been a couple of weeks and I'm getting tired of satisfying myself.'

The comment makes Mason laugh. And he recognizes that it's the first time he has laughed since he left Nordhausen. 'I must admit I haven't thought about sex for a while.' Mason looks down his pants. 'But I think that's about to change. At least now, I can see my dick again.'

'You must have experienced something really weird if you haven't been horny for a while, hm.'

'Perhaps I'll tell you about what I experienced but it may take a while.'

Under normal circumstances the arrival procedure would be to drink a couple of Pornstar Martini's at the bar inside the little terminal, then grab a taxi and drive to the apartment and have a round of sex on the kitchen table. This would be followed by a delightful dip in the ocean to remove the smell of sex before heading to the Café Casa Piran to drink the best coffee in Piran, and listen to the latest gossip. A little later they would return to the apartment to dress up and go to eat somewhere.

'Listen,' says Mason. 'Why don't we skip the drinks and head directly to the apartment? I need to freshen up.'

That surprises Yulia.

'Well … eh … okay. Any particular reason for breaking a tradition?'

'Yes. Today is the start of a new life. There are so many things we complain about. Things that are completely unimportant. When those unimportant things are gone, we become humble. Unfortunately, this only happens with life-changing events, at least, that's what I've learned in the past few weeks.'

'What happened, Mason?'

'It's a long story. How about driving directly to Café Casa Piran instead of to the apartment?.'

'You change your mind a lot.'

'I know, but I want to say thanks you to Mehdi Hananchi.'

'For what?'

'For being a man with a lot of insight.'

ON THE way to Cafe Casa Piran, Yulia asks the taxi driver to stop at a spot along the ocean, partly covered with trees and bushes. Mason, surprised at the sudden halt, sees her get out of the taxi. She makes a sign to him to get out as well. She then tells the taxi driver to continue after giving him a decent tip.

'Come, I'll show you something.' She takes his hand.

'Come where?'

'Just follow me. You'll see.'

They walk to the ocean and follow a narrow beach to something that looks like a small lagoon. It's really just a couple of square meters of sand but it looks nice and private. She lets go of his hand and points to a little wooden mini-shed, which could be in a better condition, but is good enough for her plans. She takes his hand and pulls him along.

'Come, in here, Mason,' she demands.

He follows her into the mini-shed where there is a small battered table, hardly big enough for four people to sit around, but large enough for someone to lay on their back. She hops up on it, bottom first, lies down and spreads her legs, allowing Mason to see that she is wearing no panties.

'Come, take me here. Now!'

Mason feels his dick grow.

'How did you find this little shed?' he asks.

'When I was running last week. I've been exercising a lot to get hold of my thoughts. Now pull down those pants.'

Mason does as ordered. He lies her down on the table and starts licking her pussy.

'How do you like my new haircut?'

'Did you cut your hair?'

'Not that one you fool.'

'Yes, I like it.'

'Now, do me hard! I've missed you so much and really thought I'd lost you.'

Her behavior completely throws him off his bearings. For a moment he does not know how to behave. Normally, they would kiss a little before going on, play a little around and stuff like that. Something he has heard is called foreplay. But today is different. And she is so wet that it almost runs out of her like a waterfall. He drags her closer to the table edge, making it easier to penetrate and rubbing her clitoris with his hard dick. It makes her twist from side to side.

When he finally penetrates her fully, she comes, almost crying in ecstasy.

'Wow, that was fast, Yulia! What happened?'

'Ups, sorry. I … don't know.'

'Now it is his turn! He starts moving back and forth. With every stroke he senses how unusually sensitive he is. Today, the feeling is completely different. It does not last long before he comes and it feels like the stream of vanilla syrup never ends.

'Ohh God!' he moans, looking up, thanking the heavens for making him survive that horrid experience. He lets go of her breasts and lets his head fall onto her chest.

'You have no idea how good it is to be alive,' he says. 'Believe me! There's plenty more where that came from. This was just a warm-up.'

'I can't wait,' says Yulia.

But Mason is already gone. With his head between her breasts, he has fallen asleep.

HALF AN hour later Yulia calls a taxi. While she waits, she cleans up Mason's gigantic mess between her legs. He cleans his business by letting himself fall into the ocean until he sees Yulia waving to him that she has ordered the taxi.

Half an hour later, the taxi still hasn't arrived.

'That damn Piranian taxi service, it's not what it used to be. How about if we walk?' suggests Mason.

'You really mean it?'

'Come on, it's only 5 kilometers.'

'Okay, let's go.'

IT TAKES an hour to walk to Piran. Their first stop is the Café Casa where Mason sees Medhi Hanachi up to his usual business. Entering the beautifully decorated cafe, he hears the familiar voice yell in his direction.

'Mason! So nice to see you again!' The good looking little Arabic man stops suddenly and just stands there. 'Wow, Mason! What happened? Have you lost weight? And has it already been one year?'

'Only six months,' smiles Mason. 'But believe me, it feels like an eternity. And yes, I lost weight.'

'What happened?'

'Oh, it's a long story Mehdi. But I would like to thank you.'

'Thank me. For what?'

'Remember your theory on obese people and their common denominators?'

'Eh, yes.'

'It wasn't fully snatched out of thin air.'

'I know. I've seen the photographs from Germany. I've been following the developments in the United Kingdom very closely. As you know, I too have family over there.'

'Things are definitely not good.'

'No they're not.'

'But don't you think the European Union or the United Nations will get involved soon? I mean, how can they allow such a thing to happen to a modern democracy?'

'Well, it has happened, hasn't it? And so far, it seems that neither the European Union nor the United Nations will enter into the conflict.'

'But they can't just sit back and watch and do nothing.'

'The United Kingdom is a sovereign country. They have no business interfering,' says Mehdi.

'Something must happen.' adds Yulia.

'Look at my country of birth,' says Mehdi. 'Look at how many years it took before the world got involved in Libya, and only because my former leader … I spit on his grave … pissed off the French.'

'But Mehdi, did you ever join the resistance in Libya? Did you ever do anything to change the situation?'

'No. I have to be honest. I have a wife and children, you know. They would have suffered the most if I had opposed the regime. Part of me wanted to, and although I didn't physically join the resistance, look at what happened to me. I still ended up in one of Gaddafi's prisons. It only takes one wrong word.'

'What happened? You've never really told me.'

'Not much happened, Mason. I accidentally criticized Gaddafi. And that was enough to end up with broken bones.'

'Hm.'

'But wow! You've really lost weight, Mason. How did it happen? It suits you well. Oh, you want Cappuccino?'

'Yes, please.'

'And for you too, Ms.?'

'Yes, please. My name is Yulia, by the way.'

'And I'm Mehdi.

'How's your new pizza restaurant coming along?'

'Well. It opened. But it seems people would rather eat burgers. So, now I got rid of the pizza and sell delicious burgers. And what about your business, Mason?'

'I think I lost ImplantSkills. It was sold to foreign investors. And with all that's going on at the moment, I'm staying in Piran. Returning to England is out of the question.'

'How about your business … eh … Yulia?'

'It's up and running.'

'That's good. Mason says you've worked hard for your success.'

'We all work hard. But it takes some luck, too.'

'Uh, that's really true,' confirms Mason. 'Anyway, Mehdi, if you need someone behind the counter, then give me a call.'

Mehdi does not know if it was a joke or not.

'I really meant it, Mehdi. I need new challenges.'

'Ha ha. You both are always welcome to help me and if you really need a new challenge, I'll take you up on your offer. I don't remember the last time I had a vacation.'

'Deal! Just say when.'

Mason notices that Mehdi's expression is suddenly serious. 'Hm.' he says. 'Have you heard anything about the other two? You know – Martens and

Hollister? Their wives have been asking if I've heard anything from you. You all went to Hamburg together, right?'

'Oh, that's right, Mason.' says Yulia, 'They've asked me if I've heard anything a couple of times too. They're also worried sick about their husbands.'

Mason is reluctant to answer. He thinks about it for a while and finally pulls himself together. 'When you see their wives Mehdi, and you too Yulia, you might tell them that the German government will probably be getting in touch with them. They can also call the authorities in Germany if they want answers because I'm probably not the right one to provide them.'

MIKE HORNETT called his girlfriend from a telephone booth after the incident at Heathrow Airport and told her what had happened. He convinced her to take the next plane out of London and also convinced the crew from the Lufthansa flight to take him with them on the return flight. When the plane touched down in Hamburg, he went to the airport authorities and requested asylum. They, of course, were a little baffled about the request from a British citizen who was also a citizen of the European Union. After a few telephone calls, they ordered him a taxi and asked the driver to drop him off at Hamburg Town Hall.

At the Hamburg Town Hall they were also confused and didn't really know what to do with him so they sent him with another taxi to a refugees reception center on the outskirts of Hamburg. They obviously felt that Mike Hornett must have the same rights as Syrian and African refugees escaping from war and conflict.

For Mike, the experience and the long hours of waiting were somewhat frustrating. As an Englishman coming from a modern Western society, one of oldest democracies in the world, a NATO ally and a European Union member, he felt that the Germans should have treated him a little better. It would have been more appropriate to send him to a hotel somewhere, not to barracks in the middle of nowhere to a four square meter room where he has to share a bathroom with people from all over the world. His bank accounts have now been cancelled by his government making it necessary to live off his girlfriend's savings when she arrives in Hamburg so they don't have to live in this hell hole of unhappiness with people who have lost everything they have. The 11,96 Euro per day allowance he gets is hardly enough to buy decent clothes or something to eat. Hamburg is expensive, not as expensive as London, but on such a hunger allowance, life really does stink. What a shitty situation he and the United Kingdom have ended up in.

At least for Mike who, compared to other refugees, is able to be at the airport in Hamburg one week later to pick up his girlfriend and as life occasionally has it once in a while, they turn out to be the lucky ones. Mike's girlfriend is on the third last flight leaving the United Kingdom to the European Union on a regular basis where passengers are not required to have a permit, since this morning the government in Westminster has decided to withdraw its diplomats from the European Union. Travel for regular people who are not doing business outside the United Kingdom has now become limited. Mike sees her come out of Arrivals, leaving her luggage behind and running into his arms with tears in her eyes. She throws her arms around him in relief.

'What's going on?' she cries, pressing her body even harder to his. 'Why aren't the European countries doing anything to help us?'

'The United Kingdom is in a very complicated situation. I think the last time anyone tried something like this was just before World War II. Unfortunately, our generation doesn't have the experience in how to solve a diplomatic crisis of this size.'

'Are you saying we're going to war?'

'No, that's not what I meant. I'm sure that, eventually, those in power will be held responsible for their actions. Everything will be fine.'

DENDA ESCUDOS, the President of the European Council who is responsible for holding the European Union's 27 member nation's heads-of-states together is feeling increasing pressure on his shoulders. What is happening in the United Kingdom is a disaster for everyone, and the feelings he had as a youngster and as a stud in Spain when he was in his middle thirties when Francisco Franco Bahamonde was still ruling as a dictator, are returning with one unpleasant memory after another. The United Kingdom is turning into a nightmare for the European Union. Westminster has become a disgrace to itself for what happened to obese people in Nordhausen. At least, after the awful incident, it has made populations in Poland and Hungary where the governments have for some time had aristocratic tendencies to tighten the grip on their politicians. Nordhausen clearly shows that history has a tendency of repeating itself within only a few generations. Many in the rest of the European Union's member nations have come to understand that extreme left or right-wing politics does no one a favor – except those in power.

The majority of people on the European continent no longer know what to think or what to expect of the United Kingdom. They look, they observe and then they move on with their daily lives. From being one of the strongest economies in the world and a respected nation, the United Kingdom has U-turned on itself and become a split xenophobia society that is now almost a minimum democracy and a complete disgrace to itself and the world. And in spite of this, there are still many people in England and Wales who believe that they are the ones who owe the world and that they are doing the right thing simply to keep up the illusion of still being a superior breed of people.

How can it be? And how much misery does it take to shatter a nation before it finally wakes up and recognizes that it has taken a completely wrong turn and is heading out over the cliff? The European Union has again and again been accused of doing nothing about the situation by people from the global community and also from people living in the United Kingdom and in the European Union. Smart people are leaving the sinking island, but now the government in Westminster has put a stop to this as well by limiting ferries and trains through the Eurotunnel and air traffic. Some on both sides of the Channel even blame the European Union for having caused the havoc on purpose simply to punish the United Kingdom after Brexit.

But how can the European Union assist juristically and legally to sort out what is going on in the United Kingdom? It cannot. It is an institution, a collaboration, not a country, but an entity which has instituted common rules that have been agreed to by all its member nations. The European Union does not have the authority to go to war, to invade another country, or for that matter, to interfere in other nation's affairs. Currently, the United Kingdom has still not fully left the European Union, but the new government in Westminster does not accept and obey the authority of the European Court of Justice in Strasbourg and the European Human Rights Act. So what is going on, on the other side of the Channel, is not really the European Union's problem. It is a problem for the United Nations.

But something is changing in the minds of the 27 remaining member nations of the EU Council. As European history shows, a European country running amok, asserting their own agenda is not the best thing for European prosperity and stability. The 'English Patient' ought to be healed once and for all. After Victoria Seymour, Eurocrats feel themselves confirmed in the need to integrate even further, to secure the stability of the European continent, but there are also those who would rather see the European Project dead. They think that would be a small price to pay for true national freedom and liberation.

Lately, Denda Escudos, a true Eurocrat, has had vast amounts of secret talks with officials behind closed doors at the European Union exploring how the 'English Patient' can be healed. The United Nations is, as always, split on what measures should be taken, taking into account what effect an unstable United Kingdom and European Union could have on world security, global trade, and on a world with an extremely sensitive economy. Probing has also taken place at the United Nations Security Council with its five members, China, France, Russia, the United Kingdom and the United States whose permanent seats were established in 1945 by the United Nations Charter though, of course this time, excluding the United Kingdom. Unfortunately, the Russians have objected to practically any solution since they have recently become allies with the government in Westminster Abbey and have already invested a vast amount of money in the The Party in the hope of sharing power. The consensus of the three other Security Council members are that the European Union must finally show some strength and, for once in its long history of failure and successes, show that it is capable of cleaning up its own shit to maintain stability on the European continent.

A situation of this magnitude is, from a juristic view, extremely difficult to solve. With Henry Montclair and his government continuously refusing to come to the negotiating table and discuss whatever they have on their agenda no compromise can be found in reversing the on-going madness. This is something neither Henry Montclair nor his government is willing to do, but at least, for hard-ball cases like these, there is an efficient way to proceed.

And that is with embargoes and sanctions.

MEHDI HANACHI from Café Casa Piran takes his usual orders from his jet-set customers. In winter there are not so many people in town which provides a nice break after a busy summer. But, of course, that is not so good for revenues. Mehdi goes to a woman and a man with a new-born baby who, a few minutes earlier had sat at one of the tables outside to enjoy what was left of the warm weather and the sun's rays.

'Good morning. Have you decided?'

'Yes, I think so,' says Mike Hornett.

'I'll have a Latté,' says his girlfriend, rocking the baby gently from side-to-side. 'And one of those bagels with salmon. They look delicious.'

'I'll have the same,' adds Mike.

'On its way.'

'Uhm, excuse me, if I may ask,' asks Mike. 'You're friends with Mason, aren't you?'

Mehdi turns around, returning to the table.

'Yes ... I am.'

'Is he doing alright? You probably don't remember me, but we met some time ago. I'm Mike the journalist.'

'Ahh ... yes ... I do remember you sitting here with Mason. He doesn't spend much time around here. What can I do for you?'

'Do you know where he is?'

'Why?'

'Look. I'm not here to write an article. I'm here as a private person to find out if he's all right. The last time I saw him, he was on his way to Hamburg in Germany and since then I haven't heard a word from him.'

'Oh! I understand. Mason is alright. But maybe you should talk with him yourself. He usually comes in around noon for his regular Cappuccino. Where are two staying?'

'In Lucija. It wasn't possible to get a reservation here.'

'No that's obvious. There's only one hotel in Piran. Did you come with the shuttle bus?'

'We did.'

'And how do you like Piran so far?'

'It's quite nice, actually. Not much going on. But the climate is comfortable and with what's happening in the United Kingdom, where we originally come from, we've somehow become refugees without a home.'

'Oh, I know the feeling, believe me,' utters Medhi.

'A lot of my colleagues have fled to Europe,' continues Mike. 'Some even asked for citizenship. I'm still amazed it has come down to this. How is it possible? Not so long ago, the United Kingdom was a well-renowned place … and now … It's just …'

'Oh …' says Mehdi. 'It's always the English. Their arrogance destroys whole nations. Where do you come from?'

'England.'

'Upps.'

'It's okay. I think, we're getting used to it,' says Mike, glancing at his girlfriend.

'No we're not,' she answers.

'But don't you think someone will soon try to do something?' asks Mehdi. 'The United Kingdom is an important trade, security and political partner of the European Union. I'm not sure if they'll be able to keep it up. I just read this morning that there will be sanctions imposed against the United Kingdom and an embargo on military equipment.'

'Oh my God! That means our harbours will be blocked by warships.'

'I believe something in that direction, yes.'

'But that's awful,' says Mike's girlfriend.

'Honestly, I'm not so sure if it is,' says Mehdi quite determined. 'It might make you English more humble, especially considering what you have done to others throughout your history.'

'In a way, I guess it's true …'

'You people are in for a rough ride, that's for sure!'

'What do you mean?'

'Well, if you haven't noticed, the United Kingdom is an island. I think the European Union is going to freeze you out big-time with that blockade. You people are going to suffer, that's for sure.'

'What's happening to our country?' asks Mike's girlfriend. She starts to cry. Mehdi realizes he went too far this time, but somehow it feels good to finally be able to thwart those English.

'I am so sorry,' he apologizes. 'I did not want to sound rude. But you know what? I'll call Mason and see if he can drop by a little earlier today.'

MASON is quite surprised at the news from Mehdi. He hurries from the apartment down past the town hall square, along the promenade to Café Casa Piran. When he sees Mike, he runs to him and immediately embraces him.

Mike is happy to see Mason too, but fails to return his gesture because he simply fails to recognize the man as Mason Sanders. 'Mason? Wow! I hardly recognized you. Sorry about that. You have lost weight.'

'Yes, isn't it wonderful? I even go for a run in the morning and lift some weights in the evening now. It's like a whole new life! Actually, it *is* a whole new life. But how are you doing and what're you doing here?'

'I'm … well … we're refugees without a home.'

'Oh my God,' exclaims Mason, 'how rude of me.' He gives Mike's girlfriend his hand and looks at the cute little baby. 'Oh, isn't he sweet? He looks just like his father. No hair.'

Mike laughs at the joke. 'Very funny Mason. And by the way, it's actually a girl. That's why she's wearing a blue romper.'

'Okay. So … not much into children.'

'Hey Mason, Cappuccino?'

'Yes please, Mehdi.'

'So … How's life, Mason?'

'Well, as you said yourself: A refugee without a home so I've decided to make Piran my new home and Slovenia my new country.'

'Wow! That's something. What about ImplantSkills?'

'What about it? That's all in the past; a past that'll never return. But what's the story on you two? What happened?'

'I … I got an offer to go to Nordhausen …' Mike stops speaking when he sees Mason's face turn white. He lowers his head and then continues. 'Yes I know. What you probably don't know; I was the one with the pictures in Brussels. I saw with my own eyes what was going on.'

'Well,' sighs Mason.

'You survived, amazing!'

Mason looks into Mike's eyes. 'I did. And with that guilt I'll have to live with rest of my life.'

'What happened to the two others?' asks Mike, not really wanting to know the answer. But he needs to know. 'And Chris Campbell?'

'Chris and this other guy got shot. As far as I can tell, the third one had froth around his mouth.'

'Cyanide? He's old military, he told me.'

'I see. They all are down there.'

'What happened in Hamburg?'

'I … don't exactly know,' says Mason. 'We went to this place, to this office in the middle of Hamburg in this exclusive shopping area. It was a nicely decorated office with class. We had only been talking a few minutes when I started feeling dizzy. I guess they put something in our coffee that kills, but I woke up again, and then I was on a military truck with a lot of corpses. I was pretty confused and when they started off-loading the corpses, they discovered me. They started beating me up and said I should follow them into the catacombs. That's where I bite my transmitter out. Just before they put me in a cage.'

'Oh my God! I'm getting sick.'

They both turn their attention to Mike's girlfriend. For a moment Mason had forgotten she was sitting there, too. She passes the baby to Mike and runs for the toilet.

'Whoops,' exclaims Mason. 'I totally forgot we weren't alone.'

'It's okay. It will make her a little more ashamed to be English.'

'So, what now, Mike?'

'I don't know. But Piran is a nice place.'

'Well, why don't you stay here then?'

'No, it's too expensive. We're living off Kate's savings. Hamburg is cheaper and it's a rather nice city.'

'But the sun isn't shining there right now. You know what? Yulia and I have so many free rooms in our apartment, it would be so nice to have some life around us. Why don't you two move in with us? It could be fun.'

'You mean it?'

'I certainly do.

'Wow! I think we can say 'Yes' to that. Thanks Mason.'

'Mehdi!' shouts Mason.

'What?'

'Bring out your best white wine and five glasses. I'll call Yulia.'

'You mean the Rojac Istra Malvazija?'

'That's the one, my friend. That's the one. We need to celebrate life, but more importantly, celebrate us. And then, that the European Union finally gets itself pulled together and implements those sanctions.'

EPISODE 6

THE CONQUEST FOR PEACE

CHAPTER 26

PEOPLE WHO WANT TO LEAVE THE United Kingdom can no longer leave. Ferries and aircraft are now prohibited from taking passengers on board who are not traveling on business and who cannot show an allowance that this is the case. When transportation was possible, it was utilized by clever people to get to the Republic of Ireland, France, the Netherlands, or to somewhere else in the world. But now the only choice some have is to pack their personal belongings and take the car to Scotland before it is impossible to cross the 130 kilometer border guarded by Gregg White's team that wants to prevent the southern part of the United Kingdom from draining out of competent people.

For Henry, the whole situation is turning into a huge disaster. None of what is happening should have happened. The United Nations now calls him something between an aristocrat and a dictator, though he is quite satisfied with the former names people gave him such as Montlair. Something has happened in the minds of the people because of the United Kingdom's earlier obsessive pursuit of obese people combined with what happened in Nordhausen. To his advantage, there is still goodwill among the population who still don't believe that what happened in Nordhausen actually did happen. Many think it was all staged by the European Union to discredit the United Kingdom. Unfortunately though, on the international scene, it seems the good times are over with trouble brewing practically everywhere. The European Union and the United Nations, and now also Scotland and Northern Ireland have requested that the changes made to the doctrine of Parliamentary Sovereignty must be reversed. But neither Henry Montclair nor his government take these requests seriously. The European Union wants freedom of the press again as it was before Victoria came to power.

Such requests cannot be met when the entire Kingdom is in a state of chaos. It would be the wrong thing to do at the moment, especially with the huge unrest and civil disobedience going on. The sanctions imposed by the European Union, which the United Nations supports, has hurt more than anyone in his government had anticipated. The British people are suffering as a result of European Union politics prioritizing their own interests over that of providing the most basic needs to its citizens. This has also put pressure on him from Scotland and Northern Ireland to give in and rescind the doctrine of Parliamentary Sovereignty.

But this subject is non-negotiable as it always has been. It would cost him his role as Prime Minister, which would not be good under the current circumstances. The road is full of lions and pitfalls; there is nowhere for him to hide. Does he give up the Prime Minister position and return the constitution to how it once was, causing him and the people around him to lose their immunity? It would bring the lions to the court in The Hague, making him rot in a cell in the Netherlands without his wife and children who he loves and adores. A few times, he has threatened to use military intervention to clear the sea blockade, pointing out to the United Nations, that Scotland, Northern Ireland and the European Union must adapt to politics made in Westminster, and not the opposite. They must acknowledge that the United Kingdom is a sovereign country. With the sanctions, it seems the European Union's major objective is to shatter the good collaboration between England, Wales, Scotland and Northern Ireland, making Scotland and Northern Ireland claim what they always have – that they are the ones who pay the price for England's arrogance, pride, and stupidities.

IN TRUTH, it is history that is beginning to get in the way of Henry's rule, not the sanctions. He has still not come to understand the powers he is releasing in the United Kingdom. Some historians argue that what hurt most in the relationship between England and Scotland was the corrupt Scottish noblemen who sold Scotland out to England for financial gains in 1707, forcing Scotland to dissolve its Parliament. In the process, it lost half of its wealth because of the Darien Scheme, which was an attempt to make a colony out of Panama. This ended up completely dissolving Scotland that was in financial trouble and was being abused by England who was more powerful and rich. The British monarch also did not want to risk losing his power in Scotland to a Stuart. And now it seems that history is repeating itself a couple of hundred years later. Even today, some people in England believe that Scotland is nothing but a region of the United Kingdom, as is the case with Northern Ireland. Unfortunately for England, these regions consider themselves countries. Not so long ago, Henry Montclair had to take some geopolitical beatings by an upset First Minister of Scotland who stated that a country is defined as an independent sovereign state, possessing geographic regions associated with independent people with distinct political characteristics. A region, on the contrary, is a geographical area, broadly divided by its physical and human characteristics. So, by these definitions Scotland and Northern Ireland are countries and not regions. But Henry simply said he should relax and drink a pint, because his understanding of history is nothing but propaganda of the European Union.

It was a smart move to use obesity as an excuse to come to power because obesity is free from age, marital status, economic standing, and color along with political or religious conviction. It was even smarter to purge out before people understood what was going on. But it does not change the fact that a new major clean up is required if he is to remain in power; a purge like the one he peformed under Victoria to secure her power base. At least to some extent, most people understand that the reason for their deteriorating standard of living is the European Union, making citizens sitting out the sanctions, which makes him proud of them. These real decent and respectful people know that the European Union will eventually give up reasoned internal disagreement. People will fight for their motherland and nobody should tell either him or his people what they are to do. England has always been a superpower. It has always won its battles. And it will also win this one.

There is just one obstacle at the moment, one that needs to be solved, but one he has not fully figured out how to handle.

'You cannot ask the Queen to abdicate! Impossible!' says a stunned Lisa. It would be an extreme move and one that would probably not go down well with the people.

'But I just found out she's been doing her own negotiations with the European Union,' says Henry. 'She's undermining our negotiating position not to negotiate. It's treason! How dare she fly over there and talk to a foreign power while we're trying to do everything to get the United Kingdom out of the mess they have created for us? If you don't call it treason, Lisa, then I don't know what it's called.'

'How about a quisling?' suggests Gregg.

'That's the right word. That's what she is.'

'But the Queen!' continues Lisa. 'You cannot force her to abdicate.'

'She's holding talks with a foreign power! The people understand.'

'Don't you think it's just to make the European Union ease up a little on the sanctions? People are taking some hard blows here.'

'It's the principle. And the people can hold it together, just like they did in World War II. She's negotiating in secret with a foreign power, without mine or the government's consent. So, it's treason.'

'Why don't you ask her to stay where she is for a while?' suggests Gregg.

Lisa wants to know, 'Where's the Queen now?'

'In France.'

'Well, France is nice, let her stay,' continues Gregg.

'Yes,' confirms Lisa. 'If it must be. Then let her and her family stay in France for a while. I'll have a press release written saying that she needs some time off because of health issues. How about it, Henry?'

Henry feels his ulcer acting up for the second time today. It happens more frequently these days. There are just so many things to consider. Apart from the European Union sanctions, the United Nations has issued a resolution preventing the United Kingdom from purchasing munitions worldwide. On top of that, another resolution is on its way from the United Nations regarding diplomacy, although Russia and the United States have so far vetoed it, making it difficult for the European Union to enforce one-hundred percent strict sanctions. At least, with 90 ports, 14 of which are major, and 12.429 kilometers of coastline, the European Union recognizes that it would be a huge task to maintain such trade sanctions. They know it would cost a fortune and that the citizens of the European Union would eventually grow tired of paying for them and stop the Eurocrats from wasting so much money. It's just a matter of time before the European Council falls apart on the issue due to their usual self-interest. He has tried it so often when he worked there, where especially the French have an agenda for themselves another one for everybody else. With the Royal Navy's 6 destroyers, 4 patrol crafts and 15 frigates and an aircraft carrier in action blocking the way for warships sent by the European Union, there are gaps for sneaking in cargo ships with unauthorized goods. Surprisingly though, few days ago, the European Union requested its members to increase their flotillas, asking France to provide 3 corvettes, 9 patrol craft and 5 frigates. Germany was requested to provide respectively 3, 2 and 7, the Netherlands 35 observation helicopters and Denmark 12 of their updated versions. There is a lot of traffic on the water and in the air surrounding the United Kingdom.

And it's starting to piss off Henry big time.

'By the way, how did your meeting go with the Russians?' Henry asks Gregg in a moment of silence.

'They'll support us in harassing the European blockade.'

'That's good. And our generals?'

'They'll get what they need. The Russians did have to think about it. They're concerned about sending in too much equipment which might make American take advantage of the situation. The Russians have to be careful not to provoke the Europeans too much, due to the American and European sanctions against them.'

'Oh no! You mean they are only supporting to us to put themselves in a better negotiating position with the Americans and the European Union, simply to get rid of their own sanctions?'

'That's about it.'

'I hate politics.' exclaims Henry. 'I really do! All this wouldn't have happened if those five bastards hadn't killed Victoria.'

'Stop looking back. We have 5 Russian destroyers, 35 corvettes, 5 patrol crafts and 2 frigates.'

'Okay. At least, with so many ships we'll certainly be able to make bigger holes in their blockade. That's good news.'

'We certainly will. But ... there're also warnings from our generals.'

'And that would be?'

'They say that we're playing a high-risk game. They say that if the European Union wanted to, they actually have the ability to crush us completely. There are plenty more ships where they come from.'

'Ha ha, you have to be kidding. We have the best military in the world.'

'That might be. But the European Union has 1,5 million active troops, 550 warships and 2.450 aircraft on alert, he said. I think his message was very clear: Don't piss them off.'

'They won't be able to hold it together. So don't worry. How about NATO?'

'They're doing the right thing and staying out.'

'So, they wouldn't interfere if the Russians came to our rescue?'

'I wouldn't count on the Russians. They're only in it for the money. But I think you should realize that if it gets hot, we'll be on our own. The Russians simply don't want new sanctions.'

'How much are we actually paying at the moment?'

'Around 200 million dollars per day, in gold.'

'That must be a lot of gold bars. Imagine if the European Union hadn't done this to us, what could be done for the school and healthcare system.'

'It's around 666 gold bars per day.'

There is a sudden silence. Gregg is not sure why.

'What's the matter,' he asks.

'Is there a reason for the resemblance to the devils number?

'What do you mean?'

'Why did the Russians chose that number?'

Gregg starts to giggle. 'Well, to be exact, I think we pay 666,4 gold bars per day. Let's simply round it up to 667.'

'Thank you. How much gold do we have available?'

'The Bank of England says only for a couple of weeks.'

'And what do we do if the gold runs out and the European Union still has not given in?'

'Well, for that, they have come up with a plan.'

'I'm beginning to hate these merchants. And the plan would be?'

'Here.' Gregg hands over a couple of papers to Henry. 'There are a couple of businesses they're interested in.'

Henry looks at the list. Then pulls it out of Gregg's hand. He takes his time looking at the names on it.

'I cannot believe it,' screams Henry, scrolling wildly through the list. 'There must be at least 100 companies.'

'They're pretty much all connected to financial services. I think it's no secret that the American and European Union's sanctions hurt them financially. There's an urge for hard currency.'

'They're taking advantage of our situation, those assholes.'

'What about the Chinese? Do you think they can loan us money?'

'I've already talked to them,' says Henry. 'They were stopped by France at the United Nations Security Council.'

'And the Commonwealth? They're obligated to help us.'

'They're all traitors. They say that what's going on here has nothing to do with them.'

'We'll remember that later.'

'I just hope that the European Union will break soon. At least that will put us in a better negotiating position.'

SO FAR there are no signs that the European Union is in the process of breaking up. It frustrates Henry and Gregg to know that the sanctions must be eased because they have started making an impact on people's daily lives and it is showing in the general attitude toward the government. But it is not the physical sanctions Henry fears, but rather the economic sanctions. With those, the United Nations in collaboration with the European Union, has hit a nerve in London, the heart of the United Kingdom's economy, by blocking investors and companies' ability to attain fresh capital. Because of this, the Bank of England has been excluded from raising long-term interest rates on the world's financial markets. For a Kingdom in where a great deal of the Gross National Product is financial services, this is bad news. Really, really bad news. Additionally, people like Lisa, Gregg, and himself and a dozen others from the corridors of Westminster and from the Minister of Defense, some top military generals and heads of the intelligence service and some industrialists have now had their assets frozen and are subject to travel bans.

The physical blockade of goods and the economic sanctions have sent a strong signal to Henry and his powerful allies in politics and business, that the current situation is very serious. But as things are at the moment, it seems Henry and his government prefer this rather than coming to the negotiating table. They don't seem to give a damn about what they inflict on the United Kingdom – and the European Union. The situation for both parties is a lose-lose situation – except for Russia which earns a great deal of money supporting Westminster with military assistance. The grim reality is that, in addition to the problems presented by Brexit, the sanctions have led to soaring a capital flight bringing Britain to the brink of a huge recession-and no one in government seems to care.

Unfortunately, the situation is reciprocal. Germany is starting to feel the strain because less cars and consumer goods are being imported by England. At first, Germany appeared reluctant to impose sanctions, but due to its history, it is very well aware of what must be done. All European Union nations feel some type of deceleration of their economies. And now that the financial sector is nearly inaccessible, major implications to the economies of European Union member nations can be felt. The sanctions have made the Europeans aware that the United Kingdom is not only a booming market for consumer goods but also a huge exporter of high-tech, human-skills and industrial semi-components. Food exporters, such as the Netherlands, Spain, France and Italy, are facing losses and French farmers have gone to Paris to spread the quantities of corn, cheese and milk in the streets that would normally to go to the United Kingdom, to show their dissatisfaction with the European Commission and its sanctions. Fresh fruit and vegetables, meat, dairy produce and several other foods, are all rotting in containers on ships and freight trains allowing only enough through that is required to keep a nation alive. The Eurotunnel has been closed for passengers too, and is only accessible for some goods and ferries still allowed to enter European Union waters.

It is a disaster. But for once in its history, the European Union and its members are determined to maintain a hard line and keep up the sanctions and absorb the losses. Once there was a government forcing people with a Body Mass Index over 35, to lose weight. Now, there is an embargo and sanctions and rations on food, making the United Kingdom face this objective in a way no one could ever have thought of. It is somewhat ironic, but new statistics from the World Health Organization now show that progress in the health in the United Kingdom has improved quite a bit in the last two years. The Fat Man of Europe seems to not be so fat anymore.

But not only this.

With the sanctions, regular people are getting thinner, too.

CHAPTER 27

MONICA GRIFFITH constantly feels a little hungry. Not only did she lose a lot of weight at Nordhausen, but now that food has become scarce, she is losing weight day by day. What thrills her about the food rations is that now it is no longer only people like her who are suffering, but also those who closed their eyes to this obesity thing.

A lot is going on in the minds of people these days. Many can simply not grasp that the United Kingdom is no longer capable of protecting itself and its borders. With the sanctions and the European Union's power-play, their pride is starting to crumble. Under the Brexit campaign, it was promised otherwise. It was assumed that it would be the European Union that would suffer the most when the United Kingdom left. In the months following Brexit, Victoria Seymour even promised a revival of the good old times; that the United Kingdom would become a new superpower and a region of great prosperity. But as history now shows, the exact opposite has happened, and idiots like the Foreign Minister, and the press secretary had been talking nonsense when they said that everything would be getting greater and greater by the day. No one really believes it any longer.

How are they going to feed the country on the rations they are provided? People continue taking to the streets to demonstrate but not without repercussions. When caught, Monica has heard, people may still end up in prison and similar camps like the one she ended up in. Young people lose their chance for an education, old people are thrown on the streets for opposing the government, and yet the government and its propaganda machine keep blaming the European Union for all the trouble. Some people still digest the information raw, still not believing what happened in Nordhausen, and still blaming the European Union for making fake news. It makes her toes curl and she wants to beat these naive and bigoted people's heads in.

What happened to the United Kingdom everybody used to love? Was it really that bad before? How's the future going to evolve? With serious tensions starting to show between England, Scotland and Northern Ireland, there could be a chance of a conflict escalating into something that nobody wants. And though she would like to, she is not fleeing like others because England is her country and not the property of some demagogue at 10 Downing Street hiding behind his gang of criminal henchmen. She really thought that when Henry Montclair took over as Prime Minister that there would be a roll-back of the laws on obesity and of the curfew and that The Party would release its grip on the population and finally come to its senses. But this has turned out not to be the case. On the contrary. Things are getting worse by the day. The people in power must be fought at any price.

'Hi Monica,' says Mason, picking up the receiver.

'Hi Mason. How are you coming along?'

'I don't know. I really don't. And you?'

'Well. It's difficult coming to terms with what happened in Nordhausen. I think about it every day. But believe me, being back in the United Kingdom does help a little. Now, we just need to clean up the government.'

'Did you receive the list?'

'I did Mason. I guess they want this done quickly, don't they?'

'Can your people manage?'

'I've spoken with some other groups. We've come to the conclusion that it's possible. We just to need organize our resistance a little differently.'

'So, you'd say it is possible?'

'Yes. But there are two aspects. The time frame is a little narrow, I must say. That's why we've come up with a two-phase plan. All radar stations will have their power cut at the same time as we take out the power supplies for the units. Now, Mason, this is the problem: They all have emergency power generators, just like the telecommunications networks have. We've received blueprints of many of the facilities, but not all are accessible, and it's not always possible to bribe those traitor assholes with the information we need.'

'I understand. How do you expect to cope with the installations that you have no information on?'

'Well, we're thinking about explosives. But we don't really want to kill anyone. We all agree that this must be a peaceful revolution.'

'Yes, explosives won't work. They've specifically notified me that there must be a minimum of casualties and a minimum of damage to infrastructure.'

'Sounds like the European Union knows it will have to pick up the bill?'

'Exactly. And they want to keep their reputation. It's understandable.'

'Indeed it is.'

'But how do you expect to handle places where no preparation is possible?'

'I think, in places where it's not possible to access information, we'll simply invade and threaten the people to prevent information from coming out.'

'You need weapons for this.'

'That's why I'd like to ask you to get some through the blockade.'

'That's no problem. I'll just ask them to let the ship come through. What about military bases?'

'We've been able to contact a lot of brass and non-brass, in the military, who simply want to get this over with and get back to business as usual. When the sign is given, they'll simply do nothing, perhaps go to the crapper. A couple of hours before F-day some of our contacts will vandalize heavy equipment, preventing it from leaving bases.'

Mason laughs. 'F-day, that's a cool expression. Who came up with that? But what does it mean?'

'Freedom day. Well, others call it fuck it day. It was probably one of the underground blokes from Leeds. Anyway, some of the farmers around bases are taking their harvesters and will use them to block base exits.'

'I guess they've been inspired from what's going on in Paris.'

'You mean with French peasants supporting demonstrations for Westminster?'

'Well. I'm not sure if you should believe what's on the news these days.'

'But at least, with the farmers' actions, it will provide some extra time for the European forces.'

'Very good, Monica. What about the main power supply? Have your people figured out what to do with this?'

'The nuclear power plants can't just be turned off, so we'll leave them out of the equation. The security is too high anyway. But the other power plants will be taken off the grid.

'Wow, Monica. That's excellent! You people are doing a great job.'

'But you need to send more money. And we need those weapons.'

'No issue at all.'

'When is F-day going to happen?'

'Nobody knows; whenever they're ready. But I've heard that the European Union is going to land troops in the north of Ireland. They then take the Northern Ireland border under control and cross it to sail troops and equipment to Scotland. From there, European troops will work their way down to the southern part of the United Kingdom.'

'That's a good plan. We'll certainly look forward to that. Do they need any more information right now, or do you have enough?'

'No, it's sufficient at the moment,' says Mason. 'I'm actually quite amazed at how efficient you people are.'

'Trust me, Mason. Most of us in the resistance, simply want to have it over with, like the rest of the people, and return to our daily lives like it was before Victoria Seymour.'

'I believe it.'

'I actually voted for her.'

'Many people did, Monica. Sometimes things turn out unexpectedly. How is daily life on your side?'

'It's not easy, Mason. People are suffering. Some are accepting the fact that this is their new future. We've even had people whistle blowing on us because they simply are not able to digest who is actually responsible for this damn situation.'

'How can some people be so blind?'

'Oh, you've met Gregg White in person! I think many have respect for his special teams. They're brutal.'

'Monica. You really have guts being there. In a way I feel guilty being here in Slovenia instead of back home.'

'You know what, Mason? I think we two have had it. We're all different and have different ways of coping with life and its mortality. That's probably why some are smarter than others, them getting out before the disaster hit. I think what has surprised people most is how hard the European Union has cracked down on us. No one really thought this plausible. It is a blow to our collective perception of ourselves.'

Mason sighs.

'Think about what happened to us in Nordhausen,' she continues. 'The difference between them and us is that we'll be the ones who will live with it for the rest of our lives, but the nation will only have to feel ashamed about it.'

'To be quite honest with you, Monica, if I hadn't experienced it myself, I'd probably have doubts that it happened too.'

'I know. Something like Nordhausen happening in the United Kingdom ... that's unthinkable ... and that's probably the error in thought. We've always been after the Germans for what happened to the Jews, and then it happens to us!'

'Anyway, Mason. We have a lot of planning to do before F-day. I'll ask my people to get things into place as soon as possible. Then report to you when we are ready. Is this okay?'

'It certainly is.'

'Okay, Mason. Talk soon.'

'And by the way, Monica?'

'Yes?'

'You all be careful.'

'We will. Promise.'

IT IS a long time ago that Lisa Ferguson's smile was so wide as it is right now. The Court of Justice in The Hague is all over Henry Montclair. She picks up the tray with coffee the kitchen personnel put on her desk, walking to Henry's office and to his desk, placing it beside a huge stack of papers.

'Oh boy, I have bad news for you, Henry,' says Lisa, trying to suppress her happiness.

'Get in line or take a hit.' says Henry. 'What is it?'

'A warrant for your head was issued less than five minutes ago.'

Henry looks up at her. 'You have to be kidding.'

She starts pouring coffee into cups.

'For what? What did I do?'

'For the assassination of Victoria.'

'What?' cries Henry. 'Why do they want to accuse me of the murdering of Victoria? I have absolutely nothing to do with it. Haven't they figured this out by now? I'm the one hurting from her death. Who issued the warrant?'

'The Hague.'

'But I'm not a criminal!'

'But they think you are. There's a whole list of accusations attached to the warrant. It even says you're a disgrace to humanity and human rights.'

'How dare they? Those swines! I'm not the one behind it. That was Gregg. Why haven't they issued a warrant for his head? Or yours?'

'Mine? Why, I'm just the minister of State and the Cabinet.'

'They do really try to turn the world against me, don't they?'

Lisa fails to reply. Had it not been for her double role for The Special Council, she would have gotten out of here with the last ferry or plane or simply swum across the Channel to France and hope they would fish her out. Either way, she is in no way protected by what the future may hold. There is no doubt that the world has labeled her the same type of scum as Henry and Gregg. When this ends, she will be thrown to the lions, like the rest of the bunch working at Westminster. If people just knew she is not only assisting The Special Council, but also the underground resistance who Gregg loves to hate. He is one nasty son-of-a-bitch when someone gets caught in his net. His henchmen work a little like the Nazi's did. Luckily, she has helped save some people, by providing information to the underground, being careful not to get caught in the wrong flow of information. When her two contacts in the underground resistance ask for information, she tries as well as she can to give them what they need. She is kept in the dark about their operations, which is good, because it would not go down well should her triple role be uncovered.

Luckily those in the underground resistance are a bunch of real survivors, good at working in the dark, but even better at hiding their intentions. Not even Gregg can fully understand what they are up to at the moment. Lately, there have been a lot of hacker attacks on government computer networks, which even with the Russian expertise they have available, is difficult to dismantle. It frustrates Gregg quite a bit that he still hasn't figured out how a modern resistance group works today – which is somewhat different from how they worked during World War II.

'DENDA DENDA,' shouts Denda Escudos' assistant all way down the hall from his office on the eight floor.

'What?' he screams back, sitting at a meeting table, but getting up and moving to the door to meet him.

'They've shot down one of our observation helicopters.'

'Who?'

'The English. It's a Danish helicopter.'

'Uh, that's not good. Have the Danes done anything in retaliation?'

'No. Their commands don't want to react before they get an official order to respond.'

'They're holding up to the pressure, that's good. Inform them that we'll not retaliate; that no fire will be returned.'

'What if it had been a Russian that was shot down?'

'If the Russians in any way start firing at us, we'll sink their ships, shoot down their planes and bomb all their oil fields. They understand this. You don't need to worry about the Russians. They're only in it to earn money. How is the Danish crew?'

'They were pulled out of the water some minutes ago by an Italian frigate.'

'So, no casualities?'

'No casualties.'

'Okay. Then hopefully, the English learned something too.'

'Can I come in?'

'I'm in a meeting right now. Could you please get us some coffee and Belgian waffles?' he asks. 'Then you can join us.' He returns to the table, closing the door behind him. Inside are the other four presidents of the European Union.

'As I was saying,' continues Denda, 'we need to find an efficient way to get out of this mess. The costs are starting to run high. For everyday that this damn conflict goes on, we'd be able to build 150 kilometer high-speed train network.'

'But how do we get out of it?' asks Peter Jensen, President of the European Commission and from Denmark. 'I can't believe it, by the way. That helicopter was one of our brand new ones!'

'In my opinion, there are only two ways. Either we give up or we invade the United Kingdom.'

'So, you want us to laugh now?'

'That wasn't a joke, gentlemen,' answers Dendo. I was serious and have actually established a work-group to evaluate on the risks.'

'Invade the United Kingdom? We'll never get a mandate for that, neither in our Parliament nor from the United Nations.'

'I know. But what are the alternatives?'

There is a long pause.

'I guess, Denda has come to recognize the core of Montclair's strategy,' says Marek Muranska, President of the European Parliament. 'He's playing on time, thinking our unity will disintegrate with small internal fights.'

'That's true,' confirms Denda.

'That's why he and his government won't come to the negotiating table.'

'Exactly,' agrees Denda.

'So, we'll have to keep it together this time.'

'By God, that's going to be tough.'

'I know', says Denda. 'There are already the first signs of tensions between my Council and some of the prime ministers.'

'Not good. What do you suggest, Denda?' asks Peter.

'We need to act fast, at least before Montclair's prophecy comes true. We need to invade. I see no other option,' states Denda.

'According to what NATO's intelligence has provided us, most parts of the military in Scotland and Northern Ireland are not going to intervene. They don't see it as their war. Most of the population doesn't either. The underground resistance is providing our agents with more information than we can handle. They simply want Montclair and his government to be thrown out so sanctions can be lifted.'

'Good to know that the sanctions work. So, an invasion would likely be a symbolic sign, one without bullets and rockets?'

'According to our military advisors, yes. If it comes to an actual war, we can mobilize twelve times the troops than the United Kingdom can. And due to the United Nations' weapons embargo, when they're out of bullets, the military conflict will end.'

'So, this is going to be a very short military intervention, whatever way it goes.'

'Yes.'

'Sounds like a good idea to me.'

'Then we should do it, Denda. But how're you going to convince the 27?'

'That's easy. I'll simply hold up a budget showing how much it will cost not to interfere, and then how much it will cost to invade. The difference is convincing enough.'

'Wow. I'm a little stunned.'

'Me too.'

'And me. Whoever thought it would come to invading one of our own.'

'You want the expansion of your high-speed trains across Europe or not?'

'Of course I want it.'

'Well, then start playing to our other member nations' fantasies.'

'What madness.'

'Yes. Let's end it with an invasion before people start really getting hurt.'

CHAPTER 28

THE PARTY'S PUBLIC RELATIONS department is running under the highest pressure ever, to cope with what is going on in the United Kingdom. The team is working at its best to convince the people using lies, propaganda, and the technique of using simple explanations to turn complicated issues to their advantage. And the propaganda from the other side of the Channel has, to some extent, been kept at a distance. But even Lisa knows that her new press secretary is fighting a losing battle. Not many buy into the talk of big dreams any longer. The promise of two weeks free vacation in South England with an artificial lagoon and view of the ocean from your room, free cinemas and theaters, sports facilities, a healthcare center and a daycare center has never come to fruition. Now the 'decent hard-working citizens' are happy if they can get their hands on some decent beer and imported cheese. There are still press releases and great plans available on The Party's website although everybody now knows that Efficiency Through Joy is just an insane idea from a man who has torn his country to pieces.

'How's it going with the plans?' asks Henry.

'It's going great,' his chief architect lies, not wanting to be the one to bring the bad news. 'In four months, we'll be able to start building,' he says, in the hope that in four months, all this will be over and done with.

'Have all the blueprints been completed?'

'They are nearing completion.'

'Wow, it's going to be a great place. People will appreciate this project. And they deserve it. They're really holding up at the moment.'

Henry's chief architect looks closely at his contractor with a mixed feeling of hate and sympathy. For the last hour, Henry has looked a little happy, even smiling, discussing this completely insane project, which is way too expensive and useless because people would probably rather go to Mallorca where the sun shines. Perhaps the project is taking Henry to a somewhat nicer place in his mind than what reality has to offer. By now, there is no doubt that the United Kingdom has become a little smarter about Henry

Montclair. Even he, a simple architect, is beginning to hear rumors about the European Union starting to implode on itself, politically as well as financially, because the sanctions are costing a fortune. Again it confirms what he knew before Brexit; that the European Union is all a bunch of incompetent idiots with no idea about what they are doing. So, on this matter, Henry, has been right all the time. On the rest, the man is absolutely wrong and should never have taken over as Prime Minister after Victoria Seymour's assassination.

Henry looks at the blueprints in front of him for one last time today. It is going to be a great project, this is for sure. It's just a shame that there is no time at the moment to see the project through. But soon! The latest military intelligence updates say that the European Union is rearming itself due to the Russian interference at sea. Huge troop movements and equipment from all over the European Union are going to the eastern borders of Poland, Slovakia, Hungary and Romania. The European Union obviously want to scare the Russians into pulling back their warships from around the United Kingdom. At least, with the Russian warships now supporting the Royal Navy in blocking warships from the European Union's member nations, more goods are slipping through the blockade, easing the pressure on him with his people. The Russian participation seems to work, though the costs are high. If the money had been spent on his project in Newquay in South England instead, the vision could have been double in its size. At least now with the deteriorating climate in the European Council, the decision to uphold the sanctions will fall apart as he anticipated, eventually giving him a stronger position at the negotiating table so he can remain at power.

In a way, it is kind of funny, Henry thinks. He had promised Victoria and Lisa a turning point where people would reunite and forget about fat and obese people. What he had never expected, though, was that this turning point would turn out to be himself. He moves from his huge desk between the two windows in his office to look down at Downing Street. He never intended to end up here. Not in this office. Only when he was doing Victoria on the couch. Ending up here only shows that life is full of surprises and events that we ourselves are not always in control over. It is certain that the pictures from Nordhausen are hurting him and the country, but again, he has nothing to do with the incidence. It was completely the work of Gregg, which will be sacrificed because of what the man did, when it becomes necessary. But at least the episode in Nordhausen shows how incapable the world is at reacting to situations like these, situations where unity is required, not the self-interests and carelessness of its nations.

NOBODY HAD expected a thing of this size could happen. In the late hours of a boring, rainy Wednesday afternoon, three perpetrators stormed the European Commission's building, killing seven civil servants at close hand in their offices. Denda Escudos hears the news from his young assistant on his cell phone.

'What happened?'

'Seven of our people have been shot dead in their offices.'

'What? How did they get through security?'

'I don't know. The police are here, taking tons of photographs and securing evidence.'

'Give me a few minutes and I'll be there.'

When Denda Escudos enters the building, he sees armed police forces everywhere who still don't know whether it is a terror attack, a targeted, or a random attempt to kill European Union employees. The press is all over the place, and by now, citizens are turning up to show their last respect, laying flowers in front of the big building. Denda Escudos runs through the entrance to the elevators, where his assistant is waiting. They both go up to the floor where it happened. 'We must immediately put Europol on this,' says Denda Escudos' assistant. 'Why would anyone kill seven of our people?'

'I saw the names of the dead in the SMS you send me. I can tell you why. Those seven are responsible for the possible upcoming negotiations with Henry Montclair and his government. They were the best negotiators the European Commission could ever have come up with; very professional people. By killing them, he puts us in a difficult situation.'

'You think he's the one behind this?'

'Who the hell else would it be? I'm open for suggestions?'

'So, now Henry Montclair a brutal murderer.'

'Well, that wouldn't be the first time, would it? Look at what he did to Victoria Seymour. Of course Montclair is behind this! The criminals over there would do anything to slam a hole in our blockade. You met the man when he was here. He's nuts. You heard him.'

'But the Islamic State just called and said they're responsible.'

'Islamic State? For Christ sake! The only thing they want is attention. Hezbollah will call in, too, probably. And the Rote Army Fraction from Germany, though they don't exist anymore. Don't be naive my friend. If it had been any of them, half of the building would be gone. It was Westminster. No doubt about it.'

'So, what now?'

'The police will take care of those responsible. In the meantime, we will take advantage of the situation and put Westminster in a bad light. If you haven't noticed, we're in a pretty difficult situation, here. We have the right to twist the truth a little, even it's not true. It was Westminster. And we're going to tell the world that Henry Montclair is behind this awful event.'

'SO NOW,' says Henry, getting off the toilet and pulling up his pants, 'now they're blaming me for what happened in Brussels this morning. Unbelievable! They're just unbelievable! I can't even take a shit and I'm accused of something I never did. Is it one of your sick games again, Gregg?'

'It has nothing to do with me.'

'Are you sure?'

'Yes.'

'Fully sure?'

'Absolutely.'

'Good! Because this time I would have torn off your head. What you did back in Nordhausen, was bad enough and now they're doing everything to put us in a bad light, just because of you!'

Lisa asks, 'So, why don't we negotiate now that they've just lost their negotiation team?'

'It ought to be clear to them that we won't make any changes to the doctrine of Parliamentary Sovereignty. That's what the negotiations are going to be about. And it will not change just because seven civil servants from the European Commission are dead.'

'So it's still a deadlock. And it's worth holding your country hostage only because you refuse to give up your power? That's not sustainable, and you know it!' This time Lisa knows she has leaned a little too far out the window. But once in a while, it can be difficult working with this simpleton.

'It's not in their power to tell us what to do. They're the ones who are wrong, not us,' argues Henry. 'It's about the principle. We're a sovereign state and they don't seem to be able to accept this.'

'Was it not a part of the message before Brexit, that we're not a sovereign state, but wanted to become one?' asks Gregg.

'We've always been a sovereign state. It's not my fault people don't check the facts.'

'But I thought we'd first be sovereign when we left the European Union,' wonders Gregg.

'You've always been a little brain dead, Gregg.'

'Technically, we're still members,' says Lisa to Gregg. 'We never really left,' she explains.

'Oh shut up, both of you. You two have absolutely no grasp of politics. Gregg, you go and convince some people to work for us. And you, young lady, you go play with yourself. Now please let me go back to what I was doing before you two crashed in with your rubbish.'

THE MURDER of the seven European Union officials travels the internet faster than Mr. Andrews from The Special Council in Seattle can get into his underwear. It is around four in the morning. He does what Mr. Conners always tells him to do when calling this early in the morning and goes to his office computer.

'What do you want me to write?'

'Brussels, murders.'

'Say again?'

'Brussels, murders.'

'B … r … u … s … s …'

'When … will … you … finally learn to type?'

'Well, I'm too old for that now … Holy shit!' exclaims Mr. Andrews.

'I assume you found the news?'

'Aw man! This is bad! When did this happen?'

'Less than four hours ago.'

'Who's behind it?'

'I assume your question refers to the fact that we have nothing to do with this.'

'We have absolutely nothing to do with this.'

'I thought so. Then I'm in no position to give you a proper answer.'

'What would be the point of killing seven European Union officials?'

'I was hoping you could tell me.'

'Where did they work?'

'For the European Commission.'

'The Commission? But they're only civil servants. What would be the reason to kill civil servants?'

'All I know is that they were the negotiators who were selected to negotiate with Westminster when they finally come to the table.'

'I see.'

'The European Union's President of the Council has already announced that Westminster is behind the assassinations.'

'Isn't that a little early.'

'Could it be the Russians?'

'What? No, certainly not. How would they benefit?'

'Hm,' groans Mr. Conners. 'What does this mean for the FDAR on Henry Montclair's head?'

'I don't know,' says Mr. Andrews. 'We'll have to wait and see. I'm sure the Continent Teams will get together to assess the situation.' Mr. Andews pauses and then continues. 'This show is really starting to get out of control. With the assassinations, the European Union will probably retaliate.'

'I'm worried about this too,' admits Mr. Conners. 'Please keep me in the loop regarding the FDAR, okay?'

'I will. Anyway, how's life in London?'

'It's getting difficult. I'm not sure anyone anticipated that the European Union would react as they did and be so strict enforcing the sanctions. The economic sanctions are leading to a lot of unexpected problems. In the last four decades, the European Union hasn't been able to agree on anything, and then they crack down on us like this. That's some change of mind.'

'Sounds like you guys are having a hard time.'

'They have us in a corner, that's for sure. Think how much pride we'll have to give up at the moment. It's awful. It's worse than losing a football game.'

'I hope the situation won't worsen with all those Russian warships floating around.'

'They're in it to make money. If it gets too hot, I'm sure they'll leave.'

'They're pretty smart, I'll give them that. Have you sent that interim report? I'll discuss what's next with the Old Man.'

'You'll have it in the evening if I can find some paper that hasn't been blocked by the European Union.'

DENDA ESCUDOS is nearly half the size of Henry Montclair. He is neither beautiful, nor does he have the charisma of his former colleague. Nor has he ever had sex with more than two women in his life, his wife and his ex-wife. But Denda Escudos has something else. People like him. They trust him. And contrary to his opponent on the other side of the Channel, who only has the backing of one country, Denda has the backing of twenty-seven countries. And with that, he has decided to thwart his former colleague, because Henry Montclair is not only endangering the reputation of the United Kingdom, but also that of the European Union, making Denda more than upset.

The time of thinking and talking is over. Since Montclair's takeover in the United Kingdom, more and more memories from his own time in Spain under Franco have come back. He was once in one of Franco's prisons. Though it was many years ago, he still remembers the attacks on his body and the scars they left on his soul. At least Franco was dead and Spain today is politically stable except for the Catalonian rebellion.

But now something must finally be done to solve the 'English Patient's' problems and make him well again. Denda's objective concerning an invasion can be described very briefly:

Shatter the
'English Problem',
break down English pride,
make them finally understand
they are not the masters
of the World.

A PLAN starts taking shape at the French Military headquarters a little outside Paris. In secret and without the approval of the European Parliament, as well as without the knowledge of NATO, military generals from all European Union members, have been invited to discuss how to handle the 'English Problem'. The military mission must be done quickly and neatly, and the objective is to only re-establish law and order and democracy. When the mission is completed, troops and military equipment will be withdrawn within a few days.

There are just a few technical problems that still have to be solved. Firstly; to get a mandate from the United Nations to invade the United Kingdom and clean it up. This will probably be blocked by Russia and perhaps also by the United States of America. It may also be blocked by other countries such as Pakistan and India, who would see an opportunity to let their old colonial masters rot in hell. For an institution like the European Union to invade another country would not be very popular in the USA who is not a member of the EU, but holds an observatory membership. Secondly; upholding the sanctions do hurt financially and weakens the European Union's position in the world. As Henry Montclair has recognized, it is only a matter of time before the twenty-seven members tear themselves apart because of their self-interests. Henry is playing on time for this to happen.

So,' sighs Denda, the little man with a rather powerful voice, 'Thank you all for coming today,' he says to the 27 heads-of-states. 'I'll try to keep this meeting short. The subject, of course, is the United Kingdom and Henry Montclair. I assume everybody here has been briefed that the situation now requires interference from our side. Intelligence from NATO indicates that there's an opening to act *right now*. Montclair expects us to fall apart soon – as we always do when difficult decisions present themselves. But this time, I'd very much like to prove him wrong.'

'I fully agree,' says Germany. 'We need to do something. The sanctions are costing a lot in lost trade. We can already see it in our statistics.'

'True,' says Romania. 'The money could be spent on much better things … like us.'

'We agree with Romania,' says Croatia.

'Very funny.'

'And considering what the aftermath of this crisis is probably going to cost,' remarks Bulgaria, 'it's not going to be cheap to reestablish democracy in the

United Kingdom. We all know it's going to take a while before investors are confident again.'

'Not only this,' continues Hungary. 'Industry in the United Kingdom has come to an almost complete halt. So they also need money to prevent unnecessary bankruptcies.'

'There are so many aspects of the sanctions,' agrees Denda. 'But it was the right decision to make. Now we need to finish what we've begun. What we all have in common is that these sanctions are too damn expensive to maintain. We simply need to keep it together this time to get away cheaply. Are we able to do this?'

'We need to,' says Germany. 'It's that simple. If not, the costs will run even higher.'

'Any suggestions as to how we keep ourselves together?' asks Sweden.

'I guess Denda is right. If the stars are in the right position, then we ought to act right now! It's that simple,' says Portugal.

'I'm on Portugal's side.' declares Spain. 'We came here hoping that you have the solution, Denda.'

'I do. It's something quite unusual and something that no one outside these walls may hear. If you have noticed, no one is taking dictation today.'

'Now I think you are making us all quite curious,' comments Austria.

'We'll invade the United Kingdom and simply get it done with,' says Denda not beating around the bush.

The silence that follows was expected.

'But … we can't do that,' says Finland. 'Such authority does not lie within the frameworks of the European Union. Only individual member nations can go to war.'

'That's correct,' confirms Denda.

'I actually like the idea,' comments Croatia. 'We go in, clean up the shit, save a lot of money and it's done with. We have ten times the firepower of the United Kingdom.'

'We actually have twelve times the firepower,' Denda informs them, 'not counting the reserve troops. But the intention is to prevent using firepower. Until yesterday, generals from all over the European Union have been working on an invasion plan in France … eh … something you haven't been informed about. But I wanted to first check what our options are for military intervention.'

France says, 'The generals have come up with a master plan to intervene quickly, and without sacrificing too many Europeans.'

'Does that account for British citizens as well?'

'Are they Europeans?' ask Denda.

'Well, many think they are not.'

'Living on an island, causes inbreeding. That's why they're a little strange.'

Denda continues explaining his strategy, 'Our NATO intelligence has informed me that the morale in the United Kingdom, both in the military as well as the general population, is low. Additionally, political tensions between Westminster and First Ministers of Scotland and Northern Ireland are increasing by the day. The resistance is also growing stronger by the day and is in direct contact with a group of our generals in France who are coordinating activities. But the population in the United Kingdom is still split and not everyone believes that Henry Montclair is a danger nor do they all believe that the photographs from Nordhausen are real. So you see, we need to react fast before domestic tensions intensify and a civil war breaks out. That's something we need to prevent.'

'Wow. We never thought it was this bad,' says Hungary.

'Me neither. We certainly don't want this to escalate any further.'

'No. Then it would really become a expensive for us all.'

'God! Those people!' says Germany. 'All this shouldn't have happened. Haven't those idiots learned anything from World War II? It should have been the end of conflict here in Europe.'

'Don't forget we had Yugoslavia,' tutors Greece.

'True,' confirms Denda, grabbing one of the coffee pots from the table.

'So, if I understand you correctly, Denda,' Sweden sums up. 'Montclair won't come to the negotiating table even though his position is stronger now with the absence of our seven negotiators. He's still holding on to his idea that we will fall apart?'

'Yes.'

'Bah!' says Sweden. 'This will be his downfall.'

Denda pours some coffee into his cup and offers the Prime Minister of Poland some too.

'What is the status on the murders of our seven colleagues?'

'I've asked Europol to assemble a taskforce to investigate. By now, it is uncertain if it was ordered by Westminster,' says Denda. 'At this time, I don't know any more than the rest of you.' He returns the coffee pot to the table and takes a sip from his cup. 'Damn! It would be nice if they'd learn to put warm coffee on these pots.'

'Can the murders be used to justify an invasion the United Kingdom?' asks Sweden.

'Nothing justifies an invasion of the United Kingdom, that's the problem,' acknowledges Denda. 'But … an opportunity of this type shouldn't go unnoticed.'

'Hm,' says the Prime Minister of Austria. 'The European Union was never designed to enter into conflict in this way. We've been discussing a mutual army for many years and always end up with nothing, and now within a matter of seconds, you want us to invade another member nation.'

'It's absurd, I fully agree,' says the Swedish Prime Minister. 'And I can't sell it to my people. We need a referendum on stuff like this.'

'Neither can I,' agrees Denmark.

'It might be absurd,' Denda returns, defending his position. 'But I assume it's not only I who have seen the economic figures. The sanctions are extremely costly for all member nations. The money we spend can be invested much better. Either we solve the problem now, or we'll be paying a hundredfold more in a few years. It's like pissing in our pants. First it is nice and warm, but it gets cold again, and then you need to piss again, but you can't. Are you people willing to wait or do you see what direction this is heading? That's the question I'm putting before you today.'

'They were the ones who voted for Brexit, it's their own fault.'

'Nobody could have anticipated Victoria Seymour and Henry Montclair,' argues Denda. 'I don't see Brexit as having anything to do with the current situation. They could have left in a decent way.'

'I agree' says Portugal. 'What we haven't talked about is the stability of our region. We cannot have a United Kingdom that is ruled by an aristocrat. I still remember how it was with Portugal. So, I fully agree with Denda because I know as well as he does how it is to grow up under a dictator. We should act now, and not later, and in this case perhaps forget about our standard ways of doing things.'

'I fully agree,' confirms Greece.

'In two weeks this could be over and done with,' says Denda. 'France will lead the operation. If we can agree to this and we all pull on the same rope, a military intervention will work out just fine.'

'Well, fine with me. Then let's end it,' says Finland.

'Count us in,' says the Chancellor of Germany.

Denda starts distributing a 3 page proposal. 'As you all know, I'm not able to make the decision on my own. According to the Lisbon Treaty, there must be one hundred percent agreement from all member nations.'

'But you just said this meeting isn't protocol.'

'No that's true. But in spite of that, it would be best to do this in unity.'

'So, what do you suggest?' asks the Netherlands.

'I suggest we do what's in this proposal. It could work.'

Everyone present reads the proposal carefully.

'How the hell am I going to sell this to the Danish people?' asks Denmark. 'If we do not hold a referendum on this, it will be against our constitution.'

'I'm fully aware of that. That's why we don't go to war. It's a cleanup operation. I say first we act and take the world and the press by surprise, and worry about the consequences afterward. If people complain that we have removed a dictator, even one in our union, then history will show that we were right and put them in disgrace. What matters is that the suffering ends for people in the United Kingdom, and for that matter, for us too. We've all suffered enough.'

'Ach jo!' says Slovakia. 'Either this destroys the European Union or we'll be the new unsung heroes nobody will ever appreciate.'

'So, what we need to do now,' says Denda, 'is to approve procedure on this proposal. Is anyone against voting on it?'

Not a sound from the assembly.

'Okay. Then, vote, now!'

'Thank you ladies and gentlemen. The result for military intervention, which is not a military intervention but a cleanup operation, is as follows: 26 voted 'Yes'. 1 Voted 'No'. Fellow member nations! According to Article 6 of the Lisbon Treaty a decision like this requires a unanimous decision. Come on Denmark! Reconsider your vote.'

'I'm going to get in trouble for this,' says Denmark.

'Thank you, Christian. For the unofficial records and protocol, note that all

27 European Union member nations have approved a cleanup operation in the United Kingdom.'

'Oh boy,' says the Prime Minister of Denmark, looking down at the table. 'The opposition is going to have a field day on this one.'

'Coffee?' asks Denda holding the coffee pot in his hand.

'No thanks,' replies the Danish Prime Minister.

'Don't worry,' says Denda. 'From zero to hero, faster than you click that button. Either way, it's not every day we write history.'

'Any bets? suggests Italy.

'What do you mean?' asks Croatia.

'If this will go as planned.'

'I'll vote for it going wrong,' exclaims Spain.

'Me too,' confirms the Slovenian Prime Minister.

'Okay okay, I see where this is heading. Let's make bets,' says Denda. 'What's the winner's reward?'

'One night in the Prime Minister's bed at 10 Downing Street. How about it?' suggests Poland.

'That's a done deal,' agrees Denda. 'Who thinks we'll succeed?'

The only finger in the air is that of France, the master mind of the 3-page proposal.

CHAPTER 29

HENRY MONTCLAIR RETUNS TO his desk. It was unfortunate that he could not fully bury the Nordhausen story. The damage those pictures have caused is reverberating throughout the world, and also turning into a major domestic headache. The Party's propaganda machine has managed to alleviate some of the tensions, but again, they have not been able to get the Internet under full control, making it difficult to evaluate what people actually know and think which has created a situation of uncertainty whether people support his government or not.

This only leaves him with one option. He will be forced to crack down even further on the population to ensure that the people will not rise against him and his government. He could give in and go to the negotiating table in Switzerland, but that might be seen as weakness and wouldn't change a thing anyway because any changes to the doctrine of Parliamentary Sovereignty will not be made.

Henry sees his cell phone vibrate in front of him on the desk. Currently when it does so, he is not sure whether to pick up the phone or not. But he knows he needs to pick it up.

'What?' he says.

'They're withdrawing,' he hears his Minister of Defense say.

'They're what?' asks Henry.

'The Europeans ... they're withdrawing from the blockade. Twenty minutes ago all the ships started heading back to the European mainland.'

'He he,' laughs Henry. 'I knew they wouldn't be able to hold it together.'

'We believe it has something to do with Russia. The Russians are getting upset about the European Union's armaments buildup on their western border. They think the Europeans are taking action to concentrate on the problems there because of the inteferrence in the blocade.'

'That's not our problem.'

Henry lays his cell phone on the desk and returns to the windows to look down at Downing Street. He sees Lisa entering the building and in a few minutes she is standing at the door to his office.

'Coffee?' she asks.

'No, but something else.' He walks to her and pulls her into the office, locking the door.

'You look happy,' she observes. 'What happened?'

'Something that I expected would happen.'

'What?'

'The Europeans. They're withdrawing.'

'What?'

'Twenty minutes ago, the European Union has begun pull back from the blockade.'

'That's great news!'

Henry takes her hand and puts it on his groin, then it into his pants. 'Do you feel it?' he asks.

'I certainly do. Do you want me to bend over?'

'Over at the couch. Trade will start up again in no time. I'm sure industry in the European Union must be desperate to finally get rid of their products.'

'I guess so.'

'Didn't I tell you and Gregg that they would withdraw when it got too expensive?' he says to Lisa. 'You didn't really believe me, did you?'

'I guess you were right after all.'

'Ah … yes … But to change subject … Uh! I really like your tight little pussy, did you know that?'

A COUPLE of days later troops land in the north of the Republic of Ireland. Henry Montclair listens in disbelief to his Minister of Defense.

'They what?' he screem into the telephone.

'They just landed some troops in the northern part of Ireland.'

'Where?'

'Up in Portnablagh.'

'There's nothing up there. When did they do this?'

'This morning. They're heading for the north Irish border and digging in along it.'

'You have to be kidding! Are they actually going to invade Northern Ireland? I thought that was only rumors. Those fools. How about if we send troops up there, too? How many have they landed?'

'I think around twenty five thousand.'

'That's a lot. How many would you suggest we send there? We should not allow them to invade Northern Ireland.'

'That's what we're planning to do. But to get enough troops, we need help from Wales and England. As you might well know, our Scottish allies aren't particularly reliable.'

'I've noticed. We'll deal with those traitors later.'

'Do I have authorization to send troops to Northern Ireland?'

'Affirmative. But send fifty thousand men. Let's show the Europeans that we're serious about protecting our borders.'

'Sir, with all due respect, that's one-third of our active forces. I'd suggest we only send what's necessary.'

'How many troops would that be?'

'Twenty thousand.'

'Okay. You know better than I do. What kind of equipment do the Europeans have?'

'Tanks, troop carriers, missile batteries, they have it all.'

'We should have the same then. What about military aircraft?'

'They're on their wings. The Europeans are also flying out of Ireland doing reconnaissance. According to our intelligence, they've stationed twenty-five F16 Fighting Falcons and 59 observation helicopters. But at this point, they are still on the ground.'

'Would you suggest we station some jets there as well?'

'No. If jets come from the European mainland, we need our battle stations where they are – if we want to respond fast enough.'

'What about our ships at sea?'

'I suggest we allocate them to the north. Then we can block the Europeans from landing more troops.'

'That's a good idea. Anything else?'

'Not at the moment.'

'Keep me updated, okay?'

'Yes sir.'

Henry stands for a while completely baffled.

'What's wrong?' asks Lisa.

'The Europeans are preparing to invade Northern Ireland.'

'Northern Ireland? Why?'

'Because then they can send troops and military equipment to Scotland. They're starting their invasion from the north, just as our intelligence forecast they would. But they haven't sent that many troops!'

'So you mean, they're actually going to invade us?'

'It seems so.'

'But why from up North?'

'Northern Ireland and Scotland are our weak links. They know this.'

'I find it a little odd that the European Union is doing this.'

'What do you mean?'

'Then they'll be fighting on two fronts. What's happening at their eastern border seems to be getting worse by the hour. The Russians are mobilizing, too. And now here as well? Hm.'

'They're stupid, that's the problem.'

... OR NOT. The Europeans never bothered to cross the border between the Republic of Ireland and Northern Ireland. When the troops from Wales and England arrived in Scotland, and were ferried to Northern Ireland, and positioned along the North-Irish border, European forces pulled up their tents and moved 400 kilometers further south in the Republic of Ireland. It was quite a surprising tactic of the Europeans, forcing the troops from Wales and England to be ferried back to Scotland. This took a hell of a long time. No British general had believed that European Union warships would actually have the guts to enter Scottish and North-Irish territorial waters and block the transfer of war material between the two islands.

The Europeans were well prepared. As soon as European forces arrived at their destination in southeast Ireland, troops and military hardware were ferried from Rosslare Harbour in Ireland, to the beaches of Newport on the western side of Wales. From the European mainland, troops took the direct route from Rotterdam and Amsterdam to the beaches of Great Yarmouth in England. The crossing took less than three-and-a-half hours with modern warships. The landing of European troops and equipment on the coasts of Wales and England came not only as a surprise, but also as a shock, for the military command. The intelligence networks knew that something was going to happen, but they got the European Union's intentions completely wrong. The invasion was expected to come from Scotland, working its way down from north to south. With troops now stranded in Northern Ireland, unable to return in time to join the remaining troops in Wales and England, they would not have sufficient power to strike back.

Henry cannot believe his general's reports.

'This isn't true! Tell me it isn't true.'

'Sir, we need to admit that we were simply outsmarted. With their stunt at the North-Irish border, they really screwed us over. It was a clever move to make us believe that they were going to start up there.'

'Oh God.' Henry feels his ulcer act up.

'The troop landings on the shores east of Great Yarmouth in England have made it impossible for our troops to return to England. It's unbelievable that the damn Europeans are on our border and won't let us in.'

'I'm getting sick! Have there been any confrontations?'

'The Europeans have retaliated rather fiercely to our fire with heavy shelling over our heads.'

'What do you mean?'

'They haven't been shooting at our troops, only over our heads. So, we've decided to hold fire.'

'What?'

'Sir, we don't want to start anything. They have us outnumbered in troops and equipment. It would be suicide to engage in any sort of conflict.'

'Why not?' Henry screams, frustrated at the news of his traitorous and chicken troops.

'You don't honestly believe our troops want to go into combat, do you?'

'An enemy power has invaded our country! And now you say that our troops don't want to protect their country? How the hell has the European Union managed to get all that heavy equipment landed without anyone noticing? I don't get it!'

'Well ...'

For once in the European Union's long history, it had turned its inabilities and disadvantages into advantages. As it turns out, the European Union has been pretty good at spreading its own propaganda and fake information. It was the fact that, up to the day of the invasion, no one had a hint that anything was happening and the result was a swift, quick, non-dirty and successful military mission. With the warships first removed, and then a couple of days later allocated to up-North, the blockade was lifted and the trade routes were open for anyone wanting to ship goods to and from the United Kingdom. This, of course, included companies within the European Union. During the blockade, trains were not running through the Eurotunnel and before end of the blocade, all trains used for transport through the tunnel were sent to the east-European countries bordering up to Russia. Now with all the troops, vehicles, tanks, missile batteries, etc. already there, to piss-off the Russians, the 216 passenger wagons were carrying some 15.387 troops, the large 597 Eurotunnel wagons plus 6 extra were carrying ten-thousand tons of military equipment. Residents by the Eurotunnel and along the railroads probably thought that the heavy trains again were carrying lorries with French cheese and Germany sausages.

In truth, one train after another, racing through the tunnel every 20 minutes, never stopped in Dover to unload. Instead they continued on deep into the English and Welsh countryside as well as Scotland to unload the heavy military equipment on the beaches of Great Yarmouth in England and Newport in western Wales that would be needed on F-day. When the signal was given, the troops and their equipment would leave their Trojan horses.

The underground resistance group led by Monica Griffith along with many other resistance groups, were spread out over the United Kingdom, awaiting the F-day signal. When the signal was finally received, Monica Griffith's group began to execute the orders they had received from Mason Sanders. Power cables had to be cut to the emergency station in Norwich which was responsible for the area of Great Yarmouth where the troops had landed. To their surprise, it switched to back-up power. Monica Griffith and her people could not figure out how to cope with the diesel generators, so they had to improvise. They simply decided to occupy the emergency station and prevent the people working there from relaying information to the wrong people.

'999, how can I help you,' the paramedic asks the caller.

'Europe is attacking us!' screams someone into the receiver.

'What do you mean attacking?'

'Warships, a lot of warships with soldiers coming on shore. It's crazy.'

'What do you mean with warships?' asks the paramedic.

'Warships. Ships with troops. They're everywhere.'

'Eh, just a moment ...' The paramedic looks at Monica Griffith who is standing beside him, politely, but not violently swinging a gun in her hand.

'Just tell him you'll call the Ministry of Defense.'

The paramedic returns to the call. 'Okay, so you see warships. Where exactly are you?'

'I'm in Great Yarmouth.'

'And how many ships can you count?'

'It's dark. Perhaps 20. It looks like an invasion.'

'Invasion? From where?'

'From the mainland. From the European Union.'

'Listen, I'll just contact the Ministry of Defense. Thank you for calling.'

'They're all traitors calling in like that,' says his colleague.

'You can't blame people for what's going on,' says Monica Griffith. 'If I saw troops invade our coastline, I'd probably call too!'

'It's unbelievable that we should experience this.'

Monica Griffith takes a sip of her hot coffee from the Swiss thermos. 'I'm on your colleague's side. I'd called it treason, too. But after tonight, it'll be over and done with. Then the United Kingdom can slowly start returning to normal.'

'I can't wait.'

THE INVASION was a massive logistic operation for the European Union. The French had done an excellent job preparing the missions and fulfilling the strategic requirements. With some 65.000 troops, and ten-thousand tons of heavy equipment positioned in advance throughout the United Kingdom, plus the strategy of using Northern Ireland as a decoy, resistance was kept at a minimum. There were some fights here and there from loyal British soldiers, but when buildings were shelled from European Union tanks, they quickly realized that there were better ways to die than for some idiots in Westminster. British troops never really did bother fighting nor were they prepared to sacrifice their lives for some fanatic's ideology. Too many British have enjoyed Serrano ham from Spain, French wine, Italian olives, Danish cheese and butter, Belgian chocolates, German or

Czech beer, Greek almonds, or have simply just enjoyed touring through the European mainland to be ready to fight for a future without all of those niceties. Having experienced what has happened since Brexit, first with Victoria Seymour, then with Henry Montclair, then after eleven weeks of sanctions and intense domestic politics, and now an invasion, the majority of people were caught up in unbelievable events that have evolved faster than anyone can grasp. People have finally realized their huge mistake of taking the democracy they live in for granted. They are beginning to wonder why they ever voted for this ideology that can only lead to disaster. The Scottish, Irish and Welsh have always been survivors, contrary to the English who have always been conquerors.

HENRY IS COMPLETELY baffled about what is going on. It should not be like this! He releases Lisa from his embrace with the reassurance that this will be the last time he will ever get the opportunity to shack anyone again. He gets off the couch, pulling on his underwear and looks at Gregg who is standing beside the couch.

'There are what, you say?'

'Enemy soldiers everywhere.'

'Where are they now?'

'Everywhere. They came from the west coast of Wales and the east coast of England. They're nearing London.'

How close are they?' Henry looks at Lisa on the bed, indicating she needs to get dressed too.

'The troops from Great Yarmouth at Norwick can be here any minute. They're less than 50 kilometers away.'

'Why aren't our troops holding them back?'

'They're afraid of the enemy shelling us. And they don't want old buildings to be destroyed. So, they've laid down their weapons.'

'Who gave that order? There will be repercussions! They're paid to fight and protect their country. Damn traitors,' screams Henry. 'Why did they get money for new equipment when they don't use it anyway?'

'I'll ask our generals.'

'Up yours Gregg! What's the status? Any aircraft in the air?'

'Ours or theirs?'

'Both, you moron.'

'Nothing on radar. Nothing at all. All our military installations have been invaded by people from the underground. And traitors have cut power supplies and vandalized the backup generators.'

'I never expected the European Union to actually invade us. Why haven't we heard anything from our spies in Brussels?'

'They've really kept us in the dark. I think they have kept themselves in the dark, too. I think you might have underestimated the willingness of our neighbors to interfere. Their mission is certainly outside the conventional procedures of the European Union.'

Henry puts both hands to his ears like a little child.

'I don't want to hear it.'

'The car is awaiting you,' says one of Henry's bodyguards.

'Where are we going?' asks Henry.

'We have to get you out of Downing Street,' says Gregg. 'As I said, it won't take long. They can be here any minute. I believe we have less than an hour. You need to be brought to safety, just like Lisa.'

'I'm staying here,' she says with determination.

'No, you're not. You're coming with us.'

'I'm not,' she says again.

Gregg pulls his weapon on her. 'Yes, you are. Get dressed and do it quickly.'

'Where are we going?' she repeats Henry question.

'To a heliport not far from here. I think it's best we leave the country. A jet is waiting at Northold Airforce base. But we don't have much time. And the more you two talk, the higher the chance of being caught by our own troops.'

'So, this is what our great nation has become? A kingdom of traitors, lazy soldiers, and a population that does not want to fight for their rights to be free!'

'That's right, Henry,' confirms Gregg. 'But now hurry, if you want to survive the wrath of your population.'

'Can't we just drop a couple of nukes on Brussels? Then it's settled once and for all,' suggests Henry.

'By God, you're such an idiot,' screams Lisa. 'Not only our submarines have them but France has them too.'

'You say they haven't sent aircraft,' asks Henry.

'Not yet.'

'Of course not you idiots!' screams Lisa even louder than before. 'Why do you think the European Union hasn't used their aircraft for anything other than reconnaissance? Because our planes are equipped with NATO's friendly recognition features. You guys are so pathetic. Why don't you give yourselves up?'

Only seconds later, Lisa lays unconscious on the floor. Gregg hit her hard on the head with his weapon.

'Come on, Henry. Forget about her. There are other women. We've both worked so hard for this and if we have to give it up, we should take as many down with us as we can.'

'I'm sure going to miss her tight pussy.'

'Me too.'

'What?'

'You didn't know?'

'No.'

'Well, she said, you said it was alright.'

'She did?'

'Yes.'

'So, you did her too?'

'I did.'

'How often?'

'Not as often as you.'

'But she wasn't bad, was she?'

'Nope.'

'And Victoria.'

'There really was something going on between you two. Nobody else had a chance.'

'Did you even try?'

'No.'

'Yes, Victoria was really something special. I miss her.'

'Come on, let's get out of here.'

They spit on Lisa and walked out the door of 10 Downing Street.

CHAPTER 30

THE LAST FIGHTS IN THE STREETS CEASED with a few shots. French, German and Italian forces made their way to the City of Westminster, securing and sealing off the area around Westminster Abbey, Downing Street, the Cabinet Office on Parliament Street, Buckingham Palace and the Ministry of Defense on Whitehall. The streets are empty. There are no civilians to be seen anywhere. Cars are gone, buses are not running, neither is the tube. Apart from clusters of English soldiers standing here and there smoking cigarettes and drinking coffee, nothing is going on. It is dark and windy, winter has replaced autumn, and nobody really wants to be outside pretending that they are going to repeat what happened during the Cold War, or World War II.

A German division is the first to arrive at Downing Street. The huge Leopard II tank, turns left from Whitehall onto Downing Street, ripping up asphalt on its way and destroying the security area and gate leading to one of the most famous addresses in the world. The English Special Forces are there, watching, but, like most of the nation, not even bothering to resist. When the German tank grinds to a halt before 10 Downing Street, the hatch opens and a man appears from within.

'You speak English?' shouts the Commander in charge of the English Special Forces.

'Of course,' the German Officer replies.

'Well chap, how about a cup of nice warm tea?'

'It's sure cold out here.'

The German Officer jumps down from the tank and shakes the hand of the Commander of the English Special Forces.

'Well, you finally figured out a way to invade us.'

The Officer laughs. 'I guess better late than never.'

'Come. Let's go inside. It's freaking cold out here. There must be some people who can make us a tea. How's Germany these days?'

'Aw, not that well. We feel the impact of the loss of trade between our countries. It's an unfortunate situation. And we also realize that our military isn't what it used to be.'

'Recent events have made things pretty awkward. I fully agree,' the Commander replies. 'I'm not really sure if any of us have been able to grasp that you guys have actually invaded us.'

'Nah, it's not a real invasion. But I'm sure this stunt will go down in military history as the strangest invasion ever to take place in the world.'

The Commander laughs. 'For sure.'

'But in a way …' the Officer looks at the Commander. 'Now you people will finally feel the shame my people have felt for so many centuries.'

'Yes. It's an awkward feeling this feeling of guilt and shame. It's contradicting and conflicting at the same time. It came after Nordhausen. I feel that what happened has nothing to do with me, but perhaps we could have prevented it from happening.'

'Exactly. That's the feeling we still live with in Germany. But can I give you some good advice?'

'Sure. Anytime.'

'I'd suggest you people simply get on with it.'

'Ah, here it is!' The Commander sees a soldier carrying supplies. 'Tea with sugar?' he asks the Officer.

'No thank you, but suger makes fat, you know?'

'Ouch! Be a little more diplomatic around here,' says the Commander. 'People are rather sensitive about that topic at the moment.'

'Don't mention the war … Faulty Towers,' laughs the German Officer.

'You know that episode? I'm sorry to hear that.'

'We loved that episode. John Cleese is magnificent! I don't know why you people think we hate it.'

'Oh God. Just the thought of the kick Hollywood is going to get out of this. I can already imagine the title of the movies.'

'You'll get used to it. When I watch old war movies as a German, we always think it was the Nazis who did it all. Not the German people.'

'Come, take a seat,' says the Commander.

'Where exactly are we?'

'This must be the room of our former Prime Minister.'

'Wow!'

The Commander looks around. 'I really would like to know what went on inside these four walls. This couch looks comfortable. Imagine if we could listen in … Say, would you like some English cookies? They're really delightful. Or clothed cream?'

'The last time I was here, I had it for the first time. It was great.'

'Soldier,' the Commander orders, pointing his finger at a young man beside the door. 'Could you please come here?'

'Yes Commander.'

'Could you be so kind as to see if you can find some clotted cream in the kitchen?'

'Yes Commander.'

The Commander asks, 'When did you visit the United Kingdom the last time?'

'I think it was right before Brexit. Perhaps six months before, when Europe was still intact. My wife and I were celebrating our 25th anniversary. It's a long time, you know.'

The Commander laughs. 'My wife and I, are going on our 32nd year. Now, that's a long time.'

'Certainly it is. Have you ever visited Germany?'

'I'm quite fond of Munich. It's amazing what you people have achieved since World War II.'

'I actually prefer the English way of doing things. Your black humor is just so amazing. We put a lid on ourselves after the events in the beginning of the 20th century.'

'Really! Why?'

'Well, I think if we didn't we would probably start new wars.'

'Hm.'

'Actually, now that I think of it, may I ask you a question?'

'Of course. Go ahead.'

'Did you vote to Remain or to Leave the European Union?'

The Commander laughs, 'I think we should let that one stay unanswered.'

'Commander?'

'Yes soldier?'

'I found some clothed cream and some scones in the kitchen.'

'Well … what're you waiting for? Serve them to our guest. And you know what? I'd like to have some, too. Just for the hell of it ...'

LISA FERGUSON ended up in jail, put there by the European invasion force. But it was not long before she was released again. It soon was discovered that she had had a leading role in supporting the underground resistance with information that could hurt or lead to the downfall of Henry Montclair and his government. Of the three roles she had taken upon herself, only two were revealed. Not only was she involved with the underground resistance, she had also provided information to Denda Escudos on a steady basis about Victoria Seymour and Henry Montclair and their plans. Several other civil servants were also credited for their support working against the system from within the government, its ministries and institutions. But it was Lisa who got the attention of the European Council, where it was quite obvious for Denda Escudos, that she knew the historical problems of the United Kingdom, its advantages and disadvantages. By giving her the role as interim Prime Minister and letting her select people in the government, there would be one less problem to deal with in the United Kingdom. The last thing the European Union wanted do to, was to insert its own people in power and act as an occupying force – which, in a manner of speaking, Denda Escudos actually did with Lisa Ferguson.

'So,' Denda rounds up the meeting at the European Council. 'Do we agree to put her in power?'

'Isn't she a little young?' asks France.

'That might be. But she's efficient,' explains Denda. 'Please cast your vote ... now ... Come on, France! On this one we need full unity.'

'But, we don't believe it's a good idea to let the United Kingdom rule on its own. There are still a lot of tensions, domestic as well as international.'

'Being an occupational power in a sovereign entity like the United Kingdom would not be to our advantage. It's not a path we should chose.'

'But, if they again become members of the European Union, we'll end up exactly as before Brexit with them blocking everything.'

'Then my friend, you're the only one in this building who hasn't learned a damn thing! I'm sure the English, and for that matter, the rest of the United Kingdom, have finally realized how important it is for Europe to stick together.'

'Well ...'

'Froggy! I'm asking you to change your vote. I don't give a damn about what you want or not. You French, with all your double agendas! This is not the time for national games. Please change your decision to 'Yes' before we officially protocol the result.'

'Well … But who's going to pay for the losses we've had?' asks France. 'We've got thousands of farmers spreading pig shit in the streets of Paris because they find its unfair that the United Kingdom isn't going to pay back its war dept.'

'It wasn't a war. It was a conflict. There's a difference. We'll ask the European Central Bank to print some more money. They're worthless anyway and the world is bankrupt. You'll get a pigs shit compensation injection package, okay? So, now, everyone, please vote again, thank you.'

ON THIS eventful day at the European Council, once again in the history of Europe, a decision has been made to secure the peace and prosperity of the European Union member nations, and also securing peace for the United Kingdom. When Denda returns home to his lovely apartment in Brussels, decorated in beautiful Spanish style, he pulls out a bottle of expensive French wine from his homemade wine shelf and prepares some excellent Italian antipesto. He takes the bread he bought in a German bakery a few blocks away from the European Union's office building and slices it. Then he pulls out his wife's favorite Belgian chocolates from her secret hiding place – a box he replaces every third day in the belief that she is stupid enough not notice. When she comes home from work tonight, he will seduce her passionately, something he has not done for the last two years of the ongoing Brexit crisis. He has to admit that Brexit is partly his as well as Henry Montclair's fault. In a way they have both gotten away with what they have done pretty much unnoticed.

CHAPTER 31

LAST EVENING, HENRY MONTCLAIR got extremely drunk. Lately he had been drinking a bit more than usual. He knew they would eventually get him. He was a person with knowledge not appreciated by them and that is the reason he knew he would probably not last forever. He had never pretended any different, at least not after what Lisa told him about The Special Council and the FDAR they had on his head. He knew they would do anything to keep their existence secret, so they can continue working indiscreetly to keep the world in balance.

Yesterday evening, as he was returning home, he met one of those secret people just as he was about to enter his car. Instinctively he knew that this was the last person he would ever see. It was the face of a beautiful woman he had met earlier that evening; an unknown woman with a gun with a silencer – which of course, on this fatal evening did not really matter.

'HAVE WE solved our little problem in Chile?' asks Mr. Andrews in a telephone conversation with Mr. Conners from The Special Council in London. Mr. Conners is to report to headquarters about the latest progress in the United Kingdom.

'They both have been taken care of,' informs Mr. Conners. 'Gregg White is out of the way. He fell down some stairs at his home in Venezuela. Unfortunately he leaves a wife and a child behind.'

'Who found him?'

'His daughter. Six years old.'

'Ugh, sorry to hear that. And Henry Montclair?'

'He was found dead beside his car last night.'

'What about Lisa Ferguson?'

'Aw, she's a difficult case. It seems you were right all along about her. She did change sides, although she had her reasons for doing so. It was she who disclosed the presence of The Special Council to Henry Montclair and to Gregg White, which actually almost succeeded in finding the Old Man.'

'Montclair or White?'

'White was looking for him.'

'But why did she do it? She should know it's a breach of our most important regulation.'

'Because she knew we were probably going to bring out an FDAR on Henry Montclair. She did not want to stir up more unrest by letting him assassinate. In a way she was right because it would have brought Gregg White to power, accelerating the situation even further and could have led to an escalation of the situation between the European Union and Russia. She forgot, though, that she's not responsible for strategies set up by the Continental Teams.'

'So, what do we do about her?'

'The Continental Teams have discussed her a lot. The problem is that she's responsible for the death of five people. For every assassination there's a possibility that our cover will be blown. And in a way, she's forced us to carry out assassinations that were unnecessary.'

'And they let her go.'

'She's one lucky potato,' claims Mr. Conners. 'But you have to give her a little credit. The consequences of her actions were unintentional and in a way she did the right thing. She was in a difficult situation and she knew she had to go against procedures. She was very much aware of putting her own life at risk to prevent the situation between Westminster and the European Union from escalating.'

'So, what about the others? Who still knows about The Special Council that shouldn't?' asks Mr. Andrews.

'We've nailed them all. The European Union has been good at splitting up the henchmen network of Gregg White. I've no idea how they've done this, but it's amazing! It must have been someone close to Gregg White. The European Union's report made it easy to find the ones we needed to interrogate.' explains Mr. Conners.

'That amazes me, too.'

'Did you know that there's actually a paragraph in the TSC Planning and Execution Manual that gives us the ability to take people in for interrogation and torture as soon as there's a suspicion that they have knowledge about The Special Council they shouldn't have?'

'Which one?'

'It's on page 421, Article 1 to 14.'

'Interesting. I'll have to read it later.'

'Article 7 says that Article 6 can only be used when all Continental Teams approve the evidence.'

'That makes sense.'

'At least, this time the damage to The Special Council has been minimized. And if it's any comfort, those five who were assassinated because of Lisa Ferguson, were bad people anyway.'

'Phew,' sighs Mr. Andrews. 'This time was really different, wasn't it?'

'I am also happy it's over. I've never seen The Special Council get rid of so many guilty and innocent people at the same time.'

'A comment you should probably leave out when you write your report to the Old Man tonight.'

'What's so disturbing is that the network of Gregg White's team of henchmen wasn't really that big. According to the report from the European Union, his core team consisted of less than thirty people. They had teams who took care of all the dirty stuff. And as I understood it, Gregg White, was pretty much into the operation himself.'

'Actually, the witnesses from Nordhausen, have confirmed that he's the one responsible for the deaths of Andy and Chris.'

'Yes. That fact did make our people push Gregg White a little too hard down those stairs after the interrogation.' says Mr. Conners. 'He turned into a real chicken shit when he saw our people. He talked like never before.'

'The most brutal ones are the chicken shits. Is there any paragraph on chickens in the TSC?'

Mr. Conners laughs. 'Still to be written.'

'Ha ha, that was a good answer. Please write your report and send it to me as soon as possible. Then I'll debrief the Old Man. I'm sure there'll be work for us again in the not too distant future. What are you doing today?'

'Today? I'm going to go to the supermarket with my wife.'

'I can imagine it must be nice to have access to it all again?'

'It is! But you know what I've missed the most?'

'No.'

'French cheese.'

'I'm American. I wouldn't know what real cheese tastes like.'

ADMITTEDLY, it is not one of the saddest funerals that Lisa Ferguson has gone to in her thirty-nine years. She will not particularly miss Henry Montclair and certainly not the sex. But he has perished, and that is probably the highest respect he will ever get from her. He might as well be used as an opportunity, to have some of the skeletons The Party has in its closet, buried with him in his grave. She has noticed a change in the mood of the people now that she has taken over as Prime Minister. There are hopes of a brighter future for the United Kingdom. She represents a young generation and gives hope to many that life will return to normal.

Lisa greets Henry Montclair's closest family; his wife and two children. There is also an old mother and father and two older brothers from south Wales and a few friends. She extends her condolences and sits in her assigned seat in the second row with Denda Escudos from the European Union and a couple of other high ranking Eurocrats. The family members and few friends are struggling to hold back their grief: their tears running down their faces. It seems that the only ones shedding real tears, are those in row one.

The Montclair family seems to be a limited bunch, just like her family. Most people present at the funeral, are heads-of-states. Outside the church, most people who have shown up want to show their final disgust for the man most people came to hate; some are there because they admired him. The public's interest in Henry Montclair has become headlines in the press, in the free press, with articles about his life from childhood to adulthood and his career as an entrepreneur, and at the European Union. There are articles about him as a family father, a politician, an aristocrat and a dictator.

The funeral ceremony is short. There is only one speech by the minister. It seems friends and family have no memories to share nor do they have a favorite hymn to have sung. When Lisa asked the agency to arrange Henry's state funeral she specified that the funeral be done as quickly as possible, because it is nothing but an embarrassment to the United Kingdom.

This cold, white winter day with its clear blue sky is the perfect background for the occasion and for the man it is bidding farewell to. Lisa notices that there are birds singing and that the sun's rays are sending warmth as a sign that something new is about to begin. The world will go on without Henry. It will not remember his funeral. Only what he did.

But as much as Lisa hates the occasion, etiquette demands her to visit the Montclair family to offer them her regards. She keeps an appropriate distance at the funeral, her feelings are rather mixed after two years of difficult times and triple roles. In spite of what Henry Montclair did, it would have been okay to skip his funeral and the press would have come to terms with it. She hopes that at her funeral people will remember that she had always tried to be honest, that she has always cared for others and has always tried to treat others as she would like to be treated. She hopes that her family will remember what a wonderful childhood they gave her and what a good life she always tried to lead. She hopes that she will be remembered for being a good colleague, one who was capable of building a team and never pushing or dictating actions on others. She hopes that her successes will be honoured and that she will be remembered fondly by all who knew her.

Henry being in the bubble, like many politicians are after years in the corridors of power, or businessmen for that matter, he started falling from his star without realizing that this was happening. From having had it all, the population of the United Kingdom, lost it all. And as the rule says; it is first when you have lost all that you come realize you had a lot. Henry, contrary to Victoria, failed to see who the enemy of the people was, by minoritizing the ones they should had fed on. They minoritized the wrong group, the ones who did not have it all, and prioritized the ones who had it all, but destroyed it for those. The middle-class and rich people, they are never going to start a revolution, because, they have too much to lose. Victoria and Henry, should instead had taken the very-rich and minoritized them, because when looking into history, changes that are to become permanent start otherwise, and by people who have nothing to lose. But in a society where everyone got almost everything, it is difficult to start a revolution. This is the failure the two former Prime Ministers did not understand when at power.

Before Brexit, the English were incapable of imagining their country's ability to lose a battle. That comes from a long imperial history. But this one, the battle they just fought, they lost. Hopefully, it will contribute to the same self-reflection as to what the German's experienced after World War II. Brexit, changed the landscape of the United Kingdom and when people decided to use their democratic vote as protest vote, all safety systems fell away and paved the way for people like Victoria and Henry climbing to power. Obese people were selling headlines for a long time, making the press fail to scutinize what is important, letting evil forces work in the background on their plans of persueing total power in building up an ideologoy that people only too late realized was damaging. There are many people and politicians holding extreme views, which in a way are genuinely views, but a kind of ignorant, because most such views are blinded from self-interests, not considering what these views may inflict upon the society they are a part of. With Brexit, especially Henry overestimated his nations capabilities and abilities in believing in a long gone past, being the primary reason to why the majority of a population was willing to take the risk, and put the wrong people in power.

All those thoughts, were things Lisa Ferguson considered when walking back down the path to the car awaiting her, taking them back to Westminster. She kept seeing the image of herself laying in that coffin. It was a long coffin, taking six people to lower Henry Montclair down into the pitch black. Down to where he should be.

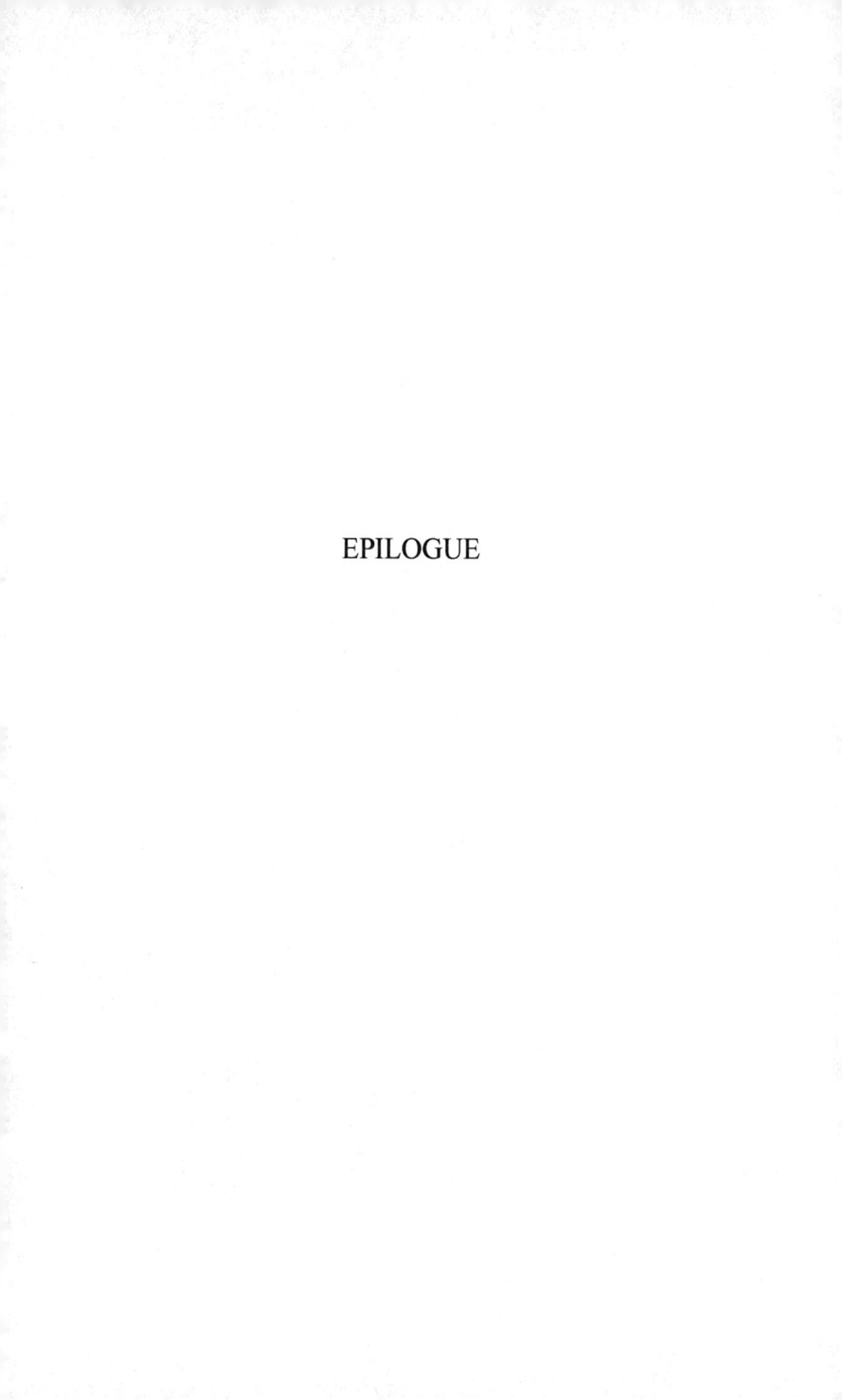

EPILOGUE

A SMALL GROUP OF EUROCRAT politicians, gather before the monthly meeting concerning the United Kingdom and its progress before and after the invasion. What should have been an easy separation of the United Kingdom from the European Union, turned into something that no one ever planned – or believed could actually happen. To begin with, the Brexit negotiations went smoothly and according to plan, though with the election of Victoria Seymour, things started turning sour and moved completely in the wrong direction. It had a major effect on the experiment engaged by the European Commission, whose objective was:

To see what would happen to a nation,
if it actually decides,
to leave the European Union?

The experiment, Brexit, was taken up by the European Union's five presidents, Denda Escudos, President of the European Council of the 27, or now, the 28 member heads-of-states. Marek Moranska, President of the European Parliament, consisting of 751 members, who were democratically selected by participants from all over the European Union. Peter Jensen, President of the European Commission, whose responsibility it is to investigate matters of importance for European cititzens. Additionally, Alessandro Giuseppe, president of the European Central Bank, and the President of the Eurogroup, Valentina Marino were also present.

The Brexit agenda was quite simple. The European Union knows it weaknesses. The five presidents provided information to an already heated debate about the future of the United Kingdom and its role in the European Union. Their information fuelled an immediate reaction when the right-wing picked up the negative seeds, doing the rest of the work for the

European Commission. As expected by the five presidents, contrary to expectations held by many politicians at Westminster, Brexit had happened and the experiment was on.

None of the five presidents thought that the Brexit experiment would evolve to the point of nearly dissolving the United Kingdom and to an almost armed conflict within 28 European Union member nations. They had released a beast, but let events take turns. They watched from the sidelines to see what would happen in the United Kingdom in terms of its political landscape, domestic tensions, the society as such, its economy, and how they would solve the problems that followed.

Who would have thought that the result would turn out so disastrously? It clearly showed that leaving the European Union would mean punishment not by the European Union itself, but by the consequences that would follow for leaving a collaboration that is economically intertwined in one of the world's biggest trade zones that insures the stability of its members. It clearly shows that the European Union has become a powerful entity. This was clearly shown by the invasion of the United Kingdom which proved that, if necessary, it has the resources to execute a lot of power, something that other world leaders and EU citizens had thought unimaginable.

Unfortunately events quickly got out of control. The Brexit experiment turned into a little 'whoops' when Victoria Seymour was elected Prime Minister in protest to the old and established political parties. Who would have thought at the time of Victoria Seymour's inauguration, that an innocent topic like fat could segregate a society as it did? Had Victoria Seymour not been manipulated by Henry Montclair, with whom she was romantically involved; had she not tried to grab power as she did, then history might have turned out differently. The five presidents could only draw the conclusion that if a member nation leaves the European Union, it has consequences for all parties, not just financially, but also for the souls of those involved.

There was no way around it. But the experiment had to be called off. The five presidents had to stop what was going on. It was expected that Henry Montclair and his government would step down and reflect on the pictures from Nordhausen. But he did not. Instead, Henry Montclair surprisingly took the transition from democracy to aristocracy. Again the five presidents failed to see a constellation between Gregg White and Henry Montclair. They should have been wise enough to know that with their former colleague on the throne, the outcome would certainly be disastrous.

In the end, there was little the five presidents could do, apart from going with the flow, now that they had called off the experiment. Under strict secrecy, they started destroying material relating to the experiment that seven civil servants from the European Commission had worked out. In the hopes of covering up their deed, with the assassinations on the civil servants, the five presidents had concocted ordering the assassination of Victoria Seymour. The orders were unanimous and in secrecy, in an attempt to stop events from spinning further out of control. In the wake of the Brexit experiment, there now seemed to be a huge price to pay, not only financially but also in human lives. Henry Montclair had taken things too far in his bet with Denda Escudos when he was not willing to stop the United Kingdom from leaving the European Union.

At least now that Henry Montclair and Gregg White were both dead, they have finally found the roles they play best: As scapegoats. Europol still hasn't been able to figure out who was behind their killings.

THE FIVE Eurocrat presidents, sit around the table in Denda Escudos office that they have been sitting around every month for the last two and a half years. At meetings like this, Denda Escudos' assistant is not invited. It is time to reflect on the past and figure out how to fix the mistakes they have made.

'I wish there had been other ways to figure out what would had happen if someone left the European Union,' says Denda Escudos sighing. 'The sooner we get the United Kingdom back up on its feet, the better it is for all of us. The Americans, Russians and Chinese are taking advantage of our weak position without the English.'

'If any of this comes out ...' sighs Peter Jensen, president of the European Commission, from Denmark, 'that we have screwed this up big time, then it's not only we, but the European Project that will be dead forever.'

'And you say we're clear on leaks and evidence about the experiment?'

'We are in the clear,' confirms Denda.

'That's good.'

'Greece was a rough enough ride.'

'At least we got that swept under the carpet.'

'Is our Support Package for England and Wales ready?'

'Like Greece, this will cost a fortune.'

'France has come up with a final proposal. They sent it out last week.'

'I haven't had the time to read it. What does it say?'

'Simply that we go in and support the industry and service sector in the United Kingdom until it has been reestablished.'

'And the conditions for the Support Package? Can all European Union member nations agree on them?'

'Actually, none of us want to pick up the bill from Victoria Seymour's and Henry Montclair's rule. But I guess we all feel obligated to do something to help the United Kingdom get back on its feet again.'

'The Commission has estimated it'll be double as expensive as rebuilding the entire East Bloc. The money could be spent on more important matters. I don't see how we can convince the other Council members to allocate the money.'

'The French argument is that the United Kingdom has been a positive contributor to the European Project for many, many years. So, in a way, it morally obligates us to provide assistance.'

'That will be hard to sell to the Council. Indeed.'

'In all fairness, there's goodwill from 25 of our 27 member nations to provide this for free – including a package for Scotland, Northern Ireland and the Republic of Ireland, which was affected too. The sanctions were pretty hard on us all.'

'Regarding to Scotland and Northern Ireland? I talked with their First Ministers, who told me they don't want to go back to the old Status Quo. Many Scots and North-Irish see the European Union as a kind of liberator from England.'

'The Commission has recommended that the United Kingdom remain as it is – at least for the moment. Things must return to the political status they were after Brexit and then they can decide how they want to solve their problems themselves.'

'Poland and Romania want to withdraw from assisting England.'

'On this issue, they'll do what I tell them to do,' says Denda.

'It sounds like they're still pissed off about how rude the English have been with their xenophobia after the Brexit referendum.'

'Yes, they still haven't gotten over it, though it was some years ago.'

'But don't worry,' says Denda. 'First they'll vote 'No' to show their dissatisfaction, but they will eventually change their vote to, 'Yes'. I've already talked to their Prime Ministers. In their hearts, they know it's the only right thing to do.'

'And if not?'

'Then we'll just decrease their subsidies.'

'I just hope we' won't see the same bigotry from other member nations as what we saw from the British when we started pumping billions into Greece. Some Europeans might see this as unfair and as a waste of money – especially after how England and Wales treated the rest of Europe after Brexit.'

'Remind me that, in the future, we need to do more to promote the European Union and explain to people what it actually does.'

'I think, with our total budget it be a drop in the water with such campaign.'

'I think that's a waste of money. People don't care anyway.'

'Anyway. Our meeting with the Council starts in 30 minutes.'

'Well. Then let's go over there.'

THE 27 prime ministers, who have turned up at the European Council today, take their seats around the rather long, oval table. It's at this table that new legislation is approved or rejected.

'Thank you for all coming today,' greets Denda, president of the Council. 'We all know that the United Kingdom, or rather England and Wales, voted for Brexit. Today, we need to decide on a Support Package for England and Wales and also for Scotland, and the two Irelands. We're obligated to assist, no matter what anyone in this room thinks about what happened in Nordhausen. The people of the United Kingdom have suffered enough under the tyranny of Victoria Seymour and our ex-colleague, Henry Montclair.'

'The first version of the Support Package is on the table,' says France. 'It's close to the previous one, which I assume everyone present has read. It's ready to be executed if you are all in agreement. The International Monetary Fund will extend us the loans as well – Guaranteed by the European Central Bank.'

'Why should we help them?' cries out Poland. 'They deserved what happened to them.'

'Exactly,' agrees Romania. 'They think we're second class people.'

'Those English always think they're superior to others.'

'And they block for every decision in Parliament.'

'I find it better they not a part of it anymore.'

'Yeah, let them sail in their own shit.'

'But in spite of that …' says Greece, 'they did help us in our economic crises in 2014.'

'Stop it!' shouts Denda. 'You sound like small children! Listen to yourselves, you spoiled brats! This is not about you, this is about the first rule of the European Union: To assist fellow member nations who urgently need help. You people seem to forget that the situation in the United Kingdom has repercussions for all of us here as well. We have losses too. Supporting the United Kingdom and assisting it to rebuild its economy, is the recipe for continued peace and prosperity for us all, making us thrive in a world that wasn't always as it is today. That's why, friends! That's why we need to help the United Kingdom. Not only because of them, but also because of ourselves. And too many of you from the East-bloc, you should be ashamed of your comments this morning. Never forget your own history of suppression and hardship. Shame on you people!'

'It's going to cost hell of a lot of money and we don't have it. That's the problem. By the way, Serbia is the next nation to join the European Union. Not the United Kingdom. They decided to leave.'

'They still haven't officially left, you people ought to know this,' explains Denda.

'I agree with Denda. It is unfair to say they left.'

'At least, until they're back on their feet, our revenge is that they become a European Union protectorate.'

'That's a sweet revenge.'

'Not if you're from the United Kingdom.'

'So … they will use the Euro?'

'That's one condition to receive the Support Package, as well joining the Schenen Agreement about free borders.'

'Wow!'

'I wonder how that will go down at Westminster and the country.'

'Oh God.'

'I already see the next war.'

'I think it was the French president who suggested it.'

'Of course it was.'

'Say, haven't you people read our Support Package?' asks France.

'So, what we need to do now,' says Denda, 'is to approve the budget for the Support Package. Are we ready? Then, vote, now.'

'Thank you ladies and gentlemen. The result for a Support Package for the United Kingdom and the Republic of Ireland is as follows: 25 voted Yes. 2 Voted No. Fellow member nations, we need a unanimous vote on a decision and budget of this size, according to Article 6 of the Lisbon Treaty. Poland and Romania! I insist on a unanimous decision. Please vote again.'

'Okay. For the record and protocol, note that the 27 have decided on a Support Package. Let's wrap it up and make the United Kingdom great again.'

'Well, this time, they might even succeed. Hopefully they've learned their lessons well, like you Germans did after World War II.'

'What happened after World War II, makes you kind of humble,' answers Germany.

'God save the Queen.'

'Yes, God save their Queen.'

'Is she and her family back in London?'

'Yes.'

'So, the next topic on the agenda,' continues Denda. 'Before adjourning, we need to decide on the expansion of the high-speed rail network to the Eastern bloc. The sooner we take care of this matter, the better. Those damn Americans are considering entering the game of high-speed trains. That's not good for our European pride. Does anyone have any objections to accepting the budget?'

- o -

Zeitfracht Medien GmbH
Ferdinand-Jühlke-Straße 7
99095 Erfurt, Deutschland
produktsicherheit@kolibri360.de